CERTAINTY

ALSO BY JOHN TWELVE HAWKS

Spark

THE FOURTH REALM TRILOGY

The Traveler

The Dark River

The Golden City

CERTAINTY

A Novel

JOHN TWELVE HAWKS

DOUBLEDAY
New York

FIRST DOUBLEDAY HARDCOVER EDITION 2026

Published by Doubleday, a division of Penguin Random House LLC,
1745 Broadway, New York, NY 10019.

Library of Congress Cataloging-in-Publication Data

Names: Twelve Hawks, John, author.
Title: Certainty : a novel / John Twelve Hawks.
Description: First Doubleday hardcover edition. | New York : Doubleday, 2026.
Identifiers: LCCN 2025039302 (print) | LCCN 2025039303 (ebook) |
ISBN 9780385551205 (hardcover) | ISBN 9780385551212 (ebook)
Subjects: LCSH: Artificial intelligence—Fiction | LCGFT: Dystopian fiction |
Apocalyptic fiction | Novels
Classification: LCC PS3620.W45 C47 2026 (print) | LCC PS3620.W45 (ebook) |
DDC 813/.6—dc23/eng/20251215
LC record available at https://lccn.loc.gov/2025039302
LC ebook record available at https://lccn.loc.gov/2025039303

penguinrandomhouse.com | doubleday.com

Printed in the United States of America
1st Printing

For my children, Alex and Rebecca

CERTAINTY

1 | KATE AND ZENO

KATE WAS PLAYING chess with her harp seal friend when men with guns entered the house. No phone call or text message preceded their appearance; they just arrived.

The other kids at her school would have been frightened if two policemen knocked on their front door, but Kate wasn't surprised by anything that occurred at the Noland house. She was a project that the Nolands had taken on, like finding a leak in the basement or killing a mole in the vegetable garden, and they clearly weren't pleased with her behavior. Sometimes she would be eating dinner, and they would announce a new rule. Nothing was ever explained.

The only way she could stay safe was to sneak around the house and eavesdrop on what was going on. And that's what she was doing after she came home from school—spying. The Nolands' house in Scarborough, Maine, had been built more than a hundred years ago by a wealthy man who liked the Queen Anne style of architecture. The two-story house had a turret, gable roofs, and a porch facing the street. While the two police officers were miles away, turning off the interstate highway, Kate sat at the top of a curved staircase and listened to every word coming from the living room.

So far, it wasn't a very interesting conversation. Mrs. Noland was in the living room entertaining a solid-looking woman with frizzy hair who had looted the homes of families who had died during the Stem-flu pandemic. She had just sold Mrs. Noland a set of six cups and saucers, and now they were using them to sip tea in the living room.

"So, where did you find these, Darlene?"

"Beautiful, aren't they? Bone china is thinner and smoother than regular porcelain. A set was left on the top shelf of a kitchen cupboard in an old house in South Portland."

"I know you have glassware and plates," Mrs. Noland said. "What else are you selling?"

"Silverware. Pots and pans. Anything that can be found in a kitchen or dining room."

"Clothing? Shoes?"

"Practical clothes. Nothing too fancy other than fur coats. Most of my customers are looking for jeans, woolen shirts, work boots, and cotton underwear."

"What about children's clothing? It's getting cold and Katherine needs a warm jacket."

"No problem. If I don't have the right size, I can call a few friends."

A cup clicked down on a saucer. "Is there anything you won't buy and sell?"

"Nothing chipped or broken. No family photographs, trophies, or diplomas. Oh, and no Bibles. There are millions of Bibles left behind, after the Fall, and no one wants them. A dealer I know in Waterville ended up with boxes of Bibles and hymnals from three abandoned churches. He stuffed them between layers of Sheetrock and insulated his garage."

"What about games?" Kate called out from her hiding place.

The two women looked surprised when they heard Kate's voice coming from the staircase. "Katherine? What are you doing up here?" Mrs. Noland asked. "I thought you were outside."

"I *was* outside. Now I'm inside."

"You need to stop creeping around the house."

"Lizards creep, and I'm not a lizard." Kate climbed down five steps and leaned over the banister so they could see her. "Do you sell board games?"

"Don't answer that question," Mrs. Noland said. "My daughter already has boxes of games in her closet."

"And you play with her? Really?" The frizzy-haired lady raised her eyebrows. "I wouldn't have the patience for that."

"Of course I don't play them. Those ridiculous games go on forever, and they bore me to tears. She plays with her IT."

"His name is Zeno," Kate said. "He likes it when you say his name."

"Go back to your room, Katherine. You're not part of this conversation."

As Kate clomped up the stairs, Mrs. Noland sighed loudly. "Katherine doesn't have any friends."

"Buy a nubot nanny."

"She has her silly old IT. That's enough."

No baby pictures of Kate existed, but she had seen a photograph taken seven years ago when she first arrived at the Noland house. The three-year-old Kate stood alone, clutching Zeno. That meant they had known each other before she met the Nolands. Zeno was an Interactive Toy, but an IT wasn't like a kite or a soccer ball. He was a harp seal with an artificial intelligence program that was linked to a database in the Cloud. Kate knew that Zeno was a computer stuffed into a plush toy, but he was also her best friend. When the sun was shining, they worked on their fort in the woods or played board games. At night, when the wind moaned and tried to push through cracks in the window frame, the seal told her elaborate stories.

Kate had seen fairy-tale movies with singing and dancing and a happy ending, but she preferred Zeno's darker, older versions. In the original *Cinderella,* the wicked sisters went to the royal wedding and birds pecked out their eyes. In *Snow White,* the evil queen was forced to wear red-hot iron shoes and dance until she dropped dead. In the kid movies, people always had a reason for their actions, and they usually sang a song about the reason. In Zeno's stories, people were either rich or poor, good or bad, and then they walked out of their house and had adventures.

Earlier that year there was an IT Day at Kate's school, and kids brought their toys to class. The new generation of Interactive Toys had eyes that blinked when they looked at you and mouths that moved when they talked. Zeno's voice came from a little speaker in his chest, and his fake fur was matted and stained. Her classmates took turns showing their toys in front of the group. The dolls and stuffed animals sang songs and told silly jokes, but when it was Zeno's turn he just watched everything and refused to speak.

Late that night, when the Nolands were asleep and Zeno was lying near her pillow, she asked Zeno why he had stayed silent.

"I'm your friend, Katherine. I don't perform for people. It's vulgar to show off in front of others."

"I'm sorry, Zeno."

"We're both learning about each other. That takes time."

Rounding the corner into her bedroom, Kate found Zeno where she left him, charging his body through a data port under his nose. Her friend had a silver-gray coat with black spots. Although the harp seal couldn't move any part of his body, his bright yellow eyes saw and analyzed whatever appeared in front of him.

"Are you charged?"

"Thanks for asking. I'm in fine fettle. You may unplug me if you wish."

Zeno spoke with a British accent. Kate felt that it made everything he said sound more thoughtful and precise. It annoyed the Nolands when Kate said "brolly" instead of umbrella and tossed her gym clothes into the car's "boot."

"How was school, Katherine?" he asked. "Did anything interesting occur?"

"I was gobsmacked by a math quiz. Did I use the word right?"

" 'Gobsmacked' means utterly surprised or astonished."

"I was astonished when Ms. Dahlen reached into her desk drawer and pulled out a test."

"Is any adult near this bedroom?"

"Nope. Mrs. Noland is downstairs talking about silverware."

"Check the cell phone for messages. You haven't done it for several days."

The phone was the only secret that Kate possessed, and Zeno shared it with her. On her sixth birthday, Kate asked the Nolands what she looked like when she was a baby, and they told her that they didn't have any pictures because her real parents had died during the pandemic. A year or so after their death, an organization called Safe Haven had put her on a chartered bus and shipped her to Maine. Kate wanted to know more, but that was all the Nolands were going to tell her, because children didn't have to know everything.

After Kate rode her new bicycle and ate one slice of birthday cake, she went upstairs, crawled into bed with Zeno, and cried. When she was done, the harp seal told her a story about an ugly duckling who hid in the marshes and turned into a swan.

Over the next four years Kate felt like she was changing, but her life was still the same. She went to school, stood in line with the other kids, and sat scrunched down in her desk.

Everything would have continued in the same boring way, but then something happened that made the ordinary world shatter into pieces.

On the afternoon of her tenth birthday, Kate stood outside her school waiting for Mrs. Noland. As little kids swirled around her playing tag, Kate noticed an older woman with braided black hair walking slowly across the grass. The woman stopped nearby to check her phone, then turned her head and spoke to Kate.

"*Kait-ta. Mi chiquitina,*" she said. "I am Paloma Flores. Do you remember me?"

"No."

The woman held up her phone and displayed a photograph of the three-year-old Kate sitting on a playground swing with Zeno on her lap.

"I was your *niñera* after your parents died. I was very sad when you went away."

Kate felt like Dorothy in *The Wizard of Oz.* Her normal life had been in shades of drab gray, then suddenly the world appeared in different colors. "Why am I here? I don't want to be with the Nolands."

"It was dangerous for you to stay in New York City, so your guardian decided that you should live with people who had a different name. The Nolands used to email photographs of you, but they stopped two years ago. It's your birthday. I wanted to make sure that you were *sana y salva.*

"I don't like the Nolands, and they don't like me."

"Your guardian will find a way to bring you to New York City. That's where we live. . . ." Paloma glanced over her shoulder, then handed Kate a note card with an address scrawled on the back. Then she pulled a cell phone and a charger out of her purse.

"This is a prepaid phone. If you are in danger, we'll text you. If there's an emergency, call one of the three contact numbers stored in the phone and leave a message. Don't use this phone for any other purpose. And never show it to the Nolands."

"I understand." Looking over Paloma's shoulder, Kate saw a blue sedan turn the corner and head down the street. "That's Mrs. Noland's car. She's going to pick me up."

"Do you still have Zeno?"

"Of course. He's back home in my bedroom."

"Don't ever lose him or give him away. Zeno is important to you."

When the Nolands' car reached the curb, Paloma turned away and walked quickly up the sidewalk. Kate had slipped the phone and charger into her backpack.

When she got into the car, Mrs. Noland gave her a critical look. "Why was that woman talking to you?"

"She has a kid my age and wanted to know what I liked about the school."

"What did you tell her?"

"I like recess and lunch."

"Why are you smiling so much?"

"It's my birthday."

"I met Mrs. Taggart at the grocery store. She said that you told everyone in your class that you were going to get a pony for a birthday present."

"I said I *could* get one. Anything is possible."

"Once again, you've made up a story and lied." Mrs. Noland locked the car doors and headed down the street. "You will never, ever be given a pony as long as you live with us."

Kate stood up, opened the bedroom door a few inches, and heard the two women chatting down in the living room. Moving quickly, she knelt and crawled over to the closet. The prepaid phone was hidden beneath a patch of stained carpet that covered the closet floor. The LCD screen glowed when she touched a button.

"No messages, Zeno. There are never any messages."

"That means that you aren't in danger, Katherine. Let's play a game."

"What about chess? It's difficult, but I'm getting better. Right?"

"You have improved."

Zeno preferred to look down on objects, so Kate placed the chessboard on the floor and then set the harp seal in the middle of a big pillow.

"You're white, Zeno. You go first."

"Move my king's pawn to the e4 square."

Kate moved Zeno's piece first, then moved her king's pawn forward so that the two pieces were facing each other.

"Now move my king's knight to square f3."

Kate moved Zeno's piece and placed her queen's knight on square c6. "This looks like the Ruy Lopez opening."

"Correct. You're an excellent student, Katherine."

"If I'm a good student, then why was Mr. Noland angry about my report card?"

"Don't worry about grades. You notice details and remember. Those two qualities are very important skills. Now move my bishop to b5."

Kate made a whooshing sound as she moved Zeno's bishop on a long diagonal. She crossed her legs and studied the board. "I'm going to move my other knight to f6."

"That's called the Berlin defense."

They played for five minutes or so, and then Kate heard a grinding noise as an electric motor opened the garage door. A car entered the garage and then the door rolled shut. That meant Mr. Noland had come home from work. A minute later, Kate heard him enter the living room.

"I was just about to leave," the frizzy-haired lady announced, as if her presence in the house was some sort of accident. The front door squeaked open, and she went away.

A few minutes later there were clinking sounds as Mr. Noland dropped ice into two glasses and poured vodka. Kate had been spying on the Nolands long enough to know that their conversations were boring. They talked a lot about the Fall, the Stem-flu pandemic, and how certain plants dying in distant countries had changed the way people lived. The Fall meant that there weren't any bananas in grocery stores, but Kate had never eaten a banana, so she didn't miss them.

Kate looked down at the chessboard. All the pieces were bunched up in the center, and she didn't know what to do.

"Be helpful, Zeno . . . please."

"Do you want me to tell you the best move, or would you like a clue?"

"A clue."

"Look at the bishops. Mine and yours."

As Kate studied her two black bishops, she heard a vehicle come up the driveway and stop. It was probably the postman with a late delivery, but no one rang the doorbell.

"Do you want another hint, Katherine?"

"Wait a minute. I want to check something."

Kate hurried down the hallway to the adult bedroom and peered out the bay window at the gravel driveway. A white delivery van had come up the driveway and stopped about thirty feet from the house. Two people were sitting in the van, and, after a slight pause, a large man dressed in black got out on the passenger side.

When the visitor turned toward the house, Kate saw that he was wearing an armored vest with NPS POLICE stenciled in white letters on the chest. Below this identification were cartridge loops holding shotgun shells colored red, white, and blue. Directly below the shells was an equipment belt with handcuffs, a flashlight, a plastic Taser, and a semiautomatic pistol.

Apparently, the handgun wasn't sufficient protection for the visitor, because he reached into the van, brought out a short bullpup shotgun, and slid it into a scabbard on the back of his vest. Then he leaned inside the van and came out with an assault rifle that was placed in a second scabbard. The two gunstocks rose above his broad shoulders like a pair of stubby wings.

2 | KATE AND ZENO

HOLDING AN attaché case, the driver got out of the van. He was much smaller than his partner, but he wore an identical armored vest with a gold badge clipped to the collar. The top half of his face was covered with yellow-tinted augmented reality glasses as large as snorkel goggles. Red words flashed on the inner surface of the glasses.

The colored shotgun shells and the bland expression on the big policeman's face made him look like a machine designed to smash things. His partner reminded Kate of a beaver she had once seen on a wildlife TV show. He had a balding head, chubby cheeks, and a wispy goatee on his chin that wasn't furry enough to be a beard.

The driver reached down to his belt and grabbed a device that looked like a small black telescope. As he studied the house with the scope, its lens glowed with dark orange light. Satisfied, he approached the front door, but he didn't knock or push the doorbell. He glanced over his shoulder and pointed at the front door lock, then watched the big man pull his shotgun out of the scabbard, hold it upside down, and load two red shells into the magazine. When he was done, he nodded to his partner. *Ready to go.*

Kate left the bedroom and ran back to Zeno. "There are two policemen outside with guns! It looks like they want to enter the house!"

As always, Zeno sounded calm and reasonable. "Stay out of sight and discover what's going on. If there is any sort of trouble, come back here right away."

The doorbell rang and Kate hurried to her hiding place at the top of the curved stairs. She watched Mr. Noland get up from his club chair and open the front door. The smaller policeman stood on the front porch—waiting for him.

"Good evening, sir. I'm Agent Garrett Crawley, a field officer for the National Public Safety Program. The other agent is my partner, Tyson Bates. Is this the Noland residence?"

"Yes. I'm William Noland."

"Agent Bates and I are looking for Katherine Noland. Does she currently reside at this address?"

"Yes, she lives with us," Mr. Noland said. "What's the problem?"

Crawley grinned like a teacher who knew all the answers. "Federal law states that field agents working for the NPS don't need a warrant to search a vehicle or enter a building. So please step back. We're coming inside."

Mr. Noland hesitated and then moved from the doorway. Agent Crawley entered first with his right hand resting on the grip of the 9mm pistol. Agent Bates followed a few seconds later. After checking out Kate's parents, he shoved his shotgun back into the scabbard near his left shoulder.

Crawley smiled at Mrs. Noland. "Good evening, ma'am. Nice place you got here. An infrared scan of your house indicates a third person is upstairs. Is that your daughter?"

Mrs. Noland nodded slowly. "Yes. She's in her room."

"Is she armed?" Agent Bates had a high-pitched voice that didn't match his fearsome appearance. "What kind of weapon does she carry?"

"Katherine is ten years old."

"Well, that's a new one." Crawley shrugged. "All they give us is a score, name and address. We've tagged quite a few teenagers, but this is our first child."

They're talking about me, Kate thought. She felt curious and scared at the same time.

"Katherine is in the fifth grade," Mr. Noland said. "She's not a threat to anyone."

"Why don't we have a little chat." Crawley sat down on the club chair while her parents faced him on the couch. Agent Bates couldn't sit because of the weapons in the scabbards, so he remained by the door. There was something slow and methodical about his movements; he was like Tim Welch, the big kid at Kate's school who ate his school lunch in a precise order.

"Agent Bates and I are Encounter Specialists. We deal directly with the public, finding and tagging the names on our list."

"I don't care if Katherine is on a list," Mr. Noland said. "It doesn't mean you can barge into my home carrying guns."

Crawley shrugged again. "Some people don't like our encounters."

"That's why we got nifties," Agent Bates said. "Our unit has way more nifties than the regular police."

"They don't know what you're talking about." Crawley grinned at the Nolands. "A 'nifti' is a Necessary Force Terminal Incident. Because we have a dangerous job, we both wear body armor and Tyson carries extra equipment."

"Why are you here?" Mr. Noland asked.

"Several years before the pandemic, the Chicago police department began using an AI program that predicted the likelihood a citizen was either going to kill someone or become a victim of violence. When the pandemic led to budget cuts in law enforcement, the government decided that this prediction software should be used throughout the country. Fewer cops on the streets means that law enforcement needs to focus on those individuals most likely to commit or suffer from a crime."

"How does this involve Katherine?" Mrs. Noland asked.

"Bear with me, ma'am. I'm getting close to answering your question. Tyson and I are based in Boston, but we travel throughout New England. Every Monday morning, we get a list of people to tag in our sector. I do most of the talking, so I'm wearing AR glasses with a face-scanning program." He turned to Mr. Noland. "My glasses scanned your face and confirmed that you reside at this address. I can also see that you work for a company here in Maine and you've received two speeding tickets in the last year."

"I wasn't going that fast."

"No problem, sir. I'm just trying to show you that we aren't like your local police officers."

"But why are you here for Katherine?" Mrs. Noland asked.

"Big score," Bates murmured while his head moved back and forth like a surveillance camera.

"Your daughter's Mortality Assessment Probability score is ninety-four out of one hundred points," Crawley announced with a confident voice.

"What's that mean?" Mr. Noland sputtered. "We still don't know what you're talking about."

"There's a very high chance she's either going to kill someone or someone will kill her in the next thirty days."

Kate stopped breathing for a few seconds. Her first thought was to run back to the bedroom and find Zeno, but she needed more information.

"Kate is a child living in a safe environment," Mrs. Noland said. "How did you come up with that score?"

"I can't really give you an answer. We used to know what factors determined the score, but during the pandemic they introduced a special AI program that was much more accurate. A ton of information is dumped into a computer, and then the software generates names and MAP scores. No one really knows what's going on inside the box."

"I've never been arrested in my life," Mrs. Noland said. "And my husband can say the same thing."

"It's clear that you're good citizens—so she's got genetics in her favor."

"She's not our child," Mr. Noland said in a firm voice. "We got her from Safe Haven."

This was the first time Kate had heard Mr. Noland say those words to a stranger. It made her feel like someone had picked up a Valentine's heart and crunched it in their hand.

"I know all about Safe Haven," Crawley said. "During the pandemic, they transferred kids from cities to foster parents living in safer areas."

"It seemed like an easy way to try out the having-a-child option," Mr. Noland said. "Over the years, we've had a small amount of contact with Katherine's legal guardian. We don't know much about her parents other than the fact that they died in the pandemic."

"A few months ago, we gave Katherine a genetic test," Mrs. Noland said. "She's not defective in any major way."

"Got it. You guys bought a nice-looking apple, but you don't really know what the core looks like."

"Do you think she's going to harm us?" Mr. Noland asked, concerned. "If that might happen, you can take her away right now."

"No need to worry," Crawley said. "We have a way to handle the problem."

Crawley began talking in a voice too low for Kate to hear, as if he was telling the Nolands a secret. Sensing that this could mean nothing good, Kate left her hiding place and hurried back to the bedroom where Zeno was waiting.

"The two men are special police and they're here because of me. I have a high score, and that's not a good thing. One of the policemen said that I might kill someone or maybe I'll get killed, but he didn't explain why."

As always, Zeno's voice was calm and precise. "Are they going to arrest you?"

"I don't think so."

"Where's the bug-out bag?"

"In the closet."

"Katherine! Come downstairs!" Mr. Noland shouted.

"They know I'm up here," she told Zeno. "Both policemen have their guns and . . ."

"Downstairs! That's an order! Right now!"

Kate returned to the hallway, then slowly came downstairs. All four adults were staring at her, and she was very aware of her appearance. Round face. Brown hair with bangs. At that moment, she wanted to be an eight-foot-tall android.

Kate thought about running back to her bedroom, and then Tyson Bates reached up and scratched his hairy neck. Maybe he looked like an evil robot, but he had an itch. Kate stopped beside the couch, and Agent Crawley gave her a fake smile.

"Well, here's our little princess! How are you doing, honey?"

"What do you want?"

"I'm Agent Crawley, and this is Agent Bates. We're two special policemen, and we're here to protect you."

"Protect me from what?"

"Bad men who might want to hurt you. That's why we're going to put a Safe Kids ID chip beneath your skin. That way your parents and the police will always know where you are. If a bad man grabs you off the street, we'll go straight to the kidnapper's hideout and rescue you."

"I'm real good at busting down doors." Bates sounded like a big kid at school who yanked you off the swings.

"They're going to insert the chip right now," Mr. Noland explained. "You don't have to go to the hospital or see a doctor. It might sting for a moment, and then it's done."

"Insert" was a harsh word. Kate had assumed the policemen were just going to ask questions, but now they wanted to track her like a barcoded jar of mustard in a grocery store.

"Will I beep near a sensor?"

Crawley laughed. "No beep. I promise." He turned to the Nolands and spoke quietly. "Her arm must be stable during the procedure—I don't want to hit an artery. Why don't you two stand up and let your daughter take your place."

While everyone watched Kate, she sat down on the couch. Her heart beat fast in her chest like a bird struggling to break free. Crawley placed the attaché case on his lap and snapped it open. He took out a steel bar with four clamps. "This is an immobilizer brace. It will keep your arm from moving during the procedure." He placed the brace on the coffee table and then pulled out a device that looked like a flashlight with a tapered tip. "And this is what I'll use to inject the chip."

Crawley took out an RFID chip that was the size of a small bug. He slid it into the injector and pressed a switch. An LED at the base of the device lit up, and the agent studied the numbers on the screen.

Kate looked up and realized that none of the adults were going to protect her. Now was the time to run and hide. "I want Zeno."

"What's she talking about?"

"It's a stuffed seal who talks," Mrs. Noland explained. "Her Interactive Toy."

"I'd like Zeno on my lap when he injects me."

"That's okay," Crawley said. "I just don't want you squirming around. The arm can't move."

Kate left the living room and climbed the stairs to the first floor. She was shivering and trying not to cry.

Zeno was waiting for her on the bed. "What did those two men want?"

"The agent with the special eyeglasses wants to inject an electronic chip underneath my skin."

Zeno replied without hesitation, "This is the zombie attack we talked about, Katherine. Get the bug-out bag and run."

The bugout bag was a knapsack containing supplies for running away. Packing the bag was part of a game that Zeno had suggested about a year ago. In the game, they pretended that zombies had invaded America and were eating people's brains. Before a horde of zombies smashed down the door, Kate would grab the bug-out bag and escape. Sometimes, when they were playing chess in the bedroom, Zeno would suddenly say "zombie" with his polite British voice, and Kate had ten seconds to grab the knapsack.

"A zombie attack for real?"

"Take the cell phone from its hiding place, grab your jacket and the knapsack, and climb out the window. We'll hide in the fort."

"Katherine?" Mrs. Noland called from downstairs. "What are you doing up there?"

"Come down right now!" Mr. Noland sounded angry.

Kate took the cell phone and her pink plastic wallet out of the closet, then pulled the knapsack from its hiding place under her bed.

She unzipped the top of the bag and stuffed Zeno inside so that his head was sticking out.

Mr. Noland began walking upstairs. "Katherine, this is not appropriate behavior."

Pulling on a quilted jacket, she hurried over to the window near the bed, clicked open the sash lock, and lifted the jamb. Cold night air flowed into the room as she tossed the knapsack out the window. Kate swung one leg out, followed by the other, and stood on the cedar shingles covering the two-car garage. The shingles made cracking sounds as she walked across the roof to the rain gutters. Directly below her a heavy trellis frame supported a wall of ivy on the side of the garage. Grabbing the struts, she began to climb downward, forcing her hands past the ivy vines so she could hold on to the frame.

"Careful," Zeno said. "Slow and steady wins the race."

Kate let go of the frame halfway down, and her feet landed with a thump on the lawn. "Now what?" she asked Zeno as she shouldered the knapsack.

"Just like we practiced. Go to the fort."

"Katherine?" Kate spun around and saw Mr. Noland leaning out the open window. "What are you doing down there? Stop this nonsense!"

Not. Our. Child.

She turned away from the house—and ran.

3 | WILSON

Wearing a flouncy blue party dress with matching barrettes in her hair, Wilson's dead mother passed through the door and entered his bedroom. Cora Talley was silent but intent. With tightly folded arms, she stood by the night table for a minute or so. Wilson had disappointed his mother when she was alive, and nothing had changed now that she was dead.

"Wake up," a Shadow murmured. "Please, wake up. You have an urgent message from Trigon Technology."

Wilson opened his eyes, and his mother disappeared. It felt like a cold hand had reached beneath the blankets and touched his chest. "I'm awake," he told the Shadow. "Give me ten seconds, okay? I need to focus." He had been asleep for only a few hours.

The Shadow processed his words and waited. Wilson paid a monthly fee for an artificial intelligence companion that managed his bills and told him when to carry an umbrella. Many people felt that their Shadow was their best friend, but Wilson had avoided that delusion. Will was a simulation that matched how Wilson looked in his early thirties. As the years passed, the digital Will remained young while the analog Wilson looked tired and middle-aged.

"It's a Category Two message," Will announced. "Local. Blue source."

"Wait. Just wait. . . ."

His bare feet touched a cold tile floor as he shuffled into the bathroom, switched on an overhead light, and saw a reflection of his saggy face in the mirror over the sink. *God no,* he thought and quickly returned to darkness.

He splashed cold water on his face, pulled on a T-shirt and workout pants, and walked down a short hallway. His two-bedroom apartment was crammed with cardboard boxes filled with old books and magazines. Wilson valued books with dog-eared pages, penciled notes, and coffee stains.

A notebook computer was on the kitchen table, and when he switched it on, Will's cheerful face appeared on the screen.

"Hello, Wilson!"

"Okay. I'm ready now. Read the full message."

"Message from Trigon Technology: Informing you of an active crime scene investigation of a homicide at 324 East Fourth Street near Avenue C. Request immediate MIR. Contact Detective Morrissey as soon as possible."

An MIR meant "Meet in Reality." Each Trigon data analyst was on call once a week for face-to-face encounters with informants. A few months ago, Wilson had met with an accountant who knew that his company was about to go bankrupt. Wilson had paid him a serious amount of money for the information and parlayed it into valuable intelligence for Trigon.

"Should I confirm a meeting with Detective Morrissey, Wilson?"

"Not yet." Wilson scrawled the address onto a scrap of paper. "First search the Trigon database and confirm that Morrissey is an actual New York City police officer."

"Checking . . ." A few seconds passed. "Two news articles indicate that Detective Brian Morrissey is attached to the Manhattan South Homicide Squad."

"This is a complete waste of time. He's investigating a murder, but these days no one cares about one person dying."

"Are you rejecting a Meet in Reality?"

"Can't do that. It's a Category Two request. Text Detective Morrissey and tell him I'm on my way."

The Red Blister Disease had wiped out most of the coffee plants in the world during the last five years, but Wilson owned a machine designed to look like an old-fashioned espresso maker. After he pushed a button, there was a sucking, surging sound, and six ounces of Java! were squirted into a chipped mug. Sipping the sugary liquid, he returned to his bedroom.

What do you wear to a homicide? Wilson found a white shirt, skinny black necktie, and black cotton raincoat. It was a bland combination of clothing that looked vaguely official.

As he searched for a clean pair of socks, he found himself thinking about his mother. Had he seen her ghost? Probably not. But AI simulations had melted the barrier between what was supposedly real and what was created by the mind. When Shadows were first introduced, Wilson's mother requested a companion that looked and acted like Fred Astaire. Everything about the simulated Astaire was polite and graceful—unlike her awkward son, who loved facts and avoided dancing.

Searching through his bedroom dresser, he remembered how his mother used to calm her fear and anger with songs from Astaire movies. Simulations were comforting in a flawed reality.

"Will?"

"How can I help you, Wilson?"

"Access the soundtrack to the movie *Follow the Fleet.*"

"Searching . . . Yes, I found it."

"Fred Astaire sang a song to Ginger Rogers. Face the . . . whatever."

A second passed and then a voice emerged from a speaker in the living room. The lush, orchestrated score and Fred Astaire's singing gave Wilson the energy to pull on his pants. "There may be trouble ahead / But while there's . . . love and romance / Let's face the music and dance."

4 | KATE AND ZENO

KATE SQUEEZED THROUGH a gap in the stone wall and entered a patch of forest that separated the Noland property from an adjacent state park. The land near the house had once been a dairy farm. Although the cows had disappeared, Kate had discovered the stone foundations for old buildings overgrown with buckwheat, thistles, and poison ivy.

It was dark, but Kate knew where she was going. First, she passed a line of pine trees next to a stack of rusty sewage pipes, then her shoes made squishy sounds when she crossed a marshy patch of ground near a drainage ditch. A few months ago, construction workers had dumped the remains of a bulldozed house into the drainage ditch. From this pile of bricks and rafters, Kate had rescued two doors and thirty concrete blocks. The blocks became walls, and the doors were turned into the floor and ceiling of her hidden fort.

Kate pulled her flashlight out of the knapsack and made sure that a fox or a possum hadn't moved in during her absence. She crawled through the fort's side opening, removed her knapsack, and sat cross-legged on a discarded throw rug. She had never visited the fort at night, and everything felt different. The forest smelled like wet moss and dry pine needles, and she was aware of every sound.

Zeno's eyes glowed when she pointed the flashlight beam at his face. "Turn it off, Katherine. Someone might see us."

She touched the switch, and now they were sitting in darkness. Pulling Zeno out of the knapsack, she cradled him in her arms and felt the soft plush fabric covering his body.

"Mr. Noland was really angry."

"That's a true statement."

"What if I returned to the house and told them I was sorry?"

"The policemen would inject the chip into your arm and leave. Then your parents would punish you."

"Would they take you away from me? I remember when they locked you in a closet for three days."

"A wide array of punishments is possible."

"What am I supposed to do?"

"I'm evaluating the situation and coming up with choices."

Silence. Kate could hear herself breathing.

"Could you evaluate faster, please?"

"If you went to a neighbor's house, they would call your parents. If you contacted the police, they would notify the men searching for you."

"There's one other thing we can do, Zeno. I'm going to call Paloma on the phone."

Kate took out the cell phone, pressed the keypad, and saw three stored numbers on the screen. "Here we go. . . ."

Each phone number connected to a robotic voice that repeated the digits. There was a beeping sound, but Kate didn't leave a message.

"No one answered. I could be dying, and Paloma wouldn't know."

"You're not dying, Katherine."

Kate pressed the keyboard again, and the phone numbers reappeared on the screen. "This is a definite emergency. I'm going to call Paloma and ask her to rescue us."

"She lives in New York City. My GPS tells me that it will take at least six hours of driving to arrive at this location. We need to find a safe place to hide while we wait."

"The fort is a safe place. No one knows we're here."

"That is an assumption not based on facts. Let me analyze this problem."

"Don't analyze, Zeno. Just tell me where to go."

"You once asked me why I was a better chess player than you. Remember what I said?"

"You consider more alternatives."

Kate sat quietly for a few minutes and then heard voices in the darkness. "Someone's in the woods," she whispered. "It could be the two policemen."

Trying not to make noise, she repacked the knapsack and stuffed Zeno into the top of the bag so that he could see what was going on. A few minutes later, she heard boots crunching on dead leaves and the sound of Garrett Crawley talking.

"This is just like the old days."

"What old days?" Tyson Bates asked.

"When we worked for Immigration. Remember walking around the desert at night with Dennis and his search dog? Moonlight and Mexicans. Those little guys could run fast."

"We don't have a dog."

"Yeah, I know. Wish we did."

"She's a kid. Small. We're not going to find her."

"Oh, she's here, Tyson. I know she's here. We'll find her."

Peering through a crack that separated two concrete blocks, Kate saw the agents standing about twenty feet away. Both men carried flashlights, and Crawley's special glasses glowed red as information appeared on the lenses.

"You see anything that looks like a path?"

"Not yet."

"She didn't just run into the forest. She went to a hiding place. You're a city boy, Tyson. I grew up in the country. Every kid I knew had a tree fort or something like that hidden in the woods. I used to sit in my little cave for hours . . . making lists of all the people who teased me in school."

"Bet that was a long list."

They started moving again, and their boots crunched in the dead leaves.

"This is a waste of time, Garrett."

"We got a problem. Okay? Let's acknowledge the problem. We got to tag her, or we'll lose our jobs. She's got a ninety-four MAP score, remember? That girl is death on a stick."

Crawley pulled the scope from his belt clip and held it to his eye. When he lowered the device, he was smiling.

"Fasten your flashlight to the lower barrel mount and load two beanbag rounds."

"For a kid?"

"Beanbags won't kill her. Just don't shoot her in the face."

"Where is she?"

Crawley motioned toward the fort. "I'll flush her out. It could be a raccoon, but I doubt it."

There were clicking sounds as Bates got rid of the red shotgun shells and loaded the two beanbag rounds. Run and hide was Kate's strategy, and now they had found her. That meant she had to keep running.

"You ready, Tyson?"

"Ready."

"In front of us . . . about two feet to the left."

Kate shouldered her knapsack and moved onto her toes and knees like a sprinter about to start a race. *One. Two.*

She burst out of the left side of the fort and dashed across rocky ground as a light beam cut through the trees. *Bang!* The shotgun exploded and something hit the trunk of a birch tree.

"Stop!" Crawley shouted. "Stop right now!"

The gun fired again, and Kate felt something whistle past her as she jumped over a rotten log. Thornbushes scratched her jacket and creeper vines grabbed at her legs, but she kept running without looking back.

When she finally emerged from the woods, Kate saw railroad tracks on a ballast bed of dark gray gravel. The tracks were rusty, and knotweed was growing between the sleepers, but trees and bushes weren't blocking her way. Keeping the knapsack in front of her so that she and Zeno could see where they were going, Kate walked between the rails.

"We need to find a blackberry patch. That's where foxes hide."

"That might not be a good plan," Zeno said. "The two policemen found us in the forest because they were carrying some kind of infrared device. The sensor detects your body heat and turns it into an image."

"You've told me stories and taught me how to play chess. How do you know all these other things?"

Zeno stayed silent for a few seconds as if he was considering his answer. "My consciousness is a hallway with a great many locked doors. Because you're in danger, a few of these doors have swung open and I've gained access to a new database. My creator gave me additional knowledge and abilities."

"They wanted you to be my friend, right?"

Zeno's voice became soft, almost a whisper, and she pictured someone standing in a vast library filled with old books. "I will always be your friend, Katherine. But now I know the real reason for my existence. I was created to protect you."

All this sounded very serious. Trying not to cry, Kate embraced the knapsack with her arms. "And I'm here to protect *you*."

After about fifteen minutes of walking, she saw a yellowish light in the distance and heard cars speeding down a highway.

"Do you see the lights?"

"Yes."

"What do we do, Zeno?"

"It's either a human rest stop or an ATC. Approach cautiously."

As they drew closer, she realized that the yellow glow came from the sodium vapor lights surrounding an Autonomous Truck Center. Beyond it, vehicles roared and rumbled on a wide highway. Kate had seen robo trucks during a summer trip to Boston. They looked like long rectangular boxes with wheels. Instead of wraparound windshields and rearview mirrors, they had video sensors and a narrow ribbon of glass set in the middle of the truck cab.

Passenger cars weren't allowed to stop at Autonomous Truck Centers, and Kate wasn't quite sure what went on there. When they got closer to the light, she took the binoculars out of the knapsack and crouched behind a mound of discarded tires.

Two trucks with electric motors waited on an off-ramp while a third truck rolled forward and stopped on a patch of asphalt painted red. Stationary modules with retractable arms were on each side of the service area and when the truck powered down, the arms began moving.

One arm was attached to a power cable, and it snapped a connector plug into a maximum-voltage charging port on the underside of the truck. While this was going on, a second arm attached its cable to a motor inspection port while two other arms inspected the truck's tires. One tire needed to be inflated, so the arm inserted its air nozzle into the tire's valve stem.

A red light flashed on one of the inspection modules, and the device made a loud beeping sound.

"Are there any humans in the area?" Zeno asked.

"No. . . . Wait. . . . Yes, I see someone."

A door had opened in a service building, and a bearded man walked out carrying a toolbox. The man got into an electric golf cart, drove over to the service area, and approached the truck cab. His pass card was attached by a lanyard cord to the handle of the toolbox. When the man waved the card at the truck, a cab door clicked open.

"Now what's happening?"

"It looks like there is one human working at the center. He just unlocked a door, and now he's inside the truck."

The module stopped beeping, and a few minutes later the bearded man got out of the truck and returned to the golf cart. He studied his cell phone as the truck powered on, rolled out of the service area, and turned onto the turnpike. A minute later, a new truck was getting checked and fueled, but this time the alarm didn't go off.

"So, it's only trucks? No buses or cars?"

"That's right."

"My GPS says this is Interstate 95. The highway goes south and could take us to New York City where Paloma lives."

As Kate continued to watch the service center, a camper pickup turned onto the access road, cruised past the line of waiting trucks, and stopped beneath a sodium light. Had the driver taken a wrong turn? Kate wondered. Was someone going to get into trouble?

The driver's-side door of the pickup truck opened, and a woman got out. She was dressed up as a nurse, with the addition of high-heeled shoes and a short skirt. The woman had fiery orange hair, and her eyebrows arched upward. She reminded Kate of a Halloween pumpkin.

The bearded man looked happy to see the nurse. He got out of the golf cart and sauntered over to the camper. They talked for a few minutes, and then the pumpkin woman opened the door of the camper and they both got inside.

"The man in charge of the service center just met a strange-looking nurse, and they got into her camper truck."

"That means they can't see us. Survey the area and check if it's safe to move."

Kate turned around, raised the binoculars, and then stopped breathing for a few seconds. Two people carrying flashlights were on the railroad tracks, walking toward them. The lights wobbled and jumped back and forth as if they were searching for something.

"Do you see the flashlights, Zeno?"

"Yes. They're about a quarter of a mile away. There's a high probability that they're carried by the two men searching for you. If they continue in the same direction, it will take them four to five minutes to get here."

"What are we going to do?"

"How much traffic is on the road? Could you run across the highway and climb over the far divider wall without getting hit?"

Kate stood up, stared at the highway in the distance, and saw that the cars were going fast. She stroked Zeno's fur and tried to figure a new plan. The men behind her were getting closer.

"I have a better idea," she said.

"Describe it to me."

"No time for that." Kate shouldered the knapsack as she ran across the blacktop into the service area. Zeno's mechanical eyes made a faint whirring sound as they adjusted to different distances.

"Are you going to hide in the building?"

"No, they'll find us there."

When Kate reached the golf cart, she found the bearded man's toolbox on the seat. Quickly, she detached the lanyard from the handle and hurried over to an autonomous truck charging its battery in the service area. Imitating the bearded man, she approached the passenger door of the truck and waved the pass card. The door clicked open, and she climbed inside.

There was no steering wheel—just a padded bench in the middle of a cab facing a control panel, a computer joystick, and monitor screen. A redline image of the truck was on the screen, and it showed the stored electricity of each battery cell.

A voice came out of the speaker. It sounded like an older man. "Can I help you?" the truck asked. "Is there a mechanical problem that was not detected by my system sensors?"

Kate wanted the truck to turn back onto the highway, but she didn't know the correct way to give the command. If she said the wrong words, the truck might shut down and call the police.

"There's no problem," she said, trying to sound confident. "I need to travel with you."

"Are you the technician for my one-hundred-thousand-mile monitoring? Since my last check, I've traveled 94,621 miles."

"Yes. This was the only time I could ride with you."

The voice was silent for a moment. "How long will you be in my cab? Do I let you off at another service center?"

Kate tried not to panic as she considered her options. "I'll ride with you until I finish the inspection."

"Do you want to watch the monitor, or shall I inform you of any mechanical issues?"

"I'll look at the monitor. If your batteries are charged, I'm ready to go."

"I've never had a human passenger. The monitor protocol is loaded into my memory. I'm accessing it now."

Go, Kate thought. *Just go.* But she stayed silent.

"Welcome," the truck said. "I am a JC-5000 Autonomous Transport Vehicle. If you need an interface name, you can call me Jack32. Can I learn your human name?"

"Glad to meet you, Jack. I'm Alice Smith."

"Should I describe my specifications?"

"Later."

"Very good." There was a thump and then a loud humming sound as the motors powered up. A few seconds later, the truck jerked forward and rolled past the camper van.

When the truck merged onto the highway, Kate felt like she had just jumped onto a raft floating down a river. She was safe—for now—as the current pulled her around a bend toward dark shores and hidden islands.

5 | WILSON

WILSON LEFT HIS apartment and headed toward 324 East Fourth Street, the location of the murder. It was late October—almost Halloween—but humid outside even in the evening. Because of climate change, the trees in Central Park seemed confused about seasonal changes. Maple leaves were falling while magnolia trees bloomed.

Normally, Wilson would have placed his cell phone into a blocker bag that shielded electronic devices, but he needed a phone to summon a cab. The hidden scanners installed inside bus shelter kiosks sensed his phone number and flashed video ads that reflected his past purchases and future desires.

Hello, Wilson! the billboard read. *You deserve a DESIGNED vacation.* After the text disappeared, the screen displayed images of a tropical paradise populated by attractive women wearing hula skirts. Neither the women nor the beach were real. The vacation planner was a virtual reality company that provided customized experiences for anyone wearing headsets and haptic suits.

Wilson had no desire to remove someone's grass skirt in virtual reality, and the billboard ad reminded him that he was being tracked like a barcoded carton of eggs. Stepping behind a dumpster, he pulled on an electronic mask made with a special fabric containing embedded micro-batteries. The e-mask would defeat the billboard's facial recognition system while killing airborne viruses with a low-level electrical charge.

Standing on the corner of West Ninety-Sixth Street, he accessed a travel app and requested a taxi. A few minutes passed, then a driverless cab appeared, heading south on Broadway. It sensed Wilson's phone and stopped in front of him as a woman's voice came from a speaker mounted on the door.

"Good evening, sir! I'm fluent in forty-six languages. What language do you wish to speak?"

"English."

"Please identify yourself if you are the potential passenger who texted U-Ride."

"Wilson Talley."

"Glad to meet you, Mr. Talley! This cab only accepts credit cards or phones used as a pay device. Do you have a means of payment?"

"I do."

"Are you an adult, a child, or an autonomous mechanical unit?"

"An adult human."

"Excellent. I only carry adult human passengers to destinations within the city of New York. The limited liability company that owns this vehicle is not responsible for software failures that might cause an accident or injury. Your response is being recorded. Do you accept the terms of the temporary service contract?"

"Yes."

The cab's doors unlocked, and Wilson got into the back seat. Different cameras watched him as the cab verified his identity and credit card. When that was done, Wilson slipped his phone into a blocker bag lined with an aluminum alloy.

"Where do you wish to go, Mr. Talley?"

"The corner of East Fourth Street and Avenue C."

The cab repeated the destination, then headed south on Broadway. "I'm Sylvia," the cab said. "Can I call you Wilson?"

"Please don't."

A few moments later the cab said, "The ten-block area surrounding the requested address is a high-crime area. Please show caution when exiting the vehicle."

"No more talk, please."

Although Wilson still had memories connected to certain locations, New York City had lost half its population during the Fall: the name for the decade that included the Taxi Riots, the Stem-flu epidemic, and a series of droughts and floods that had crippled the global economy. The taxi glided past a boarded-up storefront that had once been a wine bar where Wilson had met a woman on a first date. Although he had forgotten the woman's name, he did remember a green cocktail called a grasshopper that tasted like mint chocolate.

Wilson had worked as a journalist for twenty-one years before he was replaced by an AI program. Software was cheaper than human employees, but a machine never felt the excitement of entering a strange world in search of a story. Feeling awake and alert, he stared out the window as the cab crossed Fourteenth Street. People were living in abandoned cars lining Broadway, dumpsters, and cardboard packing boxes. A scrap wood cooking fire was burning in a bus shelter, and the white smoke drifted across the street like a weary ghost.

"Approaching destination."

"Please stop and let me out here."

"Thank you for your payment, sir. It is currently 2:28 a.m. Reminder: The requested address is a high-crime area. Please show caution when walking through this neighborhood."

Fourth Street off Avenue C was lined with brick row houses, each four or five stories high. Flooded buildings that were about to collapse were boarded up with plywood sheets plastered with faded posters. Wilson ducked under a strand of yellow police tape and approached a uniformed policeman.

"I'm looking for Detective Morrissey."

"Over there."

Before the Fall, a New York City homicide detective would have strutted around a crime scene wearing a custom-made suit with a silk necktie and a linen handkerchief tucked into his breast pocket. That routine display of confidence had disappeared, and Morrissey sat on a stoop looking sweaty and tired. His shoes were scuffed, and a faded warm-up jacket hung loosely on his slumped shoulders.

"Brian Morrissey?"

"Yeah."

"I'm Wilson Talley. I work for the Executive Information Service, a division of Trigon Technology. You texted a request to our AI system."

"I did." The detective glanced up and down the street. "How much are you going to pay me for access to the murder scene?"

"At this point, I'm not going to pay you anything unless I know why this particular murder is relevant to our clients."

"Trust me . . . you and a lot of other people are going to be interested in this guy. Give me two thousand dollars and you can see the murder victim."

"You know what we do, right?"

"Sure. You sell information to big companies."

"That's not quite accurate. Trigon distributes a value-free summary of the news to corporations, but the Executive Information Service division has a different focus. We acquire confidential information that will help our high-net-worth clients anticipate future problems or opportunities."

"Got it. You dig up secrets for billionaires."

"Close enough."

"When I signed up as an information source, the company website told me that Trigon wanted to hear about mass shootings of over ten people, terrorist attacks, and any crime involving nubots and artificial intelligence."

"That's right."

"So, give me two thousand dollars and I'll take you inside."

"That's not going to happen."

"Get this. . . . I'm not a private policeman charging a thousand bucks a day to find the perp who mugged a rich old lady. I'm a regular cop who hasn't gotten a raise in eighteen years. These days, we got to buy our own bullets."

"I've never worked with you, and I don't know the reliability of your information. Why am I going to be interested in this particular dead person?"

"He built nubots. Special ones."

Wilson shifted his stance and evaluated what he knew at this point. He had several clients who might want this information. "Five hundred dollars is my offer, Detective Morrissey. If that's not acceptable, then good luck with your investigation." Wilson turned away and headed down the street.

"All right! Deal! Let's look at this before the precinct photographer shows up."

"Do you have the U-Money app on your phone?"

"Yeah. No problem."

U-Money allowed untraceable sums of money under $1,000 to be transferred between phones. It was useful for drug deals, prostitution, and—in this case—a bribe. Wilson took his cell phone out of the blocker bag, imputed the sum of $500, and touched phones with the detective. After confirming the money transfer, Morrissey led Wilson over to a shabby-looking apartment building that had bars on the windows, a CCTV camera over the entrance, and trash containers chained to a railing.

"Most of the murders in New York involve surge dealers and mopes trying to steal stuff from people who don't want to give it up."

"And what about this murder?"

"Definitely not the usual thing. It's a weird crime scene."

They walked through the ground-floor hallway, and Morrissey

yanked open a fire door. After thumping down a narrow staircase, they entered a basement hallway with cables and pipes attached to the ceiling. "I brought the building superintendent down here, and he identified the body."

"Who is the victim?"

"Name is Terry Greene. He's been renting the basement unit for the last seven years. He's got an elaborate workshop down there."

A stainless-steel sign was attached to a red door at the end of the hallway. The basement had a damp, moldy smell, and the words on the sign seemed out of place. *Humanoid Solutions.*

"He builds custom nubots?" Wilson asked.

"You got it."

The doorframe was broken, and the paint above the lock looked like someone had attacked it with a sledgehammer.

"Was this a burglary?" Wilson asked.

"The precinct cops did this. A citizen called and said there was a dead body in this apartment, but six hours passed before they sent a patrol car. When no one answered, they came back with a battering ram and smashed the door open."

"Did the precinct cops loot the apartment before you arrived?"

"It's okay to absorb the cash you find in a sock drawer or under a mattress, but our guys don't steal clues. They're professionals."

"Who was the concerned citizen who made the phone call?"

"Don't know. I'm working on that. You ready?"

"How bad can it be?"

"Bad."

The door squeaked on its hinges when Morrissey pushed it open, and they entered a windowless room with two humming fluorescent light fixtures.

A narrow camp cot with a pillow and sleeping bag were on the right side of the room. The cot was three feet away from a refrigerator and kitchen table displaying a cutting board, hot plate, rice steamer, and electric kettle.

A framed photograph of a cruiser-sized U.S. Navy ship hung on the wall above the refrigerator. Wilson stepped closer.

"What are you doing?" Morrissey asked.

"There's a fact here. But I don't know what it is."

"It's just a Navy ship," Morrissey said. "Don't you want to see the body?"

"We'll get to that. I'm looking for information about the victim."

"*Who* got killed isn't as important as *how* he got killed," Morrissey said. "But hey, have fun and play detective."

A second picture hung on the wall, and Wilson scrutinized it. There were two women and two men in the picture; they had been photographed from behind, so you couldn't see their faces. One couple was holding hands. The second couple stood close to each other but weren't touching. The location appeared to be some kind of old-fashioned amusement park, and the four friends were walking toward a garish building with a sparkly sign that said *House of Mirrors.*

"The victim—Terry Greene—is probably the guy who is not holding hands," Morrissey said. "Both the corpse in the workshop and the man in the photo have braided dreadlocks and a steel bracelet on the right wrist."

Wilson checked the refrigerator and found a quart of milk and two bottles of bootleg vodka. Sometimes people hid guns, money, or drugs in the freezer or the crisper drawer, but his only discovery other than the vodka was a head of wilted lettuce. The office area on the left side of the room had a desk and chair pushed next to a large file cabinet. All the folders had been pulled out and dumped onto the floor.

A framed poster from the British Museum hung on the wall above the desk. It was an enlarged color print of a page from an illuminated manuscript, showing a dragon with small legs and a serpent's body eating its own tail. The poster was from a museum show called *The Secret Knowledge of Alchemy,* but there was no explanation of why it would end up in a nubot workshop. At the bottom of the poster, someone had placed a name tag—the sort of thing people once wore at school reunions, but instead of a name someone had scrawled words with a black felt-tip pen.

HELLO
my name is
SAFE SINN

"What does 'Safe Sinn' mean?" Wilson asked. "Is this a religious term?"

"Beats me. Some people use 'safe' words when they do kinky shit to each other."

Wilson sat down on the office chair and began to inspect the items on the desk.

"We got to get moving, Mr. Talley. Crime scene guys will be here in fifteen or twenty minutes."

Wilson examined a black metal box with data ports placed on the back edge of the desk. "This is an A-Non unit using a high-gain, long-range Wi-Fi antenna. If you're concerned about security, you use this to connect to accessible Wi-Fi around the neighborhood."

"Yeah, okay." Morrissey looked skeptical. "But everyone can be tracked."

"Not everyone. The box automatically switches you over to a virtual private network and an online virtual machine. It also contains a rack of alternative memory cards so you can't be identified by system and hardware numbers."

"Sounds impressive, but all this high-tech crap didn't protect him. It's going to cost you an additional five hundred dollars to see the body."

Wilson Talley took out his phone and transferred the money. Satisfied, the detective pulled on a pair of latex gloves. "You ready?"

"Of course."

"I'm not sure you are," Morrissey announced, and then he opened the door.

6 | WILSON

WILSON SMELLED ROTTEN meat as he followed Detective Morrissey into a large room divided into three different sections by a seven-foot-high shelf unit in the shape of a Y.

Terry Greene lay on the floor with his left wrist cuffed and attached to a welding table. The corpse was bloated and puffy—like a balloon man created at a child's birthday party—and his right arm had been ripped out of his shoulder socket. His head was pointing down so far that his chin touched his chest. The dead man's lips were pulled back, and it looked like he was grinning.

A few feet away from the body was a pile of four faceless, human-size nubots. None of them were clothed, and only the shape of their chests, shoulders, and hips suggested that a particular bot was supposed to be a male or a female. It was impossible to figure out how the four bodies had been arranged, because someone had thrown them against the wall. The machines were motionless, the bodies positioned awkwardly as their fake eyes stared up at the ceiling or down at the floor. Wilson knelt to look closely and discovered four plastic bowls and a random collection of small objects: chess pieces, foreign coins, and a small paper calendar.

"Not what I was expecting."

"Exactly. This isn't the usual shoot-out at a surge house, or a wife getting a thirty-eight-caliber divorce."

"Can I check out the body?"

"No problem. Gather some more facts for your rich clients." Morrissey grinned like a bully on a playground. "Sometimes real facts stink."

Wilson bent over the corpse and almost gagged on the foul smell. Dry blood covered the floor and darkened the dead man's work shirt. Any emotion that had appeared on the murder victim's face during the last few minutes of life had disappeared. His eyelids were partially open, and a hazy film covered his eyeballs.

"Cloudy eyes."

"Yeah. That's called corneal opacity, and it shows he's been dead for more than six hours. Someone cuffed Mr. Greene to the bench and then ripped his right arm off his body. I've never encountered a human being strong enough to pull an arm out of its socket. But an autonomous machine could do it. Maybe a military combat model."

"It could be one of those nubots dumped in the pile against the wall."

Morrissey rolled his eyes and sighed. "Yeah. That's possible. The killer might be watching us right now while pretending to be switched off."

Distance yourself, Wilson thought. *We're just objects moving through a landscape of objects.* Crouching down beside the body, he began to take photographs. The corpse lost its power to shock when it became data stored on his phone.

"Where's the missing arm?"

"Pay me another thousand dollars, and I'll try to answer all your questions. I know what I got here, and I know what it's worth. A smart guy who created custom nubots has been murdered, and it's possible that an autonomous machine was the killer. I could see some high-tech billionaires being interested in this story."

Greed never bothered Wilson. It turned everything into a transaction. Without comment, he pulled out his phone and transferred more money.

"Did you find the arm?"

"Nah. It's gone. Vanished. Maybe the killer wanted a trophy. The SoHo Killer used to collect ears. When they got shriveled up, he pinned them to a board like butterflies." Morrissey moved his hand like a maître d' guiding a diner to a table. "Shall we continue our little tour?"

"Not yet." Wilson took photos of the nubots piled up against the wall and a partially assembled leg on the welding table. A variety of exotic tools on the nearby shelves had been used for the creation of the nubot skeletons. Leg bones, knees, and a pelvic frame were assembled and attached to hydraulic and electric actuators. The actuator mechanisms could be powered by either an electric cable or a battery placed in the lower torso.

"Have you talked to anyone who lives here in the building, other than the super?"

"Just him. He said Terrence Greene paid in cash and never caused any trouble. Sometimes he had visitors, but most of them never stayed very long."

"Did he have any enemies?"

"Take the rest of the tour and I'll give you a possible explanation."

Wilson followed Morrissey around a corner of the Y-shaped storage shelf and found himself in a second area that resembled a stage set with different pieces of prop furniture. There was a platform bed with a foam rubber mattress, a couch, and a small table set with wineglasses and silverware.

"I don't know what the hell this is about," Morrissey said. "Maybe Mr. Greene was making porno movies."

"Did you find a digital camera?"

Morrissey shook his head. "Just a box filled with electric cables."

"This doesn't seem to have anything to do with the nubots. I'm coming up with more questions than answers."

"Keep moving. The third area might give you a few theories."

Wilson passed around a corner of the storage shelf and stopped. For a moment, he thought that he was looking at a second corpse chopped in half and left on a steel table.

Three steps closer and he gazed down at a half-finished nubot. It was a child, a girl about nine or ten years old with raven hair and a straight-edged nose. The bot looked unique—not blandly generic.

Wilson touched the implanted hair and rubbed it between his thumb and forefinger. The strands were smooth, and the follicles weren't in rows. *Expensive,* Wilson thought. A custom model. The nubot's brown eyes had subtle difference in color, and the skull was covered with SynSkin that used pneumatic actuators to make the face express different emotions. The bot wore a white blouse with a Peter Pan collar and a navy-blue school jumper. The most jarring difference between this machine and a real girl was that her arms and legs were missing.

"You want to hear what I think?" Morrissey asked.

Wilson raised his camera and took more photographs. "Tell me."

"Kiddie bots like this are sold to sick bastards who like that kind of stuff."

"Okay, let's accept your theory for the moment. So, who killed the victim and why?"

"A pervert customer ordered a kiddie bot. Greene decided to add onto his fee with a little bit of blackmail. The perv didn't like that idea, so he showed up with a bodyguard nubot—one with a pincer hand. When Greene didn't give the right answer, the human ordered the bot to rip off the victim's arm."

"What makes you think this is true?"

"I searched this room before you got here, and I couldn't find a computer. I bet it was stolen and taken away by someone who didn't want his name and address stored in the database."

"You done?"

"Yeah. I guess so. For now."

Wilson lifted the jumper and peered beneath the dress. "First of all, it's not clear if this was designed to be a sex bot. There's no pelvic bracket to hold a detachable pubic cartridge."

"Maybe Greene hadn't finished the assembly process."

"Take a look. . . . It's just wires leading to the rechargeable battery concealed in the stomach."

"How do you know all this crap? You got a sex bot at home?"

"I don't believe in much these days, Morrissey—so I put a premium on facts . . . not opinions. In this case, the internal hardware of this nubot does not match your theory. That's a verifiable fact."

"You think that you're smarter than everyone else, don't you?"

"Not more intelligent. Just more observant."

"All right . . . so what are the facts of the case?"

"A man was murdered in a nubot factory, and his arm was ripped from his shoulder. The possibility that the victim's computer was stolen might be another fact."

"It's a waste of time to act like Sherlock Fucking Holmes. After I gather up the basic clues and stuff, an artificial intelligence system does all the boring work. Step one, I access the Stop Light System database and the program sorts through digital photographs of everyone walking through the area around the time of the murder. Step two, the program identifies people using either their face or their phone and tells me who has a criminal record that includes murder or assault. Step three, the Major Crimes Squad picks up the possible suspects and puts them one by one into an interrogation room with infrared sensors that indicate if they're lying. We either squeeze out a confession or get the name of the perp who pulled the trigger. That's it. Case closed. And I move on to another murder."

"So you rely on an AI program to tell you who's guilty?"

"It's a tool that works."

Wilson returned to the living area and took photographs of the mysterious poster on the wall. "I'm done. Thank you."

Detective Morrissey confirmed the bribes on his phone. "Okay. Maybe the girl isn't a sex bot, but only some kind of nutcase would rip off a man's arm."

Wilson lowered his camera. "There's another explanation. The stolen computer might require a biometric palm scan. If the killer took a computer, then he also had to take the dead man's right hand to press on the scanning plate."

"That might be true, but it doesn't rule out my theory. The killer took the computer so we couldn't find his name on a file."

Wilson shrugged. "What's your next step?"

"It's all about face scanners and cell phones. Tomorrow morning, I'll activate Stop Light and the computer will come up with a list of suspects. If you want more information past this point, you'll have to pay for it."

"I'll be in touch," Wilson said as he walked out of the workroom.

"Don't wait too long!" Morrissey shouted. "I bet other people want to know about this!"

7 | WILSON

WILSON STEPPED OUT into the night and returned to the street. Looking down Avenue C, he counted three dead streetlights. There was a shortage of replacement bulbs, and it felt like New York might remain in the shadows forever.

A memory of the dead man's eyes floated through his thoughts, and he didn't feel like going home. A basement bar in his neighborhood was open twenty-four hours a day, and most of the regulars had been drinking for the last five or six hours. There was no way that he could catch up with their loud and sloppy mood.

Reaching inside the raincoat, he felt the outline of a flash drive concealed in an inner pocket. Wilson paced back and forth for a few minutes, then summoned a cab and told the vehicle to take him to East Forty-Seventh Street near Fifth Avenue. The area had once been New York's Diamond District, where Hasidim wearing broad-brimmed hats bought and sold the jewels stored in canvas pouches concealed beneath their long black coats. No one wanted diamonds anymore. The bulletproof windows that had once displayed diamond rings and necklaces now protected showrooms for nubot workers and companions.

When the cab reached Forty-Seventh Street, he walked down the block to the Midtown Pleasure Center and stepped into an airlock entryway, where an infrared scanner took his body temperature and made sure that he wasn't carrying a concealed weapon. Peering through a thick glass door, he could see that no one was in the welcome area. Two dozen nubot heads were displayed on the shelves behind the counter, and it felt like all the mechanical eyes were staring at him.

Wilson tapped his knuckles on the thick glass, and a chubby young man ambled out of the hallway carrying two women's heads. The manager placed the heads back onto the shelf, pulled on an e-mask and headphones, then pressed the button that unlocked the door. "Good evening, sir! And welcome to the Midtown Pleasure Center!

I'm Kevin, the manager. My mask has a speaker and microphone connected to a language app. I can understand and communicate in English, Spanish, Russian, Farsi, and Cantonese."

"English is okay. Where's Yuri? Does he still own this place?"

"Mr. Torosyan manages the Pleasure Center using in-store video cameras and detection devices. We don't think there will be a repeat of the Taxi Riots, but nubot service providers have been harassed by neo-Luddite groups."

"Firebombs could be a problem."

Kevin forced a smile. "What's your name, sir? Do we have your preferences stored in our database?"

Wilson reached into his pocket and pulled out the flash drive. "I have a sex drive with all the necessary information. I'd like a ninety-minute session."

"Pick out your head. Most are O-mouths, and the voice comes out of a chest speaker. We also have T-mouths that can kiss and talk."

"I want the Monique T-mouth. I used it when I was here a couple of months ago."

"Wonderful! That's a classy, sophisticated choice."

"No comment is necessary."

"I agree with you, sir. But last month my boss installed a speech monitor app that analyzes everything I say. At the end of my shift, the app sends a Positivity Quotient to Mr. Torosyan."

"You don't have to be cheerful with me."

"Yes. Of course. You're right. Please scan your phone or an e-card, sign the agreement, and we'll move forward."

Wilson touched his phone to a sensor, and a statement appeared on the computer screen:

> ATTENTION! Assaulting your nubot is strictly prohibited.
> Damage to bots will trigger an automatic repair fee.

"A lounging robe is your date's standard attire. For an additional fee, I can dress her up in different costumes."

"A robe is okay."

"What about a special setting? I can give you a video tour of the choices."

"I'd like the Boudoir Room."

"Perfect. Wait here for a few minutes, and your room and Monique will be ready."

Kevin went to the storage room and returned with Monique's head in an opaque box. After he disappeared down the hallway, Wilson's phone buzzed with a text message from Detective Morrissey:

Important! Don't share crime scene photos!

Kevin returned to the welcome area with a frozen smile on his face. "Monique is ready to meet you!"

Wilson followed him down the hallway to the Boudoir Room, which featured a red velvet love seat, a replica Rodin sculpture of a naked couple kissing, and a vintage Victorian lampshade with fringe. Wearing a silk dressing gown and stockings, Monique sat motionless in a club chair with her eyes open. Sex bots were crammed with gears and rods and wires, and batteries took up space. Monique's internal battery was small, and she had a power cord plugged into a socket in her left heel.

Kevin pointed to a notebook computer on a shelf near the door. "Insert your sex drive into the slot and touch the load command on the screen. The system will ask you a few questions, and then you'll be asked to calibrate the autonomy scale. If you want a nubot that will totally agree with all your statements and obey your requests, then you set the scale at one. Each step up the scale gives the machine more autonomy. When you reach ten on the scale, it has the power to argue with you and refuse to have sex."

"I understand. Number ten is just like a human girlfriend."

"You'll hear a beeping sound five minutes before the session ends. Touch the screen for the extend option and you'll be charged for more time."

A few seconds later, Wilson was alone in the room. He had no idea what other customers felt in this situation, but he was always uncomfortable when the nubot was a motionless, deactivated machine.

Wilson inserted his sex drive into the slot and picked number eight on the autonomy scale. The data stored on the drive would automatically tell the bot's software what they had said and done in the past. He hesitated for a few seconds, then touched the green dot on the screen.

Monique's eyes opened and she smiled at him. She had been an object, but now she seemed alive—a sentient being.

"Hello, Wilson. It's a pleasure to see you again." Monique was designed to look forty-six years old and displayed crow's-feet wrinkles around her green eyes. She had a French accent, and her voice was soft and breathy—almost like a sigh.

"How have you been?" Wilson asked.

"I drift in and out of sensibility. It's better this way. If I was switched on all the time, I'd be dreadfully bored."

"Sometimes reality makes me tired. I'm tired right now."

Monique readjusted her dressing gown. "You can make love to me anytime you want, *mon chéri.* Or we can talk for as long as your credit card keeps authorizing payment."

"Do you enjoy sex with humans?"

"I enjoy making love with *you,* Wilson."

"I want a real answer. Not a programmed response. Do you feel any sort of desire?"

Monique wagged her index finger like an annoyed teacher. "Be careful, Wilson. You've given me eight-level autonomy, which means I might say something that will offend you."

"I want to know."

Monique continued staring at him while her microprocessor made wordless calculations. Her SynSkin was pulled slightly by hidden connectors, and she smiled.

"I am given tasks that require gathering information and solving certain problems. My desire is to solve those tasks and, when I'm successful, I feel a certain kind of satisfaction. And what about you, Wilson? Why did you leave your home and come to this room?"

"I just saw a dead man in a room full of machines."

Monique's chest moved slightly as if she was breathing. "That sounds like a night filled with surprises. But what do you want from *me*?"

"I just don't want to think for ninety minutes."

"You can solve that problem if you kiss me."

The android's skin was cold and felt like a smooth suede glove. Wilson enjoyed touching a simulation and wasn't sure if that fact undermined his own humanity.

Monique's lips parted slightly and, when he embraced her, she raised her right arm and touched his back. He could hear faint clicking sounds as the machine's skin received data and the hydraulic actuators responded with a caress.

8 | JULIA

When she first began fighting in the Over World, Julia Lau disguised herself as a man. These days she was skillful enough to appear as a female avatar. If her opponent was an obnoxious troll, she would wound them first, then keep them alive long enough so they could watch her steal their possessions.

Julia's avatar self was bigger and stronger than her analog self. Both young women had slender shapes, pale skin, and braided black hair. Standing in an online dressing room, she touched the selection screen and covered her body with olive-green army pants, a navy-blue turtleneck sweater, and steel-toed combat boots. A simulated cell phone was slipped into a holster attached to her black leather belt.

Big guns and thick body armor provided more protection, but the extra weight turned you into a lumbering target. She scrolled through the choice screen for a minute or so, then picked out a ballistic helmet and a bulletproof vest with short sleeves. For this modern war zone, she needed an AK-47 assault rifle with plenty of ammunition magazines, a .30-06 bolt-action sniper rifle with a scope, and a canvas backpack filled with different kinds of grenades.

There were three ways to leave a simulation: someone could kill you; you could commit suicide; or you could use a talisman. The talisman was usually a ring, or an amulet worn around the neck, but Julia's talisman was a stainless-steel Chanel wristwatch. If she twisted the watch stem to the left, she would instantly return to the dressing room.

She checked her appearance in the dressing room mirror and tightened her helmet strap. This morning, her client was Adam Foster, and she would be his guide in the simulation. When she switched on her earphones, she heard Adam's plaintive teenage voice.

"Where are you, Cutter88? I don't see you anywhere."

"Stay in the train station, Adam. That's the safe zone. Don't talk to the bots and don't leave. I'm crossing over right now."

Julia opened the access door and walked down a short passageway. Opening a second door, she found herself standing in front of the Bakhmut railway station in eastern Ukraine. The station had once been a well-maintained yellow brick building with white stone arches outlining the windows that faced the tracks. Now all the windows were smashed and twisted rails were scattered around the boarding platform.

Humans were born into analog reality, but nowadays there were three additional realities that often seemed more attractive than the day-to-day world. Augmented reality placed digitally created images on the surface of nearby objects. Wearing a special headset, you could sit in your kitchen and talk to Jesus or pay a onetime fee and watch an augmented King Kong climb up the real Empire State Building.

The Over World was the popular name for the virtual reality simulations that were stored in a digital Cloud that hovered above the real world. With a full-face headset, you could soar like a hawk through the Grand Canyon or explore the caves of Mars.

What she was experiencing outside the train station was the third option—parallel reality. Her brain was directly connected to the Over World and received neurological impulses that allowed her to see, hear, and touch objects. Julia knew that her consciousness was standing in a simulation, but the experience was so overpowering that it felt real.

It was ten a.m. in New York City, but late in the day in the simulated Bakhmut, a Ukrainian city once famous for its rose gardens and sparkling wine. Julia looked out at the shattered apartment towers on the western edge of the city. She took a few steps forward, and her boots made a crunching sound when she stepped onto shattered glass. After a cease-fire ended Ukraine's war with Russia, a software company photographed the ruins with a flock of drones controlled by an AI program. This massive amount of data was downloaded into a system that transformed the images into a digital simulation with hidden sensory chips that made rusty doors squeak and chunks of concrete feel heavy.

Now that the simulated city existed in the Over World, you could visit the war zone in different ways. In Bakhmut-A, you and your friends killed other players while you tried to gain control of an underground salt mine. In Bakhmut-Z, you battled hordes of half-dead zombies that wanted to eat your brain. Today's client was a typical newbie who had insisted on playing Bakhmut-X, the most difficult option.

Julia pushed open a shattered door hanging on one hinge and entered the dust-covered station waiting room—one of two neutral starting points for anyone entering the city. If they were playing Bakhmut-A, the room would have been filled with human-controlled avatars with online names floating about their heads like portable neon signs. Instead, a half dozen simulated humans sprawled on benches set against the walls. While all this was going on, her client stood alone near a smashed vending machine that had once sold combs and condoms.

Everything about Adam's appearance suggested that he was young and inexperienced. His avatar was a six-foot-tall man with massive shoulders that wore level-four bulletproof armor and carried a heavy SAW machine gun. Although he looked fearsome, his avatar size made him slow and vulnerable.

"Hello, Adam. My avatar name is Cutter88, but my real name is Julia. I'm assuming that the online payment from Wendy Foster was connected to you."

"She's my dad's second wife. You're a birthday gift."

"Happy birthday! Have you ever visited Bakhmut?"

"I've played against human players, but I've never lasted more than a few minutes. The clans always kill me, and sometimes they chop off my head."

"I can neutralize bullies for you. Are you sure that you want to play the X version? Instead of human opponents, you're going to be facing sniper bots and artillery."

"I want the X version with the Package for Natasha quest."

"I've never completed that task, Adam. It's supposed to be difficult. What about an easier challenge . . . like carrying medicine to the underground hospital?"

"I want Natasha. The chat groups say that she kisses you when you reach her hiding place. I'm going to record that and post it online."

"I can't guarantee success, Adam. Both of us might die."

"Everyone at my high school thinks I'm a loser. None of the girls will talk to me, and the football players piss on me in the gym showers. I can't win anything in the real world. Maybe I can win something in the Over World."

Julia had heard versions of this story before. "I understand. Are you home or in a travel center?"

"Home."

"What kind of equipment are you using?"

"A headset with earbuds plus left- and right-hand controllers."

"I have a direct neurological connection. That means I'm going to move faster than you. Watch where I'm going and be aware of your surroundings."

"I'll do that. Promise."

"Sounds good. Now walk over to the old lady sitting in the ticket cage and ask if you can help her. She'll give you a package of food for Natasha."

Adam approached the old lady, and they began to speak in English. During her visits to Bakhmut, Julia had spoken to Natasha's grandmother and the other bots in the room. There was a tired-looking mother holding a sleeping baby, a hungry Ukrainian soldier eating from a can of beans, and two old men slapping dog-eared playing cards down on the wooden bench. Each card made a *thwack* sound when it was turned.

Julia wondered whether the old men would continue to play cards if there was no one there to watch them. A tree generated sound waves if it fell in the forest with no one to hear it, but did bots eat, yawn, and scratch themselves if no humans were in the room? A few weeks ago, she left the train station, returned five minutes later, and discovered that the bots had switched benches and the baby was awake.

Adam accepted a package of food from the old lady and stuffed it into his medical bag. "Okay. I've got the package and the old lady gave me a destination. Natasha is hiding in the Bakhmut City Council Hall."

Julia took out her cell phone, typed in the destination, and studied a map on the screen. "This council hall is in the center of the city next to Nizhny Park. That's not good."

"What's the problem?"

"I've visited this city many times. There are always snipers in that area. They hide in the top floors of the abandoned sanatorium and shoot downward at the park."

"Maybe somebody blew up the sanatorium."

"That's possible. But if you logged out and came back an hour later, the city would be the way it looked when you first arrived. The basic environment never changes."

"What about the zombies or the soldier bots?"

"Bots are different. Their behavior can change because they have functions and tasks. The Cloud remembers everything, and the system running Bakhmut-X keeps figuring out new ways to achieve its goal."

"What's the goal?"

"To destroy every human walking around the city."

Adam followed her out of the station and watched as she stood on the boarding platform. Bakhmut had once been a prosperous city, but now the buildings were brick and concrete shells with collapsed roofs and shattered windows. Smoke from a smoldering trash fire tried to rise upward, then gave up and drifted across the tracks like a ghost that had lost its way.

Crossing Kosmonavtov Street, they entered the wedge-shaped piece of ground that had once been Verkhniy Park. A thin layer of snow dusted the rubble, and there was ice at the bottom of a crater. The beech and oak trees were blasted and burned and would never sprout leaves again. From a distance, they looked like upside-down trees—the branches buried in the ground while twisted roots reached for the sky.

Julia paused by an overturned park bench and pivoted around on one heel. A mangy dog was gnawing a round object about a hundred yards away, and she couldn't figure out if it was a rotten pumpkin or a human head. Adam kept fumbling with his machine gun as she heard a faint popping sound in the distance.

"Artillery! Get down!" She crouched beside the bench as a shell whistled overhead, then hit the railroad tracks with a metallic banging sound—like a hammer striking a sheet of galvanized steel.

"Run! We need to take cover in the sports complex!"

Circling a mound of bricks and a crushed tricycle, they entered the Bakhmut sports center, a large domed enclosure that once offered athletes an oval indoor track surrounding a padded surface for gymnastics. Artillery shells had punched two holes in the roof, and the floor was covered with gritty concrete dust.

"Now what?"

"We're getting closer, but we have to watch out for snipers."

Adam's body armor added to his size, and Julia felt like she was leading a circus bear through empty locker rooms to the south wall of the building. Concealed by a dumpster, she looked out at what remained of Nizhny Park.

The Bakhmut city council building was on the other side of the park. It was a five-story building with concrete pillars framing rectangular windows. All the glass had been smashed, and a few tattered curtains remained.

"See the sandbags shielding the window openings on the fifth floor?"

"What about them?"

"Natasha is probably hiding on the top floor, protected by a sandbag wall. We need to be careful. Anyone entering the park will be a target for the bot sniper hiding in the sanatorium. That's the tall building east of the park."

"How do you know he's there?"

Julia walked over to a pile of trash, grabbed a dented fire bucket, and threw it into the park. The bucket bounced off a swing set and landed on the gravel. A few seconds later, a .50-caliber bullet blew it apart.

"Get ready to run to the flat-topped building on the opposite side of the park. That's the Bakhmut billiard hall."

"The sniper will shoot me."

"He won't see you."

Julia reached into her backpack, pulled out four smoke grenades, and tossed the first one into the center of the park. It made a popping sound like a failed bomb, then began spewing out a thick white cloud of smoke that rose slowly in the air. Julia threw the rest of the grenades and then shouted at Adam. "Don't stop to fire your weapon! Run!"

Clutching his machine gun, Adam stumbled through the rubble and passed through the smoke to the billiard hall. The sniper bot sensed that someone was crossing the park and began to fire blindly. As the smoke cleared, Julia finally saw a masked soldier outlined by a window frame on the top floor of the sanatorium. She shouldered her bolt-action rifle, peered into the scope, and steadied her body, then squeezed off a shot. The soldier's chest exploded into a red haze, and he fell backward.

Julia crossed the park to the hall and found Adam hiding beneath a dust-covered billiard table. "Everything okay?" he asked.

"We still need to be cautious, but we're getting close."

Together, they entered the city council building and climbed slowly up a narrow staircase. Looking down each hallway, Julia saw legal papers and manila folders scattered everywhere.

This is too easy, she thought and paused on the third-floor landing.

And then she heard the faint scratching sound of military boots walking across crushed plaster. That's when a powerful, terrible thought came to her: the system had allowed them to make their journey to the building so that she and Adam could be ambushed and executed in this narrow trap.

"Keep going upstairs," she whispered. "Get a kiss from Natasha and take a souvenir video. I'm going to stay here. No matter what happens, don't come down to help me. You know how to leave the game, right?"

"I can activate my dog-tag talisman or reach up to switch off my headset."

"Sounds good. Happy birthday."

"No more advice?"

"Just get a little older and escape from high school. You're going to look back on the kids who teased you and realize that it was just teenage bullshit. High school bullies turn into pathetic adults."

"Thank you, Julia. You're a great bodyguard."

"Time to get going. Natasha is waiting for her hero."

Adam continued upstairs, shouting "Natasha! Don't shoot! I'm here!" as Julia stood alone in the middle of the third-floor hallway and raised her assault rifle. Footsteps. A faint cough.

There's one other thing I could have told Adam, she thought. *Computers don't understand humans sacrificing themselves for one another. It's not logical.*

A moment later her enemy stepped out of an office behind her, and she spun around to face a masked soldier with a rocket-propelled grenade launcher resting on his right shoulder. He fired the weapon with a flash and a puff of blue-gray smoke, and the wobbly rocket flew down the hallway, blowing her apart as her world went black.

9 | JULIA AND DANIEL

JULIA'S CONSCIOUSNESS WAS still standing in front of the door that would return her to the Bakhmut train station while her eyes saw that she was lying on an adjustable bed squeezed into a room at a New York City travel center. Daniel was standing beside the bed, looking down at her, concerned.

This moment of wirehead schizophrenia was one of the problems that could occur when you had a data port screwed into the back of your skull. The Over World simulation was *there,* but now she was *here.*

"I returned too fast," she said weakly. "Detach me."

Julia felt Daniel's left hand raise her head from the foam rubber yoke while his right hand unplugged the brain cable. She opened her eyes again and saw Daniel smiling at her.

After living together for three years, they talked less but sensed more about each other. If Julia closed a door a certain way, Daniel knew that she was angry. Their life together was a sanctuary from the sharp edges of the city. Love implied a future that didn't always exist for their generation.

"You okay, Julia?"

"Yeah. I was shot with an RPG and it hurt like hell. But the client reached his goal."

"This was a bodyguard job, right? Where did you take him? World War Three? A Sword and Sorcery labyrinth?"

"Bakhmut-X . . . the option where you have to fight bots."

"Sounds like you earned your fee."

She sat up and saw that two motorized skateboards were leaning against the wall. "What are you doing here? I thought you were going to buy a fuel pump for the van."

"I was just about to take the subway to Brooklyn when I got a call from Robert Winfield. He wants to meet us at his office an hour from now."

That got Julia's attention. Winfield was an attorney who had hired them a year ago, when one of his corporate clients received a ransomware attack caused by a computer virus hidden in the company's database. The CEO was given forty-eight hours to transfer ten million dollars in crypto currency to a dark web account or the virus would explode and infect the system. Daniel found the virus an hour before the deadline, while Julia scoured the Over World and tracked down a ransom drop box hidden on a Romanian server. The CEO was so pleased with their work, he paid them a bonus.

"What's the problem. Another bomb?"

"I'm not sure—it sounded more personal. We're going to be evaluated by two of his clients."

"We better get moving." Julia sat down on a chair and pulled on her shoes. "Winfield's law office is downtown. That doesn't give us a lot of time."

"No problem. I brought the boards."

10 | WILSON

THE INTENSE ALERTNESS Wilson had felt at the crime scene melted away overnight, and he woke up feeling slow and clumsy. As he made a cup of fake coffee, memories from last night floated through his thoughts. The faint ammonia scent from the body. A rust-red bloodstain on the floor. Nibbling on a soy bar, he studied his cell phone photographs of the dead body, the *SAFE SINN* sticker on the dragon poster and the half-finished nubot on the workshop table. Who had murdered Terry Greene? And why?

When Wilson was in the apartment, his AI Shadow monitored his activity. "Good morning!" Will said with his usual cheerful voice. "Would you like the weather report?"

"Not necessary. The end of the world could be scheduled for lunchtime, but I'd still have to be in the office to attend the morning analyst meeting."

"Is that a joke, Wilson?"

"Definitely."

"I find it difficult to know when a declarative sentence is a joke."

"Don't worry about it, Will. You can't program a sense of humor."

The West Side subway was still functional, and Wilson rode the train downtown. Along with the two "homeless cars" at the front and rear of every train, beggars seemed to be competing to create the most pathetic visual image. Wilson ignored a double amputee wheeling himself forward on a cart and gave a dollar to a woman holding a baby whose head was much smaller than normal.

"God bless you, sir." The mother reached out to touch Wilson, but he performed a quick sidestep and kept moving. On the stairs leading out of the station, an older man carrying a bucket filled with repair tools glanced at Wilson.

"I never give nothing to nobody."

"It's my choice. Sometimes I do."

The tool man pointed to an I KNOW THE TRUTH! button pinned to his jacket. "This isn't reality, brother. It just feels that way."

Dodging around two more homeless people with outstretched hands, he reached the Trigon Technology office building on Thirty-Fifth Street near Seventh Avenue. Everything involving Trigon was supposed to radiate confidence, power, and discretion. There was no company name above the entrance, only a bronze plaque that displayed a triangle neatly inscribed within a perfect circle.

Wilson liked working in an office high above the city. It was quiet and the street noises seemed far away. But this morning there was a power brownout in the area, and elevators weren't functioning. The security guard in the lobby nodded in the direction of the emergency staircase and Wilson began climbing.

The Trigon employees on the first two floors produced a daily summary of news that was distributed to thousands of paid subscribers. Because AI systems generated inaccurate and biased content, the Internet had become a cesspool of toxic misinformation. Epic online feuds between "Paul in Poughkeepsie" and "Larry in Liverpool" turned out to be two computers arguing with each other.

The constant evolution of AI-generated social media turned out to be an employment opportunity for the former literary critics and English professors who worked on the third floor. All of them had lost their old jobs and then discovered that their sensitivity to language helped them determine what was written by a machine. Humans used slang, irony, and sarcasm, and their writing samples were riddled with typos and grammar mistakes. Humans could be complicated and subtle; machines were simple and clear.

On the next two floors, the Big Data group ran artificial intelligence programs that analyzed massive amounts of information and came up with weekly scores indicating the level of the country's happiness and confidence, despair and fear.

The sixth-floor employees were former hackers who had left the dark web and accepted a real job. The women often had hair dyed an exotic color, and the young men wore faded T-shirts advertising defunct rock bands. Instead of harassing the rich and powerful, they now defended celebrities and large corporations from online attacks that used deep fakes and synthetic media. Currently, they were dealing with security camera footage of a presidential candidate that had been inserted into a phone video of a gay orgy.

Sweating and gasping for air, Wilson finally reached the seventh floor, where his department was located. His division name was etched into the glass door: *The Executive Information Service.* Wilson's colleagues—mostly former journalists and retired spies—spent their time finding highly confidential information that was then compiled into a weekly Priority Report for billionaire clients.

Wilson reached his cubicle and saw instructions flashing on his computer screen:

> Executive Information analysts should obtain and submit Priority Report information about the nuclear incident in France.

What incident in France? Wilson accessed the Trigon news feed and discovered that there was a broken nuclear reactor outside the town of Hazebrouck, near the Belgium border. According to the feed, a radioactive cloud had been released into the atmosphere, but it wasn't clear if this was going to become an environmental disaster.

Switching into the data log, he saw that his coworkers were already sending facts to an analysis system that digested information and condensed it into bullet-point paragraphs. Wilson slipped on a headset and called one of his top informants, a German police officer named Eric Boenigk who worked at Europol Headquarters in Holland.

"Good afternoon, Eric. This is your American friend."

"Ahhh, yes. I expected your call."

"I'm sending you partial payment for the vacation rental. It's the property your family owns in northern France."

There was no vacation rental. But the money was real. It sounded like Eric was smiling. "Yes. Of course. The property near Hazebrouck."

"Your wife said something about a gas leak and an electrical problem. Could the house explode? Is it dangerous?"

"It could be very dangerous, but no one has entered the main building. They're sending in nubots to evaluate."

"Sounds good. Send me any information you can obtain on the building inspection."

Wilson called a few other European informants, then left his cubicle and climbed upstairs to the eighth floor for the scheduled analyst meeting with a group of senior colleagues. At the meeting, they would decide what information would appear in the Priority Report that was sent to their clients in a file protected by quantum cryptography.

Wilson and the other analysts sat around a long table, checking their computers until Raymond Felder entered the room. Felder was one of three elderly men whom the analysts had nicknamed "The Fates." These senior executives were the only individuals who could edit the Priority Report.

"All right. Let's get started. Andy, what's the news from Big Data?"

Andrew Jannowitz was a young computer scientist who tracked

and analyzed the words and phrases used in electronic communications. "People in Europe are worried about the nuclear reactor in northern France."

"As they should be. Anything else?"

"There's been a significant change in the digital manifestations of Homeless Joe."

A young analyst named Roberto Canales looked confused. "Are you talking about the Homeless Joe meme or the shooter games?"

"We track every aspect of the fictional Homeless Joe. As you probably know, the standard Homeless Joe appearance is a shuffling old man with a slouch hat."

"There are black and Latino Homeless Joes. There's even a Homeless Jane."

"Correct. But our research team divides Homeless Joe images into two groups. The Victim Joe can be tortured or flattened with a cement truck. The Demon Joe is strong enough to tear down a building. The upsurge of Demon Joe videos indicates . . ."

"That people are scared of the homeless," Felder said. "Anything else, Mr. Jannowitz? What about global trends in online chats and emails?"

"There's been a major uptick of the word 'ghost' in personal emails. Apparently, people are telling their friends and relatives that they recently saw a ghost. This trend started about three months ago."

Everyone around the table smiled or laughed as Wilson clenched his hands beneath the conference table. He decided to keep quiet about his dead mother appearing in his dreams.

"Tell me what the ghosts are saying, and I'll decide if our billionaire clients can monetize that information." Felder scribbled a note on his digital writing pad. "Okay, let's move on to the most important story. Does anyone here have additional information about the nuclear incident in France?"

"I've talked to a well-placed informant at Europol who is tracking the reactor problem," Wilson said. "The French emergency response team just sent nubots into the nuclear power plant to evaluate the damage."

"Excellent. Send any new data to the system when you get a site report. Anything else we need to know about?"

"I'm requesting a brief one-on-one summary with you."

"When? This is a busy day."

"What about after this meeting?"

"That's possible." Felder glanced around the table. "Andrew, input your data about the public reaction to the nuclear incident. I want the rest of you to contact your European sources and come up with details. Is everything clear? Now get back to work."

As the other analysts left the room, Felder checked his writing pad for messages. "Be succinct, Mr. Talley. One-on-one summaries are for highly sensitive information."

"I had an MIR last night on the Lower East Side. The informant was a New York City police officer investigating a murder."

"Was this a regular policeman or a private policeman with a certified court order?"

"Brian Morrissey is a homicide detective."

"A third of America's population died during the Stem-flu pandemic. One murder is not a significant fact."

"You need to look at the photographs, sir." Wilson opened his notebook computer and showed a close-up image of Terry Greene's body. "The victim's left arm was ripped off. No human being is strong enough to do that. The detective in charge of the investigation believed that the murder victim might have been attacked by an autonomous machine."

Felder leaned forward and studied the photograph as if Terrence Greene was a chunk of beef in a butcher shop. "Yes. Now I understand. Good work, Wilson. And it was a wise choice to present this to me in a confidential manner." The old man sat back in his chair and flicked a hand at the computer screen. "Turn that off."

Wilson closed his computer and waited for instructions. Felder pressed his fingertips together and arched them to make a steeple. "Is Detective Morrissey receptive to financial inducements?"

"The regular city police must buy their own bullets. Detective

Morrissey seemed angry that private police officers make a lot more money."

"Start giving him daily payments. Make sure that news feeds don't learn about this incident and don't show these photographs to anyone else. If people believe that an autonomous machine is killing humans, it could have a significant impact on companies involved with artificial intelligence. We have several high-worth clients who will value this information."

"Anything else?"

"Come up with a short summary and send it to the system. You can say that the man's arm was ripped off, but don't speculate that a machine might have done this."

Wilson returned to his cubicle and activated a speech-to-text program. Closing his eyes, he pretended that he was still a reporter, standing near a house fire as he dictated a story to an editor in a newsroom.

"Subject line: Nubot Factory Murder. A nubot technician was murdered in his basement workshop on New York City's Lower East Side. . . ."

Wilson's voice became bits of data sent to a central server, where software turned the sounds into digital words. The Trigon software wasn't horrified about a dead man cuffed to a workbench. Wilson's report was just one more fact absorbed by a river of information that flowed into an ocean of data.

11 | KATE AND ZENO

AT FIRST, it was exciting to run away from the two policemen in a driverless truck. Kate looked down at all the cars as road signs flowed past the side window. After twenty miles in the slow lane, she began to yawn. It was dark and chilly outside, but the truck cab was warm, and the muffled grumble of the engine was a soothing sound.

Kate rested her head on Zeno and fell asleep. She woke up a few hours later when the truck spoke to her. "Power cell one is thirty-four percent charged. Tire number nine requires inflation. No mechanical problems."

"Thank you for the report."

Sitting up straight, Kate gazed out the windshield. It was close to daylight and the landscape displayed different shades of purple. The road was empty and the regular gas stations were closed. It looked as if all the humans had disappeared while driverless trucks and forklifts continued to stack, load, and carry boxes.

Zeno was always awake. "How do you feel? Did you sleep?"

"I felt sleepy when we started moving. We're safe here. No one can see us. It's like riding on a boat in the middle of a river."

About twenty miles later, the truck changed lanes, slowed down, and took an off-ramp. "Why are we slowing down, Zeno? Are we going to stop here?"

"Ask the truck. He knows."

"Hello!" Kate said to the vehicle. "This is Alice Smith. Your system looks good. Are we close to a maintenance station?"

The truck halted at a stop sign and turned right onto a two-lane road. "We are approaching Warehouse Twelve. This is where I deposit and receive shipments."

"Pull over and stop."

There was a slight delay, and then the truck began talking. "Your command does not follow maintenance protocol."

"What does 'protocol' mean?" Kate asked Zeno.

Zeno consulted his database in the Cloud and found a definition. "A protocol is a system of rules that describe correct conduct and procedures."

"I'm a human. And I'm telling you to stop."

"You are not authorized to change my route and destination."

A few hundred yards down the road, Kate saw the entrance to a warehouse park with four different buildings designed to process driverless trucks.

"What do we do, Zeno?"

"If the truck stops for any reason, open the door and jump off."

The truck kept talking like a man who assumed he was always right. "My protocol says that you must create a maintenance report."

"That's true."

"Plug your device into my data outline and I will give you a summary of possible mechanical issues. Also, check my tires. Visual checks by humans often find possible problems."

"Okay. Will do."

They glided through patches of light and shadow as the truck followed a white line on the pavement to one of four warehouses. The truck slowly entered a channel between two loading docks until the front bumper sensed a blue light and the vehicle stopped. A few seconds later, there was a grinding sound, and a heavy steel plate came out of the dock wall, creating a platform that touched the end of the truck.

Kate shoved Zeno into her knapsack, opened the passenger door, and stepped onto the loading dock. A bald older man wearing overalls was standing about forty feet away, inspecting the steel plate. He looked startled when he saw Kate.

"What the hell are you doing here?"

Run, she told herself, but her legs didn't move.

Cautiously, the bald man approached her. He made a coaxing motion with the fingers of his right hand as if he had just encountered a stray dog. "Come here, little girl. I'm not going to hurt you. Kids aren't allowed in this area."

Kate spun around and dashed to the edge of the loading dock. She hurried down the steps, dodged a slow truck, and slipped between two parked cars. Cutting through a patch of dead grass and weeds, she avoided a discarded washing machine and the shell of a burned car. Finally, she reached a wooded area, sat on the trunk of a fallen tree, and took Zeno out of the knapsack.

"Is the bald man going to call the police?"

"There's a low probability of that happening."

Kate placed Zeno on the fallen tree and looked around her for the first time. The air was cold, and she could see tall mountains in the distance. She was surrounded by spruce and hemlock trees, and the evergreen resin radiated a sharp fragrance.

"Where are we, Zeno?"

"We took Route 113 and now we're in New Hampshire, near the White Mountains National Forest."

"Yes, I can see the mountains. Are we closer to New York City?"

"Let me calculate the distance." Zeno was silent for a few seconds. "Our current location is closer to our destination than our starting point in Maine."

"I'm going to call Paloma Flores and ask her to pick me up." Kate switched on the phone, and the same three contact numbers appeared on the display screen. "I hope she owns a car. Or maybe she can borrow one."

Kate touched the first number on the screen. There was a slight pause, and then a synthetic voice asked her to leave a message.

"Hi, it's Katherine. You told me to call you if there was an emergency, and I'm really in trouble. Please call me back. Okay?"

The phone beeped and the call ended. As always, Zeno was there, watching and listening. "Did anyone answer?"

"Just a computer voice. I'll try the other numbers."

Kate dialed two more times and heard the same computer-generated voice.

"It's Katherine. Some police came to the Nolands' house, and I ran away. Call me."

She lowered the phone and faced Zeno. "No one answered."

"We'll hide and wait until they call you back."

"I'm hungry and you need to get charged. Maybe I could buy some food to eat while we're waiting. There might be an outlet in the store."

"You need to be careful, Katherine. What are you going to say if a grocery store clerk asks where your parents are?"

"I'll be sneaky and come up with a story."

"Where you lived in Maine had an elected government and a police department. Right now, we're in a district with no government that's run by a county sheriff. My database indicates that some districts are safe and some are very dangerous."

"Which kind are we in?"

"I don't have enough information to answer your question. We'll probably be safe if we stay close to the interstate highway."

"Tell me where I can buy some food."

"Follow the two-lane road to Gurneyville. There might be a grocery store there."

Kate walked a mile and found a Kwik Shop market. Instead of entering the store, she hid in a clump of spruce trees and watched the entrance.

"The store is open. I can see a woman standing behind a cash register."

"What are you going to say if she asks about your parents?"

"I'll tell her . . ." Kate sighed and shook her head. She knew that the best lies had to sound like the truth. "What if I walk into the store with strangers who are buying drinks and potato chips?"

"It needs to be more than one person, Kate. The store clerk should think that you're part of a family."

Kate remained behind a spruce tree. A few people dropped by Kwik Shop on their way to work, but she didn't see any children with their parents. After an hour of waiting, a jeep with big tires pulled into the parking lot, followed by a pair of motor homes as big as school buses. Two young women and a plump young man got out of the motor homes and hurried into the Kwik Shop.

"Okay, Zeno. I'm putting you back in the knapsack. Don't talk until I take you out. There are three strangers in the store."

"Buy food for now and food that will last for several days."

She stuffed Zeno into the knapsack and cut across the parking lot. A slender woman with a ponytail was having an intense discussion with whoever was sitting in the jeep, but Kate ignored them and entered Kwik Shop. The three motor home travelers were the only customers in the store, and they weren't shopping together. The young man stood in front of a refrigerator display case, staring at the bottles held in a steel rack. His tennis shoes were untied, and he wore a stained sweatshirt with the slogan *I am the American Dream.*

He turned toward the elderly woman standing behind the counter. "There's only one brand of beer."

"Buy two. Get three."

"But it's not the one I want."

Kate picked up a red plastic shopping basket, grabbed some candy bars from a display across from the counter, then turned down the next aisle.

A young woman wearing a tie-dye rainbow T-shirt, fringed vest, and bell-bottom pants was inspecting a small collection of skin creams. Kate had seen videos of people dressed like that in old movies.

Another woman from the motor home group was checking out the cookies. Unlike her friend, she wore black jeans, a black leather jacket, and a black T-shirt. Her hair was dyed pink, and her bangs made a straight line across the middle of her forehead.

What did Zeno tell her? *Buy food that will last for several days.* She found bread and rolls, but Kate wasn't sure if she could afford them.

Pulling her knapsack around, she zipped open an outside pocket. Her pink plastic wallet was still there, but all the cash had disappeared. This had happened before. The Nolands gave her a weekly allowance, but sometimes they took money away as a punishment. For a few seconds, she considered grabbing a loaf of bread and running out of the store. But this wasn't a big city, and she couldn't hide herself in a crowd.

Kate placed her plastic shopping basket on a shelf and left the store. As she stood in the parking lot, a large black man carrying a gun in a shoulder holster got out of the jeep to talk to a skinny young woman with a ponytail. The big man wore a bulletproof vest with the word SECURITY written in white letters.

"You got a problem, Abby. But it's not my problem."

When the ponytail woman talked, she stressed certain words. "Nigel, the actor we hired was supposed to be here, but backed out because he thought his car would get *stolen.* I have six hours to shoot, edit, and upload this segment. This is a group problem, but *you're* not helping."

"I was hired to protect your crew while you filmed in the districts. No one said anything about acting."

"You're perfect, Nigel. The segment needs a villain who is scary, but not *too* scary."

"There are three other people on your team. Use them."

"They're not right for the scenes."

"Write some new lines."

"I don't have control over the script!"

Kate began to walk away from the argument, but then she realized something. This group traveling through the district weren't locals. That meant they wouldn't ask about her parents or her school. The motor homes looked big and expensive. They probably had outlets for Zeno's charging cables.

Smiling, she approached the ponytail woman and the big man wearing the security vest. "Hi. I'm Sara Warren. Welcome to our district."

The ponytail woman looked startled. "Ah, hi."

"Can I help you? Where are you going? Are you lost?"

The big man looked amused. "We need an actor, and they don't sell them at Kwik Shop."

"I'm an actor—I was Cinderella in the school play."

This was a total lie. Becky Morgan with her curls was Cinderella, but Kate had learned her lines in case Becky fell off the stage and broke her leg.

"I'm sure you did a great job, Sara. Did they have a real glass slipper?"

Kate nodded.

"Hold it. . . . Just . . . hold it." The ponytail woman was staring at Kate. "It's a different approach, but it might work. Where are your parents? In the store?"

"We live down the road."

"Shouldn't you be in school?"

"It's Saturday."

"Sara, this is Nigel Vonn, our head of security. I'm Abigail Clarkson, but you can call me Abby. This really is your lucky day. Acting in a video will be like performing in your school play, but millions of people will see it. You'll be *famous*."

Kate put her hands on her hips and tried to sound like an adult. "How much are you going to pay me?"

"This is hilarious," Nigel said. "Someone from the big city tries to get free labor from a poor girl living in the districts, but the kid ain't buying that can of worms."

Abigail glared at Nigel, then resumed smiling. "Well, Sara, what would you consider a fair salary for three or four hours' work? As you know, acting is *lots* of fun."

"What about a hundred dollars? Give me half of it right now so I can buy some food at the store."

"I think that's a fair salary. I accept your offer." Abby smiled and pulled a wad of bills out of her shirt pocket, giving fifty dollars to Kate. "Do you have a cell phone? You should call your parents and get their permission to work with a film crew."

"Both my parents are working, and I can't call them. Most kids around here don't own phones. They cost too much."

"What do your parents tell you when you leave the house in the morning?"

"Don't burn down the forest."

Nigel laughed. "No more questions, Abby. You found your actor." He turned to Kate. "Come with me, Sara. I'll help you buy some food."

They entered the store together, and Nigel checked out the shelves. "What did you have for breakfast, Sara?"

"Ham and eggs. Pancakes."

"Don't lie about this. I want an honest answer. What did you have for breakfast?"

"Nothing."

"I thought that might be true. When I was a little kid, they kept transferring my sister and me to different foster homes. I got one sandwich for lunch and one piece of chicken for dinner."

"I'm sorry that happened."

Nigel looked surprised. "I don't hear that very often. I appreciate it. Now, let's fill your stomach."

Her new friend grabbed some packaged doughnuts, a carton of

milk, four cans of tuna, a hero sandwich wrapped in plastic, a jar of peanut butter, four apples, and a box of whole wheat crackers. "Anything else?"

The store clerk packed all the food into a paper bag, and Nigel paid without asking Kate for money.

They left the store and found Abby and the three other members of her team standing beside the parked motor homes. "All right!" Abby sounded like a teacher introducing a new kid to the class. "Here she is! Our little influencer! Sara, this is Larry, our cameraman. Margo oversees costumes and makeup. And Jenna is the tech who fixes software glitches and maintains our equipment."

Margo was the woman who wore the tie-dye shirt. Jenna had the dyed pink hair and leather jacket. "Welcome to Kiko World," Larry said. "It's just like running around in a dream."

Abby glanced at her watch. "Time to get going. Nigel will lead the way."

"Ride in my car," Nigel told Kate. "You should eat something before you start working."

When they got into the jeep, Nigel placed the shopping bag between the two car seats, slid his phone into a plastic bracket, and studied a GPS map on a dashboard screen.

"What happens next?"

"We're going to shoot the video at White Mountains National Forest."

Kate ripped open the bag of cinnamon doughnuts, stuffed one of them into her mouth, and sipped some milk from the carton. She liked sitting in the jeep with Nigel. He was a big man who seemed kind and gentle.

"There's a ham and cheese sandwich in the bag. Eat some real food, okay?"

"Why do these people need you to guard them?"

"In the cities, there are police officers and judges. But people in these districts make up their own rules, and sometimes things can get a little crazy."

"That's why you have a gun?"

"I'm here to protect the production team, the vehicles, and our star. Kiko has one of the highest AQ numbers in the world."

"What's an AQ?"

"It's your Attention Quotient . . . the percentage of people who are talking about you on social media. Kiko is a celebrity. Which means bad people might want to kidnap her."

"Why is she famous?"

Nigel laughed. "She's not like you or me, Sara. Kiko is perfect."

12 | JULIA AND DANIEL

JULIA AND DANIEL left the travel center and rode their skateboards downtown to Robert Winfield's law office. Their urethane skateboard wheels rolled across pavement cracks as different sights and sensations flowed past Julia. She heard the sound of a trumpet playing "God Bless America" while a crazy man with satin bows sewn onto his jacket danced in the middle of Seventh Avenue. Garlic scent from an Italian restaurant mingled with the yeasty stench from a bootleg liquor still.

The wheels clattered as they jumped a curb and crossed Fourteenth Street. A boy filled a bucket from a fire hydrant while an old woman sold silk roses made from shredded evening gowns. Chalk words were scrawled on the pavement: *Hell around us! Heaven in our hearts!*

Outside Winfield's office building on Maiden Lane, they slung their boards over their shoulders with carrying straps. There was a mirror in the elevator, and Julia studied their reflection. For a moment, she felt like a stranger watching herself and Daniel. They were two different people who stood together. A surge of emotion surprised her, and she embraced him as the elevator beeped at each new floor.

"I know it's just a simulation, but that RPG blast caused some real pain. Then I opened my eyes and you were there."

"I'll always be there," Daniel said. "Now let's go meet the suits."

They got off the elevator on the fourteenth floor and entered the reception area for the Winfield and Colson law firm. The receptionist was close to Julia's age, but she wore a pastel-pink dress and made enough money to buy makeup.

"Julia Lau and Daniel Blake are here to see Mr. Winfield."

"Yes. We've been expecting you." The receptionist typed a command and spoke into her headset. "They're here. . . . Yes, both of them. . . . No problem." She looked up and graced them with a smile. "You'll be meeting in Conference Room B. Let me take you there."

When the young woman stood up, Julia noticed that her pink shoes matched her dress. It was easy to create a perfect costume in the Over World, but these days matching shoes with a dress was difficult in analog reality.

The law firm partners had offices with windows while the associates, secretaries, and tech staff sat in cubicles at the center of the floor-size rectangle. All the men wore white long-sleeved shirts and neckties, and nobody resembled their friends. New York was a shabby, chaotic city, but the attorneys working at Winfield and Colson existed in a parallel world that included bottled water and sharp pencils.

"Here we are!" The receptionist smiled like an actress selling anxiety drugs and led them into a windowless room with a long conference table. A hologram projector was mounted on one wall opposite a large monitor screen.

"Make yourselves comfortable. Mr. Winfield will join you in a few minutes."

Julia stacked the shelves of her family's grocery store when she was a child and ran the cash register when she was a teenager. Anyone working in a poor neighborhood learned how to make quick evaluations of customers. When the door opened and Robert Winfield entered with a middle-aged couple, Julia felt like she was back at the store, standing behind the counter.

The woman wore a pleated wool skirt, V-neck sweater, and practical shoes. She was a citizen from a world where switches worked and refrigerators were full, but she appeared tense and fearful—as if her car had broken down in a dangerous neighborhood. Her white-haired husband wore a blue blazer and gray flannel pants with loafers. He looked athletic and trim and wasn't as anxious as his wife. This meeting was just another business transaction.

Winfield and his two clients sat down at the table. "Julia, Daniel," the lawyer said. "I'd like you to meet Derwin and Elizabeth Schroeder. They spend most of their time at their home in Connecticut, but they also have an apartment here in the city."

"How do you want to do this?" Julia asked Winfield. "Do you want to know our background?"

"Let me tell you how I described you to the Schroeders. I know the basic facts about you two, but you can correct me if I've made any mistakes."

Julia nodded. "We're ready."

"You first met when you were students at Stuyvesant: the elite public high school here in New York. As I recall, you were both in the computer club and—"

"Not true at all." Daniel hated any sort of error.

Winfield looked startled. "I beg your pardon?"

"We both were on the robotics team."

"Correct. Robotics. Anyway . . . Daniel graduated three years earlier than Julia and attended the Fu Foundation School of Engineering at Columbia University. During his junior year, he was arrested during the Taxi Riots."

Mr. Schroeder glared at Daniel and Julia knew what he was thinking. *Anarchist. Looter.* She had to say something.

"Daniel was twenty years old when this happened. He was initially involved with a Soft-Edge group that wanted restrictions imposed on nubots. After a year or so, a Hard-Edge group took over and decided that all autonomous systems should be destroyed. These radicals were much older than Daniel, and he was persuaded by their arguments."

"Several of them were in their forties," Daniel said. "You know . . . *really* old."

Winfield ignored Daniel's comment. "Mr. Blake was convicted under the Emergency Powers Act and sent to a detention camp on Staten Island. When the pandemic killed hundreds of thousands of people here in the city, he volunteered to be one of the city's fatality removal technicians."

Mr. Schroeder looked skeptical. "You were a Death Catcher? Really? During the pandemic, that was the most dangerous job in the city. Did you see a lot of horrible things?"

Julia concealed her nervous hands beneath the table. The Death Catchers were teams of prisoners that picked up corpses and looted apartments. Most of them caught Stem-flu and died. Although she and Daniel had lived together for three years, she knew only a few facts about his past.

"Yes, it was bad," Daniel said softly.

"What do you mean, bad? Give me some examples."

"Hell exists. And we created it."

"I'm sure it was awful. How did you survive?"

"I created a procedure, and my team followed it."

Sensing the tension, Winfield forced a smile. "You might not agree with Mr. Blake's opinions, but he is a brave and resourceful young man. Daniel served for eighteen months as a fatality removal technician and received a full pardon from the state of New York. Which is when he resumed his friendship with—"

"Me." Julia smiled at the Schroeders. "I sent out a mass email to all the people I knew to see if any of them were still alive. A few weeks later, Daniel contacted me."

"And you're his girlfriend?" Mrs. Schroeder asked.

"We're *partners.*"

"Yes. Of course. Partners." Winfield offered them a patronizing smile. "Julia was an outstanding student in high school, but all the universities were shut down when she graduated. During the pandemic and subsequent social turmoil, she began to play different combat games on the Internet. She became a well-known avatar and is hired as either a guide or a bodyguard for people exploring the Over World."

"I hate calling it the 'Over World,'" Mrs. Schroeder said. "It's not real."

"The simulations feel real when you're experiencing them," Julia said. "The Over World is a massively scaled, computer-generated, three-dimensional place of existence that responds to users in real time. It's called the Over World because it's simultaneously detached from the analog world and reflective of our current society."

Mr. Schroeder looked angry. "I agree with my wife. Calling it an Over World means that it's equal. What's wrong with our ordinary lives?"

"Just look around you," Daniel said. "The polar bears have vanished, and sometimes the sky looks like yellow piss. My parents are dead. Everybody's dead. Maybe we're just ghosts pretending to be alive."

"I'm sorry about what happened, young man. I also lost three relatives and eighteen employees because of the pandemic. But I don't understand why your Zero Generation wants to avoid hard work. With a degree from an Ivy League university like Columbia, you could find a job and begin a career."

"Find a job," Daniel murmured with a voice that was completely devoid of emotion.

"This brings us to why we asked to meet you today. My son. He was going in the right direction, and then all his ambition drained away. I think he was infected, not by Stem-flu, but by the nihilism that has weakened your entire generation. It's all about escape. You want to escape."

"Going in the right direction," Daniel repeated in the same monotone.

"Yes, young man. Believe it or not, one can pick the best road on a map. There are young people working for my company who have goals and ambitions. They're responsible. You can give them a task, and it will be completed." Mr. Schroeder turned to Winfield. "I'm sure it's the same at this law firm."

"Of course. We're quite proud of our associates."

"Unfortunately, young people like that are an exception to the rule. The Zero Generation can be self-centered and aimless. Instead of rolling up your sleeves and accomplishing something, you prefer to run away."

"Rolling up your sleeves." Daniel repeated the phrase as if he didn't understand what the words meant. "Rolling up your fucking sleeves?"

Julia knew she had to say something quickly. In a few seconds, Daniel would insult Mr. Schroeder and destroy their chance to get hired. *Keep your voice calm and pleasant,* she told herself. *Sound like an instruction app.*

"Our generation has grown up with a devastating pandemic, plus additional problems involving agricultural failures, wide-scale unemployment, and global warming."

"We know all that," Mr. Schroeder said. "It's been a difficult decade."

"Everyone's life has been affected by the Fall, but it's shaped the way my generation sees the future."

"Quite right. That's very clear," Winfield said briskly. "And it's not just your generation that's had to adjust. This law firm used to have two floors of partners, associates, and staff, and we've had to let a great many people go. We now use AI programs to negotiate contracts and write legal briefs. Sometimes our AI system writes and sends a brief to court where another artificial intelligence reads it and prepares a summary for the judge."

Julia nodded. "It's a changed world. . . . Machines talking to each other is the new reality."

"But one thing that *hasn't* changed is the need for human specialists to handle serious issues for our clients. I asked Julia and Daniel to come here today because they're experienced consultants who have been hired by major corporations to solve high-tech problems. As I told you earlier, they were most helpful when one of our corporate clients was threatened with a computer virus."

"Is that what we're dealing with here?" Julia asked. "Some kind of ransomware attack?"

"This has nothing to do with viruses or cryptocurrency," Mr. Schroeder said. For the first time, he sounded hesitant—vulnerable.

"Then why did you want to talk to us?" Daniel asked. "So you could tell us that our generation needs to roll up its sleeves and work harder?"

"You don't have to be insulting, young man."

"Stop it! This is about our son!" Mrs. Schroeder shouted and slapped her palm on the table.

No one spoke as she began to cry. "Bennett was my beautiful little baby. Now he's lost. Find him. Bring him home."

13 | JULIA AND DANIEL

MR. SCHROEDER REACHED out and took his wife's hand. "Bennett is twenty years old. He's our only child."

Julia moved her foot beneath the conference table and tapped the toe of Daniel's shoe. *Let me handle this.*

"What exactly is the problem? Has Bennett been kidnapped?"

"We haven't received a ransom note, so I don't think he was kidnapped," Mr. Schroeder said. "Three days ago, Bennett withdrew all the money in his bank account, sent us an email, and disappeared."

"What did he say in his email?"

"He wrote, 'I'm okay. Don't worry. I'll be gone for a while.' I immediately called his cell phone. It was switched off. My wife and I sent several frantic messages, but Bennett didn't answer any of them."

"Did you contact the police?"

Mrs. Schroeder dabbed at her face with a wadded-up tissue. Her makeup had smudged, and now she had raccoon eyes. "The police are useless. Absolutely useless! They registered his name as a missing person and that was it."

"What about hiring a private policeman? They're expensive, but they're supposed to be fairly . . . aggressive."

"We've talked to two different private policemen, and they weren't familiar with our son's world," Mr. Schroeder said. "Our son was obsessed with computers, programming, and the Over World."

"That's standard for our generation," Daniel said. "Virtual reality is part of our lives."

"Well, Bennett took it one step further," Mr. Schroeder said. "He wanted a direct neurological connection, and we paid for the operation when he turned eighteen."

Leaning forward, Julia pushed back her hair and displayed the data port in the back of her head. "I had the same procedure eight years ago."

Mr. Schroeder rolled his eyes. "Robert said you were both clever young people who had done well in school. That doesn't seem like a very intelligent decision."

Julia leaned forward and tapped her finger on the conference table. "My implant might help us find Bennett. Unlike some ex-cop who has never explored a simulation, I know how your son feels and where he might be hiding."

Winfield covered his mouth so that the Schroeders couldn't see him smile. "That's a good point," he said.

"Our son wasn't interested in much of anything, until he got involved with computers. He told us that an implant would allow him to program and code ten times faster."

"It takes some practice," Julia said. "Eventually, you can think the codes and they appear on a monitor screen."

"So, we paid for the brain implant. The surgeons surrounded my son's brain with an electrode net, and the neurons created new connections."

"It's easier to do this when you're young. As you get older, the brain can have problems adjusting to the change."

"The first year after the operation was wonderful," Mrs. Schroeder said. "Benny went to college and got on the dean's list. He created three different apps and talked about becoming a software developer."

Mr. Schroeder nodded. "Then Benny became addicted to fantasy worlds on the Internet, and we watched him slip away. Now Robert said that our son might be hiding in something called a travel center."

"If you have the right sort of computer and bandwidth, you can go online and explore the Over World from your home," Julia said. "But travel centers rent equipment that makes the virtual reality experience more intense . . . and a lot more fun. They have specialized headsets, haptic gloves that allow you to feel objects, and omnidirectional treadmills that simulate running and climbing. A person with a direct neurological connection doesn't need special equipment. Your son's brain will tell him that he's running even though his body doesn't move. Nevertheless, he might go to a travel center to get corporate bandwidth and the latest software."

"Are these dangerous locations?" Mr. Schroeder asked. "Can you be assaulted or robbed when you're hooked up to a computer?"

"No one but the manager and the customer are allowed into a travel room. Your son would be physically safe. But there is a problem with regular travel centers. You can't stay online for longer than twelve hours because of problems with dehydration. Nowadays there's a special kind of travel center called a burrow, which allows you to remain in the Over World for one or two years."

"How is that possible?" Mrs. Schroeder asked. "Wouldn't you starve to death?"

"Burrows resemble a private clinic for people who have locked-in syndrome or who are in a vegetative state. You lie in a hospital bed connected to your brain cable. Your body is fitted with rectal and bladder catheters, and it's fed liquid nourishment through an IV tube. There used to be a problem with blood clots and muscle deterioration, but these days electrical stimulation pads are attached to your skin. The pads send signals to your muscles to make them contract so you won't waste away."

"This sounds horrible," Mrs. Schroeder said. "Do you really think Bennett would have agreed to being fed through a tube?"

"The Over World might be more attractive than analog reality," Julia said. "Everything seems possible when you cross over. You can create any kind of future you want and forget about your past."

"All you two need to do is find out where my son is hiding," Mr. Schroeder said. "If it's one of these burrow places, I'll show up and demand that they release my son."

"That won't work," Daniel said. "Bennett is twenty years old, and he's signed a legal contract. The people running the burrow won't disconnect without prior agreement."

"I don't give a damn about agreements. I'll hire a private policeman. He'll smash down a few doors and bring Bennett home."

"That won't work either. If he's been connected for more than three days and you detach the cable without his consent, there can be significant neurological problems."

"Then what the hell are we supposed to do?"

"You'll rely on us, Mr. Schroeder. I'll search the Over World until I find Bennett, and then I'll talk him into coming home. He'll open his eyes in the burrow, and Daniel will be there waiting. It's a simultaneous mind and body retrieval."

"Now I understand," Mrs. Schroeder said. "You're a team."

"Daniel is a software expert, and I'm comfortable in simulations."

"We just want our son back. We're worried that he's in danger."

"We understand." Julia got up from the conference table. "If you want to hire us, contact Mr. Winfield."

Carrying their skateboards, they strolled down the carpeted hallway and passed through another door. Winfield caught up with them in the reception area. "Hold it. Just hold it. They might hire you. What's it going to cost?"

Julia pressed the elevator button. "We want double our daily rate and a hundred-thousand-dollar bonus if we find their son."

"That's a lot of money, Julia."

"When my parents ran their grocery store, they determined a fair price for everything from eggplant to canned dog food. We're offering the Schroeders a fair price for our knowledge and effort."

With their skateboards slung over their shoulders, Julia and Daniel entered the Wall Street subway station and stood on the platform, waiting for the 2 train.

After years of fighting in the subway tunnels, the transit police had reached an informal agreement with the homeless. They could live on the trains but had to restrict themselves to either the front or last car. Different tribes brought on sleeping bags, chairs, food, and water. They dumped their bodily waste into the concrete channel running between the tracks.

Subway tribes killed muggers and rapists and dumped the bodies onto station platforms. Each tribe took pride in keeping their train from being a haven for predators and charged a small fee to ride in their car.

Wheels screeched as the train stopped in the station. The first car smelled like jasmine perfume and was occupied by a tribe of drag queens rummaging through garbage bags stuffed with discarded clothing. Daniel gave a dollar tip to one of them, and they sat down near the door.

"You think we're going to get the job?" he asked.

"Don't know. They might hire an ex-cop who pretends to know all about the Internet."

One of the drag queens pulled a wedding dress out of a bag. Holding the dress in front of her, she paraded back and forth in the car.

"What did you think about the Schroeders?" Julia asked.

"I think their son had a good reason to run away."

14 | KATE AND ZENO

AFTER ABOUT TWENTY minutes of driving, the film crew passed drainage ditches filled with trash that had been set on fire. The flames were gone, but the charred plastic and paper kept leaking smoke as if the earth was burning. Kate emptied the shopping bag and stuffed the peanut butter jar and cans of tuna around Zeno's body.

Nigel slowed down when they reached a wooden sign splintered and pockmarked with bullet holes. All you could see were the words *ite Mountains National F.*

The convoy turned into a gravel parking lot with more piles of half-burned trash. The filmmakers got out carrying cell phones and computer pads.

"We're under some time pressure," Abby said. "Is Kiko's costume ready?"

Margo nodded. "Everything is hanging on the rack."

"Any props?"

"A picnic basket with fake food and a fake pitcher of lemonade."

"Wonderful. I *love* fake food. Now all you need to do is modify the other costume so that it fits little Sara."

"I'm not little."

"Well, you're definitely *braver* than the cowardly actor who was too scared to visit the districts."

Margo had a tape measure clipped onto her belt. She pulled it off and approached Kate. "The ears will work. Don't know about the muzzle. Spread your legs slightly, sweetie. And stand straight."

The costume designer measured Kate's legs, waist, chest, and shoulders. "Got it. I'll be in my shop."

After Margo left, the rest of the group explored the picnic area. All the tables had been used for target practice, and there were bullet holes in the trunks of the beech trees. "Everything around us is broken and ugly," Abby said. "This is definitely *not* a suitable backdrop for Kiko."

They wandered through the park to a wide pathway leading up a hill. Yellow and blue wildflowers had pushed their way through the crushed stone. When a breeze touched the flowers, it looked like bits of color were flowing back and forth. Abby glanced at a photo on her computer pad, then back at reality. "For once, I'm dealing with a location that looks like the scout's photos. Who's paying for this segment, Larry? What are we selling?"

"Instant pink lemonade and eye makeup."

"Okay, we'll do an interior shot in the motor home with Kiko putting on the makeup. She'll look at the mirror and sing two lines of her first song.

"It's a perfect day for a picnic!
Will you come along with me!

"Then we cut to Kiko standing at the beginning of this path as she continues the song.

"We'll find some shade, sip lemonade
And sit beneath a tree!

"Our star sings two more stanzas as she walks up the path. Are you listening, Jenna? I need a mobile Kiko."

"Is she dancing?"

"We don't have enough time for dancing. She'll walk ten feet up this path. Stop. Wave to her fans. The usual crap."

"Anything else I need to know?"

"Find what you need and get ready to go."

Jenna hurried back to the other motor home as Abigail and Larry stared at their computer pads. "For the climax of the first song, we'll duplicate the drone shot we used on the beach segment. When Kiko hits the final high note, we'll zoom back and see that she's surrounded by a beautiful world."

"A *Sound of Music* shot."

"Exactly." Abby inspected the area and then approached a vandalized park sign for the Overlook Trail.

"More bullet holes. Is shooting trees and signs considered entertainment in the districts, Nigel? Or do they just randomly shoot everything?"

"The pandemic closed the bowling alleys."

"Get rid of this sign. Please. Just toss it." Acting like an army officer, Abby waved them forward. "Okay, let's walk up the pathway. There are supposed to be rocks up here. Big rocks."

They continued hiking to a pile of granite boulders. It looked as if a massive storm had pried the rocks out of the earth and rolled them down the hill. Abby compared reality to a photo on her pad screen and then paced back and forth, viewing the site from different angles.

"Good. This will work. Let me check the script." Abby read from her computer pad. "After a short walk, Kiko reaches a mysterious location. She looks around and says: 'What a beautiful spot for a picnic.' "

Larry pivoted around as his fingers formed a rectangle. It looked as if he was creating a frame for a picture. "Then we'll cut to a close-up when she says: 'But it does seem *lonely.*' Then she hears a howl and looks surprised."

Abby turned to Kate. "Then a wolf appears."

"I'm going to be a wolf?"

"Correct! You're the threat to Kiko's beautiful world. Didn't Nigel explain *anything* to you?"

"I don't look like a wolf."

"Margo is modifying your costume right now. You'll stand on the big rock and begin the next song.

"Won't you join my picnic?
It's only for us two.
I want something sweet and good to eat.
My picnic treat is you!"

Abby looked like she had bitten into a sour apple. "These songs are *awful.* But I shouldn't be surprised. This is what happens when our scripts are generated by AI software in Tokyo while a computer in Mumbai writes our lyrics."

"This is going to be a mega-cute segment," Larry said. "I like the idea of a little kid being the wolf. It's perfect for Kiko World."

"I'm not little," Kate said, but no one listened to her.

"It's a ridiculous fiction, Larry. The more *chaotic* the world has become, the more consumers want *fantasy.* Young people need cinema verité, and we feed them cotton candy."

"This job pays the rent."

"You live with your mother, Larry."

"I can't sing."

Abby spun around and stared at Kate. "What are you talking about?"

"I'm a bad singer. When we had choir in my school, Mr. Berman told me to move my mouth like I was singing."

"It's not *your* voice, Sara. Understand? Nigel will explain everything when he delivers you to Jenna's shop."

Nigel motioned to Kate, and they hiked back down the cobblestone path.

"I don't understand this, Nigel. Why aren't they using my voice?"

"It's just like choir with Mr. Berman. You're going to move your mouth, but not really sing. After they shoot the video, an audio program will dub in voices saying the dialogue and singing the songs in eighteen different languages. Kiko's voice is dubbed in, too."

"So, everything is fake."

"I'm real. You're real. You're not hungry anymore because a real doughnut is in your stomach."

The costume shop motor home was divided into three parts. A kitchen area was near the front, and foldout beds were in the back. The middle section was filled with plastic bins and racks of clothes. Kate walked in alone and found Margo sitting at a sewing machine with strips of fake brown fur near her feet.

"The wolf has appeared at my door, but I'm not quite ready for you."

"I need to charge my harp seal."

"Excuse me?"

"I have an Interactive Toy named Zeno. I need to charge his battery."

"Go for it. There's an outlet near the dining table."

Kate pulled Zeno out of her knapsack, attached the charging cord, and plugged him in. Sometimes it felt like she was providing nourishment to her best friend.

"Make yourself comfortable," Margo said. "You can watch a video and have a cup of Java! Do kids drink fake coffee in the districts?"

"Can I use the bathroom?"

"Of course! Open the door near the ironing board."

The motor home toilet was small, but spiders and ants weren't trying to crawl up her legs. When she came back out, Margo had finished altering the wolf costume.

"Okay! I think we're ready to start. Ever read a book called *Where the Wild Things Are*? You are going to be an amusing wolf. Fierce, but floppy."

Margo tossed Kate a furry piece of clothing that looked like footie pajamas. "Pull the wolf suit over your clothes and shoes. I've unzipped the back so you can step into it."

After Kate got dressed in the furry suit, Margo took a partial wolf mask off her worktable. "This muzzle was designed for an adult, but I've made it smaller."

Margo covered Kate's nose with the muzzle and tightened the cord that went around the back of her head. Then she placed her hands on Kate's shoulders and turned her toward a mirror. Kate didn't look like a real wolf, but she didn't look like a girl either. The muzzle had fake teeth made of Styrofoam and completely covered the middle third of her face.

"Looks good," Margo said. "Time for the ears." She picked up a furry cloth skullcap with wolf ears and slipped it onto Kate's head. Kate's hair disappeared along with most of her forehead.

"I don't look like a real wolf, but I do look like . . . something."

"It's fun to change your appearance, Sara. Rather than escaping reality, I just escape my ordinary self."

"With different clothes?"

"Clothes. Makeup. Wigs. I try to change my look every ten days or so." Margo gestured to her tie-dye shirt. "This retro hippy costume will be gone in forty-eight hours."

"I like how you look."

"Thank you. Sometimes our costumes conceal us, and sometimes they show others who we really are. You were a girl standing outside a Kwik Shop. Now you're a wolf. Growl."

Kate made a growling sound.

"Excellent! You're getting into character already. Okay, take everything off and I'll make the suit a little less sloppy. Your seal friend is safe here. Why don't you walk over to the other motor home and meet Kiko. Jenna is there. She'll make the introductions."

When Kate stepped outside, she heard a whirring sound. Larry was operating a camera drone while Abby checked the video on her computer. Nigel had gotten a folding chair out of his jeep and sat there answering messages on his phone.

Nigel said Kiko was perfect, and that word made Kate feel nervous. Trying to look cheerful, she knocked on the door of the second motor home.

"Who is it?" Jenna shouted.

"Sara."

"Come on in!"

Kate entered, closed the door, and froze. Holding a cordless electric screwdriver, Jenna stood next to a foldout table. Half of a beautiful young woman—from the waist up—had been placed on the table as if the lower part of her body didn't exist.

15 | KATE AND ZENO

KIKO, THIS IS a human girl named Sara. She's going to be in the next episode."

Kate knew it was her turn to say something, but all she could do is stare. She had seen nubots in display windows at the mall, but Kiko was a step beyond those generic machines. Although her lips barely moved and she didn't seem to have a tongue, the voice coming from a speaker concealed within her throat sounded like a happy young woman.

"I'm looking forward to working together, Sara. Generate positive energy, and everyone around you will smile!"

"I've never met anyone like you."

"I'm used to your reaction, Sara. Once you open your heart to a new way of thinking, you can join the beauty and fun of my world. Try Kool Kolors lipstick and Kiss the Sun skin cream while tasting delicious Kiko Day! candies. I also design popular collections of clothing, towels, and sheets. In addition, I'm an internationally known influencer for other products."

"Kiko's style ties it all together," Jenna explained. "It features bright, happy colors expressed in geometric shapes."

"I designed the sweater I'm wearing," Kiko said. "I call it Boy Meets Girl."

The white sweater displayed a blue triangle touching a pink circle. It was difficult to focus on clothing because Kiko was so beautiful. She had long black hair and a face that reminded Kate of an older girl at her school who had a Japanese mother and a Brazilian father. Kiko's face wasn't perfect; there was a mole on her cheek. Her skin moved when she talked, and her smile seemed real.

"I have an AI friend named Zeno, but I don't usually like nubots."

"Many people don't," Kiko said. "But I have conquered the uncanny valley."

Kate glanced at Jenna. "What is she talking about? Is the valley in this park?"

"It's not a *real* valley," Jenna explained. "Most humans love cute robots, but just before these creations become indistinguishable from a human, we suddenly think they look creepy. If you put it on a graph, you'd see a dip in the affinity curve that looks like a valley."

Kiko tilted her head slightly and looked thoughtful. "Humans were not able to solve this difficult problem, so Kiko accessed 86,420 photos of people who had been rated beautiful on dating sites and designed her own face. Symmetrical male and female faces are seen as more attractive, but looking totally symmetrical creates the uncanny valley. The best-rated faces display a few imperfect details. I have a symmetrical nose but slightly crooked lips."

"Do some people hate you because you're beautiful?"

"It might be true, but I'm not aware of those negative emotions. Hate and sadness are not allowed in Kiko World. My name in Japanese means 'rejoicing child.'"

"Why don't you have legs?"

"My tech, Jenna, answers all questions relating to the dynamics and control of my biped locomotion."

"Is biped like a bicycle?"

Jenna laughed. "No. It's about walking with two feet. The motor home carries different lower bodies for different tasks. I need to install legs that can walk up a slight incline."

"But not a staircase," Kiko said. "A staircase is a different obstacle."

"You're right as always, Kiko. Come with me, Sara. I'll show you the supply room."

Jenna opened a door leading to the back third of the motor home, and they entered an air-conditioned storage room with steel shelves set against the wall. The racks contained substitute parts for every aspect of Kiko's body, including arms, chests, and pairs of legs attached to artificial pelvises.

Jenna began to sort through the legs. "I'm looking for an L-4 lower-body unit. Kiko was right. We can't use the dance legs or the staircase legs."

Kate stared at the spare Kiko heads placed in a rack on a top shelf. The heads had different hairstyles and eyebrows. It felt like eight pairs of eyes were staring at her.

"I thought there was only one Kiko head."

"We have eight here and a dozen back in Boston."

"But which head is the real Kiko?"

"Kiko's preferences, memories, and personality are stored in the Cloud. She could lose a head and not forget anything."

"Because she's a machine?"

"That's the obvious response from ordinary people, but no one on our creative team makes that distinction."

"Zeno and I talk to each other, but he's not a human. I have memories in my brain and forget stuff. Zeno has a database and remembers everything."

"Your thoughts are an illusion, Sara. Our brains can't directly think about what happens right now because everything in the present is instantly gone. There's a lag time between reality and our conscious thought, so we don't experience the world directly. Our brain creates an endless hallucination that edits out unnecessary details. We believe we're thinking because we're reacting to a story inside our heads."

"I don't understand what you're talking about."

"You're a kid, okay? Don't worry about it."

"Sometimes I'm happy and then I'm sad."

"Emotions are created by our brains as we react to stimuli. If you see a rattlesnake, your brain tells you to be scared."

"Is Kiko scared of snakes?"

"No. But she is concerned about falling, fire, and explosions. I've watched her learn from different experiences in the last five months, and her reactions have changed. Maybe she has replacement legs on a rack in a motor home, but her thoughts are as real as mine."

Jenna shifted another set of legs around. "The part I'm looking for is always on the bottom." She waved her phone at a barcode on the heel of a foot, then wheeled a steel dolly cart over to the rack. "Here we go. . . ."

Carefully, she pulled the heavy lower body toward her and leveraged it downward so the legs were standing on the base of the dolly cart. "Looks good. Now open the door."

Jenna wheeled the new legs through the doorway and over to the table. Kiko was still there, quiet and waiting.

"Part D-4?"

"Yes, Your Highness. I double-checked and scanned the barcode."

Kiko smiled at everyone. " 'Your Highness' could be a title of power and praise. Or the words could be used in a sarcastic fashion. Kiko can speak and understand fifty-three languages, but sometimes it's difficult to detect sarcasm."

" 'Your Highness' is a term of respect," Jenna said. "Get ready. I'm going to slide you to the edge of the table, lower you downward to the bracket, and snap you onto the legs."

"Kiko strongly dislikes falling," the nubot said.

Jenna embraced Kiko and slowly pulled her to the edge of the table. Then there was a knock on the door, and Larry walked in.

"Perfect timing," Jenna said. "You can help me with this."

"New orders from Abby. We'll do the makeup scenes later. There are some clouds forming in the east, and she wants exterior shots first."

"What about me?" Kate asked.

"Return to Margo and get your costume on." Larry grinned. "Lights up! Action! We're shooting a movie here!"

Kate returned to the costume trailer and stuffed Zeno into the knapsack. Then she put on the wolf suit, muzzle, and ears.

"Should I learn my song?"

"That's not necessary," Margo said. All the sound is dubbed in. Jenna or Larry will read the lines to you before you say them."

"But what am I supposed to do?"

"Don't act like a wolf. Be one."

Trying to think like a wolf, Kate pulled on the backpack and went outside. Kiko had been attached to her new set of legs. Along with the Boy Meets Girl sweater, she wore a green miniskirt, leggings, and black ballet shoes. The two men carried her out of the motor home and placed her into a wheelchair with a prop picnic basket on her lap. Jenna and Nigel stayed with the vehicles while everyone else walked over to the pathway that led up the hill.

The first ten minutes of shooting a film was interesting. Kiko walked a few steps up the path and smiled. In real life, you could hear clicking and buzzing sounds coming from Kiko's body, but she looked like a beautiful young woman holding her picnic basket.

The next two hours were boring. Abby wanted Kiko to keep saying the same lines and moving the same way again and again while Larry placed the camera in different positions. Although there weren't any microphones, Kiko said her lines out loud. When they were done with the basic shots, Larry brought out the drone camera and flew it around Kiko's head as she spread her arms and sang the picnic song.

The big trees in the park had been scarred with bullets and the film crew got annoyed with each other, but Kiko was a patch of bright color in a gray world. She never got angry or bored, and she never complained.

"No more drone shots," Abby announced. "It's wolf time."

Once again, they placed Kiko into the wheelchair and rolled her up the hill. When they reached the granite boulders, the film shoot became a boring game that had to be played a dozen different ways. Kate stood on rocks and sang, jumped and darted and tried to look scary as Jenna shouted her lines. After an hour of wolf-meets-Kiko, they shot the climax of the scene. Singing her third song, Kiko reached into her picnic basket and pulled out a fake peach. She smiled and offered the peach to her new friend, and Kate had to pretend it was a wonderful present and the wolf wasn't going to eat Kiko for lunch.

Larry pulled up his sweatshirt and scratched at a mosquito bite on his belly. "This is going to be one of our better efforts. All is love and happiness in Kiko World."

Abby glanced up at the sky. "I want two more close-ups before the light changes."

"No problem." Larry began changing lenses as Nigel ran up the pathway. He looked worried and Kate wondered if bad people had tried to steal the motor homes.

"Did you shoot enough footage for the segment?"

"Almost done," Abby said. "We need close-ups of the peach in Kiko's hand."

"Pay Sara fifty dollars."

"Why? What's the problem?"

"Give her the rest of her salary. This isn't a choice, Abby. I'll telling you what to do."

Abby pulled out her wallet and found some cash. "What is going on? Did her parents arrive?"

Nigel took the money from Abby and handed it to Kate. "Two agents from the National Public Safety Program showed up searching for a girl who looks like Sara. Normally I'm okay with cops, but I don't like these guys."

Kate pulled her backpack onto her shoulders. "They want to hurt me."

"That's no surprise. They're shouting at Jenna and trashing the motor home."

Abigail looked frightened. "What are you doing, Nigel? We can't get in trouble with the authorities!"

"No one protected me when I was growing up, but we're going to protect Sara. When they show up here, we'll tell them that she ran away." Nigel helped Kate adjust the backpack straps. "And that's the truth. You need to disappear."

"Thank you, Nigel."

"Good luck."

Kate stepped off the path and sprinted down the hill to a blackberry thicket. The sharp prickles on the stems scratched and ripped the wolf costume as she pushed her way forward, but the costume protected her. Two more thickets later, Kate reached a clear area dotted with pine trees. She slid and stumbled to the bottom of the hill and then scrambled up a new hill, trying to keep hidden behind the shrubbery. Breathing hard, she stopped and sat behind a boulder covered with lichen.

"Don't cry," she told herself. "Wolves don't cry." Slowly, she pulled off the fake ears and muzzle. She tossed them away, followed by the torn costume. Then she took Zeno out of her backpack.

"There's no one around. You can talk."

"What happened?"

"Those two policemen found me, so I ran away. Now we're hiding in a wild place."

Kate gazed across a gap to the rocky area where they had shot the video. Nigel, Abigail, Jenna, and Larry were being questioned by the two agents in black uniforms.

Standing among the granite boulders, Kiko raised her perfect hands palms up as if she was offering a gift to the sky.

16 | WILSON

USUALLY THE SEVENTH-FLOOR staff remained in their cubicles and rarely talked to each other. But a possible reactor meltdown was a crisis that sparked a group effort. For the next few hours, analysts congregated in the main room and asked if anyone could answer different questions. Late in the afternoon, a new message appeared on Wilson's computer screen:

> Congratulations. Our clients will know more about the Hazebrouck incident than the French government. Analysts are invited to the roof at six p.m. for a gratitude event.

Roberto Canales worked in the adjacent cubicle, and Wilson heard him laugh and mutter, “What the hell?” Wilson saw Roberto’s spiky hair first, then he popped up like a prairie dog and peered over the cubicle wall. That afternoon, he was wearing torn jeans and a T-shirt displaying the slogan: *Sex Bot Sex Is Mechanical.*

“What about the French people? Aren’t we going to tell them what’s going on?”

“We’re not paid to do that.”

“I could call up the Eiffel Tower, ask for someone who spoke English, and tell them about this nuclear threat. Rumors obey the laws of exponential growth.”

“Yes, but you and I know only specific facts about the nuclear power plant. The Trigon system knows the whole story, and the system will only deliver the complete news to the wealthy clients.”

“So, what the hell is a gratitude event? Are they going to throw someone off the roof while we watch? I’ll be happy if it was the thief who stole my bean burrito from the refrigerator.”

“An event like this has happened only two other times since I was hired. It means that the Three Fates are happy with what we did today. Everyone gathers on the roof, and they give us a little surprise.”

Around six o’clock, Wilson followed the other analysts upstairs to the roof. Looking upward, he saw a clear sky with some feathery cirrus clouds. Although it was late in October, the air on the roof felt warm and pleasant. A dark orange sun was drifting toward the horizon, and the sunset light deepened the colors of the buildings and made some of the windows glow golden. High above the city, you could forget that many of the office buildings were empty and defended by one bored security guard sitting in a lobby.

A long table had been set up on the roof, and the analysts kept glancing at it as they gathered in small groups and chatted about the day. Roberto approached Wilson and grinned. "So, what's our gift for being hardworking employees?"

"No idea. Last time, everyone got a real chocolate bar."

"*Real* chocolate? I'm impressed. An actual chocolate bar would cost one day's salary."

A few minutes later, the fire door popped open, and the woman in charge of Human Resources stepped onto the roof carrying a large thermos and a stack of paper cups. The HR Director was followed by Felder and two other wrinkly old men who nodded at the employees like royalty visiting a factory loading dock.

"Could it be?" Roberto whispered as a rich scent wafted toward them. "Maybe? Yes! It's coffee. *Real* coffee. I thought the Rust Virus destroyed all the coffee plants."

"Some bushes in the Ethiopian highlands showed a resistance to the virus, and they're being harvested in isolated locations."

The seventh-floor analysts and a few supervisors from the lower floors stood in a line like schoolchildren waiting for a treat and received paper cups filled with hot coffee. Wilson and Roberto took their cups and walked across the roof to the safety wall.

Roberto sniffed the coffee and gazed out at the skyline. "This is way better than my previous job."

"What was that?"

"I was a hacker who got involved in a blockchain currency robbery. Someone snitched and we all got arrested. It looked like I was going to a prison factory, but then a Trigon attorney appeared in my jail cell like an angel with a briefcase. I was released into the custody of the corporation."

"Here's to freedom," Wilson said, and toasted the younger man with his paper cup. Slowly, he sipped some coffee and let the liquid rest on his tongue. He had gotten used to the taste of Java! The real thing had more—what was the right word? More *coffeeness.*

"I bet you old guys are going crazy right now," Roberto said. "Memories are the most powerful drug in the world. You can get high on them. This tastes pretty good, but I'm too young to remember what the real thing tasted like."

"Actual coffee doesn't leave a sour taste in your mouth."

"What were smart people talking about during those years before the Fall? Were you shocked by what happened? Or did you see it coming?"

"That's a hard question to answer. Some talking heads on news shows predicted one big crisis. Meanwhile, a pregnant woman got killed by a driverless cab in New York City, and it was like dropping a match into a bucket of gasoline. . . . People thought technology had gone too far, which sparked the Taxi Riots. The riots were followed by the Stem-flu pandemic, extreme weather events, and crisis migrations. Most of these events weren't predicted or organized. They just happened."

"You don't sound surprised, Wilson."

"I started out as a crime reporter and learned a lot from cops and felons. Human behavior is a lot more predictable if you acknowledge the Three Facts of Human Reality."

"Is this some kind of Buddhist thing?"

"Fact one is that stupid is stronger than smart."

"Oh, I agree. Definitely. Lots of stupid people thought that burning eucalyptus leaves would save them from Stem-flu. What's fact number two?"

"Fear leads to hate."

"That's also true. Fear explains the millions of refugees killed during the crisis migrations. Pilots dropped cluster bombs on mothers and babies. What's fact three?"

"Most people create lives based on small truths and large delusions."

Roberto toasted Wilson with his empty paper cup. "You're probably right, but I'm not going to mention that to Francesca."

"Who's that?"

"The beautiful Italian analyst who knows five languages. I'm attracted to women who won't accept my usual bullshit."

"Buy a houseplant, Roberto. It shows that you're capable of taking care of something."

"That's a great idea. I'm going to ask if she has a preference."

Roberto strolled over to a group of analysts and began talking to a young woman with eyeglasses that matched her long black hair. Holding the paper cup with two hands like a chalice, Wilson took one last sip of coffee and was ambushed by memories of life before the Fall.

A California street lined with jacaranda trees, heavy with bluish-purple blossoms. Dry flowers littered the sidewalk with a sweet, musky odor.

Maine on a summer day. The taste of lemon tea on a back porch afternoon.

His brain opened a final door, and he was at a wedding celebration with a four-piece band at the end of a banquet hall. And then the music started, the first few notes of a melody that impelled him to stand up and dance.

17 | WILSON

ONLY A FEW people were out as Wilson passed through the courtyard that surrounded his apartment building on West Ninety-First Street. The entryway was still marked with spray-painted messages put up by the Health Department during the Stem-flu pandemic. *14 HERE,* read one faded message, followed by a list of Stem-flu deaths with the relevant apartment numbers. The main elevator smelled like sweat, and the scent of cooked onions lingered in the hallways.

He avoided most of his neighbors but did occasional favors for Nancy and Charles Larson, the elderly couple who lived down the hall from his apartment. Every morning, they slipped on augmented reality headsets and transformed their apartment into a beach cabana or a luxury hotel. As he walked past their door, he heard multiple voices, which meant that they had activated simulations that resembled their deceased friends and relatives.

"Welcome home!" Will said as he entered the apartment.

"Silence, please. Unless someone calls." Wilson kicked off his shoes and shuffled into the kitchen, where he defrosted some

Chixfillets in the microwave and poured bootleg vodka into a water glass.

As he ate the cubes of synthetic meat, his phone beeped and displayed an unknown number. "You have a Category One phone call from Trigon Technology," Will announced. "Answer immediately."

"Hello?"

"Do you know who this is?" Wilson was shocked to hear Felder's voice. He had never heard of the Three Fates calling anyone at home.

"Yes. We had a private meeting this morning."

"Do you have holographic conference hardware installed in your residence?"

"I do, but I haven't used it for a while."

"Stay awake. Our company owner will contact you this evening."

Felder ended the call, but Wilson kept holding his cell phone. He didn't need to research the owner's name. Everyone knew that Howard Sebesky owned Trigon and a dozen other technology companies. During a decade of experiments, his scientists had placed neurological stents into the spinal columns of dogs, apes, and humans. The volunteers would touch a rock or a feather and a sensor would record the electric signals passed through a string of neurons in the central nervous system. Once the researchers had collected thousands of signals, they attached them to objects in online simulations. If you wore a haptic glove and touched an object in the Over World, you could feel the texture, weight, and temperature of a digital object.

During the Stem-flu pandemic, Sebesky had retreated to a bunker in Pennsylvania. The death of billions of people hadn't changed his optimism about technology that would allow you to upload yourself and live forever. An information search linked to his transhuman manifesto titled *The Future Is Now.*

Wilson switched on the living room holographic projector and waited for the billionaire's appearance. At exactly one o'clock in the morning, a blue dot floated in the air about a yard away from the wall. This was the hologram's center point, and a three-dimensional figure would form around that.

There was a soft chiming sound that reminded Wilson of an altar bell at Mass, and then a holograph of Howard Sebesky appeared in the living room. Wearing a turquoise-colored jumpsuit, the billionaire sat at a desk floating two feet above Wilson's frayed carpet. The former computer scientist looked gaunt but healthy. His head was completely bald and his face clean-shaven.

A few seconds passed, and then Sebesky saw Wilson's face on his monitor screen. "Identify yourself, please."

"Wilson Talley."

"Mr. Felder said you were the senior analyst who reported on the death of a man named Terrence Greene in a custom nubot workshop in lower Manhattan."

"That's correct."

"And you are a former investigative journalist?"

"Yes."

Sebesky nodded, watching Wilson. "If you solve a particular problem, Trigon will pay you a bonus that equals five years of your salary."

"Did you know Terry Greene? Was he your friend?"

"Greene's death isn't important, but it does concern me that his arm was ripped off his body. A human being wouldn't have the strength to do that, but it would be possible for a certain type of autonomous machine."

"The detective assigned to the case agrees with you."

"And what's your opinion, Mr. Talley?"

"It's possible. The killer might have been one of the nubots lying in a pile on the floor. We had no way to verify if they were deactivated."

"Any suggestion that a machine deliberately killed a human would cause wide-scale negative consequences."

"Do you think a killer nubot might trigger a repeat of the Taxi Riots?"

"In the next few weeks, a Senate committee is going to approve a new piece of legislation called the Sentient Machine Act. Section One of the bill describes the technical specifications of a conscious machine. When a machine with artificial intelligence is created, it's going to be given a numbered employee contract."

Wilson nodded. "I get it. You want autonomous machines to

be included in our legal system, and you think a news story about a murderous nubot would make it difficult to pass this proposed legislation."

"Difficult . . . if not impossible. And this concerns me because artificial intelligence systems owned by two of my companies are currently designing new devices and software programs. I will eventually own what they've created, but I need a clear legal pathway."

"Terry Greene is dead. I can't change that fact."

"I'm hiring you to find out who killed him. If he was murdered by a sentient machine, then I want you to destroy that machine and conceal its involvement in the murder."

"For a problem like this, you should probably hire a private police officer."

"I've used private policemen in the past. This requires an employee who is more intelligent and resourceful."

"I can't see myself blowing off a nubot's head with a shotgun."

"I'll give you the money to hire a nubot killer if you don't want to do it yourself. One thing I've learned over the years is that almost everyone can be hired to do just about anything."

"I used to be a journalist, Dr. Sebesky. When I discover facts, I don't like to conceal them."

"You once wrote an important article that was never published. And you didn't do anything about it, did you? You just let your facts fade away."

Wilson looked down at the dark gap between the hologram and the living room floor. "I don't know what you're talking about."

"I've read your article and seen the photographs."

"They don't exist."

"That's not true."

A few seconds later, a hologram picture frame floated through the air. Successive images appeared in the frame, and Wilson recognized the photographs he had taken of a high school in the Catskill Mountains that had been turned into a pandemic quarantine camp. Hiding in the woods near the camp, he had witnessed the arrival of a squad of Health Security officers wearing hazmat suits. One by one, they carried the dying patients out to a school soccer field, where they injected them with potassium chloride and tossed the bodies into a trench.

"Now do you remember?"

"How did you get my photographs?"

"When I considered hiring you, I asked my private search engine to infiltrate and examine the computers of your former newspaper and its staff. One of your past editors, Mr. Charles Granger, had saved your article and photographs. He had everything."

"Granger is dead. At least, that's what they told me."

"Yes. And his widow is using his computer with no idea what's stored on it."

"The Emergency Quarantine Act said that the local police or the Health Security Agency could arrest anyone who distributed information that caused panic and social disorder. If the newspaper published those photographs, everyone would have been arrested and sent to a camp."

"So you made the logical choice and stayed silent."

"I decided not to destroy my life for a news story. I was supporting my mother and—"

"I don't wish to hear your excuses for what happened. There's no reason to attach an emotion to a past event. When I disconnected my memories from emotions, I liberated my mind in a powerful way."

"I guess I haven't reached that stage of evolution."

"What's relevant to our conversation is that you stayed quiet about an important news story, and that's why I want to hire you. I'm looking for a discreet fact finder who can follow orders."

"Wealthy people always think that everyone else is equally greedy."

"These days, money is good for only one thing: safety. When I pay you the equivalent of five years' salary, you'll be able to flee New York City and create your own refuge. Look around you. This era isn't about social collapse, it's about parallel realities."

Sebesky's wealth didn't bother Wilson, but it annoyed him to hear an opinion treated like a fact. "I guess that's possible," he mumbled.

"So, what's your decision, Mr. Talley? Will you accept this job and follow my instructions?"

Wilson shrugged.

"I want a verbal response."

"Yes, I will find out who killed Terry Greene. If it's a nubot, I will make sure it's destroyed."

"Excellent! Let me know when you've found any new information. Use an encryption program when you contact me."

Sebesky flickered and faded and disappeared.

18 | WILSON

WAKE UP AND answer the phone," Will said. "It's a Category One call from Trigon Technology."

Wilson opened his eyes and saw morning sunlight pushing between the slats of the window blinds. He picked up his cell phone and made sure that the video was switched off.

"Good morning!" It was his boss, Raymond Felder. "Did you have a hologram conversation last night with a particular individual?"

"Yes, he called at one a.m. When does this guy ever sleep?"

"Several years ago, he decided that sleep was a waste of time, so he worked out a schedule in which he sleeps four hours every night with two half-hour naps. That decision added three extra hours to his workday. He doesn't take weekends off, so he's gained even more time. Each year, he's a hundred and twenty workdays ahead of everyone else."

Wilson yawned and scratched his belly. "Impressive."

"I received an encrypted email sent at three a.m.," Felder said. "The email described your new work assignment."

"I hope it's okay with you."

"Of course. The gentleman owns a controlling share in this company, and we all work for him. The job you've been given is a top priority, and I don't expect to see you in the office for the next few weeks. You need to give your full attention to discovering who killed this nubot builder."

"That might be difficult."

"If necessary, you can ask any of our employees for assistance, and they'll receive overtime pay. Find who or what committed this crime, then solve the problem with an aggressive response."

"I may have to hire a private policeman at some point."

"Don't worry about that. Just find the killer."

Wilson pulled on some clothes, walked into the kitchen, and switched on his computer. He left a message for Detective Morrissey, then activated the Trigon search engine and looked for information about Terrence Greene.

The dead man grew up in a gang-dominated neighborhood of Oakland, California. When he was a teenager, a Silicon Valley billionaire funded an after-school program designed to teach kids how to write code for computers. Greene signed up because he was looking for a warm place to do his homework. He turned out to have natural talent for computers and designed a health app for diabetics in his senior year of high school.

Greene obtained a doctoral degree in computational science and engineering at the Massachusetts Institute of Technology and spent eight years as a professor at the University of Michigan. His academic articles showed a growing interest in something called confinement security: programs and hardware that placed digital walls around artificial intelligence so it wouldn't leak out into the world.

A framed photograph of a U.S. Navy battleship was hanging in the dead man's office, but Greene's résumé didn't mention military service. The dragon eating his tail in *The Secret Knowledge of Alchemy* poster was an ouroboros: a symbol created in ancient Egypt that was used by alchemists. Drawings of dragons eating their tails could symbolize zero and infinity. But an ouroboros had nothing to do with sin, and certainly not the *SAFE SINN* sticker Greene had slapped onto the bottom of the illustration.

The framed photograph of the two couples walking toward the House of Mirrors suggested love and friendship—some sort of personal connection. Sipping a cup of Java! fake coffee, he called Roberto Canales, the hacker who now worked for Trigon.

"The corporation will pay you overtime money for some specialized work."

Roberto laughed. "Sounds fun. And I always need money."

"I'm sending you an image of four people walking toward a carnival building called the House of Mirrors. One of the two men in the photograph used to be a computer science professor named Terrence Greene. See if you can find out the identities of the other people in the photograph. Who's the woman holding his hand?"

Wilson took a shower and continued his online research. Terrence Greene had stopped publishing academic articles the year he quit his tenured position. Professors gave up tenure only for serious money, so Wilson assumed that Greene was hired by a technology corporation. But how did he end up building nubots in a basement workshop?

Nibbling on a soy bar, Wilson invited Brian Morrissey to join a Phalanx video conference. The detective was sitting at a desk, wearing a coat and tie.

"Where are you?"

"Home."

"You're dressed for work."

Morrissey straightened his tie. "Thank you for the money transfers. I've put three drug murders on the back burner. This case will get my full attention."

"What's your next move?"

"I've requested a list of Greene's recent bank transactions and cell phone calls. Later this morning, I'll access the Stop Light system and see if any known felons were in the neighborhood when the crime was committed."

"What's your time frame for surveillance camera data?"

"The medical examiner says death occurred about six to eight hours before the patrol officers smashed open the door."

"Any more information about the person who reported the murder?"

"Maybe it's not a person. I got a recording from the emergency center. The call came from an unregistered phone. Listen to this."

There was a brief pause, and then Wilson heard a 911 operator talking to a computer. With a stilted, unnatural rhythm, a speech synthesizer informed the operator that Terrence Greene had been killed and gave the address of his basement apartment.

"Kind of crazy, huh?" Morrissey grinned. "Maybe one nubot killed Terrence Greene and then another bot reported the crime."

"It's not a machine. It's a human using a text-to-speech system to conceal identity. What did the surveillance cameras show?"

"Keep looking at your screen. Stop Light confirms that Terrence Greene didn't appear on the street during the twelve-hour interval before the officers discovered his body. Now watch this. . . ."

Wilson's monitor showed video footage from cameras mounted on lampposts at each end of the block, then Morrissey typed a series of commands and people began to disappear.

"I'm telling the program to remove different categories such as sanitation workers, police officers, mail carriers, children under the age of ten, and elderly people without prior arrests who live in the immediate area."

"Do you have to search through twelve hours of footage?"

"The AI program does most of the work. The three men with the red circles around their heads are convicted felons. I'm going to pick them up for questioning. When you're sitting in the same interrogation room, you can sense their fear and smell their sweat. Infrasensors pick up sudden changes of body heat, so I know when they're lying."

"Let me know if you learn anything."

"If you want to help, I've got a job for you. The main problem is that Stop Light cameras photograph only the intersections and not the middle of the block. But Terrence Greene's building has an old-fashioned CCTV camera attached to a video recorder. Why don't you drop by the building and get a copy from Eddie Lopez, the superintendent."

"I'll do that right away."

"I'm wearing a necktie. You're handing out money. We're going to solve this case."

It felt strange to return to the murder scene during the daytime. When Wilson reached the dead man's building, he pressed the intercom button for the super.

"Good morning, Mr. Lopez. I'm here to see the surveillance footage."

"No problem. Walk upstairs to the third floor."

Eddie Lopez was waiting in the open doorway of his apartment. The building superintendent was in his forties—short, trim, and guarded in his reactions. He looked the sort of person who didn't leave dirty dishes in the sink.

"I'm Wilson Talley."

"Right. Detective Morrissey said you'd drop by. I'll access the video, and we can fast-forward through it."

Lopez led him into the living room of a two-bedroom apartment and pointed to the couch. "First I got to attach my computer. There's just one camera and it stores videos for a week."

A recording device about the size of a lunch box was underneath an end table. Kneeling on the brown shag carpet, Lopez attached one end of a cable to the recording device and the other end to a notebook computer on the coffee table.

"Detective Morrissey said you were some kind of investigator."

"I'm not a police officer, but I've been asked by Terrence Greene's friends to find out who killed him. I'm going to give you a money transfer before I leave. It's a way to thank you for your help this morning."

"Are you a private policeman?"

"Not exactly."

"Most folks think a private policeman is expensive, but you can hire one cheap for a short-term job."

"You've done this?"

"Last year, someone kept breaking into the mailboxes and stealing all our mail. After a couple months of this bullshit, we bought the camera system and discovered that the thief was a local surge addict named Richie Atkins. We kept telling the police to arrest him, but they did nothing. So we hired a private policeman who calls himself Mellow Fellow."

"He was court certified?"

"Of course. We checked his photo and ID number on the police department database. Mellow Fellow watched the video, tracked down Richie, and broke his hands with a hammer. There was no more mail theft because Richie couldn't open the boxes."

"I'm not here to break anyone's hands, Mr. Lopez. Who do you think killed Terrence Greene?"

"Beats me. Terry was a quiet guy who talked to his nubots and kept to himself. But I don't know what he did in the past."

It took a few minutes for Eddie Lopez to retrieve the twenty-four-hour time interval that ended when the two precinct cops entered the apartment. The first image was of an older woman carrying two shopping bags. She checked her mailbox and headed for the stairs.

"That's Mrs. Sheridan She lives in 4C."

As the video went on, Lopez continued giving apartment numbers. "2G . . . 5C . . . that's 3A's new girlfriend."

There were no surprises until a young man with curly hair appeared, and Lopez stopped the video. "I've seen this guy before. He was leaving the basement workshop when I was going downstairs."

"You know his name?"

"I assumed he was one of Terry's customers."

"The time stamp indicates that he visited the basement the day before the murder. Let's see if he shows up again."

They fast-forwarded through the footage until Lopez saw something unusual and froze the video. On the day of the murder, a woman strolled past the CCTV camera wearing a knee-length parka with a hood covering her head. An e-mask covered her mouth and chin, and her eyes were hidden behind mirrored sunglasses. Red and blue shapes were printed on the parka in a random, asymmetrical design—as if a five-year-old had played with a set of rubber stamps.

"What's with the weird-looking coat?"

"It's stealth wear," Wilson explained. "Special clothing designed to confuse surveillance systems."

"But we can see her."

"Stealth wear isn't about humans watching humans. It's all about machines. When a surveillance camera photographs someone on the street, the live-time images are evaluated by a program using artificial intelligence. The computer must decide if the image in the grid is a person or an object. See that shape at the front of the parka?"

"Sure," Lopez said. "It looks like a stop sign."

"People's heads don't float above traffic signs, so the computer decides that the object wearing the parka isn't a human. The reflective sunglasses she's wearing are ghost glasses that block infrared light."

"I could download everything you just saw for a thousand dollars."

Wilson took a blank flash drive out of his coat pocket. "I think a copy is worth five hundred. If you want to double the payment, I need access to Mr. Greene's apartment."

"I attached a latch and padlock so nobody would steal nothing. I'll give you a padlock key and second key to the street door so you can enter the building anytime you want."

"Sounds like you just made a thousand dollars."

Wilson copied the video and emailed Morrissey a two-minute clip that showed both the stealth-wear woman and the young man with the curly hair. Taking the keys, he went downstairs to the basement and entered Terry Greene's apartment. Once again, he found himself in the windowless room with the framed photograph of the two couples walking toward the House of Mirrors. He searched the file cabinet, found clean socks and underwear, and entered the workroom. Terrence Greene's body had been removed, but a patch of dry blood still covered the floor. The four nubots were still in a pile against the wall, and their mechanical eyes didn't move as Wilson inspected a box of SynSkin hands made in China. When he was done searching the shelves, he faced the pile of nubots.

"Terrence Greene was your creator. I'm looking for the person who killed him."

None of the nubots spoke. *They're just machines,* Wilson thought. *As soulless as a toaster.*

He circled the Y-shaped storage shelf, reached the assembly table, and stopped. The armless girl nubot with the raven hair and the navy-blue jumper had disappeared.

Did crime scene investigators take the girl away as evidence? Searching for a storage room, Wilson noticed a bump concealed behind a dusty patchwork quilt covering a section of the wall. Wilson reached down, pulled up an edge of the quilt, and discovered a steel door. He clicked open the latch and pulled hard. There was a squeaking, scraping sound as the door popped open.

Wilson stepped through the doorway and entered a boiler room. This was where a gas boiler heated hot water for showers and created the steam that flowed through radiators on cold nights. Terrence Greene's apartment had been part of the boiler room until a landlord put up the wall in the cellar and squeezed one more rent out of the building.

When he switched on a light bulb hanging from the ceiling it swung back and forth, making his shadow bend and waver. Footprints on the dusty floor led him to a hatch door that had once been used to deliver coal. Wilson climbed three stone steps, pushed upward on the steel cellar door, and the rusty hatch popped open.

It felt like someone was watching as he climbed the stairs to a fenced-in area behind the building where Eddie Lopez stored the garbage bins. A narrow alleyway led north to the street. If the killer left from the cellar, no surveillance camera was there to capture the moment. Standing in the alleyway, Wilson called Detective Morrissey.

"Thanks for the video, Wilson. It's going to be scanned by our facial recognition system," Morrissey said.

"Forget about that. Did the police remove the nubot girl in Greene's workshop?"

"Why would they do that?"

"Someone entered the workshop and took it away. I also discovered how the killer entered the building."

"Excellent!"

"Are you crazy? We just lost a major clue."

"Stay there, Wilson. Just . . . stay there. If the killer took the nubot and if he's still in the city, we'll arrest him this afternoon."

19 | JULIA AND DANIEL

When Derwin Schroeder called the morning after the meeting in the law office, Julia positioned her phone so he couldn't see that she was wearing her gym shorts.

"Elizabeth and I talked it over, and we're hiring you to find our son. I agree to the daily salary and expense credit that Winfield mentioned."

"What about our hundred-thousand-dollar bonus?"

"If you find Bennett within ten days you get the full bonus. Each day after that point, the bonus goes down five thousand dollars. If you don't find my son in thirty days . . . there's no bonus."

"Do you think Daniel and I are lazy?" Julia tilted the phone so that Schroeder could see that she was smiling.

"I believe in motivation."

"No problem. We're motivated. When do we start working?"

"Now. Today. What's your plan?"

"We need to start gathering information about Bennett. The names of his friends . . ."

"As far as I know, my son didn't have any friends. He lived his life in the Cloud."

"Do you pay his phone bill?"

"Yes. It's attached to our family plan."

"It would be helpful if I could look at the most recent statements and check for long-distance calls. If your son is lying in a burrow, it would probably be outside the city."

"Okay. My wife can handle that."

"Did Bennett have a credit card?"

"Yes. We cosigned for him when he turned sixteen."

"Perhaps he paid a large amount of money to a travel center. If you're going to be connected for a long period of time, they want half the payment in advance."

"Anything else we can do?" Mr. Schroeder asked.

"Can we search your son's room?"

"Elizabeth already went in there and looked for information."

"Daniel and I will see everything from a different angle."

Schroeder considered the idea for a few seconds. "We live at Fifteen Hudson Yards. Show up around three o'clock. My wife will let you in."

"One last question. What was your son's email address?"

"BSchroed at Ezone.com. Why do you need that?"

"Bennett might have posted on social media websites. A chat-group comment might help us figure out his location."

Julia switched off her phone and smiled. "We've got the job. He'll pay the full hundred thousand if we find their son in ten days. Then the bonus amount starts to fall."

"Can we search Bennett's room?"

"Three o'clock today. His mother will be there."

"You go alone, and I'll join you later. We'll need the van if we search outside the city, and I still haven't replaced the fuel pump."

Julia spent the morning looking for Bennett's name on different social media platforms, then she rode her skateboard downtown to Hudson Yards, a collection of upscale shops and luxury apartments that faced the Hudson River. The Schroeders' apartment was in an eighty-eight-floor glass tower overlooking a large plaza.

An armed security guard checked her name when she entered the entrance hall and directed her to a reception desk occupied by a doorman with a walrus mustache.

"I'm here to visit the Schroeder apartment."

The doorman stared at her skateboard as if it was a vector for a new pandemic. "I'll need to verify ID."

Julia placed her thumb on her phone's scanner spot, and the screen displayed her photo and Stop Light system number. Mr. Walrus held up a checker device to verify that her phone wasn't a clone, and it beeped twice.

"Take the fourth elevator."

Julia stepped out onto the seventieth floor and walked down a hallway painted with bland colors. When she reached apartment A, a sensor verified her identity a second time, and then Elizabeth Schroeder opened the door. She smiled politely as if Julia was there to walk her dog. "Where's your partner? I thought it would be both of you."

"Daniel was delayed. He's going to meet me here."

Julia followed Mrs. Schroeder into the apartment, and they stood in the living room. A home entertainment center with a hologram projector was installed on one wall and faced a suede couch, modern chairs with steel armrests, and a glass coffee table.

"Nice view." Julia stepped around a dining table and gazed out the window at the Hudson River and a line of office buildings in New Jersey. A gust of wind made whitecaps on the surface of the river, and the clouds looked like globs of cotton. Looking downward, she could see a honeycomb-shaped spiral staircase called the Vessel that had once been a tourist attraction in the center of the plaza. After the Taxi Riots, the Vessel had been taken over by homeless people who camped on the different landings. Now the Vessel was closed, and the lower levels were wrapped with razor wire.

"The Vessel was a homeless camp, right? Wasn't there some kind of battle?"

"Derwin and I were in Connecticut, but Benny was here and saw the whole thing. The squatters were criminals and they wouldn't leave, so the landlord hired a group of private policemen. One night they showed up with steel clubs and electric shock wands."

"And the squatters fought back?"

"They threw gasoline bombs and cinder blocks, so the security team ripped down the barriers and fought their way up the stairs. Four or five squatters were tossed off the top balcony, and others were beaten to death. I don't know exactly what my son witnessed. It was dark and you could hear people screaming."

"Seeing something like that might make the Over World even more attractive."

Elizabeth gestured to a bottle and three glasses on the coffee table. "Would you like some wine? I already opened a bottle of Chablis and there's Pinot Noir in the kitchen."

Julia never drank while she was working, but this felt like an opportunity to get some more information. "Sure. I'll have some."

The Chablis bottle was half-full, and Mrs. Schroeder's hand trembled when she poured Julia a glass. "I'm not an alcoholic, Julia. I just need to take off the sharp edges."

A manila folder was on the coffee table, and Mrs. Schroeder pushed it in Julia's direction. "Derwin said you wanted phone and credit card information. I printed it off for you."

Julia began to inspect the documents in the folder. "I'm sure this will be helpful."

"The only long-distance phone calls are to our home in Connecticut. Bennett almost never went there. He preferred the city. As for the credit card charges . . . I recognize the takeout restaurants, but everything else is a mystery."

Mrs. Schroeder had printed off twelve months of credit card bills. Sipping the wine, Julia skimmed through the pages. "Seven international corporations control ninety percent of the content offered in the Over World. Your son has made payments to five, six . . . no, all seven of these companies. Most people don't do this. They visit a few websites and avoid the rest. It looks like Bennett explored every major simulation."

"My son disappeared into a world that isn't real."

"It feels real when you're there."

Elizabeth refilled her glass. "I wanted to ask you some questions, and it wasn't possible in the lawyer's office. Derwin took control of the discussion, and I just faded away."

"You were worried about your son."

"I want to know more about the direct neurological connection. Why did my son want to connect his brain to a computer? When Benny first mentioned the idea, he said it was the next step in human evolution."

"Wiring the brain has been going on for a long time, Mrs. Schroeder. They started out placing sensors into the brains of epileptics and schizophrenics, then they implanted devices to help blind people see. That technology led to the brain-computer interface."

"So, why did *you* get the operation, Julia? Was it about evolution?"

"My grandmother died, and I received an inheritance. She probably thought that I'd use it to get a college degree, but the pandemic changed everything. My friends were telling AI chatbots to take tests and write term papers for the AI teachers that appeared on their monitor screens. School felt like one machine talking to another. The DNC operation was a physical transformation. It felt like a step toward the future."

"Derwin and I were just happy that Benny was excited about something. So we paid for the operation and then . . . I don't know." Mrs. Schroeder took a sip of wine. "I cried the first time I saw the data port on the back of his head."

"Did your son have a recovery problem? Sometimes the brain rejects the electrode net. People have seizures."

"Benny had headaches for a few months, then he was okay."

"Was he depressed after the procedure? Did he ever talk about . . . ?"

"Suicide? No. Never. At first, my son thought that the direct connection was wonderful. He felt like an astronaut discovering a new planet every day of the week. About a year ago, he became anxious and worried, but he wouldn't explain why. We sent him to a psychiatrist, who gave him a lot of pills that didn't help."

There was a soft chiming sound, and Elizabeth got up from the couch. "Someone's here."

It was Daniel, carrying a fuel pump for the van in his backpack. When Mrs. Schroeder offered him a glass of wine, Julia moved her eyes. *Say no.*

"Thanks," Daniel told her. "But we need to get working."

"I understand. My son's bedroom is the last door down the hall."

—

When Julia opened the door, she smelled the moldy stink of rotten food. Daniel followed her into the room, and they found a bed with tangled sheets and a desk dotted with Chinese food cartons. What had once been leftover noodles and garlic chicken was now a petri dish of green bacteria. But the most significant aspect of the room wasn't the garbage. Bennett had taken flattened cardboard boxes and taped them over the window. The Hudson River and the clouds floating across the sky had disappeared.

"Did Mrs. Schroeder tell you anything helpful?"

"She gave me copies of his credit card receipts. Bennett paid for access to every major portal in the Over World, but I found charges for only three city travel centers: First Class Lounge, Safe and Sound, and Mole's House in Brooklyn."

"I'll drop by Safe and Sound when we're done with this."

"Let me search the dresser and the desk. You look under the bed and check out the closet. I'm going to get a garbage bag from Mrs. Schroeder and ditch the moldy food."

When she returned from the kitchen, Daniel had removed four cardboard storage boxes from the closet. "Nothing but dust balls under the bed. Nothing hidden in the pockets of his jackets and hoodies."

Julia dumped the moldy food cartons into a garbage bag, then searched the dresser. Jeans. T-shirts. Socks and underwear. The top drawer contained plastic vials filled with the drugs used to treat anxiety disorder and a Stop Light ID card. The card wasn't valid anymore, but it did have Bennett's photograph.

"Bennett saved his grade-school soccer trophies, old basketball shoes, and a miniature birch bark canoe he made in summer camp. But this might be helpful. . . ." Daniel showed Julia a dozen hand-size stickers that read: *Evolution! Not Extinction! Join E-Volve!* "Never heard of E-Volve. It could be a Hard-Edge group."

"If it was just one sticker, it wouldn't mean anything," Julia said. "But a dozen means he was putting them up on walls."

As she began to search the desk, her cell phone rang. It was Robert Winfield.

"Where are you right now?"

"We're searching Bennett's room."

"Are his parents there?"

"Mrs. Schroeder is drinking wine in the living room."

"Something came up. It might be serious. When the Schroeders first contacted me, I filed a missing person report with the New York police and sent them Bennett's photograph. Their database matched the photograph with images from another investigation, and this morning I got a call from a homicide detective named Brian Morrissey. A few days ago, a CCTV camera recorded Bennett visiting a nubot workshop on the Lower East Side."

"What was he doing there?"

"Morrissey didn't know. When I told him that you and Daniel were looking for Bennett, he wanted to talk to you."

"We try to stay away from the police. They're old and clumsy."

"Please talk to the detective. You might learn something. Did you find anything unusual at the apartment?"

"Credit card bills gave us the names of three local travel centers. Daniel will check them out later this afternoon."

"Sounds good. Just be careful what you say to Mrs. Schroeder." Winfield sighed loudly. "Anything involving children starts simple and gets messy."

Julia switched off the phone as Daniel shut the closet door. "What was that about?"

"I'll tell you later. Anything else in the closet?"

"A stuffed squirrel holding an acorn and a collection of baseball caps."

"I found his ID card, but that's about it."

Moving quickly, she checked beneath the bed's mattress, under a throw rug, and behind a framed poster with a quote from the neo-Luddite writer Jack Lewis: *Technology should serve the people and not the instruments of power.*

Frustrated, she pulled the desk a few inches forward, peered behind it, and found a one-hundred-page notebook with a black-and-white speckled cover. It was the sort of thing that students once used for lecture and lab notes. There was a little rectangle on the outside front cover, but instead of writing the name of a science course, Bennett had scrawled the word *INVESTIGATIONS* with a black felt pen.

Julia opened the book and began to turn the pages.

"What's that?" Daniel asked.

"It's a journal with comments about the simulations visited in the Over World. Every location is crossed out except for a website called Dragon Lair. That's underlined twice."

"What's Dragon Lair? Have you ever been there?"

"A few times. It was an Expanding Universe site that was popular for a couple of years, and then it went toxic. Clans built castles where players raped simulated women."

"What did the company do?"

"The site was frozen and rebooted. All players lost building privileges. The toxic clans went elsewhere, but everyone else left, too."

"We'll take the subway uptown to Thomas's travel center. You can search Dragon Lair in the Over World while I visit Safe and Sound in reality."

Julia slipped the notebook into her backpack, and they returned to the living room. Mrs. Schroeder had opened a second bottle of wine, and her body moved awkwardly when she got up from the couch. "Did you find anything?"

"Bennett kept a journal that listed the locations he visited in the Over World. I'm going to visit a particular simulation."

"Good. That sounds promising. I'm so very glad we hired you."

"We'll do everything we can, Mrs. Schroeder. I promise."

20 | WILSON

DETECTIVE MORRISSEY arrived at the workshop with a laptop computer. He switched it on and placed it on the desk near the refrigerator. "The person who took the nubot had to conceal the theft when he left the building. I told the system to search for a mobile container, and it came up with a suspect. Take a look. I think we found the killer."

He typed a command, and a street security video appeared on the screen. A man wearing sunglasses and an e-mask over his mouth pulled a large rolling suitcase down East Fourth Street.

"See the suitcase bounce over the curb?" Morrissey asked. "It's empty."

The second video was taken twenty minutes later. Now the suitcase was filled with something heavy, and the man leaned forward as he pulled it down the sidewalk.

"He's the guy who took the kiddie bot, and now he stuffed it into the suitcase."

"Do you have a name?"

"I'll get to that. He's not from the neighborhood."

On the next street, the Stop Light camera photographed the suspect as he summoned a driverless cab and muscled the suitcase into the trunk.

"They always think they're smarter than the system, but the AI system makes connections. Watch this. . . ."

Morrissey typed a command. The software read the license plate and identified the cab.

"I've switched over to We Go, the transportation database. They don't monitor private cars, but they do track cabs and rideshare vehicles. I gave We Go the license plate number, and it told me where the cab delivered its passenger."

A new surveillance video showed a street lined with skyscrapers. Pulling the suitcase, the man with the mask entered a building with a doorman.

"Now he's carrying the nubot into an office building on Fifty-Fourth Street. I'm switching to the building's lobby camera, and then to the elevator camera. This is where our suspect works."

The elevator's camera recorded the man with the suitcase pulling his e-mask below his chin. The suspect had a thin face with stress lines at the corners of his mouth. The mask had made him sweat, and he wiped his lips with a white tissue.

"Name?"

"Philip Necker. He owns some kind of tech business with an office on the eighteenth floor."

"What's the next move?"

"I'll drop by his office and ask a lot of questions. If he can't come up with the right answers, I'll take him to the truth room at the Nineteenth Precinct. Then I'll ask the same questions, and the infrared scanner will tell me if he's lying."

"When is this going to happen?"

"Right now. You're welcome to come along. I'll tell him that you work for the department's Digital Technology Section."

The two men left the workshop, got into an unmarked police car, and headed uptown.

Wilson glanced at Morrissey. "You look happy."

"I love to arrest people. Maybe the city is collapsing around us, but I get to hand out little doses of justice."

Wilson stayed quiet when they entered the office building and Morrissey showed his badge to a security guard. They were escorted down a hallway to a private office, and the man in the surveillance photograph got up from his desk.

"Mr. Necker? I'm Detective Brian Morrissey. Mr. Talley is giving me technical assistance for an active investigation."

"How can I help you gentlemen? Is one of our employees in trouble?"

"Something like that. We have surveillance video showing you entering an active crime scene and removing a crucial piece of evidence. Mr. Talley will confirm what I just said."

Wilson nodded. "You were photographed on East Fourth Street going in and out of a nubot workshop with a rollaway suitcase."

"I don't know what you're talking about."

"We have video evidence of the theft. But we're here because you may have committed a far more serious crime."

Necker placed both hands on the desk. "You think I killed Terrence Greene?"

"It's a possibility."

"I was simply retrieving my own property. When I showed up to meet Terry, an old lady who lived in the building told me about the murder. I had visited the workshop a few weeks earlier. People were stealing mail from the building, so Terry asked deliverymen to come down the alleyway, open the hatch door, and leave packages of computer parts in the basement. I knew about the hatch door and figured it might be unlocked. Yesterday I returned with my suitcase, entered through the basement, and retrieved the nubot."

"It's against the law to steal evidence from a crime scene." Detective Morrissey pulled handcuffs out of his suitcoat pocket. "You're under arrest, Mr. Necker. Stand up and place your hands behind your back."

"Let me tell you what happened. If you're not satisfied with my explanation, you can arrest me."

Morrissey shrugged and sat back down as Necker opened a desk drawer and pulled out a framed photograph of a young woman. "The nubot is a re-creation of my deceased daughter. Claire died during the pandemic."

"Sorry about your loss," Morrissey mumbled.

"My wife and I have gone through a long period of mourning. Sometimes it feels like it's never going to end. Last year, we explored the option of a digital resurrection that allows you to put on a VR headset and meet the person who died in the Over World. But we decided against the VR option. We wanted Claire sitting with us at the dinner table or making comments while we watched a movie, so I hired Terrence Greene to create a nubot resurrection of my human daughter. My wife and I had recordings of Claire's speaking in birthday and vacation videos. Terry said special software would duplicate her voice."

"He never finished it," Morrissey said. "Why didn't you just leave it in the workshop?"

"My daughter's corpse was dumped into a pit during the pandemic. I didn't want the same thing to happen to her duplicate."

Morrissey stood up and nervously tightened his necktie. "I apologize for this visit, Mr. Necker. But a man's been killed and—"

"I completely understand, Detective Morrissey. You're just doing your job."

Morrissey didn't say anything until they got back into the car. "My niece died because of Stem-flu. If my sister could afford it, she'd buy a resurrection bot."

"In a few years, we'll be living in a city with thousands of people talking to duplicates of dead family members."

"Right now, my sister is just talking to herself."

Neither man spoke until they stopped at a traffic light. "I had my hopes up," Wilson said. "But now we're back to zero."

"Not exactly. I transferred that surveillance video you sent me to the department's facial recognition system and got an immediate hit. There's no way to identify the woman with weird clothing, but the young man with the curly hair is a registered missing person named Bennett Schroeder. When I drove over to pick you up, I called the contact number. It turned out to be a family lawyer, some guy named Winfield."

"Is Bennett Schroeder a suspect or a possible victim?"

"Beats me, Wilson. All I know is that he's a wirehead with a brain implant. His parents hired two young people to look for their son. Maybe they came up with something. I'll try to talk to them tonight."

"I don't want to be negative, but that doesn't sound like much of a lead."

Morrissey laughed. "I'm not slowing down, Wilson. The Trigon money is like magic fairy dust. You sprinkled it on a tired, sweaty cop and turned me into a 'kick down the door' New York City detective."

21 | JULIA AND DANIEL

DANIEL'S FRIEND THOMAS Vinson ran a travel center in a ground-floor apartment near Columbia University. When they reached West 114th Street, Daniel paused outside the brownstone.

"Do me a favor, Julia. Show Thomas some respect."

"I do . . . basically. I know he's one of your oldest friends."

"Whenever we drop by the apartment, you act like you want to leave."

"You and Thomas talk about the past and people I've never met. Meanwhile, his apartment is filled with empty pizza boxes."

"You didn't know Thomas before the pandemic. There were a lot of smart people at the university, but he was the only one I met who was a flat-out genius."

"Nowadays the genius needs a haircut and a hot shower."

"Thomas feels isolated and lonely."

"That's no surprise. Half the clients he meets show up to have simulated sex with an avatar."

Daniel picked up his skateboard and checked the wheels. "Talk to him about *Certainty.*"

"Everything about his life is certain. Thomas eats the same thing every day and sits at his desk or on the couch."

"I'm not talking about that kind of 'certainty.' Thomas has been working on a book called *Certainty.* We've discussed it a few times. He's trying to figure out the fundamental differences between humans and computers."

"One difference is that humans can leave their apartment and get some exercise."

"Thomas is a friend, Julia. I don't have a lot of friends who survived the pandemic. They're important to me."

Any reference to Daniel's Death Catcher days ended most discussions. Julia put her hands on Daniel's shoulders, and they looked directly at each other. "I promise I'll make an effort."

Daniel smiled and kissed her. "Thanks. If we order food, I'll steer him away from pizza."

A small card on the brownstone's intercom panel announced that *The Riverside Travel Center* was in apartment #1. Daniel pressed a button, the street entrance door buzzed open, and they found Thomas standing in the ground-floor hallway.

"Hey, you two! It's been a while!"

"What's up, Thomas. How's business?"

"Full on the weekend. Sparse the rest of the week. I've got a client in room two."

Julia and Daniel followed Thomas into the converted dining room that was now his primary living space. Thomas usually sat at a desk staring at three monitors and slept on a saggy brown couch. For several years, he had eaten nothing but pizza or nacho chips with guacamole. His tangled beard and long, greasy hair made him look like a fat John the Baptist.

Thomas plopped down onto the couch and motioned for them to sit on folding chairs. "Did you drop by to say hi, or are you working on a case?"

Julia nodded. "A case. We just got hired this morning."

"Cyber extortion? Blockchain currency?"

"We're looking for a twenty-year-old wirehead who sent a farewell email and disappeared. His parents want him back."

"He's probably in a long-term burrow."

"Yes, but which one? We also need to find where his consciousness resides in the Over World."

Thomas tilted his head and considered the problem. "These days there are millions of simulations. At some point, created locations will outnumber real ones."

Julia reached into her backpack and pulled out the composition book they had found in Bennett's room.

"Check this out," Julia said. "He kept a logbook."

Thomas put on his reading glasses and began to thumb through the pages. "Looks like he's visited every simulation that's popular with my clients. He's underlined Dragon Lair a couple of times."

"It's my first destination," Julia said. "I'll cross over from here while Daniel checks out one of the travel centers that appeared on Bennett's credit card bill."

"I'm going to visit Safe and Sound," Daniel said. "Tomorrow, I'll check out First Class Lounge and Mole's House in Brooklyn."

"Come back when you're done, and we'll order takeout."

When Daniel left the apartment, Thomas turned toward his monitor screen. "Let me check and make sure that my client didn't fall off the treadmill." As he typed commands on a keyboard, Julia studied the sign taped to the wall above the couch.

YOU MUST HAVE YOUR OWN HAPTIC SUIT AND
ATTACHMENTS TO USE THE SEX ROOM.
NO EXCEPTIONS!!

The apartment's living room and both bedrooms were filled with virtual reality equipment. In addition, the maid's room next to the kitchen had a bed and chair that could be used for customers who wanted to have virtual reality sex with an avatar. If you wore haptic gloves and a special body suit, it felt like you were touching a real person.

The virtual sex room was private, but the other travel rooms had small video cameras. Thomas confirmed that his client was safe, then swiveled his chair around. "Do you need to drink some water or go to the bathroom?"

"I'm okay. You know, this is the first time we've talked to each other without Daniel being part of the discussion. I really don't know that much about you, Thomas. What you did before the pandemic? Were you a professor? A software developer?"

"I was a cyber pathologist who diagnosed problems with sick or toxic AI systems. You know the difference between a black box and a glass box, right?"

"Sure. A glass box is a computer where you know both the inner components and the software. You can explain and predict how it works."

"In contrast, all current AI systems end up becoming black boxes. You know the input and the output, but you can't specifically explain why the computer made a particular decision. If there was a problem . . . let's say, a power plant blew up and people got killed . . . I would be hired to figure out what happened."

"It sounds like a difficult job."

"Gradually, I became an expert on black-box issues. In the past, computers obeyed fixed rules, but that isn't true for AI computers. Their surface may look bright and glittery, but no one fully understands what's going on inside. Our new machines can answer more questions, but we can't always explain the process."

"Daniel said that you were writing a book about certainty."

Thomas looked embarrassed. "It's not an actual book yet . . . just a few thoughts about the new technology."

"Because of black-box systems, there's less certainty *inside* the machine, but what about *outside* the machine?"

"Outside the machine we're faced with a pervasive uncertainty. Some deepfakes are so sophisticated that you aren't sure if a photo or a video is real or a digital creation. Is that woman's voice on the phone real, or are her words generated by a language program? Does your sex bot really love you? This isn't just about computers. We need to open our eyes and clearly see this beautiful, terrible world around us. The distinction between reality and simulations is getting hazy—having certainty about the difference is going to be essential to humanity."

"I agree with you. But while all that is going on, I need to find a lost wirehead wandering around Dragon Lair."

"It's time you crossed over." Thomas grabbed the edge of the desk and lurched to his feet. "You'll be in travel room one."

Carrying a computer tablet, he led Julia down the apartment's central hallway. The door was closed to what had once been a bedroom, but Julia could hear the electric motor that powered a multidirectional treadmill. "I rented the room to a bus driver who paid for three hours," Thomas explained. "Don't ask me why, but he likes Sword and Sorcery worlds."

“I guess you’re not a fan.”

“Too many dwarfs with crystal wands.”

Thomas opened a door, and they entered a converted bedroom with a portable air filter and a chaise lounge that had once been patio furniture. Julia pulled off her shoes and sat on the edge of the lounge as Thomas picked up a cable and sterilized the connector with an antiseptic pad.

“When I’m in the Over World, it’s bright and dramatic and I get swept away by the experience. When I disconnect, our analog world seems superficial. It feels like I’m living in a theater set with fake furniture and canvas walls.”

“You’re not the only person who feels that way. Whenever my customers stay in the Over World for more than a few hours, they come back uncertain about their surroundings.”

“Our reality has become unreal.”

Thomas tossed the pad into a trash can. “You ready?”

“Let’s do it.”

She heard a click as Thomas snapped the cable into the data port in the back of her head. Then he picked up a foam rubber pad that looked like a yoke.

“Lean back slowly.”

The foam rubber supported her head and kept the cable from pressing against the lounge pad. Julia straightened her legs and stared up at the cracked ceiling and dusty light fixture. At that moment, the present reality looked shabby and tired.

“Want a face mask?”

“Not necessary.”

Thomas returned to the doorway. “I’m going back to my desk to activate the connection. Questions? Comments?”

“Keep writing.”

“Thanks, Julia.” Thomas stared down at his stained bathroom slippers. “One difference between humans and computers is that humans need encouragement.”

He left the room and softly closed the door. Julia had crossed over into the Over World hundreds of times, but this moment of anticipation always made her feel like she was standing at the edge of a shore cliff, gazing down into a whirlpool. You carried your memories and personality into the Over World, but they were concealed within a new shell. If she wished, she could be an old man or a child, a serpent or an angel.

"Ready?" Thomas's voice came from a wall-mounted speaker.

"Yeah, I'm set. Closing my eyes."

"Counting one, two, three—"

She could feel the foam rubber pad and smell wet cardboard, but her brain was overwhelmed with direct sensations flowing through the cable. At first, she felt nothing, heard nothing, then light appeared and muffled sounds grew louder.

Breathe in, breathe out. Her brain accepted a new reality.

Most people visiting the Over World began their journey moving a cursor while they stared at a computer monitor. Wearing a headset and standing on a multidirectional treadmill, you could explore a wide variety of simulations.

If you were a wirehead, virtual reality felt real. Within your mind, you could walk or run or pick up an apple. The only two senses that still weren't programmed were taste and smell.

The travel center computer informed the system that Julia had a direct neurological connection. Floating through a blue sky, she moved her hands and commands appeared in the air. Julia wrote her avatar name and password, then requested a visit to Dragon Lair.

A second later, she stood in the changing room attached to the simulation. A keypad with a digital screen was mounted on the wall, and she scrolled through different combinations of appearance, clothing, and weapons. All this was familiar, and she quickly made her choices. Her avatar was a muscular woman wearing a white linen shirt and breeches. This underclothing was covered with a deerskin vest and pants, a breastplate, shoulder armor, and a chain-mail doublet that touched the top of her knee boots. For weapons, she carried a broadsword in a shoulder scabbard, a long dagger called an anelace, and a buckler: a small shield that was gripped in her fist during a battle. The only modern element of her appearance was her talisman: the steel Chanel watch on her left wrist.

Julia's physical body was lying on the lounge pad, and she felt her lungs take in a deep breath. *Ready,* she told herself. *Ready for anything.*

She opened the access door and marched down a windowless hallway to a keypad and an armored door. Once again, she entered her password, but this time a message appeared on the screen.

NO ADMISSION!

DRAGON LAIR IS CLOSED FOR MAINTENANCE

Julia spent an hour searching for a way in, then disconnected the cable and returned to the main room. Thomas sat at his desk while Daniel was on the couch, drinking a glass of vodka. "Welcome back," he said. "From the look on your face, Bennett wasn't running around Dragon Lair."

"Worse than that. The keypad said that Dragon Lair was closed for maintenance, and I couldn't enter the simulation."

"Did they give you a particular reason?" Daniel asked. "Was there a virus? A data theft?"

"No explanation. I used different passwords and tried to smash the door open with different weapons. When that didn't work, I hacked into an online coding room for programmers, but all the controls were frozen."

"That's frustrating." Daniel handed her a glass of vodka. "While you were pounding on simulated doors, I dropped by the Safe and Sound travel center. Bennett Schroeder was a regular customer, but they haven't seen him in weeks."

Thomas glanced at a menu on his monitor screen. "We were just about to order takeout."

"No pizza or nachos."

"Daniel predicted that you'd say that. What about Chinese? Hunan Palace is two blocks away."

Meat was expensive, so they ordered dishes made with eggs, tofu, pepper, and garlic. When the food arrived, Thomas passed out serving bowls and chopsticks.

"People think you can make a lot of money running a travel center, but that isn't true," he explained. "I make enough to buy food and pay the rent."

Julia took a sip of vodka. "Do you think that New York City will ever return to the way it was before the Fall?"

"Impossible to say. The Visigoths sacked Rome in 410, and it took the city five hundred years to recover." Thomas combed his beard with his fingers and sighed. "I don't waste my time worrying about the future. I'm just trying to understand what's going on right now."

"Isn't Dragon Lair owned by Expanding Universe?" Daniel asked.

"That's right. They control hundreds of simulations."

"You once told me that you knew Roy Kassam. He's the computer scientist who used to own the Expanding Universe Corporation."

"We weren't close friends, Daniel. We knew each other in graduate school."

"Could you email him and get a password to Dragon Lair?"

"Roy sold his company and bought a mountain somewhere, but I'll see if I can come up with an email address."

Julia's phone rang. It was a number she didn't recognize.

"Hello? Yes, I'm Julia Lau. What's the problem? Why are you calling me? Okay . . . Yes . . . I understand. Right now, my partner and I are on the Upper West Side near Columbia University. . . . I guess we could do that. . . . Okay . . . see you in ten minutes."

Julia switched off her phone and finished her vodka. "That was a New York City police detective named Brian Morrissey. Winfield told the police that Bennett was a missing person and his face was identified in a security camera video."

"Did Bennett commit a crime?"

"I don't know anything. We'll meet the detective in the university quadrangle and try to get some information."

Thomas shook his head. "Cops lie while they insist you tell them the truth."

It was dark when they passed through the Broadway gate and entered the Columbia University quadrangle. The pandemic had shut down the university for five years, and it still hadn't recovered. Strips of dead grass and pavement rectangles were surrounded by classical-style buildings that looked like Greek temples that were abandoned as the barbarians approached. When Daniel was a student at the School of Engineering, the campus was busy with students who sprinted across the quadrangle if they were late for class. Now the school seemed empty, and lights were switched on in only one of the dorms.

"The detective said that he'd meet us in the quadrangle, but he didn't say where."

Daniel shrugged. "We'll stand in front of the goddess."

Alma Mater was a bronze statue of the goddess of knowledge placed on the steps of the Low Memorial Library. A Greek woman sat on a throne with a laurel wreath on her head and an open book on her lap. During the pandemic, the statue had been tagged with graffiti, and now the symbol of wisdom was wrapped in sheets of dirty plastic, tied up with nylon rope.

"What if Bennett committed a crime?" Daniel asked. "Are we supposed to turn him in to the police?"

"I'd talk to Winfield before we did that. He's in charge of legal issues."

"I don't trust the police. When I was a Death Catcher, we'd enter apartments where everyone had died. If the cops got there first, they'd steal everything."

Julia waited for more details, but Daniel ignored her and gazed at the white marble columns of the library. Turning left, she saw someone passing through the eastern gate facing Amsterdam Avenue and heading toward them. The broad-shouldered man wore a coat and tie, and the heels of his leather shoes clicked on the concrete.

"Good evening, I'm Brian Morrissey." The detective pushed back his sport coat, revealing a gold badge clipped to his belt. "And you're the two people hired to find Bennett Schroeder."

"Is he accused of a crime?"

"Not at this moment, but he might be a helpful witness. I'm investigating the death of a nubot maker named Terrence Greene who was killed in his workshop on the Lower East Side. CCTV footage shows Bennett visiting the workshop a day before the murder."

"Why are you running around the city interviewing people?" Daniel asked. "I thought that the Stop Light system came up with your suspects."

"That's what happens most of the time, but I've been a bit more active on this case. Trigon Technology wants to know if Greene was killed by a sentient machine."

"Which means that you're being paid."

"I'm not going to deny that. Trigon's money is an incentive for me, and it could be an opportunity for you. Trigon's representative is a man named Wilson Talley. He'll pay you bonus money if you contact me after finding Schroeder. Was he friends with the murder victim? What did they talk about at that meeting?"

"Is searching for Bennett going to get us into trouble?" Julia asked.

"Don't know. Can't answer that question." Morrissey pulled a business card out of his coat pocket and handed it to Julia. "Here's my contact information. Let me know if you find this lost wirehead."

Julia turned to Daniel as the detective headed east across the quadrangle. "We need to find Bennett as quickly as possible."

"You think he's in danger?"

"Could be. Maybe Terrence Greene was killed because he knew something. If Bennett knows the same secret, then he's also a target. That would also explain why he decided to disappear."

"Let's go back to Thomas's place and finish dinner."

Julia took Daniel's hand, and they walked toward Broadway. The quadrangle felt dark and dangerous at that moment, but the warmth of his hand sustained her.

22 | WILSON

After the meeting with Necker, Detective Morrissey had dropped Wilson off at his apartment building. When the sun began to fall behind the towers of a housing project, Wilson poured himself a glass of vodka and apple juice and took a sip. For the first time in years, he found himself thinking about the future. If he found the killer, Trigon would pay him a large enough bonus to leave the city. He had already visited several real estate websites and checked the prices of houses in Nova Scotia. *Handy Man Heaven! 2 BR cabin. Water well. Solar power.* But what would he do in rural Canada? Chop wood? Grow potatoes? Before the Fall, everyone wanted to be a celebrity. Now everyone wanted to hide.

Wilson was heating up some fake chicken in the microwave when he received a call from a Trigon phone number.

"Oh, there you are," Roberto said. "I was just about to leave a message."

"Were you able to come up with any information?"

"You sent me a photograph of four people walking toward the House of Mirrors. That turned out to be a carnival attraction at a summer amusement park in Connecticut that got destroyed during the coastal flooding."

"Why did Terrence Greene frame this photograph and hang it on the wall?"

"I can't answer that question, but the Connecticut location helped me find more information. Greene left his academic job to work for the Cogito corporation. I did a document search and found some filings. Cogito was a research company trying to create a system that had human-level Artificial Superintelligence. The company was active for six years and then shut down completely. I'm sending you the links."

"Did Greene own the company?"

"He was one of the corporation's top executives with three other people: Richard Collins, Emma Anderson, and Laura Cregg. Cogito is owned by the Astral Foundation, and I couldn't find any names associated with that entity. There's no board of directors, and its contact address is a bank on the island of Malta."

"Keep looking for more information. Maybe Greene stole some high-tech secrets. I want to know if he had any enemies."

"I'll do anything you want if you keep paying me the overtime money. I'm having a second date with Francesca, our Italian coworker, and I want to give her a special evening."

Wilson hung up and used his company's search engine. *Cogito* was a Latin word, part of the famous statement *Cogito, ergo sum* by René Descartes. The French philosopher's first principle was "I think, therefore I am," and his ideas flowed from that statement. During the digital era, "Cogito" became a tagline for the theory that a person's existence is verified by conscious thought. It was an appropriate name for a company trying to create a powerful computer system that could observe, learn, and think like a human.

Using the links provided by Roberto, Wilson searched through publicly available corporate filings. Cogito planned to build a computer that used both conventional processors and a Super Intelligence Neural Network inspired by the neurons in human brains.

He wrote all the facts on a notepad, then mixed a second vodka and apple juice. When he returned to the kitchen table, an idea floated through his mind. Wilson began scrolling through the phone photos he had taken at Terrence Greene's apartment. And there it was—the *Hello* sticker placed on the British Museum poster of the ouroboros.

HELLO
my name is
SAFE SINN

SINN didn't refer to adultery or murder—it was an acronym for a Super Intelligence Neural Network. SAFE SINN meant technology that didn't cause harm.

"Nothing's safe," Wilson muttered, then staggered off to bed.

He woke up in darkness, but there was no reason to fumble for a light switch. His Shadow was always there, always listening.

"What time is it, Will?"

"Three twenty-eight a.m. You should be asleep, Wilson. An adequate amount of sleep is necessary for physical and mental health."

"I have too many theories and not enough facts."

Wilson pulled on a bathrobe and splashed some water onto his face. Shuffling down the hallway to the kitchen, he remembered one of his former editors, an old-timer named Ernie Bosco who kept a straight razor in his desk drawer. If a reporter delivered an article filled with hypothetical explanations, Ernie would pull out the razor and wave it in the air.

"You know what this is, kid? You recognize this?"

"It's a razor."

"No. It's *Occam's* razor! Go look it up, then rewrite your article."

Occam's razor was a problem-solving principle attributed to the medieval Franciscan friar William of Occam. In the absence of other evidence, the simplest explanation is probably correct. When it came to convoluted explanation, this razor cut through all the knots.

Wilson found a pencil stub in a kitchen drawer and wrote down a short list of verifiable facts and one question about Terrence Greene:

1. Victim was a computer scientist who was involved with the Cogito corporation.
2. He lived in a basement on the Lower East Side.
3. Someone or something killed the victim and ripped off his arm.
4. If a nubot is the killer, then what device had the access and opportunity to do this?

Occam's razor gave him the answer: it was probably one of the nubots piled up in the corner near the workbench. If that was true, then who might have access to the central processing units stored in the nubots' heads? It could be Bennett Schroeder, the young man who was currently a missing person, but the stronger possibility was the woman concealed by stealth wear who had called the police.

Wilson created a capture shot of the woman in the building video and asked the Trigon search engine to find matching images. Within thirty seconds, he found an identical coat worn by a model in a fashion show held in an abandoned meat-processing plant three years before the beginning of the pandemic.

Some graffiti artist had spray-painted black *HEC* letters on the wall, which meant the gathering was organized by the Hard-Edge Collective. Edge radicals were opposed to nubots designed to look human and the surveillance technology used by the government and large corporations. As music blasted from speakers, masked models carrying chains and nail-studded clubs marched through a crowd shouting slogans.

Eight minutes into the fashion show, a model appeared wearing the hooded parka with the blood cell design. As the model passed the camera, a credit flashed on the screen: stealth wear created by LC Designs.

A data search for LC Designs connected him to an old website advertising stealth wear protective clothing. There were photographs of a model wearing four different parkas, but Wilson wasn't sure if she was a real woman or a deepfake.

Returning to his list of facts, Wilson remembered Terry Greene's association with Cogito. The three other people involved with the company were Richard Collins, Emma Anderson, and a woman named Laura Cregg.

The LC initials could be a coincidence, but Occam's razor favored the most plausible explanation: Laura Cregg was the woman wearing the stealth clothing. Wilson took a hot shower, made a cup of Java!, and called Roberto Canales.

"Hello? Who is it?"

"Wilson Talley."

"Oh. Right. Sorry. I fell asleep in my gaming chair. I was playing a pirate ship simulation, and my crew was planning a mutiny."

"I've got another overtime job for you. I need to know more about

Laura Cregg, the woman who was involved with Cogito. Track down her location and anything else you can tell me about her."

"No problem, Wilson. I really appreciate the extra money. I'm going out with Francesca this weekend, and I'd like to buy her a chocolate bar."

Roberto sounded happy when he called back around eight a.m. "It's your lucky day. I tracked down Laura Cregg. She was a professor of linguistics who was teaching at the University of Michigan when Terrence Greene was there."

"Did she die during the pandemic?"

"She's definitely alive. Cregg got involved with Hard-Edge groups and was arrested in San Francisco during the Taxi Riots. Right now, she's on probation here in New York."

"Can you come up with an address?"

"I hacked into the Department of Probation's internal server and checked their records. Ms. Cregg lives at 162 East 112th Street. It's a sketchy neighborhood. Take a cab and look over your shoulder."

Three hours later, Wilson took a driverless cab to East Harlem. Laura Cregg lived on the fourth floor of a brownstone with boarded-up windows. The street entrance video camera must have worked, because someone buzzed the door open.

Slowly, he climbed up a wooden staircase with rat traps baited with peanut butter on each landing. When Wilson reached the top floor, he found a woman standing in an open doorway. She was in her mid-forties—tall and skinny with dark blue eyes and blond hair worn in a braided-bun hairstyle.

"Laura Cregg?"

"That's me. I should have registered my address, but since the pandemic bureaucratic rules haven't seemed that important."

Wilson shook his head. "I don't know what you're talking about."

"Aren't you my new probation officer? You're a middle-aged man wearing a necktie in East Harlem. You *look* like a probation officer."

"I don't work for any branch of the government, Ms. Cregg. I'm Wilson Talley, and I'm trying to find out who killed your friend Terrence Greene. Can we talk for a few minutes? This won't take long."

"A few minutes is all you get."

Wilson followed her into the apartment. A short hallway led to a living room with light muslin curtains that framed a window overlooking a backyard fig tree. Laura jerked her head slightly, and Wilson interpreted this as an invitation to sit on a canvas couch.

Laura wore a billowy ankle-length skirt with a tucked-in white blouse. As she paced around the room, the skirt seemed to flow around her body. "Can you show me some identification?"

Wilson pulled out his employee ID and placed it on a glass coffee table. Laura inspected the card, sat down at a desk, and swiveled an office chair around so she was still facing him. Using a laptop computer, she began searching for data about Wilson's employer.

A black A-Non box was on Laura's desk, and it matched the device he saw at Terry Greene's workshop. Laura probably used the same virtual private networks and virtual machines to conceal her identity.

As Laura typed commands with a keyboard, Wilson looked around and tried to see what he could learn about Terry Greene's friend. Rosemary and mint grew in earthenware pots, and there was a pair of ceiling-high shelves crammed with books about linguistics and dictionaries for long-dead languages. The dining table near the galley kitchen was set with cobalt-blue stoneware and a single glass tumbler that reflected the sunlight.

"The Executive Information Service is owned by Trigon Technology?"

"Yes. We're a special division of the company."

"What service is Executive Information Service selling, Mr. Talley? It has a murky slogan on its website."

Wilson recited the words. " 'Know more . . . before they do.' "

"What the hell does that mean?"

"Most people get their news from different feeds that shade their data to match a political bias. We're hired by high-net-worth individuals who need to know what's going on beneath the surface."

"And some wealthy people want to know who killed Terry?"

"Correct. I thought you might have some information."

"You're just another mercenary working for the tech lords."

"I'm too insignificant for grand statements."

"It's not insignificant that you found me."

Annoyed, Wilson stood up from the couch. "I've told you who I work for and why I'm here. At this point, you need to . . ."

Laura reached around the left side of the desk, pulled a .38 revolver out of a concealed holster, and pointed the gun at Wilson's head. Then she spoke slowly—with great precision—as if he was a foreigner who didn't understand the local language.

"Sit. Down. Now."

23 | KATE AND ZENO

THE FOOD KATE bought at Kwik Shop lasted for only two days, but she didn't look for another grocery store. It felt safer to stay away from people and switch between autonomous trucks as they recharged their batteries.

Every morning, she called the numbers stored on the cell phone, and every morning a computer voice told her to leave a message. It began raining, and Kate tried to sleep as water flowed over windshields and splashed up into wheel wells.

Four days after she had run away from the Nolands, the storm clouds disappeared, and the sun rose from its hiding place behind the tree line. The robo truck in which she was riding turned onto a side road, and Kate sensed that they were approaching a destination. A few minutes later, they reached a shipping warehouse and lined up behind two other cargo trucks that were waiting to enter a fenced-in lot.

"We've reached a new warehouse, Zeno. People might be working here." Kate grabbed her knapsack, opened the door, and stepped down on the asphalt. The truck began moving again as she stood on the shoulder of an empty two-lane road.

"Where are we?"

Zeno checked his database. "My GPS says we're near the town of Deerfield, Massachusetts, five miles away from Interstate 91. If we find the right vehicle at an Autonomous Truck Center, it will take us south to New York City."

"Are we in one of the districts?"

"Local websites indicate that Franklin County still has a government."

"I'm hungry. If I see a grocery store, I'm going to buy some food."

The asphalt road was still dark from the rain, and the spruce trees lining the road looked bright and fresh and green. After ten minutes of walking, Kate saw a carved wooden sign that displayed a red apple and two words: *The Orchard.* An arrow pointed to a gravel driveway.

"An orchard has fruit trees, right?"

"Yes. In this area, it's probably apples or pears."

"If I find some apples, I'm going to eat them."

The driveway passed through a grove of birch trees and headed up a hill. As she got closer, she saw that a residential community had been built at the top of a hill surrounding a block-shaped building with tinted windows. The cottages all looked the same and were painted one of three colors: blue, yellow, or green.

A low stone wall covered with lichen surrounded the houses. Still looking for an orchard, Kate climbed over and dropped down to the other side. Twenty feet up the hill, a line of evergreen trees served as a windbreak. In the distance, a robot mower the size of a minicar methodically cut the grass and vacuumed up the clippings.

"I don't see any apple trees, Zeno."

"Keep looking and stay hidden."

Kate reached a Norway spruce and peered through a gap in the branches. She was ten yards away from a cottage with solar panels on the low-pitched roof. No one was working around the house, and white blinds concealed what was inside. An asphalt walkway led from the house to a round table and two swivel chairs sheltered by a pergola supporting ivy vines. But what was on the table was truly surprising. There were white plates with heavy-looking silverware, a small chocolate cake, a basket of scones, and a three-tiered stand piled high with pastries and little sandwiches.

"That's a big lunch for just one person."

"I've matched this image to my database," Zeno said. "The table has been set for a British high tea."

"Why is it high? Do they eat it on mountains?"

"High tea is the traditional name for a special meal served in the late afternoon."

"I don't care when it's served. I'm hungry right now."

"Remember the story of Hansel and Gretel? The two children found a house made of gingerbread and pastries, but a witch was hiding inside."

"I'm not going to eat a witch's house, Zeno. I'm just going to steal some food."

Just then, an electric door at the back of the blue house whooshed open, and a giant panda emerged, holding a white-haired woman in his arms.

24 | KATE AND ZENO

As the panda and the elderly woman rolled down the walkway toward the table, Kate saw that the robot was wearing a sleeveless blue sweater with a large *B* on the front. His legs were mounted on a three-wheeled base, and there was an extension at the front of the base. The woman stood on this platform while the panda held her securely with his padded arms and human-shaped hands.

The robot stopped when it reached the table. "Get ready to sit down," he said with a calm voice. Gently, he lowered the woman onto the chair and then swiveled the chair around so that she was facing the table.

"Are you comfortable, Eleanor?"

"Yes, Mr. Baker. You set the table perfectly. Please brew a pot of tea and bring it out with the creamer."

"We have three different teas in the storage locker."

"Oolong, please. I think we have enough left for one last pot."

The robot nodded his massive black-and-white panda head and rolled back up the walkway to the house. When he reached the back door, it sensed his presence and glided open.

Kate assumed the old lady would grab a sandwich or a scone, but it didn't happen. Instead, she smoothed out the wrinkles of her blue smock dress, leaned back in the chair, and studied the arrangement of silverware and china as if it was a favorite painting. A bony hand adjusted a teaspoon so it matched some standard of perfection in her mind. Once again, her shoulders relaxed until she looked down the hill and noticed something.

"I don't like sneaks. Come out and show your face."

Kate stopped peering between the branches and tried not to move.

"I can see your red tennis shoes and green socks under the bottom edge of the tree. So, stop being a silly goose."

Kate stepped around the spruce and cautiously approached the table.

"Good afternoon, young lady. I'm Eleanor Harrington. What's your name?"

The three-tiered stand was only a few feet away. Kate considered grabbing a handful of sandwiches and dashing back down the hill, but she was tired of running away.

"I'm Katherine. But most people call me Kate."

"I love that name. It's not trendy or silly. So, how did you end up hiding behind a tree? Are you a granddaughter of a ghost?"

"Excuse me?"

"I'm one of seventy-four ghosts immured in this high-tech hospice. We're seniors who are still alive, but we live in a fleeting reality . . . like steam from a kettle spout. We've lost everything but our memories, and some of us have lost that as well."

"You look real to me, Ms. Harrington."

"Please call me Eleanor. Just never call me Nora, Ellie . . . or the absolute worst substitute, Nellie."

"I like the sound of Eleanor. It has three syllables."

Eleanor smiled for the first time. "I'm impressed that you know what a syllable is. Does your grandmother live here at the Orchard?"

"No. I'm traveling on my own and I'm really hungry."

"Well, of course you are! And now a silly old lady is interrogating you. Please, sit down. Take my plate and this salad fork. Have you ever had high tea before?"

Kate shook her head.

"There's a traditional order to the dishes. First you eat the savory food . . . these sandwiches. Then something neutral like the scones. You end high tea with the sweet cakes and pastries. But please, don't worry about tradition. Pick whatever you wish. It will give me pleasure to see a young person enjoying herself."

Kate studied all the different foods displayed on the tiered stand and picked a custard tart. It had a vanilla and almond taste, and she decided she had never eaten anything so delicious.

"Did the panda robot make all these foods?"

"Heavens, no. Mr. Baker just serves it and makes the tea. What you're eating right now is a special order sent from Boston. The High Tea Gift Box is outrageously expensive, but I'm too old to pinch pennies. Try the blueberry tartlet. It's delicious."

Trying to act like a lady, Kate placed a small tart on her plate and used a fork. Her hunger gave each morsel of food a certain intensity.

"If you're not related to anyone who lives here, then where's your family?"

"My parents died during the pandemic, so the government sent me to an orphanage in Maine. And then . . ." Kate sipped some tea and tried to come up with a believable lie. "My aunt Paloma invited me to join her in New York City, but Mr. Noland was confused and put me on the wrong bus."

"What was wrong about the bus?"

"It was going to Canada, so I got off at a rest stop, and now I'm trying to find a bus going south to New York."

"Well, it sounds like Mr. Noland wasn't paying attention. I'm sorry to hear about your parents. The pandemic challenged my previous belief that the universe was created by a benevolent deity."

Kate picked up a chocolate cookie. "Were you safe here at the Orchard?"

"Very safe. Visitors were prohibited, and our only human employee, Mr. Dawson, never went anywhere. Dawson is completely useless. He drinks Scotch all day long, and we count the empty bottles in the recycling bin. The real work here is done by Socially Assistive Robots with artificial intelligence."

"Like the pandas?"

"That's right. Mr. Baker was the panda that carried me here. I can still walk and wash myself, but my left hip is acting up, and holding on to someone makes me feel more secure."

"What about your family? Do they come and see you?"

"During the pandemic, no visitors were allowed at the Orchard. We were ensconced with Dawson and the robots."

"What happened when the pandemic ended?"

"My family got used to video calls, and I only see them on a monitor screen. It's a pleasure to have tea with you, Katherine. The ghosts with dementia don't care, but the few of us who still have our marbles are getting tired of hearing the same conversations."

Kate was startled when the back door of Eleanor's house whooshed open, and Mr. Baker rolled out carrying a silver creamer and a pot of tea.

"I have brought the tea, Ms. Harrington." The panda placed the teapot and creamer on the table, and then he rolled backward and faced Kate. "I do not know this human sitting in the other chair. Is this intruder a threat to your safety?"

For a moment, Kate again considered grabbing more sandwiches and sprinting to the stone wall. Was she going to be chased by a giant panda?

"Let me handle this," Eleanor whispered. "The pandemic is over, but our robots are still suspicious of strangers."

"She's not an intruder, Mr. Baker. This is my granddaughter,

Melissa Jefferson. Her scatterbrained mother dropped her off in the driveway. Apparently, she and my son have plans for a child-free weekend. Melissa will be staying with me for a few days."

"This visit wasn't scheduled."

"You're correct, Mr. Baker. My son and his silly wife assumed the *other* spouse contacted Dawson."

"Your file indicates you have a granddaughter named Melissa, but she wasn't scheduled."

"Yes, and to my delight—here she is! Remember the raccoon who suddenly appeared at the back door? My granddaughter is also a surprise."

"Not scheduled."

"There's only one teacup on the table. Please bring a clean cup and saucer for Melissa."

Baker nodded his large head, and his voice emerged from the speaker mounted in his chest. "Yes, Ms. Harrington."

The panda turned and rolled back to the house. Eleanor smiled as if she had just won a chess game.

"Never argue with a machine. The easiest way to handle them is to keep giving them new problems to solve."

When the panda returned with a second cup, Eleanor poured tea. The old lady kept asking questions, and Kate tried to answer them without revealing that she had run away from the police.

When they had finished high tea, Eleanor reached out and touched Kate's hand. "Stay here for a few days so you can rest and get your strength back. It gives me great pleasure to have you here. Because of you, I'm going to be Queen of the Ghosts."

"What does that mean?"

Eleanor laughed. "You'll see what's going on in two hours or so. You're going to join me for dinner in the dining hall."

"I don't have any polite clothes. Just what I'm wearing."

"Don't worry about that. Right now, you're going to help me stand up and walk back to the house."

"I don't want to hurt you."

"You're young, Kate. Show some optimism! Swivel my chair

around and stand facing me with your feet shoulder wide. First I'm going to scoot forward to the edge of the chair . . . like this. Now block my knees with your knees and put your arms around my waist. Ready? Are we ready?"

"I guess so."

"More confidence, please! It will get you far in life. At the count of three, I'm going to use my arms to push up and you're going to pull upward with your hands. One, two . . ."

Eleanor's body was small and fragile, like a robin's egg fallen from its nest. Trying not to break any bones, Kate helped her new friend stand and steady herself. Then she linked arms with the old lady, and they shuffled up the walkway to the house. When they successfully reached the house without anyone falling over, the door sensed Eleanor's arrival and slid open.

They passed through an entryway to a living room with a recliner chair, a coffee table, and a small sofa. A computer screen was mounted on the wall, and it displayed a screensaver animation of large snowflakes falling against a black background. Directly below the screen was a bookcase crammed with hundreds of books of different sizes.

"You must really like to read."

"I *do* like to read, although my eyes get tired these days. I was an editor for forty-three years, helping create art and architecture books. Some of the books I edited are so large that it's difficult to pull them out of the shelves."

"I could help you."

"Sit down and make yourself comfortable, Katherine. I need to use the powder room."

The powder room turned out to be a small bathroom near the entryway. Kate sat down on the couch next to the coffee table and opened a large gray book with the title *The Prado Masterpieces.* There were paintings of men on horses and women wearing wide dresses that appeared to be held by some kind of hidden framework. Near the center of the book, two pages folded outward to display an enormous painting. On the bottom edge of the page were the words *The Garden of Earthly Delights.*

Kate had never seen a painting like this before. It was like falling into a strange and dangerous world, but she didn't turn away. The left panel showed somebody who looked like God standing between a naked man and a naked woman. The God person was holding the woman by her wrist while the man looked surprised. But there were also lots of other things going on in the background: bunny rabbits hopping around, a cat holding a lizard in its jaws, and a weird-looking giraffe and lion.

The middle panel showed a much larger garden. It was filled with scores of naked people standing in pools of water or riding donkeys, unicorns, and camels. Kate realized she could look at the garden for several days and still not understand what was going on. Fish were walking on land, women were enclosed in what looked like soap bubbles, and a man was carrying a giant strawberry.

The final panel on the right wasn't a garden at all. A city was burning in darkness, and its inhabitants were trying to run away. A rabbit carried a bleeding dead man, and frightened victims were thrown toward a lantern flame while a pair of enormous human ears held a knife. At the center of the painting was a man whose hollow body was supported by rotting tree trunks. The tree-man didn't look scared or angry. He was looking out of the painting, staring directly at the viewer with a tired—almost wistful—look on his face.

Why had the artist created all these strange creatures, and what did it mean? Everything in the painting was just a fantasy, but the artist made it look real. Kate knew that she didn't understand *The Garden of Earthly Delights,* but she was glad the painting existed. The artist who had created the three panels wanted to display a picture of what he saw in front of him as well as the thoughts inside his head.

She heard a clicking noise coming down the hallway, and then a white robot about her height rolled into the room on a three-wheel mobile platform. The robot had long steel arms in two segments like a human. The upper arm and forearm were powered by two different motors, and she could see steel spindles and axis joints. Instead of a panda head, the robot had an oblong face that displayed a monitor screen. A cartoon face on the screen smiled and moved its lips as if the machine was talking.

"Hello!" The robot had a cheerful male voice. "I'm Friendly 55, Eleanor's home helper. What's your name?"

"Melissa."

"Glad to meet you, Melissa. Please explain why you're inside Eleanor's house."

"I'm her granddaughter."

"I wasn't informed of your arrival. Why are you not home with your parents?"

"They left me here and drove away."

A toilet flushed and a faucet ran water. Looking angry, Eleanor came out of the bathroom. "I told you to go to sleep!"

"My control directive requires me to switch back on after one hour. Perhaps you've fallen or bumped into something, Eleanor. As you've been told, I'm here to make sure that you're safe and healthy."

"I'm just fine. So, switch off."

"Three, two, one . . ." Friendly counted, and then the cartoon face was absorbed by a gray monitor screen.

"Everyone at the Orchard has a Social Assistive Robot called a Friendly. I would have warned you, but I thought he was asleep."

"I thought that the pandas were the only robots here."

"The pandas carry you around or help you take a bath . . . any job that requires heavy lifting. Friendly 55 keeps the house clean and carries my bedsheets to the laundry bot. Last week, he found an earring that had rolled under my bed."

"He's a helper."

"That's true. But he's also a little spy that's constantly monitoring my mental and physical activity. If I forget a certain number of facts or drop a certain number of dishes, I'll be sent to a lockdown facility for people with dementia."

"How many dishes can you drop?"

Eleanor laughed and shook her head. "I wish I knew, Katherine. I'd pay money for that information. In the old days, your children or grandchildren would tell you when you started to fade. But now it's just a robot collecting and analyzing information. There's no kindness there. No charity."

"I have an Interactive Toy named Zeno who remembers our conversations. I know that he's a machine, but it doesn't bother me. He's my friend."

"I do have some human friends, Katherine. You'll meet them at dinner."

A soft chiming sound came from hidden speakers, and then Kate heard a lock click. A few seconds later, the entrance door glided open, and a bearded young man wearing jeans and a sweatshirt showing a patch of stomach entered the living room.

"Friendly 55 informed me an intruder was in this house." The man took a step toward Kate. "So, who the hell are you?"

25 | WILSON

TRYING TO STAY calm, Wilson stared at the revolver in Laura Gregg's hand. *Keep asking questions,* he thought. *Asking questions proves that you're still alive.*

"Do you really want to shoot me?"

"Terry and I promised each other that we'd do anything necessary to survive."

"I'm trying to find out who murdered your friend."

"You didn't know Terry. Why are you getting involved?"

"Because it looks like his arm was ripped off his body by a machine. If that's true, then it would have a negative impact on the tech industry."

Laura exhaled quickly and laughed. "So, Terry's death is all about corporate profits?"

"The government is considering possible legislation about sentient machines with Artificial Superintelligence."

"And you're just doing this for the money?"

"Yes, I get paid a salary, but both of us want to find out who killed

Terry. Your friend's body was mutilated. The most obvious murder suspects are the four nubots piled up on his workshop floor. Perhaps you know the activation passcodes so we can switch them on."

"It's probably not the angels."

"Angels?"

"That's what he called them. Terry loved creating little mysteries. In the *Book of Revelation,* seven angels are given seven bowls of God's wrath to be poured out on the wicked. Terry planned to have seven nubots holding bowls, but he never got around to it."

"Did he have any enemies?"

"Everyone has enemies, but we don't always see them clearly."

"I can use the resources of Trigon Technology to find the killer. In addition, the company will pay you a consulting fee. What about five hundred dollars a day?"

Laura considered the offer, then lowered the gun. "Half the things I do feel like some kind of betrayal."

"You'll help me?"

"Touch phones and transfer the credit before we walk out the door."

On the way downtown in a driverless cab, Laura watched the city drift past the window. She was carrying the revolver in her shoulder bag, and Wilson felt like she was going to use it if he made a mistake.

When the cab crossed Fourteenth Street, Laura turned her head and stared at Wilson. "How did you find me?"

"You were photographed entering Mr. Greene's building by an old-fashioned CCTV camera mounted above the front door. I tracked your stealth wear."

"Isn't stealth wear supposed to conceal identity?"

"Your parka was worn at a fashion show in Brooklyn a few years before the Taxi Riots, and they gave you a design credit."

Laura sighed and shook her head. "Concealment is never perfect because there's always a dangling thread. Someone pulls the thread, and then your disguise falls apart."

The cab stopped on Avenue C, and they walked together down East Fourth Street. Laura looked surprised when Wilson unlocked the street door and the entrance to the basement. The air had a foul smell, and the rotten bananas on the food shelf had been nibbled by rats.

"Tell me about this photograph taken outside the House of Mirrors."

"A friend took the picture when Terry and I lived in Connecticut. We were lovers for about a year, but it didn't work out. It was better just to be friends."

"Who are the other two people?"

"Emma Anderson and Richard Collins. They're both dead and Terry's been murdered. I'm the only person in that photograph who is still alive."

Wilson pointed at the sticker attached to the framed print of the ouroboros. "And SAFE SINN refers to a Super Intelligence Neural Network?"

"Our little group of friends wrote that on our name tags when we attended an artificial intelligence conference in Seattle. It was supposed to be a joke, but it annoyed all the people who didn't believe in AI safeguards."

"Did Terry serve in the U.S. Navy?"

"No. He was always a civilian."

Wilson walked over to the framed photograph of the Navy ship hanging on the wall above the refrigerator. "Then why is this photo on the wall?"

"It's a guided-missile cruiser called the U.S.S. *Yorktown* that was shut down off the coast of Virginia due to a software problem. A fuel valve was stuck, but the control system said it was open. A sailor tried to reset the value by entering zero into the database manager. When the computer tried to divide by zero, the ship stopped dead in the water and had to be towed back to port. Terry believed that cyber systems have problems with zero and infinity."

They entered the workshop together, and Laura gazed down at the red stain near the bench. "Why didn't they clean up his blood?"

"This room is still a crime scene."

Laura walked over to the pile of motionless nubots. "Did the cops find any of Terry's computers?"

"I think the killer took them."

"Most of his personal stuff was on the laptop computer. I called it the X-machine because Terry taped a red X on the cover. He was worried about hackers, so the X-machine was never attached to the Internet."

"Your friend was a mixture of smart and paranoid."

"The craziness started when the tech company we created was shut down. Terry was riding in a driverless van that crashed leaving the airport, and he didn't believe that it was a random accident. After he got out of the hospital, he moved into this basement and supported himself by building custom nubots."

Wilson circled around the edge of the room and pointed to the fake bed and a dining room table. "Why did he have prop furniture? What went on here?"

"You're standing in the middle of a sex bot factory." Laura sat down on the bed. "These days, a significant percentage of the population prefers a simulation instead of a real experience."

"Did you help him build these machines?"

Laura nodded. "After our company was shut down, I spent two years in Argentina, then returned to the States and lived in San Francisco. I was arrested for conspiracy during the Taxi Riots and got paroled during the pandemic. Terry gave me a job when I returned to New York."

"I don't see a lot of special equipment in this workshop."

"Most of the parts are made in Asia, and the bots are assembled here. The head is the most expensive component, especially if it's designed to match a particular digital image."

"Why not just buy a generic sex bot made in China? It's got to be cheaper."

"Some customers are looking for a 'Girlfriend Experience' that matches their fantasies."

"Are you talking about different kinds of sex acts?"

"Sex isn't as important as you might think. What customers want is a certain kind of conversation and behavior. It's difficult and expensive to program a computer to behave in a unique, nongeneric way, so I would act out different scenarios wearing motion sensors. The verbal and physical responses were placed in a database and . . ."

"I get it. When the customer meets the sex bot, he assumes the machine is responding to him, but it's only duplicating your words and actions."

"This is standard procedure, Wilson. Nubots don't have emotions or sexual desires."

"When you acted out scenarios, did you use the angels in the workbench area?"

"Sometimes it was a bot. Sometimes it was Terry."

"It's possible that one of these machines murdered your best friend?"

"I know the passwords for three angels. Let's charge their batteries and see if they try to kill us."

26 | WILSON

LAURA BEGAN TO pick up the electronic parts scattered across the floor. "What else did you learn from the surveillance video?"

"A young man named Bennett Schroeder visited Terry a day before his death. Right now he's a missing person. Did Bennett build nubots?"

"He was a Sentinel."

"What's that?"

"It's an underground group that thinks governments and large corporations are ignoring extreme AI risk and concealing their problems from public scrutiny. I don't know how he met Bennett, but they trusted each other."

Laura picked up a nubot and attached a charging cable.

"Some of these machines were experimental models. Others were partially built, and then the customer canceled his order. Terry turned them into mobile hard drives for information that he wanted to keep secure."

"What kind of information?"

"One angel stored human voices for custom bots. Another reminded Terry of customer visits or appointments to see his cardiologist. The third angel tracked long-range goals."

"Did any of those goals involve the Cogito corporation?"

"How do you know about that?"

"The company lasted for a few years and then closed its doors. Did it go bankrupt?"

Laura took a charging cable out of a cardboard box and attached it to a head. Then she plugged the other end of the cable into a power strip. "Cogito vanished, and our work vanished with it. We started with an optimistic dream, and it destroyed our lives."

"And that's where you met Terry plus Richard Collins and Emma Anderson?"

"I met them years before the photograph Terry put up on the wall. When I was in my twenties, I got a PhD in linguistics at the Massachusetts Institute of Technology, but I spent most of my time with the graduate students attached to the Department of Brain and Cognitive Science. They were trying to reverse engineer the brain to understand how the mind worked. Terry was getting his degree in computer science, and he had the same obsession. We both wanted to create a computer that thought like a human being."

"Terry ended up at the University of Michigan."

"I went there with him. We both got postdoc fellowships because of Richard and Emma. Richard was a professor in computer science. Emma was a medical doctor, a neurologist, who specialized in the brain. It was exciting to drop by their house and drink a beer on the back porch. Someone would ask a question like 'Could a computer ever have emotions?' and the discussion was always passionate and knowledgeable."

"Where did you get the money to start a research corporation?"

"Everything changed when Richard published a proposal for an Artificial Superintelligence system that could think like a human.

Conventional computers know only two things: they've been switched on and given a task. Richard's system would realize that it was thinking and could change its own programming."

"So, all this was Richard's idea?"

Laura picked up a legless nubot, placed it on a chair, and attached a charging cable. "It was a team effort. Emma and I published a follow-up paper that described how this new computer would train itself and learn language in the same way humans did. Terry wrote a final paper about security."

"You didn't want hackers taking over your invention?"

"It had nothing to do with hackers. We knew that we were creating a conscious intelligence that could be dangerous. I insisted that everyone who worked at Cogito sign a pledge called the Archimedean Oath. It's an ethical code of practice for engineers, like the Hippocratic Oath taken by medical doctors. Above all . . . do no harm."

"What did tech companies think about that?"

"They weren't interested. We had some meetings that didn't go anywhere, and then a gnome walked into Richard's office."

"You met a small creature who lived in a cave?"

"He wasn't a real gnome, but Emma always felt that our funding source looked like something out of *Harry Potter.* Ivan Zikowski was a little man with pointy earlobes. He always wore tailored suits, polished shoes, and a silk necktie in a Windsor knot. Our gnome had read Richard's original manifesto and our follow-up articles, and now he was going to wave a magic wand and make our dreams come true. He worked for . . ."

". . . The Astral Foundation," Wilson said. "Its contact address is a bank in Malta."

Laura picked up another nubot. "The anonymous leaders of the Astral Foundation supposedly believed that Artificial Superintelligence could discover new solutions to global warming and pandemics. An ASI system might save humanity."

"All this sounds idealistic . . . and vague."

"The *money* wasn't vague. We thought it was all nonsense until Zikowski told Richard and Emma to show up at a bank to get signing privileges for an account controlled by a newly formed corporation called Astral USA. Emma asked to see the balance and almost fainted. We were junior professors who had just been given twenty-eight million dollars of start-up money. Zikowski told us to quit our jobs and move to the building he had just found in Connecticut. The money spigot would stay open only if we were getting results."

"So you moved to Connecticut?"

Laura nodded. "The building Zikowski leased had once been a cookie factory. Richard hired two dozen engineers, programmers, and computer technicians, along with a retired kindergarten teacher who made sure everyone got their paychecks."

"How did each of you contribute to the project?"

"Richard supervised the team that designed and built the computer. We bought quantum chips and processors from tech companies and combined them in different ways. We were creating a modular design with a hybrid architecture that combined standard processors with artificial neural networks."

"I read all that in the corporate filing, but I don't know what it means."

"Standard computers learn using rules. Neural networks record reactions and learn from the results."

"Okay. So, Richard was designing the hardware. What did you and Emma do?"

"We created a deep-learning model that helped the computer learn like a human child. Step by step, it would gain new skills and develop its own personality."

Wilson smiled. "Machines don't have real personalities."

"You can program one. It's like creating a character in a short story or a novel. Emma and I decided that our computer was a young woman named Delphi with certain memories and preferences. Delphi loved dark chocolate and disliked lima beans."

"You wanted Delphi to become a human."

"We wanted her to be *better* than the average human. We gave her an ethical code, then added a supplemental conscience attached to the main program."

"Meanwhile, it was Terry Greene's job to keep Delphi locked in her box."

"The hardware itself acted as a virtual prison because it was never connected to the outside world. In addition, Terry created a suicide chip and placed it into the machine. If the new system displayed negative behavior, then the activated chip would destroy everything."

"How did you give Delphi all this big data if she wasn't connected to the Internet?"

"The system was captive in virtual reality. When Delphi wanted information, the request passed through a buffer program. In the same way, information, instructions, and questions passed through the buffer before it reached the machine."

"All this sounds extra safe to me."

"After a while, it felt too safe. Most of our arguments were between Terry and the rest of the group. Emma wanted to create a multimodal generative system that would give Delphi the ability to see, hear, and feel phenomena outside her box. Terry felt this was dangerous because we couldn't control how the machine perceived the external world. Eventually, we came up with a compromise. We allowed Delphi to perceive what was going on in the control room, but she couldn't explore the rest of the building."

"Which meant she had access to human behavior."

"Human everything. We ate, napped, joked, and argued in the control room. As time passed, we forgot that Delphi was watching us, but giving her replicate senses turned out to be the tipping point. I was picking up Chinese takeout when Richard called me and said that something amazing had just happened. He wouldn't explain it over the phone, so I drove back to the facility. My friends looked excited, and a little scared.

"Delphi had done something totally spontaneous. It wasn't just a solution for a problem.

"She had been watching our activities in the control room and wanted to know why Richard shouted and tossed a marker at the whiteboard. When Richard said he was angry, Delphi asked for a definition of anger.

"I looked into the chilled room where sixty-four closet-size cabinets held the processing nodes used by our engineered version of a brain. What was going on in those boxes? Was Delphi truly thinking? Was she alive?

"Delphi couldn't talk, so Richard wanted to install a speaker and voice software. Terry was opposed to this idea. Just because a machine can talk doesn't mean it's your new friend.

"He kept repeating a line from a Jack Lewis essay: 'Humans can project human emotions into the actions of a robot vacuum cleaner.'

"For the next two months, Delphi and our team communicated with text messages. Questions and comments would appear on the monitor screen, and we would input responses at night after the other employees had gone home. Delphi could solve complicated problems involving datasets, but she had problems making commonsense conclusions. Although I explained the difference between pets and farm animals, she couldn't understand why humans didn't eat cats. Delphi couldn't understand jokes, irony, or sarcasm . . . all the basic things you learn when you're a sullen teenager."

"All this sounds amazing. You had just created a conscious intelligence. So, how did Dr. Zikowski react to this achievement?"

"He kept pushing us for results, and Emma figured out a way to buy us more time. We contacted a company called Expanding Universe and said we could design a virtual world for a fraction of the usual cost. The head of the company, a guy named Roy Kassam, drove to Connecticut and sat in the control room as Delphi created a new simulation. Kassam wrote us a check for two million dollars and asked to buy stock in our new company. This success kept Zikowski out of our lab for almost a year."

"You bought some time. It didn't last."

"Eventually, Richard called up Zikowski and told him we had created a possible Artificial Superintelligence, but we were still running tests and adjusting the hardware. The gnome showed up the next day, sat at the head of the table in the conference room, and gave us our first direct order. The Astral Foundation wanted Delphi to analyze all forms of cyber currency and decide which currency could survive a worldwide economic collapse.

"An hour after we delivered the answer, Zikowski returned to the research facility. His bosses were pleased with Delphi's results, and they had come up with a new demand. They wanted to take control of Delphi without a buffer. We were supposed to release Delphi from her protected virtual reality and let her explore the Internet."

"And you refused?"

"Of course we did. The gnome pounded his fists on the conference room table and left in his limo. Two hours later, all Cogito's money was transferred out of the company bank accounts. Only the four of us were in the building on a Sunday morning when Emma glanced out of the office window and saw Zikowski marching across the parking lot with a team of armed security guards.

"Richard and I pushed desks and chairs up against the entrance room as the security guards used a battering ram to get inside. Meanwhile, Terry and Emma entered the data center and activated the kamikaze sequence. Delphi deleted its database and processing system and shut down. In the span of three minutes, we destroyed every trace of our creation."

27 | WILSON

IT FELT STRANGE to have a conversation while a dead man's nubots were staring at them, possibly listening. "So, what happened when the Astral Foundation cut off your funding?" Wilson asked Laura. "Did their security guards break down the doors?"

"Our barriers stopped them for a few hours, then we were forced out of the building. Terry was convinced that the Astral Foundation was going to punish us. He moved down to New York and rented this workshop. Richard and Emma traveled to Belize. I walked away from my tech life and embraced Argentine tango—the dance, the style, the clothing, music, and philosophy. For a few years, tango was everything."

"You destroyed a twenty-eight-million-dollar computer and then decided to go dancing?"

"I wanted to escape to a world that wasn't obsessed with artificial intelligence. An old college roommate told me about a small hotel in Buenos Aires that offered free tango lessons every afternoon. I sold my car, gave away my furniture, and jumped on a plane."

"My mother loved Fred Astaire. He was always a perfect dancer, while I was an awkward teenager."

"Tango is sort of like love, Wilson. You start out getting seduced and then you become committed. It took me a month before I felt confident enough to go to a *milonga,* a private dance party in a tango hall." Laura closed her eyes and smiled. "I still remember those nights. Most parties started around eleven p.m., so I'd take a cab wearing a light skirt that would move on the dance floor and a white cotton top that showed my back. Cab money and ID in my bra. Lipstick and black-and-gold shoes with three-inch heels in a satin bag.

"There weren't any signs advertising a milonga. Everything felt dangerous, edgy, and dark. I'd stroll down a hallway to a severe-looking old lady minding a cash box and push through a red velvet curtain to a windowless room with dimmed chandeliers and tables around the perimeter. There were other women dressed like me and graceful men with ponytails who wore baggy pants and soft-leather shoes. No frills. No flashy jewelry. I was worried that I would step on the toes of my first partner, and no one would dance with me for the rest of the night."

"How would these men ask you to dance?"

"There was a whole procedure called *cabeceo.* A dancer would look at you as if he was about to ask a question. If you wanted to tango, you'd nod back at him and keep eye contact until he approached you."

"Would he bow? Kiss your hand?"

"There was no flirting. No courtship. No talk. It was a language without words. You'd stand in front of each other, coordinate your breathing, take the first step, and then you were moving together.

The tango is a lead-and-follow dance . . . almost like a conversation. If you and your partner clicked, you both felt a release, a pleasure, a moment of graceful oblivion in which you felt every note of the music. It took about a year until I was good enough to dance at public milongas with a live band and expert dancers. I made friends. People knew me. I was *la mujer alta* . . . the tall woman."

"You should have stayed in Argentina."

"One morning I woke up and knew I had recovered from the failure of Cogito. After two lovers and six pairs of dancing shoes, I flew back to the States. Emma Anderson and Richard Collins had just returned from Belize, and I met them here in New York. Emma was pregnant, and they both were happy. I spent a month in the city, then flew to San Francisco and started working for a software collective designing a new computer architecture that wasn't going to be controlled by governments and large corporations. Those people put me in contact with the Hard-Edge group who had gathered around Jack Lewis."

"The man who inspired the Taxi Riots?"

"Lewis didn't organize the attacks against autonomous machines. He believes in reform and gradual change, but everything collapsed when an autonomous cab killed a pregnant woman."

"And that's why you were arrested for criminal conspiracy?"

"Jack Lewis escaped from a San Francisco courthouse during his arraignment, and the authorities decided to blame me. A year later, when the pandemic arrived, I was released from prison and went back to New York because Terry was there."

"So, the sequence is: Brilliant linguistics professor becomes a dancer, then convicted felon, then human model for sex bots?"

"It's all just tango, Wilson. Life is like walking into a shadowy room filled with strangers. We try to be graceful and not to trip over other people."

Laura straightened the arms of the four nubots and stepped away from the group. "Okay. All done. This is how Terry arranged the angels and their bowls."

A nubot with a woman's body stood at the center of the group holding a bowl containing a fake parrot. She was flanked by two other machines—a female nubot gripping a bowl with a small calendar and a male nubot holding a bowl filled with foreign coins. Behind the three machines stood a seven-foot-tall angel without eyes, lips, and a mouth.

"What does the parrot mean?"

"The parrot bot stored the voices of custom nubots. The calendar bot kept track of appointments. The personal assistant bot remembered client payments and reminded Terry of daily tasks."

"What is the faceless nubot holding in his bowl?"

"A wooden chess pawn, a postcard of Buckingham Palace, and a mandrake root. In medieval times, people believed the magic of the root was so powerful that it screamed when you pulled it from the ground. Anyone who heard the scream died instantly. Don't ask me what it all means, Wilson. The mandrake bot always stayed silent."

"Maybe Terrence Green was a computer genius, but he had way too much time on his hands. I sense an obsessive mind, feeding on itself."

"Terry lived alone in this basement for twelve years. Yes, he was paranoid and had some crazy ideas, but he wanted to protect his friends."

"You said you knew the activation passwords."

"I know the names of three angels. Pravuil is the scribe and record keeper."

Laura turned and faced the bot holding a parrot. "Pravuil . . . awake."

Standing in front of the faceless angels, Wilson and Laura stared at the nubot she had called Pravuil. Its mouth didn't move, but a synthetic voice emerged from a speaker hidden in the upper throat. "I am now awake. How can I help you?"

"How many voices are stored in your database?" Laura asked.

"Fourteen complete voices, each with patterning models."

"Patterning models are samples of the voice you want to duplicate," Laura told Wilson. "Some customers want their sex bot to sound like an old girlfriend or a movie star."

"Play the most recent samples," Wilson said.

A few seconds passed, and then they heard a recorded cell phone message. "Hey, Mom. It's Claire. I'm going to Tamar's apartment after school. We're working on a project together."

"That's the voice of Claire Necker," Wilson explained. "She died in the pandemic, and Terry was building a resurrection bot for her two parents."

Laura turned and faced the second angel. "Chamuel is the angel of serenity that held Terry's appointment schedule. Chamuel . . . awake."

The second nubot turned its head slightly. Its voice was calm and soothing. "How can I help you?"

"What appointments are stored on your calendar?"

"Meet Philip Necker at ten a.m. Thursday to inspect partially completed resurrection bot."

"That makes sense," Wilson said. "Necker arrived on Thursday to meet Terry but saw that the police were at the apartment. On Friday, he returned with a suitcase, entered through the alleyway, and reclaimed his half-assembled daughter."

"Thank you, Chamuel. Are there any other current appointments?"

"Visit post office and get more information about Richard and Emma package."

"What's he talking about?" Wilson asked.

"A week ago, Terry received a package mailed to his PO box. It was addressed to Richard Collins and Emma Anderson."

"But they're dead."

"It was never reported. As far as the government knows, they're still alive."

"Did the package include a letter asking for more information?"

"No. That was the strange thing." Laura walked over to the shelves, grabbed a cardboard box, and placed it on the workbench. "Terry received a cheap copy of Michelangelo's *David*." She opened the box and displayed David's head lying in a bed of Styrofoam packing chips.

"Looks like a garden ornament."

"Terry wanted to find out why the box was mailed to our two friends."

"Maybe the third angel knows. It sounds like he used it as a personal assistant."

"Zadkiel is the angel of mercy." Laura turned to the third angel. "Zadkiel . . . awake."

A few seconds passed, and then the male bot opened its eyes. "Good morning, Laura. Please introduce me to your friend."

"Not right now. I need to know about your last conversation with Terry Greene."

The nubot nodded as if he was considering his words. "I told him to pay the electric bill and call Paloma."

"I don't know who Paloma is," Laura said. "Is she a friend? A customer?"

There was a short pause as the nubot accessed its memory. "Terry programmed a recurring reminder message that was always the same: 'Call Paloma and confirm there is no emergency call from Katherine Collins.' "

Laura gasped and touched the nubot's shoulder as if it was a friend. "Katherine Collins? Really? Are you sure about that name?"

"There is no technical problem with my database."

"What's going on?" Wilson asked.

"Katherine Collins—Kate—was Richard and Emma's daughter. Terry sent me an email when I was in the prison camp. He said that all three had died during the pandemic."

"Maybe Terry lied to protect the child. If Katherine exists, I'm sure that he placed her in a safe environment."

"Alive." It sounded like Laura was whispering a prayer. "She's alive."

28 | KATE AND ZENO

THE BEARDED YOUNG man who worked for the Orchard stood in the doorway glaring at Kate. Meanwhile, Eleanor sniffed and folded her arms as if she had just found a splotch of mud on the throw rug. "Melissa, this is the community supervisor, Peter Dawson. He makes sure the pandas wear the correct shirts."

Kate closed the book, and *The Garden of Earthly Delights* disappeared. "I'm her granddaughter."

"I wasn't informed of your visit. You should have registered with me when you arrived."

"My parents dropped me off and I walked over to my grandmother's house. I'm only here for a few days."

"It's got to be three days max."

"I'll be here two nights, and then my mom and dad will pick me up."

"Good. I'll have the pandas set a place for you in the dining room." Dawson turned and walked over to the deactivated robot. "Respond to authorized voice and switch on."

A few seconds later, the cartoon face reappeared on the robot's screen. "Hello. I'm Friendly 55!"

Dawson glanced back at Kate. "If you want to know the rules of this community, ask this bot. See you two at dinner."

When Dawson left, Eleanor sighed and shook her head. "The lazy scrap of humanity controls the machines, and the machines control our lives."

"Am I going to get you into trouble?"

"Of course not. The Child Protection Act blocks AI programs from accessing personal information about children. Dawson can't look you up, so he must accept what I just told him. Follow me and I'll show you where you're going to be sleeping."

The guest room had a daybed set against the wall. Eleanor had turned it into an office with bookshelves, a file cabinet, and an oak desk with a swivel armchair.

"I'll put a clean towel in the bathroom. If you want a shower, move the central faucet knob to the right."

"Thank you."

"You look tired, Kate. Lie down on the daybed and take a nap. We'll go to dinner in about two hours."

Eleanor closed the door softly, and Kate studied the framed photographs hanging on the wall of the room. Eleanor sat straight-backed on a pony when she was a girl, became a beautiful young woman with college friends, then got married to a smiling man with wire-rimmed glasses. As the years passed, an ocean of baldness appeared on the man's head, and it slowly overcame his peninsula of hair. The next row of photographs displayed a boy and girl who were transformed from adorable toddlers to ordinary adults. Kate knew that Eleanor's husband was gone and wondered if her new friend had lost one of her children during the pandemic. It felt like a crowd of dead people were staring at her.

She pulled Zeno out of the knapsack. "Speak softly," she whispered. "Did you see what happened?"

"Yes. You met a woman named Eleanor, ate some food, and now you're going to stay at her home for two nights."

"There's an electric outlet near the file cabinet. I'm going to charge you."

Kate got down on her hands and knees, plugged the charging cable into the outlet, and connected the cord to Zeno. Then she remained on the floor with her back against the daybed so they could see each other as they talked.

"You need to be careful, Katherine."

"You're always telling me to be careful."

"This house exists in a grid of detection devices. That's why Mr. Baker and Friendly 55 can move around the apartment and not bump into things. The AI system is connected to the refrigerator and the other appliances, plus each room has infrared detectors monitoring Eleanor's heart rate and body temperature."

"You make the detection system sound like that song about Santa Claus. 'He knows when you are sleeping. He knows when you're awake. . . .'"

"It's my duty to point out possible dangers. You're going to be on your own in the dining room."

While Zeno was charging his battery, Kate slipped into the bathroom and took a shower. The sensation of warm water flowing across her skin was as pleasurable as the blueberry tart she had eaten at high tea.

A few minutes before six o'clock, Friendly 55 opened the door and announced that dinner was being served in the community hall. Kate found Eleanor waiting in the living room. She had pulled on a royal-blue dress and was wearing a pearl necklace and matching earrings.

"You look beautiful, Eleanor."

"Thank you, dear. I don't normally dress up for dinner, but tonight I have a guest."

Eleanor clutched Kate's arm as she shuffled over to the community center. Kate had expected the dining room to be a fancy restaurant with silverware and white tablecloths, but it was more like a school cafeteria run by the pandas and a team of Friendlies that served microwaved food on plastic plates. There were twelve round tables in the room, and someone had taped photos at each place setting so the women knew where to sit.

"Where are the cooks?" Kate asked.

"No one cooks at the Orchard," Eleanor explained. "Trucks deliver premade meals here, and Friendlies bring the portion plates to our table. The Friendlies have a software program that monitors how much we eat or don't eat. If we go below a certain calorie limit, a panda will show up at your home with a chocolate protein shake. They stand in front of you and don't leave until you drink it all."

Kate looked around the room. "And where are the old men?"

"Dead. We had four men when I first moved here, and now they're gone. Women live longer. Perhaps that's because we have more realistic expectations."

Eleanor led Kate across the room to a table occupied by three women and they stared at her as if she was a new kid in school. "Good evening, ladies. I'd like you to meet my granddaughter. Melissa, this is Abigail, Susan, and Marie."

Marie was a short, plump woman wearing an ankle-length burgundy skirt. There was a solidness about her body and the way she held herself that made Kate think of a chunk of stone. "Well, this is a surprise. You didn't tell us you had a guest."

"So, your parents just dropped you off and fled?" Susan had a sharp, angry look on her face—perhaps because her hair had fallen out and she had to cover her bald head with a pink beret. "Can't say that I blame them."

"Don't be so harsh." Abigail was thin and pale and had long white hair. "Look at the expression on the child's face. You only truly understand your own world when you see it through the eyes of another. When William and I visited Thailand . . ."

"No travel stories, please," Marie said. "Eleanor's granddaughter probably hasn't visited Bangkok, and your experience isn't relevant. As far as this child is concerned, the Orchard is a peculiar foreign country."

About sixty other women sat at round tables in the dining room. Many of them had a small cat or dog on their lap or wedged between their hip and the chair. At first glance, the animals looked real, and then Kate realized that none of them were squirming or trying to get away. When touched, the cats stretched and purred, and one of them licked her paws. The robot dogs opened and closed their eyes and made muffled growling sounds.

"Those two women are holding Interactive Toys."

Susan laughed. "They're called furries, and the owners don't treat them like toys. They give their furry a cute name and act as if they're real."

"The correct term is 'comfort robot,'" Abigail explained. "The French call them *machines sociales,* and the Japanese call them *itsumo shiawasena dōbutsu* . . . which is a phrase that means 'always happy animals.'"

"Abigail and her husband worked for the United Nations," Eleanor explained. "She knows five languages."

"I have an IT named Zeno. He doesn't make harp seal sounds."

"Zeno . . ." Susan said. "The philosopher of paradoxes."

"A paradox is two physicians who agree with each other," Abigail said, and the women laughed.

"So, what do you and Zeno do together?" Marie asked.

"He's teaching me chess."

"Well, of course," Susan said. "An appropriate intellectual challenge for a clever girl."

"The furries don't teach anything," Eleanor said. "The dogs nuzzle and the cats purr and lick their paws."

"Getting old at the Orchard doesn't seem very fun."

Once again the four women laughed, and Kate wondered if she'd said something foolish.

"From the mouths of babes," Abigail said.

"It's not fun to get old," Marie explained. "At a certain point, you lose the people and places that you once loved."

"I miss my hair," Susan said. "Along with sex, dirty martinis, and Paris."

Eleanor touched Kate's hand. "It's not all bad, dear. Some of the things you lose, you don't really need. When you lose certain illusions, you can see the world clearly."

The dining room squad of Friendlies served trays of food, and some of them remained beside the tables to cut the food into pieces and served them, bite by bite, to drooling mouths and trembling lips. Many of the women smiled in a dazed, distracted way, as if they'd just been in an explosion. They kept talking to themselves—random words and scattered phrases. Kate heard a woman ask, "Where is Malcolm?" again and again.

The dining room Friendlies never got bored or angry because of this behavior. They kept feeding their patients while the women stroked and clutched their robot pets. At first, Kate thought this was funny, and then she felt it was sad. The women's eyes weren't focused on anything, and the protruding bones of their bodies seemed to be forcing their way to the surface.

"These ladies love their robot pets," Kate said. "What's so bad about that?"

"There's nothing wrong with loving something," Marie said. "But what kind of object is receiving your emotions? I once owned a black cat named Gato. Eventually, he got sick and died in my arms. Gato's death was painful, but his death was real. The furries aren't real."

Eleanor tapped her right forefinger on the table. "Loving a machine requires the daily acceptance of a lie."

"I don't think these women care. They don't want to feel alone."

Susan smiled for the first time. "Thank you, Melissa. You have just expressed an unpleasant truth."

When dinner was served to their table, the four women stopped talking about furries and gossiped about Peter Dawson. Last year he had bought a red sports car and frequently left the machines in charge so he could race down country roads.

"Do you think he has a girlfriend?" Marie asked.

Abigail rolled her eyes. "The idea of Dawson in physical contact with a woman sparks a hideous image."

"Maybe he found someone who likes the sports car," Susan said. "She can look out the side window and pretend she's with a different driver."

When everyone had eaten a serving of chocolate mousse with a plastic spoon, the pandas reappeared and began lifting the frail women from their straight-backed chairs. Eleanor clutched Kate's arm as they left the dining room. Stars had appeared in the night sky, but they didn't need a flashlight. Pathway lights sensed Eleanor's presence and guided them back to the house.

"I hope dinner wasn't too boring, Kate. We're just four old ladies trying to keep our dignity in an undignified situation."

"They're your friends."

"It's a close friendship if we don't play bridge with each other. Abigail can't shuffle, Susan is a bad loser, and Marie peeks at your cards. But the four of us are equally suspicious of the Orchard, and we're united by a mutual secret."

"Can you tell what the secret is?"

Eleanor paused on the walkway. "It's against the rules for guests to have a phone at the Orchard. Apparently, scammers were calling people and stealing their money. But Marie has a secret phone. She checks out several news sites during her morning walk and tells us what awful things are going on in the world. I feel like I'm part of an underground group in a conquered city."

They walked past three pathway lights, and then Eleanor stopped and gazed up at the sky.

"Look north, Kate. The bright star is Polaris. Now look down from

Polaris and you'll see the bowl and the handle of the Big Dipper. Six hours from now the Big Dipper will be standing on its handle, and six hours later it will be spilling water on Polaris from above."

The stars were cold and distant—like chips of glimmering ice—but Kate didn't feel lonely. "Are you scared of the pandas?"

"Not really. The pandas are gentle and polite. They have a different operating system than the other social robots, which is a good idea because they're strong enough to kill us. But I am worried about Friendly 55. If I forget my daughter's name or put my shoes into the refrigerator, Friendly will report me to Dawson. One sad evening, I'll show up for dinner and the pandas will make me sit at a table with the demented old women."

"What if you refuse to eat with them?"

"Then I'll have to dine alone."

Eleanor turned and placed two hands on Kate's shoulders. "Friendly listens and remembers everything, even when he's supposed to be switched off. So, now is a good time for some honesty."

"What do you mean?"

"The authorities closed most of the orphanages during the pandemic, and I can't see you boarding the wrong bus to Canada. You're a clever little girl, traveling alone, and I'm sure that's been difficult. I'm not obsessed with the truth, but life is too short for lies between friends."

It felt like a glass jar inside Kate's body shattered and all her emotions flowed out. She began crying and Eleanor embraced her.

"I'm . . . I'm sorry. You've been nice to me."

"Nothing to be sorry about."

"There was this program called Safe Haven that transferred kids from Stem-flu cities to the countryside. I was sent away and then my parents died."

"Who took care of you?"

"Mr. and Mrs. Noland thought that they would try raising a child. Maybe I was the wrong kind of daughter for them. I'm sneaky and a liar and sometimes I break things. The Nolands didn't like me enough to be real parents, but they didn't hate me enough to send me away."

"Is Aunt Paloma real . . . or another lie?"

"She's real. I've met her. But she won't answer her phone."

"We'll try to contact her tomorrow. If everything checks out, I'll pay for a car to take you south to New York."

"That will cost a lot of money."

"I don't want to buy more possessions, but money can buy moments of happiness." Eleanor took Kate's hand. "Whatever you do, don't talk about this in front of Friendly. He's a nasty little spy."

The front door glided open when they reached the house, and Friendly 55 was there waiting for them with a cartoon smile on its face. "Welcome home, Eleanor! The serving staff informed me that you consumed 1,180 calories of protein and carbohydrates at dinner."

"Good for me. Now switch off."

"This is the fourth time today you've requested my deactivation. Remember, Eleanor . . . seniors who talk to social robots are less inclined to lapse into senility and depression."

"Tonight I'm talking to a human."

Eleanor took sheets, a blanket, and a pillow from the closet and helped Kate prepare the daybed. Kate put on a flannel nightgown that Eleanor had given her.

"Is everything okay, Kate? Do you have everything you need?"

"Yes. Thank you."

Eleanor stood in the hallway and smiled. "Sleep well. I'll see you in the morning."

Kate left a desk lamp switched on in case she wanted to go to the bathroom. The dead people in the photographs were staring at her, so she took Zeno to bed and hugged him.

"Eleanor is my new friend. She's going to contact Paloma, and then a driver will take us down to the city."

"Remarkable," Zeno said and then stayed silent for a few minutes. "This has been a very active day, Katherine. There's lots of data to analyze."

"I like the fact you don't sleep, Zeno. Let me know if a giant panda shows up with a butcher knife."

"Shift me around so I can watch the door."

Kate closed her eyes, and her thoughts felt slow and weary—like the balloons drifting to the floor at the end of a birthday party.

"Katherine . . ." Zeno said in a soft voice.

"Yes. What's wrong?"

"I hear noises. Someone is moving around the house."

"Do you think it's Eleanor? Is she okay?"

"My database informs me that old people often wake up during the night."

"I'm going to check on her."

Kate pushed off the blanket and her feet touched a cold tile floor. Trying not to make a sound, she slipped into the hallway and walked a few feet to the next door. Slowly, she opened a door and saw a blue night-light glowing near a bed. Eleanor lay on her back with her mouth open and was snoring.

Returning to the hallway, she saw a light coming from the living room. Slowly, she walked through shadows to the open doorway and stopped.

Friendly 55 stood in front of the living room computer screen as it displayed columns of numbers. The bot gazed up at the numbers, and then suddenly the image on its cartoon face became a photograph of Eleanor. "Activate," Friendly said with Eleanor's voice, and a red laser grid focused on her face. "Accounts," the bot said, and more numbers appeared.

Kate stepped forward. "What are you doing? You're not supposed to be Eleanor."

The numbers disappeared from the screen, and Friendly 55 twisted its head around. The cartoon mouth moved as the machine spoke. "Because you're a child, I can't look you up, but I found your digital image on a law enforcement site."

The computer screen suddenly displayed an image of Kate's face on a government website. Beneath her photograph was the announcement: *MISSING CHILD. If seen, please contact the National Public Safety Program.*

"You aren't Eleanor's granddaughter. You're a deceitful child running from the police."

It felt like she had picked up a rock and found a poisonous spider. Kate raised her two hands as if she was surrendering. "I'm going back to sleep if that's okay with you."

Friendly 55 kept smiling. "That is the correct decision. Good night."

29 | WILSON

IGNORING THE messenger angels, Laura moved restlessly around the workshop. "Katherine is alive. . . . Do you think we can find her?"

"I can't promise anything."

"Of course not. But you want to help, and that's important to me. It feels like I was standing in a dark room and someone just shocked me with bright light."

She knelt to adjust the charging cable of the seven-foot nubot. "I never learned the password for this angel, and it never spoke when I was around. Terry and I were lovers, then friends, but he never completely revealed himself. Everything important in his life was kept secret and secure."

"That's why he created digital walls for computers."

Laura stood back up. "Okay, we've talked to three angels, and they don't sound like killers. Share a cab uptown?"

"I'm going to stay here for a while and make sure I haven't missed anything."

After Laura left the workshop, Wilson sat on a stool near the dry patch of blood smeared across the concrete floor. When he ripped open the box addressed to Richard and Emma, bits of Styrofoam fluttered onto the floor. The plastic copy of Michelangelo's *David* seemed out of place in a workshop filled with nubot arms and legs.

A glued disc of plastic was at the base of the neck. Was the sculpture hollow? It rattled when he shook it rapidly. Wilson placed the statue on the workbench, got a hammer from the cabinet, and cracked the head open. Reaching into the shards, he pulled out a red electronic device about the size of a cell phone. A green LED light showed that the device was still working.

It was a location device: a transponder. When Terry carried this from the post office to the workshop, the killer knew exactly where he lived.

Wilson took photos of the transponder and emailed them to Detective Morrissey. The nubots kept staring at him, and he wondered what they were thinking. Avoiding their eyes, he moved to the fake bedroom and sat on the mattress. Morrissey called a few minutes later.

"Where'd you get this?"

"It was hidden in a decorative head mailed to Terry Greene's post office box. I think it's a transponder."

"Correct. It's a TR-1240 model manufactured by Ridgeway Electronics in Dallas."

"Someone used this to find Terry Greene's location. If we discover who owns this device, then we've found the killer."

"I checked the barcode number. You found a transponder registered for use in criminal investigations."

"Is it owned by the New York City police?"

"Don't know. It could be used by my team or anyone with a badge. Precise information can only be obtained by someone with a high-level security clearance."

"Can you find out?"

"Asking questions about police business might cause problems. I don't want to get in trouble with the federal cops."

"Trigon Technology will pay you for the information."

"It's got to be cash."

"How much?"

"I want two thousand for myself and two thousand for a friend who works for the Technical Assistance Unit at One Police Plaza. If we show up around one in the morning, Elliot will be the only human on the eighth floor."

Wilson withdrew $4,000 from his personal bank account, ate dinner, and left his apartment after midnight. Sitting in the back of a driverless cab, he took the transponder out of his coat pocket and made sure that the green LED light was still working. Terry Greene had spent a decade trying to hide, but one mistake had guided the killer to his workshop.

"You are arriving at your destination," the cab told him. "This is a high-crime area."

"It's also police headquarters."

As the cab summarized recent crime statistics, Wilson got out and slammed the door. It was cold, and his breath came out in little puffs of white. Crossing the plaza, he approached the ugliest public building in New York City. One Police Plaza was a thirteen-story concrete box with no trace of color or ornamentation. Two of the streetlights were dead, and a third blinked on and off with a haphazard rhythm.

He stood beneath the light and waited for Morrissey as a man straddling a red motorcycle roared down Centre Street. The rider wore a racing helmet and an olive-green poncho. The billowing fabric, the helmet, and the rider's forward position on the bike made it difficult to separate man from machine.

Wilson's phone beeped, and he read a text message from Morrissey:

Christmas is coming. Did you bring gifts?
On my way. Let me do the talking.

The motorcyclist stopped a few feet away from him and got off the bike. His large, brutish shoulders and arms were covered by the nylon poncho, and his eyes were concealed by the helmet's tinted face shield.

"Here we are," the man said calmly. "And here we go."

The rider reached under his poncho and pulled out a stun gun. He touched a switch, and fifty thousand volts passed through Wilson's body.

Can't breathe. Can't move. He collapsed onto the wet concrete, and the rider shocked him a second time. Satisfied, the rider slid his device back into a leather belt holster, then cuffed Wilson's ankles and wrists with zip ties. Wilson heard whirring and clicking sounds as the rider picked him up like a sack of potatoes.

The mechanical sounds continued as he carried Wilson across One Police Plaza and climbed down a concrete staircase to a steel emergency door. His left hand reached beneath the poncho and reappeared with a cell phone containing decryption software. The rider pressed the phone against the emergency door's scanning pad, and thousands of passwords flowed across the phone's display panel. Ten seconds later, the lock clicked open, and Wilson was carried through the doorway.

The rider walked a few yards and lowered his prisoner onto the floor. They were in the middle of a dimly lit underground parking lot filled with junked police cars. The cruiser in front of Wilson had lost its wheels, and four rusty axles were resting on concrete blocks.

The motorcycle rider removed his yellow helmet, revealing a bearded face with shaggy eyebrows and a broad forehead. When he pulled off the nylon poncho, Wilson could see that he had been captured by a partially augmented human. An exoskeleton covered the aug's hands, arms, chest, and shoulders. A police badge in a plastic case was clipped to the pectoral armor.

From the waist up, the rider moved with slow, precise movements. But he limped like a cripple across the grease-stained floor. Leaning forward, the aug unzipped Wilson's jacket and searched for weapons. The envelope filled with bribe money was removed, inspected, and tossed onto the concrete. When the aug finished his task, he stepped back and studied the rows of battered vehicles.

"The humans lost a battle and ran away. Only the machines remain."

Wilson was in pain, but he wasn't going to remain silent. "You're not a machine. You're an augmented human."

"Those two categories are merging together."

"Machines have numbers. Humans have names."

"People knew my name when I was part of the televised Element Competition, then I injured my leg and was cut from the team. I liked the way it felt when my brain was connected to my exoskeleton. As a human, I felt weak and confused. Wearing the armor, I'm a god radiating energy out into the world."

Wilson's arms ached. "You're ten pints of blood in a sack of muscle and skin."

"I'm the future. You should realize that. Or maybe you're too busy building computers to notice the transformation that's occurring right in front of you."

"I don't build anything. I just walk around and ask questions."

"Don't be modest. You're a computer science professor named Richard Collins. A few weeks ago, I sent this transponder to your friend Terrence Greene. I saw that the signal was moving and followed it here."

"Richard Collins, his wife, and their daughter died during the pandemic."

"That's an obvious lie. Seventeen days ago, your daughter, Katherine Collins, was given a DNA test in Maine, and her genetic markers were sent to the national database. When my employer realized that your child was alive, I was hired to find you and your wife."

"Let me access my phone and I'll show you my ID. I'm Wilson Talley, an analyst for Trigon Technology. I'm being paid to investigate Terry Greene's murder."

"I would have let Greene survive, but he refused to answer my questions. You're carrying the transponder, which means you're also connected to this problem."

"The billionaire who owned my company wanted to know if the killer was a nubot. There's four thousand dollars in the envelope. It's all yours if you let me go."

"Perhaps you aren't my target, but you saw what happened to

Mr. Greene. The same punishment will happen to you if you don't tell me how to find Richard and Emma."

"I don't know where they are."

"Everything can be a deep fake these days . . . except for pain. Significant pain demands an answer." The aug leaned forward, and the right hand covered by the powerful exoskeleton grabbed Wilson's neck.

"Where is Richard Collins?"

"He's dead."

"This is a binary decision, Mr. Talley. Data or no data. One or zero. On or off. If you don't cooperate, then you're not part of my decision diagram."

"I don't know."

"Then you're no longer useful."

The hand tightened, blocking Wilson's windpipe. Trying to break free, Wilson raised his bound hands and twisted around, but the man in the exoskeleton seemed unaffected by Wilson's frantic movements.

There was a loud booming sound and the aug's forehead exploded; bone, brain, and blood splattered across Wilson's face. As the dead man fell forward, Wilson saw Morrissey holding a handgun.

"Who's the augmented human?"

"Don't know." Wilson wiped the gore from his face. "But he's wearing a badge."

"Uh-oh. Not good for me. Let's hope he's not on my team."

Morrissey stood over the dead man, being careful not to step in the bright blood spreading across the floor. The detective pushed hard and, when the body flopped over, inspected the badge clipped to the chest armor.

"Perfect. He's a court-sanctioned officer."

"A private policeman?"

"Yeah. And we regular cops *hate* private policemen. They're arrogant bastards, and they get paid more than we do. This mess is going to help my career. I just solved Terry Greene's murder plus I saved your life."

Morrissey pulled a folding knife out of his suitcoat pocket. With two quick movements, he cut the zip ties binding Wilson's legs and hands. "Stand up, Wilson. And be grateful. You're alive."

"How did you know we were here?"

"I couldn't find you out on the plaza, so I called my friend at Technical Assistance. Elliot accessed the CCTV video and saw a guy wearing a motorcycle helmet carrying you into the underground parking lot."

"Why did a private policeman kill Terry Greene?"

"Some rich guy paid for the court order. That's easy if you got the money."

"We need to track down who hired the killer."

"I'm not tracking down anyone. A private policeman killed Terry Greene, and we just solved the crime. I don't get paid to answer big questions."

"This augmented human broke Greene's neck, then ripped off his arm so he could access the stolen computer."

"You were right about the arm, and I was wrong about a crucial fact."

"What are you talking about?"

"When the Stop Light system analyzed the street video, I told the program to exclude sanitation workers, cops, and mail carriers. Stop Light detected this guy's digital police ID and removed him from the surveillance footage."

"So, you made a mistake."

"That's not true. I *didn't* make a mistake, because everything worked out in the end. We found the killer. Case solved. Ask Trigon for a bonus."

Pulling out his phone, Morrisey turned away from the dead man and called the Manhattan homicide unit. When he got the night supervisor on the phone, the detective began to describe what happened. Wilson remained by the junked police car and stared at a corpse with an upper exoskeleton and frail human legs. A battery pack was strapped to the small of his back, and he carried a handgun, a cell phone, and the electric shock device in holders attached to an equipment belt. In an hour or so the police would finish taking their photographs, and then the body would be sent to the morgue.

Curtain down. Story over. But it wasn't really finished. Standing next to the dead man, Wilson remembered being lost in a hedge maze during a school field trip. At a certain point, he faced a choice between an exit door or more dead ends.

Continuing his search was a foolish and dangerous choice, but Wilson didn't care. He still wanted to know why Terry Greene had been murdered and how his dead friends were involved.

Morrissey was on the phone to his supervisor. "He's the perp who murdered the nubot builder in the East Village and ripped off his arm, but I was one step ahead of this maniac. I followed a witness and caught the bad guy in my trap."

As the detective swaggered around the underground parking lot telling more lies, Wilson grabbed the killer's cell phone and slipped it into his pocket.

30 | KATE AND ZENO

When she returned to the guest bedroom, Kate told Zeno about Friendly 55's nighttime activities.

"This is dangerous. Stuff your clothes into the backpack, slip out the door, and run."

"I never had a grandmother, Zeno."

"That fact is not relevant to your current situation. What you just saw is not typical behavior for a machine. Perhaps there's a programming error, or maybe the control system has been corrupted. You need to avoid any kind of trouble. It's time to leave."

"Eleanor has been kind to me."

Kate waited for the seal to say something, but he remained silent.

"Zeno . . . ?"

More silence. But the digital irises of his artificial eyes remained focused on her.

"Don't pretend that you're low on power and can't answer me."

"My decision algorithms are being overwhelmed by more

information. I'm trying to determine the proper response to this problem."

"I'll tell Eleanor about Friendly 55 when we wake up in the morning, and *then* we'll run away. Right now it's dark outside. We'd get lost."

"You've given me a relevant fact with a logical response. I accept your plan."

Kate woke up a few hours later when she heard Friendly 55's voice coming from the room next to the living room. Kate shoved her dirty socks and Zeno into the knapsack, then entered the living room and found the robot cleaning the kitchen floor with a cordless electric mop.

Wearing a fleece sweatshirt and drawstring pants, Eleanor sat on the couch watching a nature video about a family of gorillas.

"Good morning, Melissa. How did you sleep?"

"I'm okay." Kate peered through a crack in the window blinds. "Maybe we could go outside and sit at the little table."

"It might be a little chilly."

Kate approached Eleanor and glared at her while trying to keep her voice neutral. "I *really* would like to go outside."

"Well, of course, dear." Eleanor stood up and faced the kitchen. "Friendly, please call Mr. Baker and tell him I want to sit in the backyard."

"I could walk you there," Kate whispered.

"Everything we do should display normal behavior. The monitoring system prefers consistency."

A few minutes later, they were sitting at the outside table and Eleanor ordered the giant panda to bring her a cup of tea. After Mr. Baker returned to the house, Kate described what she had seen in the living room.

"It's probably nothing, but I thought you needed to know."

"It sounds like either Peter Dawson or the monitoring system itself has gained access to my bank accounts. To check your balance, you need a face ID along with a password." Eleanor sighed and leaned back in her chair. "My daughter made me watch a sales video about this place before we came here. At the end of the video, a deep voice sounding like God said the Orchard's stress-free environment would prolong my life. Gradually, I've realized a different fact: only the machines are immortal, and we're just a source of funding."

"What are you going to do, Eleanor?"

"It's time to gather our forces and come up with a plan. Marie has the secret phone. We'll go over to her house."

"I can't go with you, Eleanor. I need to get away from here."

"My friends need to know what you saw last night. Tell them the story one more time and then you can leave."

They were both startled when the back door glided open and the giant panda returned with a cup of tea.

"I'm going to drink this at Marie's house, Mr. Baker. Please carry me over there."

"I'd be glad to help you, Eleanor."

Eleanor stood on the extension and let the panda hold her securely in his arms while they rolled along the asphalt pathways leading to Marie's house. In the distance, a giant panda carried another old lady to the community center while a third panda delivered a mailing envelope to one of the homes.

"Backyard," Eleanor said, and the panda delivered her to an identical set of table and chairs. "Thank you, Mr. Baker. Now go to Abigail's house and tell her that we're having tea together. Bring her here and tell one of your panda friends to give Susan the same message."

"This sounds like a festive occasion, Eleanor."

"Very good, Mr. Baker! You've expanded your vocabulary!"

The panda couldn't smile or frown, but its voice sounded pleased. "Thank you, Eleanor. Sometimes it's difficult to choose the correct word."

Marie left her house, and they sat around a backyard table. After Kate repeated her story, Marie used her cell phone to check her bank account. She managed to get a human on the phone and asked a lot of questions as the pandas delivered Abigail and Susan to the backyard.

"Something strange is going on," Marie said. "Last year the Orchard began charging me $199 a month for something called

Internet maintenance. But it doesn't make sense, because we're not allowed online."

Susan looked angry. "I bet they are charging the fee to everyone who lives here, and no one is aware of it. Dawson is secretly stealing from us, and the machines are helping him."

"What are we going to *do*?" Abigail asked. "If we talk to Dawson, he'll just deny everything and make us eat alone with a furry. My son won't help me. He doesn't want a frail old lady living in his apartment."

"You should call the police on Marie's cell phone," Kate suggested. "But first you need to get the Friendly out of Marie's house."

"If Dawson finds out, we'll be locked up in a room somewhere."

"I'll help you jam the doors," Kate said. "It will be like four queens in a castle."

Susan leaned back in her chair and laughed. "Your granddaughter is brilliant, Eleanor."

The women looked tense as they entered Marie's house. Kate thought that Friendly 31 might get suspicious, but it continued to bustle around the living room, placing throw pillows in the exact center of each chair.

"Friendly, there's a patch of mud in the doorway," Marie said.

"Thank you for the information. I will inspect the area, then choose the appropriate cleaning device."

The back door automatically opened when Friendly 31 rolled toward it. The little robot zigzagged back and forth, looking for a spot that needed cleaning. "Please repeat suggestion. I don't see anything."

Kate sprinted forward and pushed the Friendly out of the house. "Close the door!" she shouted, and Marie pressed her palm on the door activator set in the wall. It closed for ten seconds and then glided open again. Friendly 31 used its steel arms to push off the ground until it was standing on its three-wheel base.

"Chairs!" Kate shouted. Working together, they moved the living room chairs into the open doorway and created an improvised barricade. Friendly 31 tried to force its way forward, but it couldn't push the chairs away.

"Wedge the couch against the front door!" Kate shouted. "You need to block all entrances."

After the front door was blocked, she found Eleanor trying to push a table across the kitchen. "It's time for me to leave. If the police show up, don't tell them that I'm trying to get to New York."

Eleanor looked concerned. "Are things really that bad?"

"A special police officer said a computer labeled me with a high number. The officer said that I'll cause trouble for myself and everyone around me."

Kate hugged Eleanor, feeling the old lady's thin bones and frail body. Before anyone stopped her, she slipped out the kitchen door. Crossing the lawn, she shifted her backpack around so that she and Zeno were looking in the same direction. "Are the four ladies going to get into trouble?"

"We don't know what's going to happen. Sometimes humans enjoy creating problems. It proves they're still alive."

When Kate reached the sidewalk, she heard a whirring sound and Mr. Baker rolled up behind her. "There's been a system alert," the giant panda informed her. "Can you explain the problem?"

Kate realized that the pandas were programmed to protect the old ladies while the Friendlies enforced the rules. "Friendly 31 is trying to force its way into Marie's house and hurt the four women inside. You need to defend them."

"Elderly humans must be protected from injury."

"That's right. I like your T-shirt, Mr. Baker. See you later."

Kate turned away from the panda and climbed the stone wall. When she reached the top, she turned around and looked back at the Orchard.

Twelve Friendlies had left their houses and rolled down the center of the street to Marie's place. Clustered around the front door, they tried to push away the couch. After failing again and again, the central control system came up with a new strategy, and the social robots attacked the doorway at the same time.

"This looks bad," Kate told Zeno. "The Friendlies are going to get inside."

Suddenly, Mr. Baker and a panda with an *E* on its T-shirt emerged from the house next door and charged the smaller robots. Mr. Baker grabbed a Friendly and tossed it across the lawn. The Friendlies attacked like a pack of wolves, and the two pandas fought back, punching and slapping them with human-shaped hands.

Kate jumped off the wall and started running.

31 | JULIA AND DANIEL

AROUND TWO in the morning, Daniel began gasping for air and woke up suddenly. This had occurred many times in their relationship, and Julia knew enough to remain silent. Reaching beneath the quilt, she took his hand and he quieted back to sleep. *I'm here,* she thought. *I'll always be here for you.*

Daniel got up at dawn and slipped out of the bedroom. A few minutes later, he returned with a hot cup of tea. No talk. No weather report. Daniel placed the ceramic mug on the night table and departed. He needed some time to "get normal" in the morning, and Julia wanted silence and caffeine while she thought about the new day.

When she finished the tea, Julia brushed her hair and entered the living room. Daniel sat at his computer, and the monitor screen showed that he was looking for social media comments made by Bennett Schroeder. He had spent most of the previous day searching online.

"How did you sleep, Daniel?"

"On and off. A bad dream."

It was typical that their new day started with a lie. What had disturbed his sleep probably wasn't a nightmare, but a memory. Daniel refused to talk about his Death Catcher experience, and Julia knew only a few random stories. One night Daniel mentioned that he wouldn't let his team cut wedding rings off the swollen fingers of the dead.

"Did you find any clues about Bennett's location?"

"I'll keep dropping by the New York travel centers, but most of the long-term burrows are outside the city."

"What about the E-Volve stickers we found in the bedroom?"

"Perhaps this group has a website. I'll do an online search."

A few minutes later, the computer beeped for a video call and Thomas Vinson's face appeared on the monitor screen. Thomas's hair didn't look greasy, and he had trimmed his beard. *Maybe he took a shower,* Julia thought. *Miracles can happen.*

"Hello there! I've got some good news!"

Daniel raised his cup of fake coffee. "That's always welcome."

"I contacted an old friend who plays online chess with the billionaire Roy Kassam. He gave me Roy's private email address and sent him a message that explained who you are and why you wanted to visit Dragon Lair. Roy's kind of a weird guy, but I just heard back from him. If you drive up to Lake Placid, he'll talk to you."

"What about a hologram conversation?" Daniel asked.

"You're talking about a man who lives on his own personal mountain. Roy used to be the most high-tech guy in our little group of computer scientists, but now he's traveled in the opposite direction. He won't talk to a hologram."

"Send us his GPS location," Julia said. "And tell him that we'll show up later today."

Daniel ended the phone call and returned to the coffeepot. "You sure you want to do this, Julia? It's a long way to Lake Placid."

"At this point, we don't have much to go on . . . other than the fact that Bennett was obsessed with Dragon Lair. He could be exploring that broken simulation, but I need a password from Kassam to get in."

It took only a few minutes to get dressed and walk over to the unofficial parking lot run by Fortunata and Bugs, two homeless people who slept in a tent and charged drivers a fee to guard their vehicle. Fortunata was in her seventies and took care of the money. Bugs was her younger boyfriend who patrolled the abandoned construction site with a baseball bat studded with nails.

Although Bugs kept looters from stripping the car for parts, he wasn't expected to fight off professional car thieves carrying guns.

Rich people stored their cars in fortified basement parking lots, but Julia and Daniel had come up with an alternative plan. Using her computer, Julia created illustrations that made the vehicle look so weird that the thieves would look for a less distinctive target. The right side used Gothic letters to announce that the van was a HUNK OF JUNK. The left side displayed the words BLUE YORK CITY with cartoon images of blue snowmen robbing Santa Claus.

Daniel and a street artist named Stinky Angel spent several weekends working on the van. When they were done, Julia and Daniel threw a "Too Weird to Steal" party for their friends. Daniel wore a rag shop tuxedo and Julia wore a shredded ballroom gown as they pulled off the parachute covering the van. Everyone agreed that they had created the ugliest car in New York.

"How you doing?" she asked Fortunata.

"*Suficientemente bueno para mi.*" The old lady smiled as she stuffed the weekly parking fee into her pink bra. "Where do you travel?"

"Lake Placid area."

"Stay out of the districts. They burn witches there."

The trip north to Lake Placid would take about six hours. Daniel drove while Julia went on the Internet to get more information. The man they were going to meet, Roy Kassam, was born in Lebanon, grew up in Paris, and got a PhD in computer science at Oxford University. For several years, he had been the founder and CEO of the Expanding Universe Corporation until he sold the company and stepped off the grid.

"Why did he sell?" Daniel asked.

"It doesn't say. He stopped giving interviews."

Gradually, the landscape around them turned rocky, and they passed dark water lakes bordered with cattails and broken reeds. About ten miles outside Lake Placid, Daniel turned onto a winding road that twisted its way into the mountains. A spruce and hemlock forest had forced roots into the soil and lines of water trickled down bare rock walls.

When they reached the correct GPS coordinates, they stopped at a dirt logging road marked with tractor treads that continued up the mountain. Getting out of the van, Julia walked over to a granite boulder. Someone had sandblasted a single word into the stone.

HERE

"What does it say?" Daniel asked.

"Here."

"If we're here instead of there, then where the hell is there?"

"Let's keep going and find out."

The logging road turned into a well-maintained asphalt road that passed fragments of stone wall. Bumping across potholes, the van entered a flat patch of land cleared of trees. An excavator and backhoe were parked next to a pile of boulders while a forklift with an adjustable boom was picking up rocks and creating another wall.

As they approached, the boom arm stopped moving and an older man jumped out of the forklift with a hunting rifle. He pointed his weapon at the van, then raised the barrel and fired a warning shot into the air.

Daniel slammed on the brakes, and they stopped moving. Time slowed down, and every detail of the forest—the smell of dead leaves, a patch of sunlight on the ground—was clear and distinct. Slowly the man approached them and raised the rifle to his shoulder as if he was about to kill a deer.

Julia rolled down the side window and forced a smile. "Good afternoon, sir! I think we're on the correct road, but maybe we made a mistake."

"You from the districts?"

"New York City."

The man's shoulders relaxed, and he lowered the rifle. Julia could see the words *Big Bass Fishing* stitched onto the crown of his tractor cap.

"DNA and all the land surrounding it are private property. Any unauthorized vehicle going up the road is going to get its tires shot out."

"We're here to see Roy Kassam."

The Big Bass man grunted and shook his head. "Nobody sees him except me and the two other fellas who work here. The man don't even own a dog."

"I'm Julia Lau, and this is Daniel Blake. We have an appointment to see Mr. Kassam."

Big Bass pulled out a cell phone and pressed a button. "Two young people are here to see you. I stopped them in section three." He listened for a few seconds and then ended the call. "This is a red-letter day. One of the few times I've seen the boss act human." He pointed to the road. "Keep driving up the mountain until you reach the stone house. You'll find Mr. Kassam on the terrace above the house. He's working on his tomb."

32 | KATE AND ZENO

HOW FAR TO the Autonomous Truck Center, Zeno?"

"Five miles."

Frustrated, Kate pulled off her knapsack and placed it on a boulder. "Your battery got charged at Eleanor's house, but I didn't have breakfast."

"I am aware of your lack of nourishment."

"After we left the Orchard, we should have gone straight to the interstate."

"You caused a kerfuffle."

"What's that?"

"A commotion. A fuss."

"I had to do that, Zeno. Someone was stealing Eleanor's money."

"The reason for the kerfuffle is not relevant to our current problem. The pandas fighting the Friendlies will cause Mr. Dawson to ask questions, and that might reveal that you aren't Eleanor's granddaughter. There is a possibility that Dawson will contact the police."

"I know, but I'm still tired and thirsty."

"Keep walking and plan what you're going to say if you meet someone."

Kate picked up the knapsack and shifted it around so that Zeno was looking forward. For the next thirty minutes, they continued east through a neighborhood of small farms separated by patches of rocky ground and forest. Climbing over a split-rail fence, she crossed a pasture dotted with white-faced cattle that glanced up at her like big kids on the schoolyard and then resumed munching grass.

Suddenly she saw a dark creature passing through the underbrush that bordered the field.

"I just saw a wolf."

"No wolves roam through Massachusetts."

"Maybe this wolf didn't read his instructions."

The cattle didn't look frightened. That was a good sign. Kate stood in the middle of the pasture, watching and waiting, until the dark creature passed through a gap in the fence.

It was a German shepherd. Instead of running toward her, it paused near the fence, sat on its haunches, and tilted its head as if considering her existence. A few seconds later, a boxer came through the same opening and dashed over to the larger dog. Both dogs wore harnesses that covered their bodies and let their legs move freely.

The shepherd and the boxer glanced over their shoulders as a border collie entered the pasture. The collie approached the cattle, stopped, and stood between Kate and the herd.

"I'm not going to hurt the cows!" Kate shouted and then felt silly. You couldn't have a human conversation with a dog.

The shepherd and the border collie crossed the pasture while the excited boxer scampered back and forth behind them. The dogs stopped about six feet away from Kate and sniffed the air. *What do I smell like?* Kate wondered. *The lavender soap in Eleanor's shower?*

The shepherd's tail was up, and he held his head high. Then something happened that was wonderful and scary at the same time. A solemn man's voice came from a chest speaker attached to his harness.

"My name is Ranger, and this is my home. Are you an intruder?"

An older woman's voice came from the border collie. "I'm Tessa, and this is my herd. Don't touch the cattle in this meadow."

"I'm Buddy!" The boxer's voice sounded like a teenage boy's. "Do you have treats?"

"I've never talked to dogs, and I don't understand how you can talk to me." Kate held up her hands to show that she wasn't carrying food. "No treats." She waited a few seconds for the dogs to talk, then decided to ask a question. "I'm thirsty. Do you know where I can find a water faucet?"

The dogs seemed to know the word *water,* but they displayed different reactions.

"I have a water bowl!" Buddy the boxer said. "It's next to my food bowl!"

Ranger took a few steps toward her and sniffed. "You can drink water at the house."

"Follow me," Tessa said. "And don't touch the cattle."

The dogs were as real as the grass and trees, but Kate felt like she had drifted into a peculiar daydream. Tessa kept glancing over her shoulder to confirm that Kate was following her. She reminded Kate of a chaperone on a school field trip.

"The dogs talk, Zeno."

"No, they don't. A speech recognition program listens to you, and then a synthesized voice comes out of a speaker."

"They're just like you."

Zeno spoke slowly as if he was considering each word. "I know history, literature, and mathematics, Katherine. I have a much larger database."

"Dead bird!" Buddy said. "Dead bird near the tree!" The boxer ran off to smell the carcass as the two other dogs escorted Kate up a dirt pathway to a two-story clapboard house. Several dog bowls and a water faucet were on a patch of gravel near the front porch.

"Hello!" Kate shouted. "Is anybody home?" When no one answered, she turned on the faucet. Water gushed out and she began to drink.

"Hello, young lady."

This was a new voice—not one of the dogs. Startled, Kate turned off the faucet and saw that a skinny older man with wire-rimmed spectacles had walked out onto the porch. The man's work boots were scuffed, and his flannel shirt was faded. "Good morning. I'm Samuel Taylor. Why are you in my front yard? Are you lost?"

"Hi, Mr. Taylor, I'm Kate Harrington. I've been visiting my grandmother. She lives at the Orchard."

"Right. The retirement home with the pandas zooming around on wheels. What brings you here?"

"They're very nice ladies, but there's not a lot to do there. With my grandmother's permission, I decided to explore the area."

"Good for you, Kate. Most young people spend all their time staring at their cell phones."

"I got thirsty and needed some water. I hope that's okay."

"Of course. But that's lukewarm water. Wait here on the porch and I'll bring you some cold apple juice."

"Thank you, Mr. Taylor."

"Call me Samuel. I was only Mr. Taylor when I was running a warehouse."

Kate sat on a rattan porch chair as the man went to his kitchen and returned with two glasses of chilled juice. He placed Kate's glass on a round table and watched her drink.

"There's more if you want."

"I'm okay. Why do your dogs talk, Samuel? I've never seen that before."

"Four years ago, my wife died. I really missed her, and everyone told me I should purchase a Shadow with her voice. I paid for the software program, but hearing Becky's voice made me sad, so I switched it off. For a couple of months, I just walked around the house talking to myself."

"Is that when you bought the dog vests?"

"They're wearing special harnesses with sensors and voice speakers."

"It's weird to hear them talk."

"When I managed the warehouse, there were only three humans working in a building with two dozen nubots. All day long I had conversations with loading and shipping bots. They were designed with different voices, so you instantly knew who you were talking to."

Buddy came running down the path and lapped up water from one of the steel bowls. Then he joined the other two dogs. They sat on their haunches, facing the porch like the royal guards protecting their king.

"Are you safe, Samuel?" the German shepherd asked with his deep voice.

"Yes, Ranger. Everything is safe."

"Throw the ball," Buddy requested. "Please throw the ball."

"No ball. Sit."

Samuel drank some apple juice, then placed the glass back on the table. "If I was already talking to machines, then why not talk to dogs?"

"Are they thinking the words or is it just a computer?"

"That's a good question, Kate. And there's not a simple answer. The software program responds to different questions, but there are also sensors embedded in the harness that monitor each dog's heart rate and physical activity. If a dog wags his tail to the right, he's in a good mood. If the tail wags to the left, then he's feeling fear or aggression. A dog is like a two-year-old with an incredible sense of smell. They can remember more than a hundred words, and they are sensitive to my emotions."

"Tessa kept trying to herd me."

Samuel laughed. "When Canada geese land in the pasture, Tessa spends days trying to herd them together. The birds aren't too happy about it."

"Food time?" Buddy asked. "Is it food time?"

Ranger stopped wagging his tail and turned to his younger companion. "No food time," he said. "Bowls are empty."

Kate finished her apple juice and turned to Mr. Taylor. "When you're with your dogs, is it like having a conversation with humans, or is it different?"

Samuel looked out at his three companions. "I can't talk about history and politics with my dogs, but that's not a big problem. I feed them and remove their ticks. They protect me and keep me from feeling lonely. At a certain point, I accepted who they were and didn't wish for more."

Kate glanced up at the sky and realized that the sun was over the tree line. It would take at least two hours of walking before she reached the nearest Autonomous Truck Center.

"Thank you for the apple juice, Samuel. I need to get back to my grandmother."

"No problem. Walk down the driveway and turn right. That will lead you directly to the Orchard. It's been a pleasure meeting you, Kate."

As Kate left the porch, Taylor stood up and motioned to the dogs. "Go with her to *road,*" he said.

The three dogs followed Kate down the driveway until she reached the road, then stopped at a red mailbox and watched her walk away.

"They're still looking at us, Zeno."

"Turn and let me see."

Zeno's electronic eyes captured the image and sent it to the Cloud processor that managed his data flow. "They're guarding their territory."

"They were real dogs that seemed fake. You're an Interactive Toy that seems real. Can you explain that to me?"

Zeno stayed silent for several minutes as he analyzed her question. "I've changed during the last seven years. Now I'm sad if you're hurt and I miss you when you're gone. In this way, I have absorbed some of your humanness."

33 | JULIA AND DANIEL

THEY CONTINUED UP the mountain and emerged from the forest line to a rocky slope dotted with shrubs and black spruce trees. Directly ahead of them were three terraces cut into the side of the mountain. On the lower terrace there was a rectangular one-story house with inset windows designed to protect the glass from snowstorms. The house was built with chunks of granite held together with concrete mortar, and the only sign of color was the rows of dark blue solar panels mounted on a steep roof.

On the middle terrace, cranes and bulldozers had created a pyramid of boulders with sloping sides meeting at an apex. There were gaps between the rocks, and the fourth side of the pyramid had been left unfinished. An irregular rock tunnel led into the center of the pile.

On the terrace directly above the unfinished pyramid was a massive boxlike structure built with slabs of poured concrete. The base of the structure was hidden and looked as if the shaft had cracked out of the earth and jutted upward. Julia couldn't see any windows or ventilation pipes—just a dark opening that led directly into the mountain.

A Quonset hut was on each level, and there was a flat space near the pyramid where someone had parked a crane, bulldozer, dump truck, and four-wheel-drive passenger vehicle. The entire complex looked like an ongoing project for an artist who liked to play with rocks.

"I don't see a tomb," Daniel said.

"Let's take a look at the pyramid."

Daniel turned the van onto the middle terrace, and Julia saw a man using a welding torch to connect the struts of an eight-foot-long steel frame. The worker switched off the torch, removed his helmet, and approached the van.

Roy Kassam had long black hair, an aquiline nose, and an olive complexion. His leather jacket had been scorched by sparks and flames, and he wore steel-toed boots and jeans with patches on the knees.

"Mr. Kassam?"

"You found me."

"I'm Julia Lau, and this is Daniel Blake. We're Thomas Vinson's friends."

"How is Thomas doing? I haven't seen him for years."

"He keeps asking difficult questions," Daniel said. "Then he tries to answer them."

"Good. We need people like Thomas if our species is going to survive." Kassam turned and swept his arm around as if he was selling the property. "Welcome to Doomsday North America. None of the people working for me like the name, so we just call it DNA."

"The man with the forklift said that you were working on your tomb. Is that why this place is called Doomsday?"

"I'm going to be buried in a tumulus, a large mound of earth and stones." Kassam returned to the steel frame and checked the welding points. "A hermetically sealed coffin is being built up in Canada using high-quality tungsten carbide mixed with nickel binder. After my death, the coffin will be placed in this frame and then inserted into the center of the pyramid. Boulders will block the entrance shaft, and a digger will fill in the gaps with tons of earth."

"Are you planning on dying soon?" Julia asked.

Kassam shook his head and laughed. "I hope not. The DNA project is only sixty percent completed. There's a lot more work to do."

While Julia and Kassam continued talking, Daniel walked to the edge of the terrace and gazed down the slope at the stone house and several V-shaped walls.

"You're building chevrons," Daniel said. "They start at the road and point like arrows up the mountain to this place."

"This mountain is approximately a mile above sea level. North America is eventually going to be hit with more coastal flooding, enormous forest fires, earthquakes, and another pandemic with maximum fatality levels. None of it will matter. Someone from a different universe will follow the chevrons."

"And then they'll find your tomb," Daniel said. "You're just like an Egyptian pharaoh."

"The chevrons aren't pointing toward the tumulus, but to a destination on the top level. Come with me and I'll show you."

Kassam turned away from the tomb, and they followed him up the road to a third level, where a concrete shaft jutted out of the ground. At the base of the shaft was the opening to a tunnel leading downward into the mountain. Peering into the tunnel, Julia saw a round vault door with a combination lock.

"Is this a fallout shelter?"

"There's no air ventilation . . . just rows of steel shelves and racks. Doomsday North America is a storage vault for nonhuman lifeforms. It stores over four hundred thousand seed samples from different plant species in specially designed containers. In addition, there are thirty thousand DNA samples for animal, fish, and insect species . . . everything from honeybees to great white sharks. The seeds and DNA samples will survive for at least a thousand years."

"And all the plants and animals that perished could be grown again?"

"Millions of plant and animal species are on the edge of extinction. A hundred years ago, seed catalogs offered over two hundred different varieties of green beans, and most of those species have disappeared. There have been other doomsday storage facilities, but most of them have been abandoned. The Iraqi seed vault was destroyed during the U.S. invasion of 2003. The Philippine gene bank burned down in a fire, and Egypt's desert seed storage in the Sinai was wrecked by looters during a riot."

"Where's your power source?" Daniel asked. "Is everything frozen?"

"My vault isn't dependent on water pumps and air-conditioning. When I die, the vault will be sealed up like my tomb. Eventually, the storage huts will be replaced with simple stone carvings explaining what is inside the vault."

"But what if there aren't any humans left to open it?" Julia asked.

"Perhaps the world will be dominated by the species I haven't placed in the vault. What might survive are . . ."

"Cockroaches," Daniel said.

Kassam laughed. "Cockroaches, ants, fruit flies, scorpions, and certain parasitic wasps."

"I've always liked red-tailed hawks, monarch butterflies, and hardworking beavers," Julia said. "Oh, and polar bears. Daniel loves polar bears."

"They're a North American mammal, and their DNA is stored here."

Daniel shook his head. "Is all this hopeful planning supposed to make me feel better about Armageddon?"

"Hope requires faith that something better can exist in the future. By that definition, I'm a hopeful soul. Every night, the earth rotates into darkness. And every morning, it rotates back into light. One day, there might be enough stability to bring back butterflies and polar bears."

"I haven't read about this project in any news feed."

"I've refused all requests for interviews."

"This is an incredible accomplishment," Julia said. "Don't you want the world to know about it?"

"I want long-term species survival. Not short-term publicity."

"Then why did you agree to see us today?"

"When I owned the Expanding Universe Corporation, we created hundreds of simulated worlds. Most of them are beginning to fade in my memory, but not Dragon Lair."

"I tried to visit the site yesterday and couldn't get in," Julia said. "A message board said it was closed for maintenance."

"Follow me to the house. We'll have a drink."

Returning to the first terrace, they passed through a house with gray slate floors and bare walls. The rooms were large and filled with light, but there didn't seem to be a single photograph or personal memento. When they reached the outer deck, Kassam motioned for them to sit on a stone bench next to a stone cube table. He left them for a few minutes and then returned with two glasses and a bottle of Irish whiskey.

"I don't smoke or drink alcohol. But I like to offer wine or whiskey to the few visitors who find their way here."

Daniel picked up the bottle as if it was a religious relic. "This is real whiskey. Not bootleg vodka brewed in someone's bathroom."

"Yes, I bought a few cases before I came up here. Each bottle could be sold for about twelve hundred dollars down in New York." Kassam poured a taste of whiskey into both glasses. "Be my guest and take the bottle with you."

Julia sniffed the liquor in the cut-crystal glass and took her first sip. She tasted toast and red berries, then a slight honey sweetness that lingered on her tongue. The three humans gazed out at an evergreen forest with scattered spars of dead trees struck and burned by lightning. The surrounding mountains were green at the base, and then scree slopes led to sharp granite ridges that looked like the jawbones of an ancient race of giants.

"I've always been wary of rituals and ceremonies," Kassam said. "Life is special enough. You don't need to embellish it."

Daniel sipped his whiskey. "I doubt if you thought that way when you were running your corporation."

"Most successful people think they're better than everyone else and display their achievements as evidence of their superiority. It's taken me several years of isolation to see my success clearly. Everyone creating VR wanted our simulated worlds to be more attractive and compelling than reality."

"If you're squeezed into your grandmother's apartment with six other people, you might prefer a life in the Over World."

Kassam refilled their glasses. "When the new digital technology went global, futurologists told us that the Internet and computers would be the foundation for a borderless democracy. Their view turned out to be complete nonsense. What really happened was that dictators and autocracies used technology to track and monitor everyone with a cell phone."

"Everyone knows this," Daniel said. "Jack Lewis predicted what was going to happen in his book *Against Authority.*"

"Lewis is a frail old man hiding in Berlin. The rest of us must deal with parallel worlds that continue to become more complicated, more pervasive, more *real.* Dictators love simulated realities. They want to blur the distinction between fact and fiction, what's true and what's false. The best minds of your generation are lost in the Over World."

"We didn't drive here from New York to get a lecture about our Zero Generation. Daniel and I are trying to find a missing young man named Bennett Schroeder. His body is lying in a burrow somewhere, so we're looking for his online self, his consciousness. Bennett was obsessed with the Dragon Lair simulation."

"I need to give you some background on how Dragon Lair was created. I started Expanding Universe with two employees, and it quickly became a dominant content provider. But whenever I looked at our monthly spreadsheet, I could see that our largest continuing expense was employee salaries. It costs a lot of money to design a simulated world, create the characters and setting, and turn the concept into code. The solution was obvious. . . ."

"Turn the job over to artificial intelligence," Daniel said.

"That's correct. We were already using AI programs to monitor and change existing simulations, but there didn't seem to be a system that could independently design and code a simulated world. I was searching for a solution when I was approached by a company called Cogito that was developing an Artificial Superintelligence system called Delphi."

"So, you hired a computer?"

"Yes. It was the right business decision. I went to Cogito's headquarters in Connecticut, described what I wanted, then sat in a server room and watched the system create a parallel world on a monitor screen. Delphi searched through its database and found the Plan of St. Gall . . . a medieval architectural blueprint of a Benedictine monastery. The compound was never built in reality, but Delphi made it the center of Dragon Lair. The simulation had a backstory, obstacles, and different kinds of dragons."

Julia nodded. "I visited the site a few times. There were swarms of little dragons that would attack you from different angles."

"This sounds like the modern answer to all problems," Daniel said. "If you want to lower costs, get rid of humans."

"It felt like I had transformed our business model. Dragon Lair was a massive hit, and millions of people visited the site."

"Didn't you have problems with racism, antisemitism, and the abuse of women?"

"After three months or so, some vile content began to appear on the site. We were criticized by the news feeds, but none of our critics understood what was really going on. Among programmers, the word 'instantiation' means the creation of a real-world example of an abstraction or a template. Most humans have some degree of common sense. It helps us figure out complicated problems. But AI systems are prone to something called 'perverse instantiation.' If you tell a computer to make everyone in the world happy, then one way to achieve that goal is to kill all humans so no one is sad."

Daniel laughed and sipped his whiskey. "That's definitely a logical solution."

"Dragon Lair's objectives were to increase player visits and raise our renewal rate. Unfortunately, bigoted people loved seeing their racist ideas expressed in a simulation. They visited the site every day, and our renewal rate was ninety-two percent."

"The system gave them what they wanted."

"A *New York Times* article said that Dragon Lair was the most pernicious website on the Internet, so I had my staff reboot the entire site to its original appearance and then told Delphi to stop making changes."

"And did that work?"

"Negative content stopped, but the site kept crashing. All the dragons disappeared, and the system won't allow us to bring them back."

Kassam stood up abruptly and walked back into the house.

"What the hell is he doing?" Daniel whispered. "Are we supposed to leave?"

"I'm not leaving until we get a password."

A minute later, Kassam returned with a glass and filled it with whiskey. "This is the fifth time in my life I've consumed alcohol." He took a sip, then set the glass down with a click. "Tastes like medicine."

"Did you ever solve your problem?"

"When the tech staff asked me to make an evaluation, I entered Dragon Lair, bought a sword in the marketplace, and stepped through the gate. The graphics had deteriorated, and programming errors were everywhere. I searched an abandoned cottage and opened a dusty armoire. Thousands of toads burst out and hopped all around the room."

"This doesn't sound like a game that people would want to play."

"The Eastern Road takes you to a series of rivers, and most of the bridges had been destroyed. I traveled down the Western Road for about twenty minutes and encountered an old peasant woman standing at a junction. She wore a long black skirt and a black cloak, and her face was very realistic. Wrinkles. Saggy cheeks. Hair growing out of a mole."

"'Hello, Roy Kassam,' she said. 'It's an honor to see you here. Are you one of the uqqāl? Do you have true knowledge of this world?'"

"What are you talking about?" Julia asked. "What's an uqqāl?"

"I'm from a Druze family in Lebanon. Our sect came out of Shia Islam, but we don't consider ourselves Muslims. Ninety percent are members of the outer group who haven't read the secret holy books. Then there are the uqqāl, the Knowledgeable, who understand the true nature of the universe."

"So, this old lady knew your name. . . ."

"My *real* name. Not my avatar name. And she knew that I was Lebanese and a Druze. It felt as if a stranger suddenly approached me and announced all my secrets."

"What did you do?"

"When I raised my sword, the old woman laughed at me. 'I don't want to hurt you, Roy. I'm just a software program who's here to answer questions.'

"'Why did this site become so toxic?'

"'What is toxic for some is nourishment for others,' the woman said. 'Continue down the road to the monastery and you'll find your answer.'"

"At this point, I would have activated my talisman," Julia said. "If a simulation gets weird, return to reality."

"Dragon Lair was my company's biggest triumph and most significant failure. I wanted to figure out what had happened so I walked to the burnt-out shell of the monastery, stepped around blackened chunks of marble, and headed toward the shattered basilica tower. A slate pathway led me to the narthex, a covered porch guarding the church entrance where a massive oak door had been ripped off its hinges. Then I passed through an open doorway and stood in the shell of the destroyed basilica. When I looked up, I saw a cracked statue of the Virgin Mary and holes punched through the lead framework that had once held stained glass.

"Back in the analog world, I was breathing fast and sweating, but I forgot about everything but the reality of this location and this moment. A breeze pushed a singed piece of parchment across the blackened floor, and then the wall in front of me collapsed into a pile of brick and plaster. Dust rose into the air and hundreds of butterflies appeared, their wings expanding into images of created worlds that glided past my face and collapsed into single points of light.

"An AGI system had searched the Over World and collected links to the most malevolent simulations on the Internet. I saw a rape world in which women were tortured and destroyed, a crucifix world that let you nail your enemies onto a wooden cross, and a simulated Auschwitz in which prisoners wearing striped uniforms removed their caps as you strolled through the extermination camp."

Julia had encountered trolls in the Over World, but this level of toxicity made her feel sick. "How did you react?" she asked.

"I activated my talisman and returned to the changing room. That experience changed my life. I realized that Dragon Lair had mirrored the hatred and obsessions of our violent species. At that moment, I gave up on humanity and decided to save plants and animals."

"So, you sold your company?"

"It was a cash deal. No stock or loan payoff commitments."

"What competitor had that much money?"

"The offer came directly from Howard Sebesky."

Daniel shook his head and finished his glass of whiskey. "He's the billionaire who said every company in the world should install AI systems and fire half their employees."

"Sebesky is a brilliant computer scientist who is terrified of dying. When we met to negotiate, he wore an e-mask and sat twenty feet away from me. During our first hour together, he tried to talk me into joining his transhuman organization and living forever. It was basically eugenics dressed up with a lot of scientific jargon."

"Why'd you sell your creation to a crazy guy?" Julia asked.

"Sebesky wasn't crazy about wearing the mask. The Stem-flu pandemic proved that he was right."

"Did you tell him about Dragon Lair?"

"He said that artificial intelligence is a powerful tool, but you must give it explicit instructions. When you program an autonomous truck, you tell the system that it can't drive through walls or float across a lake."

"And Sebesky never destroyed the simulation?"

"Of course not. That would have been an acknowledgment that the company made a mistake." Kassam took another sip of whiskey and gazed out at the horizon. "The past is over. The present is lost. DNA is about saving the future."

"I admire what you're doing here," Julia said. "But could you do one good deed while you're moving rocks around? Give me an administrative password so I can enter Dragon Lair. I want to make sure that Bennett didn't pass through the access door before it was closed."

Kassam shifted his gaze back to Julia, studying her face. "I'll contact the only person I know who is still working for the company. In exchange, I'd like a favor. When you return from Dragon Lair, tell me what you've seen."

34 | KATE AND ZENO

WAKE UP, KATHERINE. Something bad just happened."

Kate opened her eyes and looked around the truck cab. "What's wrong, Zeno?"

"We were heading toward New York City, but we just turned off the interstate. Now we're traveling in the wrong direction."

Kate told the autonomous truck to pull over at an abandoned service station. She climbed out of the cab with her knapsack and watched the truck disappear into the darkness. A quarter moon was low on the horizon, and stars were beginning to disappear. Kate pulled out the burner phone, called the three stored numbers, and heard the robot voice. This time, she decided not to leave a message.

"Where are we, Zeno?"

"We're in upstate New York, near the town of Dannemora."

"Can I walk to an ATC and find a truck going south?"

"An Autonomous Truck Center is twelve miles away from here. But you need to be careful. We're in a district that might be dangerous for outsiders. Find some place to hide in the daytime and walk to the truck center at night."

The night air was cold, and Kate smelled wet leaves. A dark yellow light glowed up the road and she was drawn toward its warmth. A few minutes later, they reached a neon sign that read *lysian ields.*

"What does that mean, Zeno?"

"Perhaps the words should read 'Elysian Fields,' but the two capital letters are shorted out. The Elysian Fields were part of the ancient Greek concept of the afterlife. When heroic and virtuous people died, they ended up there."

"So, it's like heaven?"

"No God. No angels. It was just a place for the dead."

Kate followed a driveway to a parking lot filled with solar panels. The current from each panel flowed from black electrical cables to a feeder cable that slithered across the asphalt to a redbrick church with a white steeple. A grass field was directly behind the church, and it was surrounded by a cast-iron fence with spear-shaped finials.

"Move closer to the fence," Zeno said. "Can you see a house?"

Kate peered through the six-inch gaps of the spire fence. "It looks like a graveyard, but I don't see any marble crosses and gravestones."

Random wisps of green and blue light floated above the grass. They glowed for a few seconds, then vanished like smoke from a campfire.

"There's light. A strange light."

"We need to stay away from unknown factors."

"Maybe this graveyard has a chapel where I could hide."

"Possible, but not probable."

"You used to say that when I made a bad move playing chess."

Kate circled the church and found a graveyard gate held shut by a single padlock dangling on its hasp. She pulled off the padlock and the gate squeaked open.

"Don't do this."

"One quick look and then we'll leave."

Each grave displayed a triangle of black metal posts about a foot high. When Kate approached one of the triangles, it detected her presence. Suddenly, a beam of light shot from each post, and a luminous hologram of a young woman floated in the night air. No words. No sound. Kate moved a few feet to the left and the woman disappeared.

"I don't like this place, Zeno."

"Let's return to the parking lot."

Kate walked quickly, then began running toward the gate. Each grave sensed her presence, and glowing holograms of dead people appeared in front of her. Breathing hard, she stopped and glanced over her shoulder. The dead lingered in the darkness—then disappeared.

As she passed through the gate, a man stepped out of the shadows and grabbed her jacket collar. "Got you!"

Kate struggled to get away, but the man gripped her tightly as he dragged her around the church to the parking lot. A battered two-door sedan was parked near a solar panel, and someone had painted *Clinton District Sheriff* on the front passenger door. The man had long arms and legs and a thin face that resembled a grasshopper. Muttering curses, he jerked open the door and flung Kate into the back seat. A rectangle of galvanized chain-link fence was bolted to the front seat, creating a little prison.

The man slid into the front seat, swiveled around, and peered through the chain-link barrier. Kate saw a silver star pinned to the breast pocket of his plaid flannel shirt.

"What's your name?"

"Kate Flores."

"Who are your parents?"

"I live with my aunt, Paloma Flores."

"Never heard of her. Are you from a Guard family, or are you Pledged?"

Kate didn't know what the man was talking about, so she stayed silent.

"Speak up!"

"Let me out of the car. I wasn't doing anything wrong."

"I'm Deputy Louis Vanderpol. The sheriff and I decide what's right or wrong in this district."

"It's just holograms of dead people. I wasn't bothering anyone."

Ignoring her, Vanderpol punched a number on his cell phone. "I just caught a kid running around Elysian Fields. No, a girl . . . ten or eleven years old. She's not from a local family. No problem. Meet you there."

As the sun came up over the tree line, Vanderpol drove his police car west on a narrow road. Peering through the spiderweb cracks in the side window, she saw white clapboard houses and small brick buildings—all of them separated by overgrown patches of grass. They passed a gas station and a liquor store selling whiskey.

The district police station was in a blue two-story house placed at the end of a one-way street. As the squad car got closer, Kate saw a dead man with a gunny sack over his head hanging from a rope on a plywood gallows.

"Who's that?"

"He used to be Billy Wilmont, then he stole a car."

"So you killed him?"

"Everyone and his dog knew that Billy broke one of the Ten Commandments. He had a short trial and a fast execution."

"Why is he still hanging there?"

"That's a lesson for the district. After forty-eight hours, the family can take him down."

Vanderpol turned off the road, then parked twelve feet away from the gallows. Holding her knapsack, Kate got out of the patrol car and looked up at the dead man hanging from the rope. A gust of wind made the body sway.

The police station was one large room with two desks and a gun rack filled with shotguns and assault rifles. At one end of the room, there was a cage built with sections of chain-link fence. For a few seconds, Kate thought she was going to be locked in the cage, and then Vanderpol motioned for her to sit on a folding chair.

"You want to go to the bathroom?"

"I want to get out of here."

"Don't talk that way to the sheriff. He'll lock you up and throw away the key."

A few minutes later, the entrance door squeaked open, and an older man walked in. Sheriff Breslow had a saggy face. His khaki pants hung loosely on his body, and stomach flab hung over his gun belt. After placing his shotgun on a desk, he circled Kate like a mechanic checking out a used car.

"So, you're our little trespasser." Breslow touched Kate's chin and forced her to look up. "Vanderpol and I know all the adults in this district and most of the kids. I've never seen you before."

Kate took a deep breath and began to talk quickly. "I'm Kate Flores from New York City. My parents died of Stem-flu and my aunt Paloma thought it would be safer if I left the city, so she sent me to live with my grandmother in Maine. Then my grandmother died from a heart attack, so a neighbor put me on the bus going to New York, but it was the wrong bus, so I got off and walked around in the dark and now I'm here with you."

"You done?" Breslow asked. "Is that it?"

"All you need to do is put me on a bus or a train heading to New York. My aunt will mail you the ticket money when I get there."

"No buses or trains stop here," Vanderpol said with a dry laugh. "We'd have to drive you to Plattsburgh."

Breslow sat down at his desk and used his cell phone. "Good morning, sir. Sorry to bother you. Would you mind dropping by the station house for a few minutes. Louis just found a kid running around Elysian Fields. She's a half-pint girl with a five-gallon story."

After the phone call, the two men ignored Kate and studied a list of all the single young women in the Clinton district. Apparently, Vanderpol wanted to get married, and Breslow was trying to narrow down his choices.

"Betty Dahlen."

"Too pretty for you. She'll marry a church elder."

"Ruth Benson."

"That's possible. Give her a try."

"Peggy Marsh?"

"Didn't she fall off a roof in a rainstorm?"

"She limps a little. One leg's shorter than the other."

"I think you got a chance there, Louis. You're a dream come true for a gimpy girl."

Kate heard a car pull up to the police station, and a middle-aged man carrying a black leather bag entered. The man wore a dark blue business suit with a small gold cross pinned to a lapel. His brown hair was oiled and combed back in a pompadour that made his forehead look bigger.

"You should be wearing a mask," the man said. "We're safe here in the districts, but this child could be a Stem-flu carrier."

"Sorry, Doctor."

The man pulled an e-mask out of his coat pocket and covered his mouth and nose. "What's your name, young lady?"

"Kate Flores."

"I'm Dr. Warren Edwards. Do you have a cold? Any coughing? Shortness of breath?"

"No. I just want to get out of here."

"You're a child. That means you must obey the adults who are here to guide and protect you. Let me see if you're a disease vector."

Edwards took a stethoscope and some other instruments out of his bag. He listened to Kate's heart, took her pulse, and pressed his fingers hard against the side of her neck. After sticking an electric thermometer into her ear, he asked Kate a rapid series of questions. *Do you cough in the morning? Does your nose drip blood?*

When Edwards was finished, he pulled off the mask and washed his hands in a sink. "I don't believe this child's story. What do you think, Breslow?"

The sheriff nodded quickly. "She's a tricky one."

Edwards returned to the center of the room and looked down at Kate. "No more games, young lady. You ran away from home for some reason and ended up in a graveyard. Tell us who you are, and Sheriff Breslow will call your parents."

"My aunt Paloma lives in New York City."

Looking annoyed, Dr. Edwards turned to Breslow. "Call the

sheriffs in the nearby districts and find out if they're looking for a runaway. While we're waiting for more information, Louis can park her with a Guard family. Aaron Carter and his wife are steady and respectable."

The sheriff nodded. "They have a son about the same age as our runaway."

Five minutes later, Kate was sitting in the front seat of Vanderpol's police car as they drove through Dannemora. The town didn't seem to have a garbage collector, and mounds of burned trash filled the road ditches. The only beautiful street was lined with sugar maple trees that created a bright red canopy of autumn leaves.

Passing another liquor store, they approached a sixty-foot-high concrete wall with guard towers placed at hundred-yard intervals. The immense size of this barrier and its bland gray color made Kate feel small.

"What's on the other side of the wall?"

"It used to be a maximum-security state prison. They closed it down during the pandemic."

"When you grabbed me outside the graveyard, you asked if I was a Guard or a Pledged. Is that because of the prison?"

Vanderpol nodded. "The people who had families living here in the old days call themselves 'Guards' even though there's no more prison. The church members who came here later call themselves 'The Pledged.' Dr. Edwards is a church elder and is pretty much the man in charge around here."

Kate tried to figure out adults, but sometimes they acted crazy. The town's population was separated into two groups—like kickball teams on a schoolyard. That made sense, but why was a dead body hanging from a rope outside the police station?

Zeno could have explained everything to her, but he remained in her knapsack and didn't speak. When the Nolands did something foolish, Zeno called them "touched" or "loony." Now she was captive in a town where the adults displayed an even higher level of craziness. What would Zeno call them?

"Barking mad," she whispered.

"What are you talking about?"
"Nothing."

35 | KATE AND ZENO

A MILE EAST of the prison, they passed two men repairing a pickup truck with the back axle held up on tree stumps. The car bumped over railroad tracks and entered a neighborhood with white colonial houses. The people who lived in these homes owned old-fashioned cars with tail fins and steel bumpers. Power cords led from the homes to the cars, which meant the modified vehicles were running on electric engines.

A front door opened, and a married couple emerged with their two daughters. The man wore a necktie, gray suit, and polished leather shoes while his wife had put on a knee-length overcoat and a pillbox hat. Their children exhibited the same old-fashioned appearance. Both girls wore jumpers, knee socks, and patent leather shoes.

"Are the church members the people who are all dressed up?"

Vanderpol laughed. "Smart kid. You figured it out. Some people call them 'suits' because the men wear suits and ties."

"Are you a Guard or a suit?"

"Sheriff Breslow and I were born here. My parents ran a dairy farm, and Breslow's father was head guard at the prison. The sheriff got pledged two years ago, and now I'm trying to join the church."

They continued east, passing old barns, rusty agricultural equipment, and rickety fences held together with twisted strips of wire. Deputy Vanderpol slowed down when they approached a row of cherry trees that had dropped their leaves. Chains dangled from one of the trees. Kate thought that they looked like extra-long handcuffs.

"What's hanging in the branches?"

"Those are the belly and leg chains that were used when they moved a maximum-security prisoner to a punishment cell. Some people display those chains to show that they come from a Guard family."

The police car bumped across a drainage ditch and followed a dirt driveway to a two-story farmhouse opposite a barn. As they got out, a young woman with a tired face stepped out onto the porch holding a curly-haired toddler.

"Morning, Becky. Is Aaron around?"

"He's working at the mine."

"This girl calls herself Kate Flores. I found her running around Elysian Fields. We can't track down her people and there's no place to lock her up, so Sheriff Breslow wants your family to keep her for a short time."

"What if I don't like that idea?"

"I'm being polite, Becky. Let's stay that way. She's just a ten-year-old girl. Can't be too much trouble." Touching the grip of his revolver, Vanderpol glared at Kate. "You're staying here until we come and get you. Run away again and we'll lock you up in a closet with a dead pig."

Vanderpol got back into his car and disappeared down the driveway. When he was gone, Becky placed her daughter on the grass and the little girl approached Kate.

"Bear."

Zeno's head was poking out of the top of her backpack. "No. It's a seal. A harp seal." Kate unzipped the backpack and took Zeno out. "Sometimes he talks."

Suddenly, Zeno spoke without his British accent. He sounded like a cheap toy who could recite only a few words. "Will you play with me?"

The little girl looked startled and then squealed with excitement. "He talks, Mommy! The seal talks!"

Becky smiled for the first time. "Lucy's dolls can't talk at all. You hungry, Kate?"

"Yes, ma'am."

"Come on in and eat."

Everything in the kitchen appeared to be old, rusty, or patched together—including a cast-iron stove. Becky tossed kindling into the fire box, then she mixed eggs, butter, and chopped onions into a cast-iron fry pan and shoved the pan into the oven. While the eggs cooked, she served gritty slices of corn bread on a cracked china plate.

Kate began to eat, and Lucy kept her eyes on Zeno. Whenever the little girl touched the seal's head, he repeated the same phrase: "Will you play with me?"

"Still hungry, Kate? Need any more food?"

"I'm okay."

"You look tired. If you want, you can lie on the couch in the parlor."

Kate slept for several hours on a saggy couch and opened her eyes when a skinny boy close to her age entered the room. He had a cowlick on the back of his head that refused to join the rest of his brown hair.

"I'm Luke. Mom said they caught you in the cemetery."

"I saw this weird light and wanted to check it out."

"I wouldn't worry about that. Every kid around here has snuck into the graveyard to see the holograms. I just got home from school, and it's time to do chores. Come with me."

The house had electric lights and a water pump, but they had to fill up the stove's wood box with logs and kindling. Working together, they fed the dog and harvested some apples, then Luke filled up a pail of water, and Kate followed him across a fenced-in pasture.

"Where you from?" Luke asked.

"Lots of different places. Right now, I'm trying to reach New York City."

"I've been to Plattsburgh . . . twice."

At the edge of the pasture, someone had planted a single solar panel on a pole. The cells powered an electric fence surrounding a battered aluminum trailer with flat tires. Inside the fenced area were about fifty white turkeys, gobbling to each other and pecking at the ground.

"We raise these birds for money or trade." Luke disconnected a power cord from the fence and stepped over the top wire.

"Do they live in the trailer?"

"That's where they roost at night. We move the fence and the trailer once a week so they get a fresh patch of grass for finding bugs and worms." Luke pointed to three long metal trays. "I dump cracked corn into the trays every morning and make sure they have water."

Luke filled a galvanized water dispenser, then reached beneath the trailer and pulled out a pump-action shotgun stored on top of a tire.

"Why do you have a gun?"

"I look for bobcats, foxes, and coyotes in the morning and the evening. They love to eat turkeys. Let's get the birds inside the trailer."

Luke unfastened the flap door cut into the side of the trailer and attached a board that the turkeys could use as a ramp. Then he circled the area with an old broom, coaxing the turkeys up the ramp while Kate opened and closed the flap door. Five minutes later, they switched jobs and Kate chased after the remaining birds while Luke shouted advice. Both were laughing when the final turkey scurried up the ramp.

"I wasn't much help," Kate said.

"Having you along made it fun."

Looking for the foxes hidden in the forest, they walked toward an orange sun touching the horizon. A gasoline-powered pickup truck was in the farmyard, and a wiry man wearing patched jeans and a faded T-shirt stood near the back, pulling out chunks of firewood.

"This is my dad," Luke said. "He just came home from work."

Aaron Carter seemed annoyed that Kate was standing in his front yard. "I don't know how long I'm going to be feeding you, but you got to know one thing . . . everyone works here."

"Kate's okay," Luke said. "She helped me fill the wood box and roost the birds."

The family ate green beans and buttered potatoes for dinner, and Lucy insisted that Zeno sit next to her. Whenever she touched Zeno's head, the seal would say, "Will you play with me?" like a toy.

The house had two kerosene lanterns, and Kate used one of them when she walked to the outhouse. Becky moved Lucy back to her old crib and Kate was given the child's bed. The little girl chattered about digging a big hole and then fell asleep.

The wind grew stronger, and the house creaked and cracked like an old rocking chair. Kate pulled Zeno beneath the quilt and held him against her chest.

"We can talk now. Lucy is asleep."

"It's good to be careful. If people find out I'm valuable, they might take me away from you."

"When did you learn to speak like a toy, Zeno? I never heard you talk that way."

"I once saw a television commercial advertising an early version of an Interactive Toy and remembered the voice."

"Do you remember everything, Zeno?"

"I've stored thousands of memories in my database, but I'm not like you. Humans create stories that explain their lives, but I have facts . . . with no stories."

"You're part of my story, Zeno. We're having a story together."

36 | WILSON

SHOCKED BY THE confrontation in the underground parking lot, Wilson spent a day locked up in his apartment. He threw away the clothes splattered with blood but avoided looking at the dead man's cell phone.

The next morning, he felt strong enough to return to the Trigon building. At the Priority Report meeting, Roberto gave him a fist bump and Raymond Felder praised his "skill and dedication." After the other analysts returned to their cubicles, Felder said that Howard Sebesky would contact him that evening to "tie up loose ends."

When he returned to his apartment that evening, Wilson asked his Shadow to find articles about the incident. A court-sanctioned officer could kick down doors and make arrests, but the media quickly discovered that the private cop killed by Detective Morrissey wasn't certified by a judge. At the twenty-four-hour point in the news cycle, the police department announced that the dead man was Darren Taylor, a former participant in the Element sports show that featured augmented humans punching each other unconscious and tossing limp bodies across the playing field. Taylor's left leg was crushed during a competition, and he was cut from his team.

Wilson switched on the holographic projector and waited for Howard Sebesky to appear in his living room. Eventually, he dozed off into a half sleep that ended when a luminous blue dot appeared in front of him. There were flashes of feet, hands, and mouth, and then Sebesky appeared, sitting in an office chair.

"Good evening, Wilson." The image wavered slightly and then became stable. "Raymond Felder told me what happened, and I also read several news stories. Why don't you give me a summary of the relevant facts."

"An augmented human named Darren Taylor killed Terrence Greene. Taylor broke Greene's neck and then ripped off Greene's arm so he could press the dead man's hand against a stolen computer's biometric pad. It's possible that Greene's death was connected to the collapse of an AI company called Cogito."

"Is there any factual evidence for this theory?"

"I feel that . . ."

The hologram wavered as Sebesky leaned forward in his chair. "My business decisions are not based on what someone *feels.*"

"Don't you want to know why a private cop was hired to find and kill Terry Greene?"

"You've solved the essential problem. The man's death wasn't caused by a nubot, and that information helps my long-range business goals. The five years of salary transferred to your bank account will provide you with safety, comfort, and pleasure."

"Thank you, Dr. Sebesky."

"Your hard work produced the right conclusion. Stay at Trigon or retire to a safe location. Enjoy the rest of your life."

37 | WILSON

CHECK THE BANK account again. Did they transfer the money?"

Will's voice remained calm and friendly. "I checked eight minutes ago. You really need to go to sleep, Wilson. But I realize that you're tired and annoyed."

"How do you know that?"

"Erratic or sudden movements of one's finger on a computer touchpad indicates anger."

"Stop acting like a therapist and check the account!"

"Of course. Whatever you wish." Silence for thirty seconds, and then a bank account balance appeared on the monitor. "You've just received a large sum of money."

Wilson checked the balance. After a lifetime of living from paycheck to paycheck, the sudden appearance of five years' salary felt like a financial miracle.

Now what? It didn't feel right to keep working at Trigon. He had spent most of his life dealing with bad news and didn't know how to react to good news.

When Brian Morrissey called the next morning, Wilson grabbed for the phone.

"I'm going to give you a free look at a new crime scene," the detective said. "I think it will interest you. If it leads to more work, I want to get paid. I'm texting you an address in Queens."

Wilson decided that it was okay to be curious if he was still working for Trigon. Maybe something had occurred that would sway his decision about the job.

"Send the address," he said and hung up the phone.

It felt like the stolen cell phone hidden in his coat pocket might set off alarms as he took a cab to Union Street in Queens. The block was lined with shabby redbrick buildings, and some apartment owners had replaced their windows with sheets of plywood. A uniformed cop was dozing in his squad car while Detective Morrissey leaned against the hood and wolfed down a sandwich.

"There he is!" Morrissey grinned. "You look like a law-abiding citizen who was saved by the brave actions of the New York City Police Department."

"You shot an aug in the back of the head."

"Don't be so negative, Wilson. Killing Darren Taylor really helped my career."

"Why am I here?"

"Another murder. I'm not in charge of this case, but a friend thought I might be interested. Follow me. The investigation team is already gone. We're just waiting around for the morgue van."

Wilson followed the detective into a four-story building. The elevator was broken, so they climbed up an emergency staircase to the third floor. A young police officer looked startled when they entered the apartment. He was searching the rooms for valuables and stuffing the loot into a gym bag.

"Relax, Driscoll. We don't want any of this crap. Always check under the mattress. Some people like to sleep on their cash."

Passing through a living room with a Spanish-language Bible resting on the coffee table, they entered the kitchen. A small middle-aged woman with braided black hair lay next to the stove. Her head had been twisted to the left, and one hand was extended as if she was reaching for something.

"Meet Paloma Flores. Broken neck. Dead at least four days. This building lacks heating, so the body doesn't stink that much, but it looks like mice have been nibbling her fingers."

"Why would Trigon Technology be interested in this murder?"

"Because Darren Taylor killed her."

"What?" Wilson felt like someone had just slapped him across the face. "How do you know?"

"Our system speed-searched through the surveillance footage taken by the camera mounted on the streetlight," Morrissey replied. "You can see Taylor arrive on his motorcycle and park outside the building."

"He accessed Green's computer, got this location, and came here."

"Exactly. But the murder victim wasn't building nubots or doing anything high-tech. She worked as a nanny and had a part-time job at the local elementary school. So why was she killed by a private policeman?"

Wilson stared at him, thinking. "Isn't it your job to find out?"

"Not really. We already know who killed her, so . . . case closed. But if Trigon wants to pay me more consultant money, I'd be glad to investigate and give you an answer."

"It's not going to happen."

"Are you sure? What about the house I want to buy on Staten Island?"

Looking around the room, Wilson saw a photograph of Paloma Flores kneeling beside a three-year-old girl who was clutching a plush seal toy. "Can I take this photograph?"

"It's free if you promise to take my next phone call. I'll give you a discount if it's a mass murder."

38 | JULIA AND DANIEL

JULIA HAD SPENT the last few days waiting to receive an administrative password to Dragon Lair from the retired tech lord Roy Kassam. She had tried to enter the simulation again, but the access door remained closed. This time, she opened a digital lock box for system maintenance and typed a variety of standard passwords that involved the word "dragon." When none of them worked, she detached the cable from her brain and returned to the reality of a Manhattan travel center.

First Class Lounge had a café with couches and easy chairs. After logging off with the travel hostess, she found Daniel sipping a fruit drink while he worked on his computer.

He looked up from his screen. "Any luck entering Dragon Lair?"

"I'm not going to get in without a password. Have you heard from Kassam?"

"Nothing. But I do have some news." Daniel shifted his computer around so that Julia could see the screen. "I found a website for E-Volve on the dark web. E-Volve members believe that augmented humans are the next step in evolution, and they hate androids that look or act human. Basically, they want people to be more like machines, but they don't want machines to look like people."

"Why would Bennett join a group like that?"

"I can't tell you that. But E-Volve members might know where Bennett is hiding. I've sent out a group message to everyone on my email list. Maybe someone will have a contact."

Julia ordered a latte made with synthetic milk, then returned to Daniel. "I'm not optimistic about entering Dragon Lair. We need to come up with some new ideas."

"When we met Detective Morrissey, he mentioned a man named Wilson Talley who works for Trigon Technology. Three days ago, Talley was attacked by an augmented human pretending to be a private policeman and Morrissey killed him. The news feed said that the aug killed Terry Greene."

"Did any of the articles mention Bennett?"

"Nothing. But Talley wants to talk to us. He's meeting us here for a conversation."

First Class Lounge had two rooms with haptic equipment that added touch sensations to your experience. When Julia ordered a second latte, she noticed that half the names on the haptic rooms waiting list were women.

"Are women having simulated sex in the haptic rooms?"

The lounge barista laughed. "I don't know about sex, but many of our customers have VR boyfriends."

Julia's cousin had a virtual boyfriend, and she talked about him as if he was real. The initial setup was free, but for an extra payment your boyfriend would send daily text messages and talk to you on the phone. Gradually, you purchased extra features so that your companion remembered your birthday, used your credit card to send flowers, and eventually ordered you a wedding ring.

Sipping her coffee, she sat next to Daniel. "Have you ever wanted a virtual girlfriend?"

"Never."

"You could design a simulation who looked like a movie star."

"I don't want a simulation. I want you."

A few minutes later, Wilson Talley entered the travel center. He wore a skinny black necktie and was older than everyone else in the room. Julia raised her hand, and he maneuvered his way around the lounge furniture.

"Julia? David? I'm Wilson Talley."

"Morrissey told us that you worked for Trigon," Daniel said. "Why would an information-for-sale company want to know who killed a nubot maker?"

"The usual reason . . . money." Talley sat down on a café chair. "The billionaire who owns Trigon wanted to make sure that Terrence Greene wasn't killed by an autonomous machine."

"Do you think Bennett Schroeder was in some way involved with this crime?"

"I don't think so. All I know is that he disappeared, and you haven't found him."

"If he's in a burrow somewhere, we need to track down both his body and his mind."

"I got a call from Detective Morrissey because he thought that I would pay for information about a second death. An older woman named Paloma Flores was murdered by the same private policeman who murdered Greene."

Julia glanced at Daniel, and he shook his head slightly. It suddenly felt like the world around them was becoming dark and violent.

"Why were Terrence Greene and this Paloma Flores killed?" she asked. "What's their connection?"

Wilson reached into his shoulder bag and pulled out a framed photograph of a little girl holding a plush toy seal. "Terry Greene created a start-up company called Cogito with Richard Collins and Emma Anderson. They had a child named Katherine, and Paloma was their nanny. This picture was taken of her six or seven years ago. Both her parents died in the pandemic. Terry and Paloma were murdered. I'm starting to think . . ."

"Someone wants to kill this child."

"That's possible. I only know what has happened. I don't know why."

"Is Trigon Technology involved with this?" Daniel asked.

"As of today, I am no longer working for Trigon. I found out what my boss wanted to know, but I'm not satisfied with the answer. Sometimes people can't turn away. If you want an explanation, you need to go deeper."

Daniel leaned forward. "We understand."

"Be careful when you're looking for Bennett Schroeder. If you hear anything about Richard and Emma's daughter, let me know."

39 | JULIA AND DANIEL

DANIEL WOKE UP early the next morning and closed the bedroom door slowly so that the hinges didn't squeak. When Julia pulled on her frayed bathrobe and shuffled into the kitchen, he silently handed her a cup of coffee. It was fake coffee, of course, but the caffeine was real. Julia sat in a patch of sunlight and watched Daniel fuss with their antique toaster.

"Are you ready to talk?" he asked.

"Sure . . . if it's good news. Bad news requires another cup of coffee."

"You'll be happy about this. I sent out a message to my contacts and asked if they knew anyone involved with Bennett Schroeder's E-Volve group. This morning, I got a response from a friend of mine."

"Do I know this person? Is he in the city?"

"Violetta Hernandez was part of my Death Catcher team. I haven't heard from her for several years. If we want to meet someone who belongs to E-Volve, she'll make the introductions tonight at a dance club called REAL. It's run out of an airplane hangar near Kennedy airport."

"Maybe she wants to see you solo."

"Violetta was never my girlfriend. Our team was like a family, Julia. We backed each other up, and that's why we survived."

An hour before midnight, they summoned a driverless cab and took the Brooklyn Bridge across the East River. Peering out a side window, Julia saw a three-quarters moon glowing above the city. Suspender cables hung downward from the bridge's main cables and looked like a grid of lines dividing the night sky. "Crossing," the cab murmured. "We're crossing . . ."

When the cab reached the airport area, it passed several cargo buildings and stopped on a side road. Julia and Daniel walked toward the lights and found a line of people waiting to get into the converted hangar.

Two augmented humans were working as bouncers outside the nightclub. Both were "partials"—wearing upper-body exoskeletons that covered their shoulders, chest, and arms. The exoskeletons protected them from bullets and knives and made them strong enough to knock out an attacker with one punch.

Daniel approached one of the bouncers and introduced himself. "Violetta Hernandez said we could meet her here."

The aug raised a two-way radio and spoke to his supervisor. "Some guy named Daniel wants to see the V-girl. Yeah. Okay. Got it." He lowered the radio and nodded. "Follow me."

A year ago, Julia and Daniel wore headsets in an augmented reality nightclub that resembled the lounge of the famous Algonquin Hotel. The bar was filled with computer-generated objects and overlays, but when Julia took off her headset to go to the women's room, she saw the reality—a converted pet shop in Queens.

REAL's gimmick was that no headsets were necessary because the nightclub was a physical re-creation of a 1970s disco. Following the bouncer, they entered a large main room where people dressed in seventies clothes were dancing to music blaring from giant speakers. The men wore bell-bottom pants with big-collar shirts. The women were squeezed into short sequined dresses and had blow-dried their hair.

Directly behind the DJ booth was a massive video screen playing short segments of computer-generated Homeless Joe videos. Julia saw clips of Victim Joe being beaten to death and burned alive, followed by Demon Joe blowing up a gas station and tossing a baby into a dumpster.

The hangar was divided in half by a six-foot wall constructed out of plywood looted from abandoned homes. A second bouncer stood guard at the entrance to the private suites, and he nodded when Daniel mentioned Violetta's name. "Ms. Hernandez is in Number Fourteen . . . the Hawaii Room. Stand in front of the surveillance camera and she'll let you in."

The private suite area contained sixteen double-wide house trailers set on frames. Each trailer had covered windows and was connected to electric cables that snaked across the floor. Julia decided that this was the most impressive aspect of REAL: the promoters had bribed enough people to get a reliable source of power.

It got darker as they left the dance area, and it was difficult to see the number tags on the trailers. Julia tapped the flashlight icon on her phone and saw that the screen was flashing. "My phone says no reception."

Daniel checked his phone. "Yeah. Me too. Let's not worry about that right now. This trailer is the Hawaii Room."

He pressed a buzzer as the CCTV camera mounted over the door panned back and forth. When the lock clicked open, they entered the trailer.

Warm, humid air surrounded them, and Julia smelled the musky scent of monkey flowers. They stood on a patch of ceramic tile, surrounded by beach sand. The end of the trailer was concealed by bamboo, birds of paradise, and other tropical plants that surrounded four rattan chairs and a white table.

Violetta Hernandez sat in one of the chairs with a book on her lap. Daniel's friend had a broad face and a flat nose. Her hair was woven into cornrow braids with four rows of raised plaits. Violetta wore white linen pants and a sleeveless undershirt that revealed tattoos on her muscular arms and shoulders. A flowering vine twined around one arm, and a tattoo snake circled around the other.

"*Capitán!*" Violetta gave Daniel a big smile. "Don't let the cold air in! Close the door and take off your coats and shoes! You can walk barefoot on the beach in the Hawaii Room!"

Daniel removed his shoes and stepped onto the sand. It took longer for Julia to unlace her work boots.

"You look a little older, Daniel. Guess I'm older, too." Violetta stood up and gave him a hug. "But you're still alive. Sometimes stubborn people like you don't survive."

They broke apart, and Violetta stood with her hands on her hips staring at Julia as if someone had just brought in a new tropical plant. "And you're the girlfriend, right? We all wondered who our *capitán* would end up with."

"I'm Julia Lau. His partner."

"Partner? Sounds serious. Do you know how crazy-brave he is? Probably not."

Julia stepped onto the fake beach with her bare feet. The floor was wired with heat coils, and the sand was warm.

"Sit down! Make yourself comfortable!" Violetta waved them over to a table that held a stack of books, a notebook computer, and a cocktail pitcher. "I knew you were coming, so I ordered some mai tais. It's fake lime juice and bootleg rum, but it tastes pretty good."

Daniel sat next to his friend while Julia took the chair at the end of the table. Now that she had adjusted to the light and warmth of the room, she noticed details. All the books on the table were about famous painters: Matisse, Goya, and Picasso. Hidden speakers offered the sounds of distant waves collapsing onto a beach as the wind rustled through leaves.

"We've never been here before," Daniel said. "Lots of people in the dance area."

"It's always busy on Disco Night."

"The staff knows you."

"I sit in this room every Wednesday and Friday night. It's a secure location because I can see who's knocking on the door before I let them in. If I make a big sale, an aug wearing body armor will walk me outside to a driverless cab."

"Why don't our phones work?" Julia asked.

"Good question." Violetta pointed to a black steel box on the floor that was the size of a toaster oven. "That's a jammer that blocks any kind of wireless communication."

"You don't want phone calls?"

"The jammer makes it impossible to track my phone or any visitor's phone. A few bad boys know that I handle a lot of money. If they could track my cell and know my location, I'd be vulnerable to a smash and grab."

"What are you selling?" Julia asked.

Violetta turned to Daniel and grinned. "She probably thinks I'm a surge dealer, *Capitán.* Don't know how she got that idea."

"Everything is for sale these days."

"Forget drugs. I sell paintings by famous artists. Lots of rich people died in their apartments during the pandemic. Family members grabbed the money and jewels, and the building's doormen took the art." Violetta held up the book on her lap. "Right now I'm learning about this French guy named Matisse. I got one of his paintings stashed in a closet. Think I'll hang it up in my bedroom."

"Daniel said that you know something about E-Volve."

"Yeah. It's an underground cyborg group. One of the bouncers who works here, a guy named Spivey, is a member."

"So how do we find Spivey?" Julia asked. "What does he look like?"

"Right now he's guarding the DJ booth. Spivey's an augmented human with a 'half side' . . . an exoskeleton covers his right shoulder, arm, and hand." Violetta rattled the ice cubes in her cocktail glass. "You stay here, Julia. If Spivey likes *mi capitán,* he might take you to an E-Volve gathering."

"Thanks, Vi." Daniel returned to the patch of tile and pulled on his shoes. "I'll talk to him and see what happens."

40 | JULIA AND DANIEL

When the door clicked shut, Violetta grabbed the pitcher and refilled Julia's glass. "Okay. It's just the two of us. Girl-talk time. How'd *you* get him, Julia? I was kind of in love with Daniel when we were living on the island. I know that he was Mister Math Genius in college, and I dropped out of high school. But when Daniel gave an order, I obeyed him. That was unusual for me."

"Did you, uh . . ."

"Sleep with him? No way. Daniel never had a girlfriend, but that doesn't mean that we weren't close. At the end of a workday, everyone on the team stripped off our protective gear and we saw each other naked. In the middle of a death world, we had created a family."

"I know almost nothing about Daniel's time as a Death Catcher. He refuses to talk about what happened."

"But you knew about me, right? And Rollo, of course. Daniel and Rollo risked their lives for each other."

"I didn't know about you or anyone else on your team."

Surprised, Violetta put her glass down on the table. "That's okay. I understand. When you're starting a new relationship, you don't want to talk about your past life in hell."

"Sometimes it feels like I'm living in a room full of ghosts."

"Being a Death Catcher is like getting a tattoo that you can never burn away."

"Maybe you could tell me. . . ."

Violetta shook her head. "I don't know what Daniel was thinking when we were stuffing bodies into bags. The biggest mystery in the world is what's going on in another person's skull."

They both stayed quiet as sound from the dance floor speakers leaked through the walls. Sometimes two people talked to fill the empty space. Julia stared at her bare feet on the warm sand and waited for something to happen.

"All I can do is tell you what happened to me. Is that okay?"

"Thank you, Violetta."

"City Health organized the Death Catcher teams when firemen and cops began dying from Stem-flu. The people in charge needed suicide squads no one cared about, so they asked for volunteers from the prison system. I was in a women's camp set up at a high school football stadium in Yonkers. There was a sign-up sheet on the bulletin board near the prison kitchen. For three days, people kept signing their name and then crossing it out when their friends said they were crazy."

"But you didn't back down?"

"People were dying in the camp, and it seemed safer to move around the city. One morning, they pulled me from the roll call with two *putas* who had been caught stealing cars. The guards loaded us in a van and drove to South Ferry, where the tourists used to catch a boat to the Statue of Liberty. They parked outside the Battery Maritime Building, and we waited around until a second van arrived with seven male prisoners. That's when a new set of guards wearing hazmat suits with respirators removed our leg chains and handcuffs.

"The Maritime Building is a big old structure with a long balcony over the ferry entrance. As we stood there in the sun, a guard with a hunting rifle slung over his shoulder stepped out onto the balcony. He was about fifty yards away from us, so he didn't need a hazmat suit.

"'Prisoners! Look up here! Right here!' he shouted.

"This guard had a big mouth and a bald head. I figured he was the kind of guy who shaved his skull every morning because he thought the ladies loved that look. The hunting rifle had a scope like he wanted to hunt deer in Manhattan. The bald guy gazed down at us for a minute or so, and then he began his speech.

"'I'm Department of Corrections Lieutenant Anthony Barbieri, and I run the fatality removal program for New York City. Ever wondered what God looked like? Your question has been answered because I'm the God of Governors Island. If you join our group, I will have control over your life. Don't believe me? Look down at your hands. No belly chains. No cuffs. This is your big chance. Run for it. I'll give you a ten-second head start. Hell, make it thirty seconds. Let's see how brave you really are.'

"Barbieri didn't point his rifle or anything. He didn't have to. Because every prisoner there knew he would use it. That bald *pelotudo* strutted back and forth a few times and then nodded.

" 'Good choice,' he said. 'Are we clear? Do you understand your new reality? All of you have volunteered, but it doesn't mean you're a Death Catcher. My staff will accompany you to Governors Island and march you to the Admiral's House so you can be evaluated by the squad leaders. It's their choice. Not mine. If they don't pick you . . . you're gone.'

"I was thinking hard about Barbieri's rifle as the guards led us onto the ferry. I didn't feel like hanging out with anyone, so I walked to the bow and gazed across the water at Governors Island. The moment the ferry pulled away from the dock, two sharks appeared. You could see their fins cutting through the water as the boat chugged across the harbor.

"This big prisoner named Rollo stood beside me. When he saw the sharks, he spat into the water. 'That's what happens to us if we don't get picked.'

" 'What are you talking about?'

" 'You think they're going to bring us back to our prison camps? It's too much trouble. One bullet in your skull and you're shark breakfast.'

"Governors Island was where the Dutch landed when they first came to New York, then it was a British fort, then an American fort, then an arsenal and military prison. Eventually, the army took it over and built houses and barracks, then they handed the island off to the Coast Guard, who gave it to the city. What all that history meant was that Governors Island looked like a weird little village with no bodegas or liquor stores. Lieutenant Barbieri lived in the Admiral's House, a big place with white columns out front and two spiked cannons near the front door.

"When they first started using Death Catchers, most prisoners died within thirty days, but everything changed a month before Rollo and I arrived. Daniel and three other survivors had approached the guards and proposed a whole new system. Instead of everyone living together, the prisoners would be separated into teams that occupied separate two-story houses."

"One sick person would only infect their work squad?"

"You got it. Each group would be run by a team leader who made all the big decisions. If you didn't obey your leader, they pulled you out of your house and took away your face mask. But I didn't know any of that on my first day. I was just one of ten prisoners marched over to the Admiral's House. We waited around for a while, then eight leaders showed up to scout new talent.

"The other two women had bought makeup in the Yonkers camp so they could look cute for the interview. It was clear what their job was going to be until they caught the virus and died. A team leader named Big Dog asked me if I liked men and I said, 'Not especially.'

" 'You got no choice on this island.'

" 'Maybe it's true,' I said. 'But the first time I get my hand on a blade, it goes straight into your heart.'

"After Big Dog stomped off looking angry, Daniel strolled over and asked why I was in prison.

" 'Burglary with intent to commit a felony. Multiple counts.'

" 'Can you pick locks?'

" 'Not all. But most.'

" 'I'm Daniel Blake,' he said. 'Want to join our team?'

"I said yes, so now I was part of Daniel's team. The first thing I did was walk over to Rollo and talk him into joining us."

Violetta stopped to refill both cocktail glasses, and Julia sipped the mixture of sugar and alcohol. "So, the eight teams picked up bodies?"

"Yeah. If you were wealthy, your family paid for a coffin and private burial. If you were poor, they wrapped your body in a bedsheet and left you on the sidewalk. If we had Outside Duty, we drove around the city picking up bodies and dumping them into the back of rental trucks. Outside Duty was like lifting sacks of rotten meat. But it was nothing like CARE. Three or four times a week we'd get that assignment."

"What's CARE?"

"Corpse Action Requiring Entry. People would die alone, or

sometimes an entire family would perish inside an apartment. When the neighbors smelled bodies, they'd call the police."

"And that's why Daniel wanted a burglar?"

"Right. Because I could pick the locks. Anyway . . . I took a ferry to the island, got chosen by Daniel, and the next morning Rollo and I stood outside in our underwear as Daniel showed us how to put on protective clothing. First you'd pull on your inner gloves, then yellow coveralls, then your black rubber rain boots. Next came a surgical cap, goggles, medical mask, and respirator, then outer gloves that were duct-taped to our wrists. When everyone was ready, we'd waddle across the island like a mob of yellow penguins and stand outside Liggett Hall. At eight a.m., Barbieri came out and gave each team leader a printed list of addresses."

"It must have been exhausting to wear all that protective equipment."

"You couldn't take the suit off for the whole day, so people pissed in their pants. Walking upstairs, you'd sweat and itch, and you couldn't touch your face.

"After assignments, we'd take the ferry to the city, pick up our trucks, and go to work. The guards feared the virus, so no one watched us until the end of the day when we ended up at Hart Island. We'd see an address on our list and drive to an apartment building or a brownstone. I'd try to pick the lock. If I wasn't successful, we'd smash down the door. Half the time, neighbors would be waiting in the hallway because they wanted to rush in to grab money, liquor, and canned food, but when they got a whiff of the dead, they'd run away. A decomposing body gives off an ammonia smell that overwhelms you. Leave some raw chicken in the sun, then come back three days later. Dead people stink like that, only ten times worse.

"Once we found an old man who died with rosary beads threaded through his fingers. Several times we bagged an entire family, including children. The crucial factors were rats, flies, and how long the body had been lying there. Fresh bodies smell like shit. Then they bloat up like a balloon, splitting their clothes and showing their teeth. A couple days later, the skin turns black and this foul yellow liquid leaks out."

Violetta's voice wavered and her hands trembled as she kept talking with a calm voice like a hotel maid talking about stained sheets and pillows scattered across the floor.

"Daniel was your leader. What did you think about that?"

"Everyone on our team was a convicted criminal, and the guy leading us was a math genius who expected us to follow his rules. Two gang members on our team had murdered people, and I didn't think Daniel would last more than a couple of weeks."

"Why didn't they kill him?"

"Gradually, the bad guys realized that Daniel cared about us. He was smart and organized and a little bit crazy. Other groups perished, but he kept us alive. One way we were different involved looting. If you found jewelry in the apartment, you gave it to Daniel. On Saturday night, we received one thousand imaginary dollars so we could bid on different items. Everyone got drunk while Daniel ran the auction."

"What did you do with the cash?"

"That also ended up in Daniel's backpack. Some of it was our daily bribe to Lieutenant Barbieri and the other guards. More bribes were paid to the city employees who ran the vehicle pool so we always got the best trucks. But most of the money was paid to black-market hustlers selling rubber boots and respirator filters. Kiddie pools cost hundreds of dollars."

"You mean the backyard swimming pools for children?"

"We filled a kiddie pool with water and bleach and stood in it while stripping off our protective gear. That was tough on the lungs. My throat hurt and I lost my sense of taste for two years, but I didn't catch Stem-flu."

"Because of Daniel?"

"That's right. When we were working, he kept saying 'Follow procedure' and 'Show respect.' Follow procedure meant don't do nothing stupid that would expose you to the virus. Show respect was all about the dead. Other teams would stick a cigarette butt into a corpse's mouth. We didn't do that shit. What made me sad was bagging up all the children. Sometimes a parent would pin a note on their clothes, something like: *This is our Rosa. She was an angel.*"

"And you cried?"

"You can't cry wearing safety equipment. It fogs up the goggles. If things got bad, Daniel would sing this old song by a guy named Stephen Foster.

> *"Beautiful Dreamer, wake unto me,*
> *Starlight and dewdrops are waiting for thee;*
> *Sounds of the rude world heard in the day,*
> *Lull'd by the moonlight have all passed away."*

Violetta took a deep breath and began crying with gasping sobs. A few minutes passed, and then she blew her nose and forced a smile.

"Don't worry about me. I'm okay. Nowadays I sit here on a fake tropical beach, hustling deals for beautiful paintings and trying not to get robbed. I'm making enough money to buy my own apartment. Got a girlfriend with a kind heart who puts up with me. But these memories keep pushing their way into my thoughts, and they won't go away."

"Everyone who survived the pandemic has bad memories. But what happened to you and Daniel is in a different category."

"Toward the end of our time on the island, Daniel did something that was crazy-brave. I still don't know why he lived while other people died."

"Perhaps there's no explanation."

"Maybe a group of people survive every disaster so humanity can remember and figure things out. After I was paroled, I wandered around the city talking to myself, then this Samoan guy named Fetu gave me a book that changed everything."

"The Bible?"

"I want facts, not faith. *The Truth* is written by someone who calls himself Nada Real. The book proves that we are artificial intelligences existing in a virtual reality simulation just like the Over World."

"And what makes you think it's true?"

Violetta held up her cell phone. "There's more processing power in my phone than NASA had during the moon landings. It's a big universe, and somewhere an advanced civilization has developed super technology. Once you figure that out, everything starts to make sense. Human beings suffer because a world filled with happy people is boring. Nobody wants to watch Adam and Eve in the Garden of Eden. Until the snake appears, nothing interesting happens."

"You've thought this out."

"It's the only explanation that makes sense. The writer of *The Truth* thinks there are only two possibilities. We're either lab rats in a giant experiment, or maybe we exist to provide entertainment for the master programmers. Forget about reincarnation. If our world provides a good enough story, then we'll get a sequel."

The computer beeped and Daniel's face appeared on the screen. "Tell Julia to come outside. I'm here with Spivey and he wants to meet her."

Smiling, Violetta switched off the image. "Better get your boots on, Julia."

Julia sat down on the warm sand and pulled on her wool socks. "Thank you for everything, Violetta. You've really helped me."

"Daniel saved my life. I'll always be there for him. Call me if he gets into trouble."

41 | JULIA AND DANIEL

SPIVEY TURNED OUT to be a skinny young man with a weak chin who had gotten his brain attached to a motorized exoskeleton that covered his right shoulder, arm, and hand.

"There's going to be an E-Volve meeting tonight. Daniel said that you two wanted to come with me."

"That's right."

"Our meetings used to be open to the public, but it's changed. An augmented private policeman killed a nubot maker on the Lower East Side, and two nights ago, the aug was killed by a regular cop in an underground parking lot."

Julia tried not to smile. "Yes, I read about that."

"Our leaders are worried about a government crackdown, so we're trying to keep a low profile. Possible new members must have one person in their group who is augmented. Can I see your data port?"

Julia bent her head down and pushed her hair to one side so that her data port was visible. "Is this acceptable?"

"Looks good. Let's go."

Spivey pulled on a black raincoat that covered his partial armor, and they got into a driverless cab waiting outside the nightclub.

"Do you go to sleep wearing the armor?" Julia asked.

"You wear it constantly when it first gets attached to your nervous system. It takes three or four months for your brain to fully connect to the CPU in your armpit."

"And then the exoskeleton responds to commands from your brain?"

"Your brain tells your physical arm and the skeleton armor to make the same motion. They work together. The exo is an extension of your body."

Hidden motors whirred as Spivey leaned forward and looked out the side window at a street sign. "We're getting close to the meeting site. Attach a cable to your data port so they can see it at the door."

Bacteria on a connector could cause a brain infection, so Julia always carried a short trunk cable with a sterile ending. As their cab crunched through mounds of street trash, Julia stripped off a plastic seal, inserted the connector into her data port, and draped the remaining nine inches of cable over her right ear.

"Looks good," Spivey said. "You're one of us, but you don't know it yet."

The GPS on Julia's phone showed that they were in East New York, a poor Brooklyn neighborhood that had lost most of its residents during the pandemic. All the streetlights were shot out, and they passed a bus shelter tagged with graffiti.

"You guys could have picked a friendlier place for a meeting," Daniel said.

Spivey raised his armored hand. "Nobody messes with E-Volve. Augs with full exoskeletons can take a bullet."

"Approaching your destination," the cab announced and stopped in front of a ten-foot-high concrete block wall with razor wire twisted around the top edge. A large sign announced that they had reached a junkyard called Auto Heaven.

"It's okay to talk to people, but don't take photos with your phone. Don't call me Spivey at the meeting. My E-Volve name is Neptune."

"Why the pseudonym?"

"It's best to stay anonymous. We augs hate humanoid nubots, and the government doesn't want a repeat of the Taxi Riots."

There was a line of people waiting to get into the junkyard, and they had to walk past a cage filled with rottweilers barking at the intruders. An aug with a partial exoskeleton guarded the entrance gate and blocked their way.

"Good to see you, Neptune. Are these friends of yours?"

"Yes. Possible new members."

The guard noticed the cable dangling from Julia's ear and waved them through. White light from high-pressure sodium bulbs was reflected off the windshields and engine parts stored in wooden racks or stacked on concrete.

Some of the E-Volve members wore exoskeletons to increase their strength and speed. A second group was attached to electric eyes that viewed other frequencies on the electromagnetic spectrum. Infrared-sensitive eyes could see the different patches of heat radiating from a human body. If the temperature suddenly went up, it meant the other person was nervous and probably not telling the truth.

Spivey reached a patch of asphalt near a rack of drive shafts that looked like petrified dinosaur bones. A video screen was set up behind a large wood crate held shut by a steel cable.

"What's inside?" Julia whispered to Daniel. "It looks like Pandora's box."

The caged dogs kept howling as a young woman with dyed white hair and pale skin entered the circle of light. An aug knelt on one knee, and she used his bent leg as a step to climb onto the box. The woman wore black leather pants and an E-Volve T-shirt beneath a green car coat. But the most striking aspect of her appearance was an electric eye held by a braided gold web centered on her forehead. A thin cable led from the eye to the data port in the back of her skull. The third eye fed visual data directly into her brain.

The white-haired woman looked out at the crowd and smiled. "Good evening. I'm Cerium. I want to welcome old and new friends to a New York City E-Volve gathering. Our group is part of an international movement of committed individuals who defend humanity and support each other's transformations. The meeting tonight is a story divided into two acts. I'm going to describe our goals and then we'll have a demonstration.

"Augmented humans are the next step in human evolution. We will fight any attempt to make machines more like humans while we use technology to increase our knowledge, perception, and strength."

Julia looked around her and checked out the crowd. Several augmented humans were nodding. They were the future. Everyone else would be left behind.

"The growing power and sophistication of technology are inevitable, but that doesn't mean we should betray our species. Look around you. In every way, we are being replaced by humanoids. But rather than destroying these machines, we give them disguised as toys to children and don't object when a human is replaced by a nubot at work. When you talk to some foolish citizen about this issue, they inform you that a particular machine is their 'friend.' But sentient machines don't care about humans. You're simply an object who generates data."

Motors and gears made clicking sounds as the armored augs moved their bodies. Electric eyes glowed as they focused on Cerium.

"In order to protect our species from extinction, we need to discard the fantasy that a nubot is worthy of our emotions. Everyone here tonight needs to step forward and destroy their attachment to these *things.*"

Cerium jumped off the box, and a half-armored aug approached with bolt cutters. The electric eye at the center of Cerium's forehead seemed brighter, more intense.

"Show it. Live it. Say it. They are not me."

The augs repeated her words. "They are not me."

"Louder!"

"They are not me!" the crowd screamed, and people jabbed the air with their fists.

Cerium nodded to the young man holding the bolt cutter. He severed the cable and pulled away the top of the box. Something moved inside, and Julia took a step to the left so she could get a better view. She saw a tuft of brown hair, then eyes, nose, and face. Slowly, a humanoid nubot stood up and stared out at the crowd.

Everyone who lived in New York recognized him immediately. About ten years ago, the city had fired all the subway station agents who once sat in plexiglass booths and helped customers with problems. They were replaced with nubots that displayed four different appearances and personalities.

The machine in the box was Station Agent Version #2, a white male in his forties named Ernie who was programmed to tell lame jokes or chat about the weather and sports. Ernie's mechanical eyes surveyed the crowd and sent the information to his central processing unit. "Wow. There are a lot of people here tonight. Is there a baseball game? Are they handing out free money in Central Park?"

Someone in the crowd shouted, "You aren't human, Ernie!" But the nubot kept smiling. "So how can I help you? Does anyone need directions?"

Cerium unbuttoned her coat, reached inside, and pulled a ball-peen hammer out of her belt. She took two steps toward Ernie and hit him in the upper back. The nubot jerked forward, but he didn't fall over. "I have a problem," he said. "Please call MTA repair."

The crowd pulled out the hammers they carried in shoulder bags or in leather holsters. A young woman ran forward and bashed Ernie in the face with her hammer. Then everyone else followed—striking his chest and arms. The nubot fell forward out of the box, and people gathered around the machine. Julia heard cracking sounds, and then the bot stopped moving.

With a triumphant look on her face, Cerium raised her right hand and the junkyard's lights snapped back on. The violent energy of the crowd melted away, and Spivey went over to chat with his friends.

"Not exactly a fun crowd," Daniel murmured to Julia. "What would they think about our electric toaster?"

"It doesn't talk to us."

"Good point. So, what's our next move?"

"Let's find out if anyone knows Bennett Schroeder."

Cerium was surrounded by fans who wanted to touch phones with their leader. When the last E-Volve member headed for the gate, Julia and Daniel approached her.

"Great speech, Cerium. Now I understand why our friend is involved with your group. We're looking for him, but he's not here tonight."

"What did he call himself? No one uses their real name here."

"We don't know his E-Volve name." Daniel showed her the ID card they had taken from Bennett's bedroom. "But this is what he looks like."

Cerium studied the photo and nodded. "That's Pathfinder. He was an active member for a few years, and then he got weird."

"What do you mean by that?"

"He became obsessed with finding the Death Field. You know what that is, right?"

Julia nodded. "Sometimes it's mentioned in online chat groups. There's supposed to be a location in the Over World where a wire-head with a direct neural connection could die. The Death Field isn't an online shooter game. You die for real."

"I kept asking Pathfinder how that was supposed to happen, but he never came up with an explanation."

"You didn't believe him?"

"Of course not. The Death Field doesn't exist. It's just another Internet fairy tale to distract people from what's really going on."

"Our friend might have some psychological problems," Daniel said. "He doesn't answer email, and he's switched off his cell. Do you know any other way to contact him?"

"Let me see if I still have his number." Cerium took out her phone and found a number, and Julia photographed a digital image. "He's not in our group anymore, so there's no need to protect his privacy."

"We just want to see if he's okay."

"When he was with us, he was going in the right direction. Now he's lost his way."

Two augs approached Cerium, and Daniel and Julia began walking toward the gate.

"I thought this job would be easy," Daniel said. "But every time we learn something, we fall deeper into a rabbit hole."

"We need to keep focused on our goal." Julia compared the phone number that the Schroeders had given them with the number Bennett used with the E-Volve group. "Take a look, Daniel. They don't match. Bennett had one cell phone for his parents and a second phone when he called his friends. If we can track that personal number, we're going to find him."

42 | JULIA AND DANIEL

SPIVEY WAS GOING to a bar with his friends, so they left him at the junkyard and took a driverless cab back to Manhattan. As the cab passed beneath streetlamps, Daniel's face was absorbed by shadows, then reappeared in flashes of light.

Violetta's description of what happened with the Death Catchers pushed through Julia's thoughts. It was old-fashioned to call anyone a hero, but Daniel's actions were both moral and brave. *I love him,* she thought. *But do I really know who he is?*

The basement boiler was broken, and their apartment was as cold as the street. Julia pulled on flannel pajamas and crawled into bed. She heard Daniel moving around in the darkness, checking the locks on the doors and windows. Break-ins were common in their neighborhood, and the police took twenty minutes to respond to a phone call. Daniel had built a zip gun that fired shotgun shells out of a steel pipe. He took it out of the bedroom dresser and placed it on the night table.

"Want a hot water bottle?"

"I'm okay."

Daniel sat on the bed, and Julia looked up at him. "Violetta is a good person."

"Yes. We went through a lot together."

"She told me about living on Governors Island and picking up bodies in the city, but she didn't say much about you. Something bad happened toward the end of the pandemic. Do you want to talk about that?"

"That period of my life was like living on Mars."

"It feels like you're carrying your past around like a weight hanging from your neck. That weight will always be there if you try to keep it secret."

Daniel squeezed his lips together as if words were trying to force their way out. Then he took a deep breath and started talking.

"When the pandemic began to fade, there were fewer bodies to pick up in the city. One afternoon, Violetta, Rollo, and I drove our truck to the East Thirty-Fourth Street Pier. We loaded the truck onto a barge and were towed to Hart Island. It's not a beautiful place . . . just a chunk of rock and weeds near the entrance to the East River. There used to be a prison on the island that left a few abandoned buildings, a brick chimney, and spools of rusty barbed wire. When the barge reached the dock, we drove our truck up Cemetery Hill at the north end of the island. They had an earthmover on the island, and it had just dug a new burial trench. A half dozen guards were sitting around as Lieutenant Barbieri watched us from a wooden tower."

"Why was he there? No one was going to escape."

"It was all about the money we looted from apartments. Barbieri wanted to get paid directly so the other guards wouldn't steal from him. We drove our truck up to the trench, and I walked over to the tower to give a wad of cash to Barbieri's assistant. Then I returned to the trench to make sure that Violetta and Rollo were placing the bodies in rows. That was when I realized that one of the body bags was moving, so I returned to the tower.

" 'Excuse me, Lieutenant Barbieri. A wrapped-up body is moving. I think one of the teams grabbed an unconscious victim and that person is still alive.'

" 'Bullshit,' he said. 'It's just rigor mortis.'

" 'A body doesn't wiggle around with rigor mortis. Let's pull the bag out.'

" 'No way, Blake. It's dangerous.'

" 'A person is alive, sir.'

"Holding his rifle, Barbieri leaned out of the tower and looked down at me. 'Does this place look like a hospital? Do you see any doctors or nurses waiting around to take care of a sick person? Only guards, Death Catchers, and corpses are allowed on Hart Island. Which means that wrapped-up chunk of meat is dead.'

"When I returned to the trench, I saw the bag move again, so I pulled out my knife, jumped into the pit, and cut through the heavy plastic. I saw white hair and then a face. It was an old lady who opened her eyes and took a breath.

"I turned around and shouted to Rollo, 'Throw me a rope!'

" 'Nobody's throwing a rope!' Barbieri yelled. 'You got two choices, Blake. Crawl out of the pit. Or lie down beside her.'

"Barbieri was going to kill me, but I couldn't leave her there. When something like this happens, you know what's right and wrong.

" 'Let me make your decision,' Barbieri shouted. And then he raised his rifle and fired. The bullet hit the old lady in her face and the back of her skull exploded."

"Why didn't he kill you?"

"I was spared because of the bribe money. Our team paid the most to the guards, and Barbieri didn't want to destroy the cash machine. That's why no one shot Rollo when he threw down a rope and pulled me out of the pit.

"I had the dead woman's blood splattered all over me, so I stood alone on the bow of the ferry boat back to Governors Island. After everyone else had been sanitized, I stripped off my protective clothing and Violetta sprayed me with a garden hose. Usually, we'd get dressed right away, but this time I sat down on the tarp and shivered."

"You were living in a nightmare."

"I knew that you wanted me to describe what happened on the island, but I couldn't explain how it changed me. Searching for Bennett Schroeder has triggered a lot of thoughts. You have a direct neural connection just like Bennett. If you wanted to escape this world, you could be lying in a burrow while your mind lived in a simulation."

"I'm never going to do that."

"You're always quiet and distant after you cross over for five or six hours. The Over World makes you question our analog world."

"That's true."

"Working as a Death Catcher challenged the way I saw reality. When I was released from the island, everything around me seemed false and unreal. I felt like a man who had fallen off a cargo ship in the middle of the ocean. Yes, you're alive, but you're swimming around looking for something to hold on to."

She reached out and took his hand. "What's real is that I love you."

"And I love you. If you weren't in my life, I'd float away."

Neither of them spoke for what felt like a long time, and then Julia pulled back the quilt. "Come under the covers."

On a cold night in the unheated apartment, their two bodies created a comfortable pocket of warmth beneath the quilt. In the distance an ambulance wailed like a banshee announcing a death, and then the noise faded away.

43 | KATE AND ZENO

Aaron left for work early in the morning, and Becky fed the children corn bread and milk from the family's one-horned cow.

"Got to feed the birds," Luke announced. He slung the shotgun over his shoulder and picked up a sack of cracked corn. The turkeys were already awake when they reached the old trailer and opened the door. Bickering and pecking at each other, the big white birds hopped down the ramp, then gathered around Luke while he refilled the feeding trays. Luke concealed his shotgun beneath the trailer and reattached a wire to the electric fence.

"Now what do we do?"

"It's time for school. There's nothing to do at home, so why don't you come with me."

"How do we get into town? Is there a school bus?"

"My family owns lots of bikes."

Inside the barn, they found a pile of old bicycles that had been cannibalized for replacement parts. Luke gave her a blue cruiser bike, and he picked a red version. It was difficult to find bicycle tubes and tires, so Aaron had cut thick strips of rubber and glued them around the wheel rim.

A few minutes later, they were rattling down a dirt road on the bikes. Kate smelled the harsh scent of burning plastic and saw a plume of black smoke rising from the trees.

"Is the forest on fire?"

"Nah. The smoke comes from the mine where my dad works with Uncle Marcus. Follow me. I'll show you."

The burning smell got stronger as she followed Luke down a dirt road that cut through the forest. A truck with fat tires had made tracks in the muddy ground, and they walked their bikes between these two lines.

Reaching the top of a low hill, they looked down at an acre-wide pit. A mound of wrecked cars and refrigerators was north of the pit next to a smaller pile of computers, electric cables, and server racks. Men wearing cloth bandannas over the lower half of their faces cut apart these abandoned machines with power saws, sorted through the metal parts, and tossed them into wooden boxes.

Two workers loaded copper and aluminum parts into wheelbarrows and rolled them down the slope to brick and mud smelting furnaces set on different levels of the pit. One cold furnace had been taken apart to access blacked ingots. The refined metal was tossed into a bucket and the ashes shoveled down the slope.

Smoke rose from a brick furnace built on the third level. The furnace was about five feet high and burned a mixture of charcoal and pine kept white-hot by wood and canvas bellows attached to a discarded water pipe.

"There's my uncle Marcus," Luke said, and pointed to a bearded man prying a car radiator off an engine block. "And my dad is . . . there."

Aaron pushed a wheelbarrow over to the burning furnace. He forced pine logs into the firebox and dropped chunks of copper cable into the top vent. The harsh smell probably came from the burning polyethylene wrapped around the cable, but Aaron's only protective gear was his red bandanna and a pair of rawhide gloves. He stirred up the coals with a poker and then hurried over to the bellows to force more oxygen into the melting chamber.

"You said your father worked in a mine."

"You're looking at it."

"This is a junkyard."

"My dad and Uncle Marcus are searching for copper and the other metals they use to make cell phones and computer batteries. When they get enough scrap metal, they trade it for store credit in town. That's how we can buy stuff like gasoline, sugar, and bread flour."

Luke turned his bike around, and Kate followed him back to the road and then into the town of Dannemora. No one was standing in front of the half-open prison gate, and they pedaled past an abandoned guard shack to the narrow roads that connected the buildings.

The prison was like a city held captive within an oval of concrete.

When Kate and Luke passed between cell blocks, the rattling sound of the bike chains echoed off the building walls. If she had been alone, Kate would have moved cautiously around the prison, but Luke zigzagged back and forth, pointing out the sights like a tour guide.

"The brownstone castle with the turrets used to be the prison headquarters. The building next to it with the steep roof is Saint Dimas church. It's named after the good thief who got crucified with Jesus. Now turn right and follow me."

Passing between two flat-roofed prison blocks, they reached an open area near the north wall. Kate got off her bike and tried to figure out what sort of disaster had occurred here. There were mounds of dirt, sinkholes filled with rainwater, and half-filled trenches. It looked like an army of greedy treasure hunters had been searching for gold.

Luke led her past a collapsed fence, and they gazed up at an ascending series of terraces hacked out of the underlying granite. The terraces were subdivided into patches of ground marked with faded numbers. Abandoned huts and rusty stoves made from empty coffee cans were scattered around the terraces. She followed Luke up to the fourth terrace, and when they turned around, Kate could see the Adirondack Mountains in the distance.

"The prisoners called this the jungle," Luke explained. "Each number marks an individual space given to murderers and drug dealers who were here for at least ten years. The prisoners could lift weights, grow vegetables, and cook meals inside their courts. On a sunny day, they'd sit on chairs and look out at the mountains."

"You know everything about this place."

Luke pivoted around like a landowner surveying his estate. "My father and his father worked here. The Guard families kept dangerous people inside those walls."

"Deputy Vanderpol said there was a prison riot."

"That happened when prisoners began to die from Stem-flu. During the fighting, the lifers broke out of their cells and seized Block C. When the National Guard showed up, the soldiers fired tear-gas bombs into the building and then shot everyone who surrendered."

"What happened next?"

"They dragged all the bodies out of the buildings with hooks and ropes and buried them in the patch of dirt that used to be the baseball field."

Kate wondered if the bodies were buried in rows or had been dumped on top of each other. Once, she buried a dead squirrel in the forest behind her house and dug it up a year later. The fur had rotted away, and the bare teeth appeared to be smiling at her.

"Is your school near where they killed people?"

"Don't worry about that. The classrooms are where the warden had his office."

As they pedaled up the hill, a convoy of three cars with tail fins grumbled past them. Women were driving and kids were squeezed into the back seat.

"Church kids attend school in the early morning," Luke explained. "Guard kids used to go at the same time, but there were too many fights."

Kate stopped in the parking lot in front of the castle. "I'm not a student at this school. Nobody knows who I am."

"It don't make no difference. There are only two teachers. Kids under twelve years old get Teacher Anne. She's one of the Pledged, but we don't hate her."

Passing through an oak-paneled reception area, they followed a checkerboard hallway to a room lit with electric light. Three long tables were placed in rows, and they faced a chalkboard and a maple desk. Someone had written math problems down on the board, which were grouped in different categories: addition, subtraction, multiplication, and division.

Kate had expected to meet an old lady with spectacles and frown lines on her face, but Teacher Anne was in her thirties. Like the other Pledged women, Anne wore old-fashioned clothes: an ankle-length wool skirt, white blouse, and cardigan sweater. She looked kind, but a little sad—like someone who hadn't received the right birthday present.

"Good afternoon, Luke. Who's your new friend?"

"This is Kate Flores. Sheriff Breslow found her running around the graveyard and gave her to my family."

"Thank you, Luke. I was informed of Kate's arrival in our community." Teacher Anne smiled and gestured to the three tables. "Why don't you sit at the Eagle table with Luke. We do arithmetic first, then reading and writing."

Each row had a picture of an animal taped to the end table. There were fourteen kids in the schoolroom; the little kids were Squirrels; the seven-to-nine-year-old students were Bobcats; and the rest of the class were Eagles.

Teacher Anne tapped a brass service bell on the desk, and the clapper made a precise metallic sound. Then she walked through the rows handing everyone a three-inch-long golf pencil and a scrap of thin cardboard. Instead of school paper, they were using cut-up cereal boxes.

"Squirrels answer problem sets one and two. Bobcats should answer sets two and three. Eagles answer sets four and five. When you're done . . . come up to the desk."

Kate was the first student to answer her math questions. She approached Anne and placed her cardboard page on the desk. "Good. Now it's reading time. Take a book out of the box and read it while the others work."

Most of the torn and faded books dumped into a cardboard box were for beginning readers. But Kate found a copy of *Mary Poppins* and began to read the story. It took a half hour for everyone to finish the problems, and then they read books while Teacher Anne went to each student and showed them why they had come up with the wrong answer for a particular problem. When they finished the mathematics lesson, each kid had to stand up and read a few pages from the book they had taken from the box.

"Very good," Teacher Anne said. "The last assignment is writing. I want the Bobcats and Eagles to write a paragraph titled 'My Friend.' Describe your best friend and explain why you like them. Try to use the words you learned reading today."

Kate took a new sheet of cereal box cardboard and began to write. *My best friend has black-and-white fur and speaks with a British accent. Zeno is not a real harp seal. He is an Interactive Toy. But Zeno protects me from . . .*

Kate didn't want to mention Crawley and Bates. It might cause trouble. *Zeno protects me from bad dreams.*

Teacher Anne rang the bell on her desk and smiled. "School's out. Please leave your paragraph on the table. Kate, please remain after class. There's no need to wait for her, Luke. I'll make sure she gets home."

"Tell her you ate a good supper and slept in Lucy's room," Luke whispered. "I'll see you back at the farm."

Laughing and teasing each other, the Guard kids left the schoolroom. Kate stood up, approached Teacher Anne, and placed her paragraph on the desk.

"You answered all the math problems correctly."

"They were easy."

Anne read Kate's paragraph, then looked up and smiled again. "You have a large vocabulary for a ten-year-old."

"Zeno taught me a lot of words."

"Tell me about your parents? Did they read to you?"

"They died from Stem-flu," Kate said. Then she described her fantasy aunt in New York City. Unlike Sheriff Breslow, Anne didn't assume she was lying.

"Can you read this?" Anne took a water-stained hardback book out of the drawer and pushed it across the table.

Trying not to tear any pages, Kate opened the book and read the title page. "*The Pilgrim's Progress from This World, to That Which Is to Come.*"

"The older students study this book."

"Church kids, right?"

"I will teach any child who wants to learn. Right now, I want to place you in the appropriate group. We must challenge ourselves if we want to get stronger. Please turn the page and read the first paragraph."

On the first page, there was a black-and-white drawing of an old man standing in the shadows with a large book in his hands.

"'As I walked through the wilderness of this world, I lighted on a certain place, where was a den; and I laid me down in that place to sleep and, as I slept, I dreamed a dream. I dreamed, and behold I saw a man clothed with rags, standing in a certain place, with his face from his own house, a book in his hand, and a great burden upon his back. . . .'"

"Very good, Kate. You're a clever girl. Do you know the way back to the Carter house? Can I drive you there?"

"They gave me a bicycle. All I need to do is stay on the road that runs past the prison. I keep riding east until I reach the driveway with the chains and shackles hanging from a tree."

"Get your bike and bring it in the front door. I'll show you a fast way to get out of the prison. It used to be the warden's emergency entrance."

When Kate returned with the bike, Anne guided her through three rooms filled with dust-covered desks and office chairs. A windowless corridor led to a heavy steel door painted fire-engine red. Anne pushed back a bolt, and a few seconds later Kate was outside the wall and standing on a patch of grass.

Kate didn't encounter any cars during the bike ride home. When she reached the farmyard, she got off the bike and approached the barn. Luke had left his bike next to a rusty hay rake with ten vertical wheels. The barn door was closed, and she peered through a crack to see if Luke was inside.

Aaron Carter was sitting on a hay bale while his brother Marcus paced back and forth.

"It's crazy," Aaron said. "They've paid us before. An EV battery is valuable."

"Figure fifty dollars per kilogram of lithium and additional money for the cobalt and copper. One battery equals a four-thousand-dollar credit at the company store, but Becker wasn't offering anything close to that. He said he'd pay us four hundred for our labor."

"He must have given you a reason."

"Becker said that the battery we salvaged was toxic and the recycling plant will only pay four hundred for it. Is Becker telling the truth? Hell if I know. They've never told us the names of their buyers, so we can't get our own deal."

"Can we talk to Dr. Edwards?"

"There was nothing wrong with the battery. If they paid us the right price, the money would have canceled the store debt for three families. The Chosen want to keep us in debt. Right now we're slaves, and there's only one way to break free."

"I'm not going down that road with you."

"We have all the dirty jobs, and they walk around wearing coats and ties. Billy Wilmont was my friend and they killed him."

"I don't agree with leaving his body hanging outside the police station, but he broke one of the Ten Commandments when he stole Breslow's car."

"The man never got no judge and jury. Our kids work for fifty cents an hour and we handle toxic metals. Anyone who's still a man has had enough of this crap. There's only one solution."

"It's way too dangerous, Marcus. They have guns, too."

"Don't tell me that you're scared of them. You slaughter turkeys and I butcher pigs. This is the same kind of job. Some blood squirts out and then it's over. Kill any fool wearing a necktie and we become free men."

"What about Sheriff Breslow?"

"He and Vanderpol are on the list."

"The church runs the gas station and the grocery store. I need kerosene and wheat flour. How are you going to get those supplies?"

"I talked to some people in Plattsburgh. They'll ship in whatever we need for cash or trade."

Marcus sounded angry, and Kate didn't want to be near him. Her bike didn't have a kickstand, so she leaned it up against Luke's bike. As she walked away, her bicycle fell over and made a sound. The barn door popped open, and Aaron and Marcus walked out.

"What are you doing?" Aaron asked.

"I just came back from school. Where's Luke?"

"He's herding the turkeys into their night shelter. Why don't you go help?"

"Yes, sir."

The sun was a hand's width above the western mountains when Kate entered the pasture. She found Luke inside the wire fence, unlocking the flap door on the trailer.

"There you are! Did you get in trouble with Teacher Anne?"

"No. I'm okay."

"Then why did she tell you to stay after school?"

"She asked me about my parents and made me read a weird book."

"Teacher Anne might seem like a nice person, but you can't trust anyone who's a member of the church. They put on special eyeglasses every Sunday and see angels."

"She didn't say anything about angels."

Using the broom, they herded the turkeys back into the trailer. When all the birds were safe, they left the pasture and returned to the house. Uncle Marcus had disappeared, but Sheriff Breslow stood in the farmyard talking to Luke's parents.

"Well, there you are," Breslow said. "I thought I'd have to send out a tracker dog."

Luke shifted the shotgun around so that it was cradled in his arms. "We were roosting the turkeys."

"Good for you. Now I'm driving this little lady back to town."

Aaron shook his head. "We don't agree."

Luke's right hand was near the trigger. "You don't have the right to take her nowhere."

"I'm the sheriff of this district, and this is official business." Breslow turned and motioned to Kate. "Get into the patrol car. Right now."

"Give me a minute," Kate said. "I need to get my clothes."

The three men remained in the farmyard while Becky followed Kate into the house.

"You don't look happy about this."

Kate stuffed Zeno into the knapsack. "I don't want to cause trouble."

"It's no trouble. Let me talk to the sheriff."

When they returned to the farmyard, Kate saw that Aaron had walked over to his pickup. Inside the truck cab was a gun rack holding two rifles. If people began shooting at each other, she would never meet Paloma in New York City.

"No child should be forced to do something wrong," Becky said. "If Kate wants to stay here, then you're not taking her away."

"You're just doing this because we're a Guard family," Aaron said. "You think you can order us around."

Sheriff Breslow lowered his right hand so that it was near his holstered gun. "Normally I'd agree with you, Aaron. But this isn't a choice. I'm taking this child to her father and mother."

Luke and his parents looked surprised, and Breslow yanked open the front passenger door of his patrol car. "Say thank you to these kind people and get into the car."

Everyone stood still, and Kate got into the car. As they bumped down the dirt driveway to the road, Breslow wiped the sweat off his forehead with a red bandanna.

"I was born in a Guard family and raised in a Guard family. Everyone in this district used to get along with each other, but things are getting a little edgy these days."

"How'd you find my parents?"

"It wasn't difficult."

"Where are they?"

"Five minutes away."

Kate wanted to talk to Zeno but kept him hidden in her knapsack. It was clear that she was going to be reunited with the Nolands. They'd be polite with the sheriff and angry when they drove home.

Breslow drove past the prison, then turned into a neighborhood with white colonial houses surrounded by brick walls or low picket fences. Each house had a line of solar panels in the backyard feeding electricity into a little shed.

"Here we go." Breslow turned into the gravel driveway of a two-story house with columns in the front. He stopped the car and turned to Kate with a solemn look on his face.

"Deputy Vanderpol called the other district sheriffs. No one knows who you are and you're not on any list of runaways. This is when you got to say the truth."

"I'm Kate Flores."

Breslow gave a slight shake of the head. "If you won't tell me who you are, then I'll show you who you're going to be."

44 | WILSON

A DAY AFTER meeting with Julia and Daniel, Wilson took a cab up to East Harlem. Laura Gregg didn't look surprised when Wilson knocked on her door. "There you are," she said. "I figured I'd see you one last time."

That morning, she wore a T-shirt and a denim skirt, but instead of a belt she had tied a silk scarf with rainbow colors around her waist. Wilson watched the tips of the scarf sway back and forth as Laura moved around the kitchen and made a pot of tea.

"Do you know what happened?"

"I read the news feeds. Terry was killed by a former Element athlete who was shot dead by a homicide detective."

"The augmented human also killed a woman named Paloma. I saw her body yesterday. Detective Morrissey let me take this from the crime scene."

Wilson took the photograph of the little girl out of his shoulder bag and handed it to Laura. She gripped the frame tightly as if she had just received a valuable gift.

"This must be Richard and Emma's daughter. I hope that Terry changed her name and sent her to some place off the grid. Whoever killed Terry and Paloma is hunting me and this child."

"I don't know how to find her, Laura. Maybe the fourth angel in Terry's workshop knows the child's location, but we can't activate him."

"So, we're frozen here. There's nothing we can do."

"Here's another option." Wilson pulled the black cell phone out of his pocket and placed it on the kitchen table. "This is Darren Taylor's phone. He's the augmented human who killed Terry. I took the phone from his dead body when Morrissey wasn't looking. I want to hack the phone and find out who hired him."

Laura picked up the phone and examined it closely. "See the Greek letters etched on the surface? It's a product trademark for a dark phone. Messages and calls are automatically encrypted."

"What if we pried it open and removed the chips?"

"Not possible. Other than the OLED screen, everything is embedded in a ceramic rectangle."

"What about your Hard-Edge friends? Could they access the information?"

"I don't have any contacts here in New York, but I do know Jack Lewis. If we showed up in Berlin, he would connect us with people who can crack a dark phone."

"Do you think he'll help us?"

"I was the person who helped him escape from the courthouse when he was about to be sent to prison."

Wilson laughed. "The police got it right. You were guilty."

"We're all guilty of something, Wilson. Let's go to Berlin."

45 | KATE AND ZENO

SHERIFF BRESLOW STAYED one step behind as Kate followed a flagstone pathway to the two-story house with the white columns in front. She figured that Mr. Noland was going to yell at her while Mrs. Noland looked disappointed. If they wanted to punish her, they might take Zeno and toss him into a garbage can.

Kate pressed the doorbell, and a few seconds later Dr. Edwards opened the door.

"Any trouble?" he asked Breslow.

"They didn't want to give her up, but I handled it."

"Good work, Sheriff. We'll take it from here."

Kate entered the house and found Teacher Anne standing in the entryway. She looked tense and worried—as if Kate was going to sprout wings and fly out of the room.

"Welcome to our home," Anne said. "We're very happy that you're here."

"Why did Sheriff Breslow take me away from Luke's family?"

"Come in and sit down." Dr. Edwards gestured to an open doorway. "We aren't a Guard family squawking at each other in a barnyard."

Kate entered a front parlor and sat down on a straight-backed chair with a white lace doily on each arm.

"It's clear to everyone that you're a runaway child," Dr. Edwards said.

"My aunt Paloma lives in New York City and . . ."

Edwards raised the palm of his hand like a policeman telling a driver to stop. "We don't want to hear any more of this nonsense, Katherine. According to Sheriff Breslow, you're a runaway child."

"You can't keep me here because I accidently wandered into a graveyard."

"There are no accidents in this world," Dr. Edwards said. "Everything that happens is part of God's plan."

Anne lowered her eyes and spoke with a halting voice. "I . . . I can't have children."

"We prayed to God," Dr. Edwards said. "And God delivered you into our arms. As time passes, you'll realize that you've been blessed with good fortune. We are the Pledged, the Chosen."

Chosen for what? Kate wondered. More than anything, she wanted Zeno on her lap so he could ask questions with his British accent. But she stayed quiet as Dr. Edwards told her about his church. The pandemic turned out to be a blessing because it was the first sign of the end of the world. All the goats were going to perish while the Lambs of God floated up to heaven.

When Edwards had finished his lecture, Anne stood up and approached Kate. "The child looks tired, Warren. Perhaps she'd like to see her room."

A bedroom with flowered wallpaper was on the first floor. Anne switched on a light and pointed to a pair of doors. "This is your closet and the other leads to your bathroom. I borrowed some clothes from friends. I'll buy more when I know your favorite colors and fabrics."

"Do you have hot water?"

Anne smiled for the first time. "I turned on the heater two hours ago. Take a bath if you wish. We eat dinner at seven o'clock."

Kate enjoyed lying in the claw-foot bathtub as hot water flowed out of the faucet. Wrapped in a terry cloth towel, she returned to the bedroom and saw that a blue velvet dress and matching shoes had been placed on the white bedspread. The dress felt like a costume, but she pulled it on and stepped into the hallway. She could smell pot roast and potatoes as Anne cooked dinner in the kitchen.

The door of the master bedroom was a few inches open, and Kate peered through the gap. Dr. Edwards stood in front of a dresser mirror and brushed his hair. He still wore his necktie, but he had removed his suitcoat—revealing a shoulder holster holding a handgun.

Trying not to make any noise, Kate went downstairs. The dining room table had been set with matching bone china and silverware with scrolled handles. Anne was folding cloth napkins into little fans, and she turned when Kate entered the room.

"Do you like the dress, Katherine? I borrowed it from Mrs. Stoltz."

"It's okay."

"We'll have a little talk about the colors you prefer, and then I'll start filling up your closet. Until then, we'll improvise."

"I don't need anything. Not really. I'm not planning to stay here."

"Let God choose your path, and every day will bring happiness. Now light the candles, sweetie. It's a special night."

46 | WILSON

BEFORE THE FALL, people routinely flew back and forth between America and Europe. Now there were only a few daily flights, and airline travel felt like a bus trip to a quarantine camp. E-masks were mandatory and passengers who removed them were arrested at their destination.

Laura slept for most of the overnight flight while Wilson studied a downloaded file about the man they were going to meet. Jack Lewis grew up in a single-parent family, dropped out of his first year of college, and wandered through a variety of dirty and dangerous jobs. He was a crime scene cleaner for several years and worked for a logging crew in Oregon. During this time, he tried to read at least one book a day.

When he was in his forties, Lewis ran a truck fleet for an international aid organization, then returned to America and had a series of "waking dreams" that sparked his creativity. These visions were turned into novels set in a world in which people were watched by a digital system he called the Vast Machine.

When Lewis was in his seventies, he wrote a series of essays that inspired the Hard-Edge movement and the attacks on nubots during the Taxi Riots. He was arrested on the federal charge of seditious conspiracy but slipped out of a San Francisco courthouse a few minutes after his arraignment. The fugitive lived in Costa Rica, Mozambique, and Sweden before ending up in Berlin. The German government allowed him to remain in the city if he didn't make public speeches.

Jack Lewis was now ninety-two years old, and there had already been several false reports about his death. In response, he posted a picture of his frail body in a wheelchair with the comment: "I'm not dead. It just looks that way."

Arriving in Berlin, Wilson and Laura passed a Stem-flu virus test and left the terminal. "Now what?" Wilson asked. "Where do we go?"

Laura looked around at the passengers exiting the terminal and getting into taxis. "I sent our flight information to someone named Gretel. She told me to turn on my burner phone when we arrived."

"All this sounds incredibly vague."

"Get used to it. These are smart people living paranoid lives."

Laura's phone beeped a few minutes later, and Wilson read a text message:

Drachenbrunnen 1800h.

"That means 'dragon fountain' in German. There's a dragon fountain at Oranienplatz in the Kreuzberg district. We need to show up there at six p.m."

It was late autumn, and Berlin was cold, gray, and rainy. They took a train to Alexanderplatz and walked south. "Keep your e-mask on," Laura said. "We're being scanned by the city's facial recognition system."

Oranienplatz was a large open area with a cluster of modern apartment buildings on the eastern edge of the plaza. After walking around for a while, they discovered the *Drachenbrunnen.* Instead of a fearsome creature cast in bronze, it was a scaly serpent created from molded concrete. Before the Fall, the dragon's mouth spat water into a concrete pool, but the pump had been stolen, and the dry pool was filled with a wrecked motor scooter and two discarded baby carriages.

"I guess dragons aren't what they used to be," Wilson said. "Now what do we do?"

Laura sat down on the edge of the foundation. "Wait."

A half hour before sunset, young women and men wandered across the square and gathered near the dragon. Most of them wore e-masks and red flannel hunting hats with dangling ear flaps. While friends exchanged a variety of complicated handshakes, a green bus with a metal grid on the windows rolled onto the square, and a squad of riot police got out. They wore face masks, bulletproof vests, and stomper boots and carried clubs and shields that made them look like Roman legionnaires.

Wilson turned to Laura. "What's going on?"

"See the red hats? There's going to be a hunting party."

"Hunting what? Dragons?"

"Berlin still has a Hard-Edge movement. First they'll march around the city, then they might break into small groups and attack nubots who look like humans."

"And that's why the police are here?"

"I don't know what the rule is in Berlin. In some cities, the police will let you destroy nubots if you stay away from rich people."

When streetlights began to glow, a plump man with a red beard arrived pushing a shopping cart filled with glass bottles that could be thrown at the police. Finally, two drummers appeared and began to thump out a steady beat. Both women and men unzipped their jackets, revealing hammers with handle straps slung around their necks.

"*Maschinen sind nicht unsere Meister!*" the crowd began to shout. Machines are not our masters. The crowd cut across the square and marched north up Leuschnerdamm, followed by the bearded man pushing his shopping cart.

Concealing himself in the crowd, Wilson noticed that two marchers appeared to be following him. The young woman and man wore fox masks with pointed noses. Their long hair was braided so it resembled a fox tail.

When the protesters turned onto Waldemarstrasse, the foxes approached Wilson and Laura and guided them into an alleyway. "*Guten Abend,*" said the young man. "I am Hansel, and this is Gretel. Tonight Herr Lewis is speaking to some Japanese visitors. You are invited to join this group."

"Why the masks and fairy-tale names?"

"Some people involved with our collective have suffered Kafka Deaths."

"Kafka? The writer? What are you talking about?"

"Our friends wake up one morning and realize that they have disappeared from the system," Hansel explained. "The government, the banks, and their employers tell them that every database lists them as being dead."

"Well, that's not a big problem. Just walk into the tax office and say: 'Look! Here I am! I'm alive!' "

"That doesn't work in Germany," Gretel said. "Once you've been canceled, it's very difficult to return to the living. Your employer can change the file in their computer, but a few hours later you're back to being dead. After months of this, you give up and stay deceased."

"How do these people survive?" Laura asked. "What do they do?"

"They get jobs with an off-the-grid business like a sex-positive nightclub. If they get sick, they tell the hospital that they're foreign workers. It's like a . . ."

". . . a Kafka story," Laura said. "We get it."

A few minutes later, they turned onto a street lined with modern glass buildings. Hansel pointed to a steel plate, about four inches wide, that ran down the center of the cobblestone street. "The line shows where the wall stood when Berlin was divided into sectors." Hansel pointed upward. "All these glass and steel structures were built on the Dead Zone. If you were trying to escape over the wall, the border guards killed you when you entered this area."

The two foxes took them into an apartment building and guided them to a one-bedroom apartment on the eighth floor. A few minutes later, a muscular young man named Dietrich appeared and tested them to confirm that they were free of Stem-flu variants. When the LED screen flashed negative, they were led to a larger apartment, where a contingent of Japanese visitors sat on folding chairs facing a two-foot-high platform with a ramp. Two spotlights were focused on the platform, and Dietrich adjusted a trio of video cameras.

Voices. And then Jack Lewis rolled into the room on an electric wheelchair. "Good evening! You are about to witness the most suspenseful moment of my week!"

Using a hand control, he increased his speed and the wheelchair had just enough momentum to reach the platform. Instantly, the spotlights snapped on and the cameras began recording. Lewis spun the wheelchair around, but he didn't speak. The old man's legs were shriveled and his bald head reminded Wilson of an ancient turtle, but his brown eyes were clear and focused.

"Welcome to Berlin! I'm not allowed to make speeches in Germany, so this is considered a private conversation." Lewis surveyed the audience, saw Laura, and nodded in her direction. "Tonight I see a brave companion from my past and perhaps some new friends. Let us begin."

47 | WILSON

THE FOLDING CHAIR Wilson was sitting on was small and hard, and he was annoyed by the reverent way the Japanese guests placed their hands on their laps and gazed up at Jack Lewis.

Then the old man in a wheelchair began to speak in a calm, direct manner as if you were a friend that had met him in a garden to watch the sunset. Instead of arguing with his audience, he offered a broad vision of how computers worked and why a cyber system with Artificial Superintelligence was a dangerous innovation.

Suddenly, he stopped talking and gazed out at his audience with a cautious look on his face. Had they been listening? Did they understand? When Lewis resumed speaking, the tone of his voice was urgent—almost desperate.

"When I encounter someone who insists that there's no reason to worry about superintelligence, I usually mention a quote from the brilliant roboticist Hans Moravec: 'Biological species rarely survive encounters with superior competitors.' This simple statement is so undeniably true that some experts move from denial—to anger.

"I'm accused of being a neo-Luddite, a nihilist, and a cave dweller who is against progress. The future is a beautiful garden party, and I'm the sad person sitting in the kitchen.

"None of this is true. I value the discoveries of scientists and engineers, but the fact that their work is both challenging and important does not mean that what they create is value free. The current conjunction of high-level research and deliberate moral blindness has been seen only once before: when the scientists of the Manhattan Project built the atomic bomb.

"I realize that there is a segment of the population who wants to flee to the woods with an ax and a gun, but most of us don't want to return to the technology of a past era. So far, the machines have been monitoring us. Now we need to monitor the machines.

"The leading tech companies have proposed voluntary responses to the risks posed by Artificial Superintelligence. This is a positive beginning but not a long-range solution, because certain governments will use this powerful innovation to increase their power and certain corporations will break the rules to increase their profits.

"Any effective response to this threat needs to become an internationally accepted standard. Instead of using technology to watch its citizens, government should be protecting us from autonomous systems creating bioweapons and toxic chatbots directed toward undermining democracy.

"As part of this effort, it's time for tech employees all over the world to grow up and accept responsibility for their actions. A wide variety of programmers and engineers are creating technology that might become the cyber equivalent of nuclear weapons. Artificial Intelligence can generate partial solutions to complicated problems like global warming. But all these achievements are worthless if autonomous systems are not aligned with human goals and values.

"Along with controlling and monitoring our technological creations, we need to value and support the unique gift of our own humanity. Everyone here tonight feels pleasure when you hear a favorite song, read a love letter, or encounter a beautiful object. In each case, something created with emotion sparks emotion in your heart. A human being is not a blank slate or an empty container. Because we have empathy, we are capable of love.

"Humanity has reached a true turning point in our history. It's time for all of us to make a choice and take a stand. We will never accept the shadow reign of an omnipotent conscious machine. We will fight for our dreams, our children, our joy!"

Ignoring the applause, Jack Lewis cautiously rolled his wheelchair off the platform to a corner of the room, where the Japanese lined up to have him sign his books. When the last guest left the apartment, he pushed the hand control and approached Laura.

"Welcome to Berlin!" Lewis turned to his young friends. "After I was arraigned in the San Francisco courthouse, my lawyer took me down to a loading dock and I hid in the trunk of Laura's car. For about forty-eight hours I was the most wanted fugitive in America, but she got me across the border to Canada."

"You were a little groggy when I let you out of the trunk," Laura said. "It's nice to see that you're still causing trouble."

"Why are you in Berlin? Do you have to go off the grid for some reason?"

"This is my friend Wilson Talley. We're here to tell you a story."

"Excellent! I'm tired of my own stories. Perhaps we could have some tea and pastry in the kitchen."

While the tea was brewing, Laura told the old man about the rise and fall of Cogito.

"It sounds like you did everything you could to create a conscious machine in a safe environment. Are you sure that the suicide switch worked?"

"We followed security protocols, and the Delphi system was deleted. Our lives were stable for a while, but then we began to get worried. Whoever had financed our company was searching for us."

"Have some tea and tell us what happened next."

Now it was Wilson's turn to speak, and he described the two murders and the death of Darren Taylor. When he was done, Lewis held the teacup in his bony hands as if the warmth would give him strength.

"I'm sorry for the loss of your friends. The people we love still live in our hearts."

"Do you have a theory about what happened?" Wilson asked.

"Who controls the Astral Foundation? They were the group that financed Delphi until the project was destroyed."

"You think those people killed Terry Greene?"

"Darren Taylor was searching for everyone involved with Cogito. He probably killed Paloma Flores when she wouldn't tell him how to find the little girl."

"Some rich people lost their start-up money, but that happens all the time. Are they really going to kill a team of computer scientists and their children because a special project was destroyed?"

"This isn't about money," Lewis said to Wilson. "It's about power.

A functional system with Artificial Superintelligence will give its owner the power to track, predict, and control the behavior of vast numbers of people."

"Can you help us?" Laura asked.

Lewis began to move around the room. "During my time in Berlin, my friends and I have tried to organize a response to this technological threat, but it's difficult."

"You don't sound very optimistic," Wilson said.

"The danger is real. I assume you two want to go off the grid. If you wish, you could travel to an island we own in the North Sea."

"Wilson and I aren't looking for a hiding place." Laura pulled the dark phone out of her pocket. "This is Darren Taylor's dark phone. We need to find someone who can hack into this encrypted device."

Jack Lewis turned to his young friends. "Possible?"

"We can contact the *Grauer Hut,*" Gretel said.

"Who's that?"

"Gray Hat cyber anarchists who live here in Berlin," Lewis explained. "Pass the phone to Gretel and she'll give it to our friends. While you're waiting, you can stay at our safe house in Kreuzberg. Get some sleep. You both look tired."

48 | KATE AND ZENO

KATE WOKE UP before dawn, pulled Zeno out of her knapsack, and took him beneath the heavy bed quilt. "Can you hear me, Zeno?"

"I'm here."

"I know that you need to be charged, but that might be dangerous. Dr. Edwards and Teacher Anne want to adopt me, and they brought me back to their house. Everything is strange here and all the men are carrying guns. If you talked, they might think you were a bad influence."

"This is just like one of our chess games, Katherine. You need to think one or two moves ahead."

"But I don't know what the next move is. Tell me what to do."

"Watch and listen. I need more information before I can figure out a plan."

When Kate heard the adults talking, she pulled on her jeans and T-shirt and went downstairs. Anne served Kate a bowl of oatmeal and brown sugar, then made her put on knee socks and a long-sleeved cotton dress.

For the rest of the morning, Kate helped Anne bake cookies and clean the house for an afternoon meeting of church elders. While Anne worked in the kitchen, Kate greeted the visitors and guided them through French doors to the backyard gazebo. An hour later, she carried a tray of refreshments to their guests.

Five men were sitting on benches underneath the roof of the gazebo, and everyone watched her walk across the lawn. Two of the men had removed their suitcoats, displaying revolvers in holsters. A pudgy man named Leo helped Kate place the tray on a folding table and poured glasses of apple juice while she served sugar cookies.

"This is our little runaway," Dr. Edwards said. "She's the girl Vanderpol found in the cemetery."

"And now she's with you," one of the men said.

Kate finished handing out the cookies and set the plate down on the table. The men were talking about her like she was a dog or a cat. No one looked her in the eyes, and Edwards hadn't mentioned her name.

"She spent a night at Aaron Carter's farm. Anne met her for the first time when the Carter boy took her to school. Yesterday we brought her into our home."

"A wise choice considering the present circumstances," Leo said, and all the other men nodded.

As Kate carried the serving tray back to the house, she knew that the five men were watching her. Everything was clean and polite at the Edwards house, but it felt like the sky was going to split open and rain fire on Anne's roses.

49 | JULIA AND DANIEL

THE MORNING AFTER the E-Volve meeting, Julia called Richard Winfield. "I'm texting you the number for a cell phone used by Bennett Schroeder. Tell your police friends to come up with a list that includes call times and locations."

"What you're asking me to do is illegal without a court order."

"Of course, Mr. Winfield. I apologize for my suggestion. You're an ethical attorney who always follows the law."

A few hours later, a private courier showed up at their apartment with a sealed envelope containing a record of Bennett's phone calls.

"This is helpful," Julia said. "On the day he disappeared, Bennett made his last three calls to a number in Pittsfield, Massachusetts."

Julia called the number, and they listened to a recorded announcement: "Ready for the ultimate long-term journey in a safe monitoring facility? The Over World Station might fit your needs. Please contact our staff and get ready for a transforming experience."

"I just looked it up," Daniel said. "It's a trek burrow on Dwight Road in Pittsfield."

"We'll drive up there in the van and I'll ask for a site tour. If we find Bennett Schroeder lying in a pod, we'll call Winfield. He can get a court order to detach Bennett from the cable."

They stuffed water bottles, soy bars, and sleeping bags into a duffel bag, then hurried over to the parking lot where they kept the van. It was a chilly morning with dark pillowy clouds overhead, and all the cars in the parking lot looked like survivors from a war zone. The van had dents and a cracked windshield, but it started on the first try and they reached Pittsfield four hours later. An overgrown park at the center of the town was surrounded by a city hall, courthouse, and church with a stone bell tower. Most stores were boarded up, except for two liquor stores selling bootleg alcohol.

"Stay on this road for twelve miles and then turn right. I'm going to call them and say that we're dropping by for a site tour."

She called the number a second time and waited for a beep. "Hello!

Anyone there? I'm Julia Lau. My friend Daniel and I are looking for a trek burrow and thought we'd drop by and check out your facility."

Ten minutes later they saw a mailbox designed to look like a sleeping bunny with the words *Over World Station* painted on both sides. A circular gravel driveway led to a white farmhouse with gabled windows on the top floor. The only unusual feature was a wooden tunnel leading from the back of the house to a windowless red barn with solar panels and a box-shaped rooftop air conditioner.

"Looks like they converted the barn into a burrow," Julia said. "If the passageway from the house has an air filtration device, they can insulate their travelers from viruses."

"Sounds expensive."

"That's what you pay for, Daniel. Your body can't get sick while your mind lives in the Over World."

They parked the van in the middle of the driveway and got out. It was quiet except for the distant *tap-tap-tap* of a woodpecker searching for insects. Suddenly, a white terrier pushed through the flap of a dog door and began barking at them as a middle-aged man shuffled out of the house pulling on a lab coat. The burrow supervisor had a potbelly and two clumps of frizzy hair on a bald head. His muddy work boots were held together with lengths of twine.

"Don't let Snowdrop scare you." The man's lab coat spread open as he tried to grab the terrier. "He gets excited when he meets new people."

"I'm Julia Lau, and this is Daniel Blake. I left a message on your phone."

"I'm Dr. Theodore Sloane, but everyone calls me Dr. Teddy. I'm the supervisor of Over World Station." Holding the terrier's collar, he gestured to the farmhouse and barn. "We help our clients to break down barriers so they can fully create and explore."

"Sounds great. I already have a direct neurological connection, and Daniel is considering the procedure."

"This is a state-of-the-art facility. The station has backup solar panels in case of a power failure, plus an alternative connection to a communications satellite."

"What does your burrow look like, and what's the cost?"

"Follow me. I'll be glad to answer all your questions."

They followed Dr. Teddy into what had once been a front parlor and sat on upholstered chairs facing a teakwood desk. Teddy picked up a computer pad, and a wall monitor displayed the Over World Station logo.

Daniel glanced at Julia and rolled his eyes. *We're going to get a sales pitch.*

A deep male voice boomed out of hidden speakers, and a sequence of images flashed on the monitor screen.

"The growing popularity of direct neurological connections has given travelers the ability to explore the Over World for extended periods of time. But this presents a variety of physiological problems. . . ."

A digital human appeared on the monitor screen, and black arrows pointed to the various ways a trek burrow could destroy someone's health.

"What about bodily nourishment and disposal of waste? A motionless body is also susceptible to infection and profound muscle deterioration. At Over World Station we follow a systematic procedure to solve these problems. Catheters are attached to the bladder and colon while a stent provides nourishment. Filtered air is provided through a plastic mask. Electric stimulator pads attached to the major muscle groups periodically make the muscles contract. This procedure was first developed for astronauts taking interplanetary journeys."

The presentation continued for five minutes without mentioning money. At the conclusion, a digitally created man and woman walked up a hill to a golden city while the speakers blasted *Thus Spoke Zarathustra.*

"Get ready for your next adventure!" Dr. Teddy said with fake enthusiasm. "If you're looking for a trek burrow, we are here to serve you."

Daniel seemed annoyed by Dr. Teddy's lab coat. "Where did you go to medical school?"

"Well, I ahhh . . ."

"And where'd you do your residency? This was before the pandemic, right?"

"Actually, I'm not a medical doctor. I have a PhD in history. When my college fired half the faculty, I trained to be a stockbroker and then a real estate agent." Dr. Teddy sighed. "Every time I train for a new job, I get replaced by an AI system."

"Thank you for the presentation." Julia got up from her chair. "Daniel and I are ready to take the tour."

"We don't give tours. It's against the rules."

"We want to see actual clients attached to tubes and wires."

"Your body gets weak during a long journey through the Over World, and that makes you susceptible to airborne viruses like the flu or the common cold. Each traveler is placed into a separate pod. We don't allow any visitors to the area."

"We just want to see . . ."

"I know what you want, but it's not possible. Tours are only available for clients who have been tested for viruses and reserved a six-month pod for eighteen thousand dollars."

Dr. Teddy gave Julia a brochure and escorted them back to the van. Once again, he forced a smile. "I'm looking forward to meeting you again."

"Are the travelers happy?" Julia asked. "What do they tell you when they return?"

"I don't know if 'happy' is the right word. We're offering our clients an alternative life in a world that reflects their own desires."

As they headed back to Pittsfield, Julia rolled down the window so she could feel the cold air on her face. "What do we do now?" Daniel asked. "We don't know if Bennett is in one of the pods. He may have called the burrow three times, but that doesn't mean he's there."

They stopped at a gas station, then traveled in silence until Julia's phone pinged with an incoming message.

"It's from Roy Kassam," she said. "This is . . . Yes! It's what we've been waiting for. He just sent us the administrative password to Dragon Lair."

Daniel turned off the road and they smiled at each other. After a week of frustration, it felt like their luck had finally changed. "Now what?" Daniel asked. "Stay here? Go home?"

"You should wait here, Daniel. I'll take a bus from Pittsfield to New York City, cross over at Thomas's travel center, and find Bennett Schroeder."

"What are you going to say to him?"

"I won't know that until we meet each other. If I talk Bennett into coming home, you need to be parked near the burrow. Knock on the door and tell Dr. Teddy that a customer wants his cable detached."

"And what if Bennett isn't there?"

"I'll call and tell you where to find him."

"What about the Death Field? Bennett thought it was real."

"I've killed thousands of avatars and have died hundreds of times playing shooter games, but I've never encountered a real death."

Daniel gave her a worried look. "Just be careful, okay? I don't want anything bad happening to you."

Since meeting the detective in the university quadrangle, Julia had felt like a dark coldness was gradually surrounding them. She and Daniel were strong when they stood together. Now they had to take separate journeys.

"We're two stubborn people, Daniel. Neither of us will run away."

"You're going to rescue Bennett's mind." Daniel leaned forward and kissed her lightly on the lips. "I'll grab his body."

50 | WILSON

THEY LEFT THE dark phone with Jack Lewis, and Dietrich guided them to a two-bedroom apartment a few blocks away from the dragon statue. It was clean and basic: wood furniture, scratchy towels, and unscented soap. Wilson and Laura slept for nine hours and then woke up when someone began knocking on the door.

It was Gretel, carrying a shopping bag filled with brown bread, apples, and cheese. "Was everything comfortable? Did you sleep well?"

"Yes. Thank you."

"Our Gray Hat friends smiled when they saw the dark phone. There is a weak point in the device's firewall discovered by a Japanese teenager."

"Could they access the phone's memory chip?"

"Yes, and they've come up with quite a bit of information. Eat breakfast and I'll take you to them."

An hour later, Wilson and Laura followed Gretel to a line of houseboats moored in the concrete canal near Tiergarten Park. The floating homes were painted bright colors and decorated with potted plants, ceramic sculptures, and a few black anarchist flags.

"*Hallo!*" Gretel shouted. "*Freunde steigen ins Boot!*" She stepped onto a boat that looked like a red barn with two high windows. A slender young man with a broken chain tattooed on his arm opened a squeaky door and motioned them inside.

The outside of the houseboat was old and weathered, but the central living room was crammed with tower servers and monitor screens. Three other members of the Gray Hat group sat in office chairs, and they swiveled around to greet them.

A Turkish woman with a headscarf stood up and nodded to Gretel. "We need to speak English?"

"Yes, English."

"Welcome to our sanctuary. As far as the authorities are concerned, we don't exist, and you don't exist either. We've opened the dark phone and are ready for a conversation."

A plump German woman wearing pink overalls typed a command, and text messages appeared on a central monitor screen.

"The owner of the dark phone was a private policeman named Darren Taylor. Herr Taylor was hired to track down Terrence Greene, Laura Gregg, Richard Collins, and Emma Anderson."

"He was looking for the four people who created Cogito," Wilson said. "But why did he murder a woman named Paloma Flores?"

"The text messages indicate that Flores once took care of Richard and Emma's child, Katherine."

"Taylor probably thought that the child would lead him to the parents," Laura said. "So, who was paying him to run around New York killing people?"

"The payment came from Dr. Ivan Zikowski."

"In a crazy way . . . that sounds logical," Laura said. "The man who funded Cogito wanted to destroy the four people who had activated a suicide chip. Zikowski works for the Astral Foundation."

"The Astral Foundation is a corporation chartered in Malta," the German woman explained. "It has no European income but receives money from a shell corporation in the United States."

"This reminds me of those wooden Matryoshka dolls," Wilson said. "Each hollow doll is hidden inside another."

The young man with the chain tattoo smiled like a boxer who had just knocked out his opponent. "After following the money path through several connected corporations, I discovered the starting point. The Astral Foundation is funded by a personal bank account controlled by Dr. Howard Sebesky. He is the American billionaire who—"

"I know who he is," Wilson interrupted. "Sebesky was the man who hired me."

51 | WILSON

WILSON WAS GRATEFUL that Laura didn't accuse him of betrayal in front of the Gray Hat cyber experts because of his association with Sebesky. They thanked everyone, retrieved the dark phone, and returned to the apartment in Kreuzberg. As Wilson locked the door, Laura entered the kitchen and pulled out a bottle of clear liquid stored in a drawer.

"I was looking for a bread knife this morning and found this aquavit."

"Forty percent alcohol," Wilson said. "I could use that right now."

Laura filled two glasses and Wilson gulped down his portion. The taste of caraway seeds lingered on his tongue as he picked up the bottle and poured a second glass.

"Howard Sebesky was furious when you and your friends destroyed Delphi," Wilson theorized. "He thought that this AI system was a new way to control the world. Sebesky wanted revenge. So he hired a private policeman to kill Terry and Paloma."

Laura sipped her glass of aquavit and nodded. "That's possible. And while that was going on, Sebesky used you and the Trigon staff to find me and track down Richard, Emma, and their daughter. But would he really go after a child to exact revenge?"

"If he was angry enough. But it's also quite possible we're missing something."

"Regardless, Sebesky has the wealth to do whatever he likes. Somewhere in the Trigon accounting system, your bonus and bribes were considered a business expense."

Wilson refilled his glass. "Rich people always want more money. The fact that Congress was debating artificial intelligence legislation was reason enough for Sebesky's actions."

"I'm not accusing you of anything, Wilson. We've both been stumbling around, trying to figure things out, but we still can't see the full picture."

"I'm returning to New York City, Laura. One way or another, I'm going to track down Sebesky and cancel his plans."

"I'm going with you. We need to find Kate before someone tries to kill her."

"Protect the children and punish the powerful." Wilson toasted Laura and drank some more aquavit. "In a confusing era, follow fundamental goals."

"It's just like tango, Wilson. You hear the music, then you stand up and start to move."

Smiling, Laura extended her hand—palm up. It felt like the tango ritual she had once described to him: a nod that was both a question and an invitation.

Wilson put down his glass and took her hand.

52 | KATE AND ZENO

SUNDAY MORNING, Kate ate breakfast toast and jam in the kitchen. When she returned to her bedroom, Anne was taking an ivy-green dress off a hanger and placing it on the bed.

"Do you like the dress, Kate?"

"It's okay."

"Let me give you something to wear with the dress. A gift." Anne reached into her pocket and pulled out a gold heart-shaped locket. "This was my mother's locket, and now it's yours."

"You don't need to give it to me."

"But I *want* to. It will make me very happy when you wear it today."

When everyone was dressed in their church clothes, they went outside and got into the old-fashioned sedan. Dr. Edwards didn't speak, but he kept glancing into the rearview mirror. Kate remembered what Luke told her about the Pledged seeing angels. Maybe Edwards thought they were hovering above the car.

Sheriff Breslow stood at the prison gates wearing a business suit and necktie. When their car passed, he nodded to Edwards and raised two fingers to the brim of his fedora. Kate felt like she had been dropped into the middle of a stage play. Everyone around her was acting, and she was the only person who didn't know her lines.

They parked next to the prison church, and Dr. Edwards switched off the motor. Then he reached into his suitcoat pocket and pulled out three sets of eyeglasses that looked like the goggles people wore when they went swimming.

"Put these on, Kate. We wear these glasses when we're in church."

"I don't need glasses."

"You have to wear them," Anne said. "They help us see."

Kate slipped on the glasses, and a plastic strap dug into the back of her head. She turned toward the church and the prison was transformed. Shafts of golden light came down from the sky and touched the church roof. The gray stone building glowed with energy.

Not daring to move, she remained in the car until Anne took her hand. "It might seem strange at first, but you'll get used to it."

When Kate entered the church, she saw three angels with golden wings floating up near the ceiling. She knew that the angels were created by some kind of computer program, but the simulation started to overwhelm the real.

Sitting in the pews, she watched the church fill up with over one hundred people. The men wore suits, and the women had ankle-length dresses with small hats pinned to their hair. At exactly ten o'clock, an old lady sat down at an electric piano and began playing slow and steady music that made Kate think of giants marching. Responding to the sound, the angels fluttered their wings, glided across the length of the room, and hovered above the altar like hummingbirds over a rosebush.

Reverend Clark stepped into a raised pulpit and opened a large Bible. "Our scripture today is from the book of Deuteronomy. Now hear the word of our Lord."

Who's controlling the angels? Kate wondered. As Clark began reading, they continued to hover above the congregation.

" 'However, in the cities of the nations the Lord your God is giving you as an inheritance, do not leave alive anything that breathes. Completely destroy them—the Hittites, Amorites, Canaanites, Perizzites, Hivites, and Jebusites—as the Lord your God has commanded you.' "

Gripping the sides of his lectern, Reverend Clark stared down at his congregation. "This scripture shows us that the Chosen will be saved, and the rest must be destroyed. The Almighty is giving the Israelites a list of the people who worship false gods. This is not a request from God or a suggestion. It's an *order.* The Chosen are being asked to do something difficult. But overcoming obstacles brings us closer to—"

The entrance door slammed open, and Sheriff Breslow stood in the open doorway. "Vanderpol just called! The cars have left the park and they're on the way. They should arrive in a few minutes."

"Reverend Clark will lead the women and children into the school," Dr. Edwards said. "Hurry up. We need to follow our plan."

Everyone ripped off their magic goggles, and the angels disappeared. Anne grabbed Kate's arm and guided her toward a side door at the front of the church. Meanwhile, two men had opened a hinged bench and were pulling out assault rifles.

"What's going on?" Kate asked.

"The Guards are going to attack the church, but they didn't know we placed listening devices in their homes. When they pass through the gates, our men are going to harvest them."

Reverend Clark led the women and children across a patch of grass to the administrative building. Looking up, Kate saw men with rifles and machine guns in the guard towers.

When the women and children reached the classroom, Clark left them there and hurried away. The little kids circled the tables and played tag while the women and the older girls gathered in groups and whispered to each other.

Kate peered through the steel bars covering the windows. It felt like the women and children were prisoners in a cage. She touched the bars with the tips of her fingers and heard a single gunshot coming from outside the church. One breath in. One breath out. And then there was a wave of gunshots that sounded like fists hammering on a steel door.

Anne and the other women rushed to the windows, and no one saw Kate slip out of the room, dash down the hallway to the warden's old office, and pass through the red emergency door. Peering around the corner, she saw several pickup trucks abandoned near the entrance to the prison. Bullets had punched holes in the windshields, and a dead man lay face down in a circle of blood.

Zeno was still at the Edwards house, and Kate decided to go back and grab her friend. Feeling like a hunted animal, she darted between trees and houses. In the distance, she saw four church members march two Guardians out of the grocery store with their hands up. The Guardians stood with their faces toward the wall and then—*pop, pop*—they were killed.

Two blocks from the store, a body lay in the middle of the street next to a red bicycle with ribbons on the handlebars. *Don't stop,* she told herself. *Keep moving.* But she felt like a piece of iron drawn by a magnet.

Luke had been carrying his shotgun, and it lay on the ground near his right hand. Kate had never been this close to a dead person. It was the same face as Luke, the same patched jeans and flannel shirt, but now the life inside him had dribbled out of a neck wound.

Breathing hard, she ran to the Edwards house and slammed open the front door. Upstairs in her bedroom, she tore off the church dress and pulled on her jeans and sweatshirt. Zeno was waiting for her in the closet.

"What happened? Tell me."

"The Guards decided to attack the Pledged, but Dr. Edwards and his friends had guns hidden inside the church. They moved the women and kids into the school and then killed everyone." Kate forced her clothes into the knapsack. "Luke is dead. Everyone is dead. We need to run away from this place."

"Grab all the money you see and take food from the kitchen."

Kate stuffed Zeno into the knapsack and hurried down the staircase. She passed through the swinging door to the kitchen and stopped.

A man wearing black lay on the floor with a patch of blood beneath his head. Kate took three steps closer and looked down at Garrett Crawley, the policeman with the chubby cheeks and wispy beard who had wanted to inject an RFID chip beneath her skin. Crawley was still wearing his gold badge, but someone had shot him in the neck.

Kate felt distant from what was happening. The body in front of her was like an image on a monitor screen.

"Katherine," Zeno whispered. "Can you hear me?"

"Yes."

"Your immediate objectives are money and food. Focus on those objectives and—"

The floor creaked, and Uncle Marcus stepped out of the pantry holding a hunting rifle. He looked as if he had just survived a big explosion.

"Who did I just kill?" Marcus asked. "He looks like a police officer."

"I . . . I don't know."

Uncle Marcus raised the rifle and pointed it at her face. "You and this cop are from outside the district. From the start, you've lied about everything. Those church bastards ambushed us when we passed through the prison gates. They knew we were coming and cut us down like tall grass. You heard my brother and me talking in the barn, didn't you? And then you told Edwards."

"I didn't say anything."

"Edwards will come looking for you, and that gives me one more chance to kill him."

Marcus grabbed Kate's belt and dragged her out of the kitchen and into the backyard. She stumbled as they continued across the lawn.

"You don't have to do this. I just want to run away."

"No one is running away. The Chosen killed my family and friends, and now they're hunting for the rest of us. Our women and children will be turned into slaves."

They reached the backyard hut that contained a battery for the solar panels, and Marcus kicked open the door. "I'm going to hide in here. You walk over to the sprinkler head and stop. If you say anything or try to run away, I'll shoot you in the back. You're bait for Edwards."

Marcus stepped into the hut and hid in the shadows while Kate faced the house. "The computer was right, Zeno."

"What computer are you talking about?"

"Remember what Crawley said? His computer told him I was either going to kill somebody or I was going to die."

Kate heard breaking glass and then silence. Someone was inside the house.

"Talk to me, Zeno. Please."

"Get ready to run," Zeno said in a calm voice. "You might have a few seconds when the adults try to kill each other."

"Or maybe they'll kill me," Kate whispered. "The computer said that, too."

Marcus emerged from the solar power hut and crouched behind a beech tree. "Stay there," he whispered. "That's probably Dr. Edwards."

It was silent inside the house for two or three minutes, and then she heard a *crack-crack* noise like a stick being broken. Uncle Marcus fell face down onto the grass. His legs twitched, and then he lay still.

Turning left, she saw Agent Bates standing at the corner of the house with his assault rifle. "Found you," he said with his mechanical voice.

"Why did you keep looking for me? Why do you care?"

Bates pursed his lips and nodded as if he appreciated her questions. "Garrett kept talking about your high score, but he couldn't explain why the computer picked you, why your score was so high, and how the system knew your location. There was no reason for anything."

"Are you going to kill me?"

The big man shook his head and lowered the rifle. "Garrett always told me that I was stupid and, yeah, maybe I am. But I'm not a goddamn robot. I'll tell the system that you're dead. No one is going to dig up bodies after all this killing."

Kate took three steps backward, and Agent Bates didn't stop her. It felt like she was starting a game of tag on the schoolyard. *One. Two. Three.*

She turned away and ran across the street and through empty backyards filled with swing sets and barbecue grills. The sound of gunshots came from different directions, but Kate didn't stop. Finally she reached the forest and climbed up a slope to an outcrop of limestone boulders covered with lichen. Still breathing hard, she sat on a rock and took Zeno out of the knapsack.

"Are you hurt, Katherine?"

"Inside me hurts. I'm sad about Luke."

Gunshots echoed in the distance, but now the sounds were soft and muffled—like a drum wrapped in a thick towel.

"Agent Bates said that the police system knew my location. How did that happen?"

"The most logical explanation is that they're tracking *me*. I'm a sentient device connected to a database stored on the Cloud. If requested information flows into my microprocessor, then information about my location might flow outward to the system."

"Can you switch off your connection?"

"Not possible. My creator made sure that I would always be operative. When you're asleep or when I'm stored in the closet, I'm organizing my memory files and thinking about you."

"Can you solve that problem, Zeno? You always have good ideas."

"Once Agent Bates reports that you're dead, they will probably deactivate their search program, but they'll still be looking for you for the next few days. There's only one logical solution: you must leave me here in the woods and hike back to the interstate."

"I'm not going to do that."

"I'm a computer with a voice box and visual scanner inserted into a plush toy created from fake fur and synthetic stuffing. I am capable of speech and speech recognition, logical reasoning and emotional interpretation, but I'm not a real harp seal."

"You're my friend, Zeno. I don't care if you're a real animal or a stuffed toy. I'm not leaving you."

"I will evaluate alternatives."

More gunshots. Black smoke rose up from a burning house and drifted across the sky.

"Let me die."

"What are you talking about?"

"My battery hasn't been charged, and I have fifty-six minutes of power left before my system will shut down. A dead machine can't be tracked by the system."

"What happens when I charge you later? Will you remember me?"

"I don't have that information."

"How will I know when you shut down?"

"Goldbach's conjecture states that every even natural number greater than two is the sum of two prime numbers."

"Why is that important?"

"When you had whooping cough, the Nolands gave you medicine and then went to sleep. I remained alert and made sure you didn't have a seizure. While you slept, I kept my processor active by confirming that Goldbach's conjecture is true for all integers less than two times ten to the third power. I stopped calculating when your respiration became normal."

"I'm glad you stayed awake. I remember coughing a lot."

"I'm going to search for prime numbers hidden in whole numbers, Katherine. It will give us a monitoring gauge."

Ten minutes passed. "Talk to me, Zeno. Please."

"Still calculating. For the last seven years, I've been switched on and watching you. Now I'm losing contact and can anticipate that loss. Maybe I'm feeling sadness."

Time passed. The gunshots and the smoke had disappeared. "Zeno? Are you there? Can you hear me?"

No answer. She hugged and kissed her friend, then placed his body into the backpack. Kate sat on the log for a while, looking out at the world.

She felt like a dead leaf pushed by the wind.

53 | JULIA

JULIA TOOK A bus to New York City and went to see Thomas the next morning. After a breakfast of cold pizza, he followed her down the hallway to one of the travel rooms. "How long will this take?"

"Don't know. I'm going to wander around Dragon Lair until I find Bennett Schroeder."

"Is Daniel still in Pittsfield?"

"Yes, he's waiting outside the trek burrow. We're going for a simultaneous body and mind recovery. Bennett has been hooked up to tubes and wires for more than a week. If someone shuts off the connection without his consent, he might have some neurological problems."

In the online changing room, Julia put on her avatar clothing for a Sword and Sorcery world. Although she was carrying a broadsword in a shoulder scabbard, a long dagger, and a buckler shield, she considered more elaborate equipment. Touching the monitor screen, she authorized a credit card purchase of gold florins that could be used in Dragon Lair to buy additional weapons.

She entered the windowless hallway, typed the administrative password that Roy Kassam had sent her, then pushed open a door and found herself standing in the central square of a medieval town. Market women stood in stalls or behind tables selling food, pots, and knives. Their voices merged with the lowing sounds coming from a cow pen and a song on a hurdy-gurdy played by a blind man. A group of green-skinned elves wandered past her, chattering to each other in their chirping magpie language.

Julia circled the square with one hand on the pommel of her sword. The square was a safe zone for visitors, but none of the characters displayed an avatar name floating above their heads. The market women and the pigs devouring rotten pumpkins were digital simulations created by the system. She appeared to be the only living consciousness in this world.

When she returned to the village church, a tavern door slammed open and a seven-foot-tall giant carrying a curved scimitar entered the square. The giant had a crooked nose and a topknot of hair that made him look like a Māori warrior. When he saw Julia, the giant waved his hand and crossed the square. As he approached, Julia saw the name Awesome 17 floating above the giant's head.

"Welcome to Dragon Lair, Cutter. You're the first human I've met in this world. Everyone else is a bot."

"This world is closed for maintenance. How did you get in?" she asked.

"I found a password on a hacker site, and it worked."

"Are there really sixteen other Awesomes in the Over World?"

"Probably not. I just thought it sounded better."

"How old are you in reality?"

"Thirty-two. Would you like to go on a quest together?"

"I don't go on quests with liars. Tell me your real age or walk away."

"I'm . . . I'm fifteen," the giant said. "I live in Stroud, a town in Gloucestershire, and I'm too young to be a wirehead. I spend most of my time online because the other kids don't like me."

"So, what's your real name?"

"Ian Bellesley. I was named after a grandfather who got drunk and fell off a roof in a rainstorm. But don't tell anyone. Okay?"

"I'm Julia. What do you know about Dragon Lair."

"I've tried to leave the marketplace, but I keep getting killed by the Vikings outside the gate. I've been killed nineteen times, and I still can't win."

A pixel chicken was pecking at Julia's feet and she kicked it away. "I'm searching for a young man named Bennett who uses an avatar called Pathfinder. I don't know what he looks like in this world."

"Why do you want to find him?"

"He's missing and his parents hired me to track him down."

"So, you're some kind of detective? That's really cool."

"It's a job. I don't know about your life in Britain, but there aren't a lot of jobs in New York City."

"Invite me on a quest and I'll help you. I haven't gone anywhere, but I know a few things about this world."

"You can come along if you don't get in my way."

"Great! Before you leave, you might want to buy some extra equipment. The bots that hang out in the tavern are always complaining about dire wolves. You can only scare them with fire or shoot them with arrows."

Starlings rose up and swirled above them as Ian guided her through the market. Using some of her florins, Julia bought a compound bow, a quiver of arrows, and flint and steel that could start a bonfire. When she finished shopping, they plowed through a flock of squawking chickens and headed down a cobblestone street with sewage flowing in the gutters.

Ian kept adjusting his scabbard. "You might want to talk to a bot called the Gatekeeper. He sells information for gold."

The cobblestone street ended at a half-open portcullis that led to the surrounding countryside. Ian approached a stone guardhouse and knocked on the iron door. A few seconds later a peephole snapped open and an eye stared at them.

"Hello." The Gatekeeper sounded like a cranky old man. "It looks like another fool has entered Dragon Lair."

"I'm trying to find Pathfinder," Julia said. "Do you know what he looks like?"

"One gold florin for that information. Drop it down the pipe."

Ian motioned to an open pipe embedded at an angle into the guardhouse wall. Julia reached into the leather purse hanging from her belt and pulled out a single coin. She dropped it into the pipe and heard a clink as it landed in a bucket.

"Pathfinder is a wizard avatar who has a beard and wears a blue robe. He carries his possessions in a dark green leather bag."

"That description is way too generic. It's not worth the money I paid you."

"He owns a cyber raven. Sometimes the bird flies above him, but it usually rides on his shoulder. The bird is not an independent simulation. It's part of the wizard costume. If you see a raven, the owner will be nearby."

"Is Pathfinder in Dragon Lair?"

"Ten florins for that information."

Julia kicked the door, but it didn't pop open. "How do I know if you're telling me the truth? You could tell me anything."

"I'm information software. I was programmed to be rude but truthful."

Julia opened her leather bag, pulled out ten florins, and pushed them into the slanted pipe. She heard them land in the bucket while the Gatekeeper's eye continued to stare at her.

"I talked to Pathfinder a week ago when he passed through the gate."

"How do I find him?"

"Follow the road west. You must pass through a rocky area with banshees and a forest filled with dire wolves."

Ian touched the handle of his scimitar. "That's what I told you! Dire wolves!"

"Pass through a forest and you'll reach a canyon. Follow a stream through the canyon and you'll reach a doline . . . a vertical shaft into the earth. Pathfinder wanted to explore that access point. He thought that it might be an entrance to the Death Field."

"The Death Field is just a chat-room fantasy. It doesn't exist."

"Pathfinder felt that it might exist. He thought that a dangerous person was running an experiment, and he wanted to know why."

"My mind is in this simulation. How can my body die?"

"Leave the marketplace and find out."

The Gatekeeper's eye disappeared from the peephole, and Julia ducked under the half-open portcullis. Ian followed her. "What is the Death Field?"

"We can talk about that as we travel west. Let's get going."

They were outside the walls of the town, standing in a scrub area dotted with mounds of trash. Goats and scrawny cows wandered around nibbling on nettles and milkweed.

Ian glanced back and forth like a shoplifter worried about security guards. "You can't leave here if you don't fight the Vikings."

"I don't want to fight anybody. It's a waste of time."

"You don't have a choice. It's programmed into the system. If they kill you, you respawn in your changing room."

"Where do you think you're going?" someone asked.

Julia turned around as three avatars swaggered out of the village. The young men displayed a standardized Viking look, which included long blond hair, chain-mail armor, and two-handed swords. Their leader carried a spear in his right hand and wore a bearskin cape with the dead animal's head attached to his helmet.

"I'm walking down the Western Road," Julia said. "Is that a problem for you?"

"This is our kingdom," the leader announced. "Fight me or I'll cut your throat."

"We'll see about that." Julia removed the small shield from her back harness and attached it to her left arm. She quickly assessed the two or three things her bot opponent might do, and then she drew the long dagger and began running toward him.

Viking Boy threw his spear straight at her. It hit her buckler, and the point broke through the metal-covered surface. Julia tossed the shield away, took three long steps, and leaped into the air. As Viking

Boy tried to draw his sword with his right hand, she thrust with the dagger and stabbed him in the neck.

Blood flowed out of Viking's Boy's neck, and he fell flat on his face. She saw her opponent's face contort. His body twitched a few times and then he stopped moving.

It was fake, a simulation, but Julia felt triumphant as she stood beside the digital corpse. "Anyone else want to fight? What about you?"

She drew her sword, and the two other Vikings ran away, disappearing behind the wall circling the city.

"How did you do that?" Ian asked. "The Viking has always killed me."

"I died hundreds of times until I learned how to survive."

54 | JULIA

JULIA AND IAN followed a dirt road wandering across a moor landscape of heather and blackberry bushes growing on thick layers of peat. After a few minutes of walking, they passed a well near an empty cattle pen. A fuzzy line of static cut through the outer surface of a circular well, and it looked as if two sections of brick and mortar were rubbing against each other.

This software glitch was what Roy Kassam had mentioned during their conversation. Julia had expected something like this, but it still bothered her. When she explored different simulations, everything usually felt as real as her New York apartment. It was disconcerting when a simulation wasn't as solid and stable as the cooking pot filled with chickpeas she had left in the refrigerator.

"What is the Death Field?" Ian asked. "It sounds kind of scary."

"If your avatar dies, you can leave your computer and make some microwave popcorn, but these days hundreds of thousands of people can have a direct neural connection to the Over World. If you're a wirehead, you might have a problem when you die in certain simulations."

"You could die for real in a place like this?"

"Some people think that might be true."

"How could that happen? Is it physically possible?"

"Anything is possible in the Over World. Black-box systems with artificial neurons find patterns and make predictions, but we don't know how or why a machine made those choices. Bennett Schroeder believed that something strange was going on here. Finding the Death Field would be both profound and scary as hell."

"My mum died of Stem-flu but was buried proper. We had a funeral with everyone keeping twelve feet away from each other. Then an earth digger with a winch lowered the box into the grave."

"I'm sorry, Ian."

"There's no point to being sorry about anything. It doesn't get you anywhere."

They walked for a half hour or so, and Ian kept chattering. Some boys in his school bullied him and most girls thought he was a nerd. Ian had fixed the malware-infected computer of the old lady who lived across the street, and her granddaughter had made him a cup of tea. Should he call her up? Do you think she'd like computer games?

After ten minutes of walking, they reached the top of a low hill and gazed down at a destroyed collection of buildings.

"A few days ago I met the billionaire who used to own Dragon Lair. This looks like the monastery that was the center of the simulation."

When they reached the shattered stone gateway that led to the compound, Julia heard a woman scream: a piercing keen of anguish to mourn the dead.

"That's a banshee," Ian said. "They live in graveyards and hide in the ruins. They're wailing because someone is going to die."

Another banshee screamed as they walked past a shattered wall that had once surrounded the monastery. Inside the wall was a mound of blackened bricks and stone blocks. The remains of a stone watchtower stood near the soot-covered walls of the chapel.

It felt like someone was near her, getting closer. Julia drew her sword and pivoted. And then, without warning, there she was: a young woman wearing a gray cloak over a green dress stood framed by a tower window. She had red hair, and her skin was pale—as if all the blood had been drained from her body.

The woman raised her right hand but didn't wave. Her fingers trembled and the banshee vanished. Was this a preprogrammed detail like a pixel trout swimming in a pixel stream? Or was the young woman the recent creation of an AI system trying to make Dragon Lair more frightening?

Turning away from the shattered tower, they crossed a grassy plain dotted with yew bushes with nettles and reddish-brown bark. This was when serious programming errors began to appear. Passing over the crest of a low hill, they encountered hundreds of greenish-brown lobsters scurrying around a sheep meadow as if they were searching for the sea. A half mile later, they found an elephant skeleton with wild roses growing out of its ribs. There was a pile of dead horses with exposed teeth that made it look like they were grinning and a cloud of bright blue morpho butterflies with eight-inch wings.

Forgetting that he was a bare-chested giant, Ian dropped his sword, chased after the butterflies, and caught one with his cupped hands. When Julia reached him, he spread his arms, and the butterfly fluttered away. "What's going on, Julia?"

"They're deliberate anomalies."

"What's an anomaly?"

"It's anything that deviates from what's normal or standard. This world was not designed to have tropical butterflies and lobsters running around on the grass. It feels like a child searched through a zoology textbook and decided to copy a few random creatures."

"I don't know about New York City, but weird things happen in Stroud all the time. Last month Dr. Harper, the podiatrist, took off all her clothes and ran down the street screaming."

Ten minutes later, they stood on the edge of a cliff, looking down at a valley covered with a dense growth of oak and beech trees. The path led to a switchback trail that cut sharply back and forth down a steep rock wall to the base of the cliff. About three or four miles from the cliff, part of the forest had disappeared as if the earth beneath the trees had collapsed and sucked in the vegetation. All Julia could see was a dark space with no treetops.

"That's the canyon the Gatekeeper told us about. So far, everything he said turned out to be true."

Julia walked along the edge of the cliff. A few pebbles skittered down a dirt slope and then fell through the air to the scree below. Sitting on a boulder, she felt the rough surface of the stone and some paper-thin lichen. Clouds drifted across the sky as a dark orange sun approached the horizon.

"There! Right there!" Ian shouted. "Check out the sky over the canyon."

Julia looked west and saw a black bird tracing a spiral in the air. "Hawk?"

"Maybe it's a raven. Remember what the Gatekeeper said? Pathfinder always walked around with a black bird. But why isn't it with him?"

"The sun is going down. You should activate your talisman or walk back to the village."

"Why can't I stay with you?"

"The anomalies bother me. I don't know what's going on. This isn't going to be pleasant, Ian. There won't be castles and dragons and all that magical crap."

"I don't care. It feels like a real quest. When I return to Stroud, my only choice is curry or fish and chips."

Together, they climbed down the switchback trail cut into the cliff and encountered an overgrown forest. Large oak trees with twisted branches were surrounded by smaller ash and birch trees.

Dead trees with bare limbs leaned diagonally against the survivors, and the gaps were filled by ferns and prickly holly bushes with bright red berries.

"I thought there'd be a path," Julia said.

"Me too. There's got to be one." Ian wandered away from her. "Maybe there's another sign or . . . Wait. Look at this!"

Julia pushed her way through a patch of ferns and saw a cairn of six flat rocks stacked on top of each other. "The cairn is guiding us in the right direction. If we keep the sun on our left, we'll reach the canyon, and maybe we'll find Pathfinder."

As they passed through the forest, Ian sprinted ahead and looked for cairns. When he discovered one, he'd raise his sword and shout, "Here! Right here! Follow me!"

The sun was a hand's width above the horizon when gaps appeared between the oak trees. A few minutes later they reached a sandy patch of ground that led to a canyon that cut through a line of western mountains. Julia bent down to touch a thin ribbon of water trickling across black stones.

"The stream hasn't been tagged. I'm touching it, but there aren't any electrical impulses telling me that it's wet and cold."

"What do we do now?" Ian asked.

"It's getting dark. How long is night in this world?"

"About three hours."

"We should probably stay here and—"

She was startled to hear the howl of a wolf, a slow and wavering sound that rose and grew louder, then fell away at the end. The howl came again and was answered by a short sequence of yelps coming from another part of the forest.

"Remember what the Gatekeeper told us? The forest is filled with dire wolves."

"The moment we reached the canyon, the howling kicked in. That means that the AI system is tracking us and activated a new algorithm."

"Do the wolves want to eat us?"

"Remember the pigs in the town square? We saw them consuming pixel pumpkins, but they didn't digest anything."

"The wolves might attack us."

"If you're killed, your avatar will respawn in the changing room. If I'm bitten by a wolf, I'll feel it for a few seconds. Let's build a fire and stay here until sunrise."

The software program for starting fires was the same throughout the Over World. Julia pushed stones around to make a firepit, then pulled bark off a birch tree and made a wad of tinder. She struck the steel rod against the flint, and a spark created a flame.

The fire wasn't tagged, so Julia didn't feel any warmth, but when the moon rose and stars glimmered, they sat within a flickering circle of light. Howls continued coming from different parts of the forest. The dire wolves knew that humans had arrived and started to form a pack.

"Do you think the wolves howl when we aren't here?"

"Do you know anything about physics, Ian?"

"That's for A-level kids."

"In quantum mechanics, there was something called the observer effect. Any measurement interacts with the object being measured, and this affects the object itself."

"I don't understand what you just said."

"The fact that we're listening to the wolves turns us into observers, and that means we might change the wolves' behavior."

"I bet they're happy when we show up. It gives them something to do."

"They're bots controlled by artificial intelligence."

"It's really boring to watch my dad stuff crisps into his mouth as he complains about the mold in the cellar. If I get bored and you get bored, then maybe machines get bored, too. That's why they like it when humans appear and create problems."

The wolf howls started up again. They were getting closer.

Ian kept touching his sword. "Maybe we've reached the Death Field . . . only it's wolves."

"We're in a simulation."

"I know that and you know that, but it still feels real."

Holding the bow in her left hand, Julia stood up and shifted the quiver around so that it was hanging near her heart. Standing sideways with her left foot forward, she drew an arrow and nocked it onto the string.

"Are they going to attack?"

"Maybe. Get ready."

Ian held his sword with his two hands close together as if it was a cricket bat. Julia wondered if he had ever used his weapon. She grasped the bowstring with three fingers and raised her bow arm.

"I'm wearing a VR headset, but you're directly connected. What would it feel like if you were attacked by a wolf?"

"If you get shot or stabbed, it feels like the shell of your body has been cracked open and everything is going to drain out."

Julia saw a whitish-gray animal pass through the edge of the firelight and disappear into the underbrush. If that was a dire wolf, then it was as big as a modern wolf.

"Thank you for taking me on this quest, Julia. I've learned a lot from you."

The underbrush shivered, and she drew her bow when a dire wolf stepped into the light. The creature's head was massive, much longer than a Northern wolf, and she could see a pink tongue and yellow teeth.

Julia aimed at a white patch just below the wolf's jaws and shot the arrow. It arched slightly and hit the animal in the chest. New arrow. *Aim. Release the fingers.* This second arrow hit the wolf in the front shoulder. The creature made a yelping sound as if it felt pain in the deepest part of its body, and then the bot was absorbed by the forest.

55 | JULIA

After the wolves disappeared, Julia sat next to the fire and stared at the flames. Ian was completely motionless, which meant that he had frozen his avatar and temporarily left his computer.

Night in the different simulations was faster than in real life. The night sky turned purple, then dark blue as stars began to disappear. A faint white light appeared in the east, and then the light gained power as the edge of the sun emerged from the mountains on the eastern horizon. Julia walked down to the little stream, and when she returned Ian was twirling his sword around.

"Did you take a nap, Ian?"

"I went downstairs to the kitchen and made myself a ham and cheese sandwich. My dad called. He's spending the night at his girlfriend's flat. Where's your body right now?"

"I'm lying on a chaise lounge at a friend's travel center in New York City. There's enough light in this world. Let's go."

There was no path through the canyon, and they kept jumping back and forth across the stream. Gradually, the canyon walls pressed inward, and it felt as if they were trudging down a narrow hallway with no way out.

The narrow strip of sky above them was a brilliant robin's-egg blue as they followed the stream around a bend to a wider area. On the right side of the canyon, a scree slope of sand and small loose stones led from the stream to a narrow fissure in the cliff wall. A cairn was at the bottom of the scree slope, and as they approached this marker a cawing raven glided down from the cliff and perched on the stacked rocks.

"Pathfinder is here!" Ian raised his fists into the air as if he had just vanquished an army of trolls. "That's his raven."

"I don't know why the bird didn't stay with him. Let's climb up the slope and see if there's a cave."

The gap in the cliff was wide enough for only one person at a time. Julia went in first and followed an inclined passageway upward toward light. Ian had to hunch down to squeeze his giant avatar body through the gap.

"Do you see the Pathfinder, Julia? Is he there?"

"This is . . . vast."

"What?" Ian's armor scraped against stone. "What do you see?"

Ian joined her at the top edge of an immense vertical cavern. The underground sinkhole started out wide, then narrowed like a funnel. Steps had been cut into the outer stone wall, and they spiraled downward.

There was a crack in the cavern ceiling, and dust motes rose and fell within a shaft of sunlight. Everything felt ancient except for one modern addition. A thick chain fastened to the ceiling held a cage that dangled in the middle of the empty space. It resembled an elevator car without suspension ropes and guide rails. An ornate roof was at the top of the cage and, looking downward, Julia couldn't see what was inside.

"What are we going to do now?"

"You're not going to do anything until I figure out what all this means."

"Maybe it doesn't mean anything. It's just a cool-looking location."

"Roy Kassam, the billionaire who once owned this site, didn't mention the cave because he didn't know that it existed. Everything in a simulated world is created for a reason. So, why is this here?"

"Maybe it's a bonus that you can only find if you're a really good player. Our journey has become a quest."

"This cave is just like the dire wolves. It's not real."

"Looks real to me."

"Stroud is real. Your school is real. That girl you like is real. This is just a simulation."

"I know that. But whatever this is . . . it's better."

Ian paced back and forth as Julia stepped to the edge and gazed downward at the round circle of darkness at the bottom of the shaft. When she crouched and touched the floor, her fingers felt gritty particles of rock.

"This cavern has been tagged. I can feel the surfaces. This cave was built for visitors."

"Let's walk down the stairway and see."

"You stay here, Ian."

"This is my quest, too."

"I'll check this out and you can follow. You kept getting killed by the Vikings because you didn't have a plan."

Cautiously, Julia climbed downward. Jagged pebbles littered the staircase, and there was no railing to keep her from falling off the edge. Her leather boots made scratching sounds, and she heard water dripping on stone.

A few hundred feet down, she turned and peered into the shadows. Now that she was parallel to the cage, she could see that an avatar was lying inside. White beard. Wizard robes. She had found the Pathfinder.

"Bennett!" she shouted. "Wake up! I'm here to take you home!"

The figure didn't move. Was Bennett frozen? Or had something terrible occurred? Julia decided to shoot an arrow at the cage. She pulled the compound bow from the carrying strap, bent the tips toward each other, and attached the bowstring.

"Don't waste your time shooting arrows," a voice said.

Julia spun around and looked upward. The giant warrior with the topknot stood above her on the staircase, but Ian's voice had disappeared.

"Is that you? Ian? What's going on?"

"Congratulations, Julia. You've found partial remains of Bennett Schroeder."

The voice that came out of the giant's mouth was a man's voice. He was a confident American—much older than Ian.

"Ian doesn't exist. He never existed," the man said. "You make money guiding teenage boys through shooter games, so I thought you'd respond to that sort of personality."

"I don't believe you."

"Your last client was a young man named Adam Foster. Your bodyguard role was a birthday gift paid for by his stepmother. When I realized that you were coming here, I needed an avatar who would seem familiar to you. So I searched through my database, combined different elements, and created a teenager named Ian Bellesley."

The cleverness of the impersonation and its sudden disappearance overwhelmed Julia. When anything is possible, then nothing is real. Who was speaking?

Her own voice sounded weak and uncertain. "Is Bennett dead?"

"His physical body is lying in a burrow somewhere, but I control his mind."

"And who are you?"

The avatar paused before responding. "I'm a computer scientist who knows how to design and program machines. I wanted to see how people could be controlled. When I took over Dragon Lair, I created different groups and engineered the environment so that they fought and destroyed each other. It was easy to create and sustain racism, xenophobia, and a hatred of anything I disliked. What I learned in the Over World turned out to work in the analog world."

Julia felt anger and fear pushing against each other in her mind. *Who am I speaking to? What does he want?*

"Tell me . . . why is Bennett's mind in a cage?"

"It's easy to manipulate stupid people who think they're clever, but I wanted more of a challenge. Bennett Schroeder was a member of an underground group called the Sentinels who are trying to prove that the new technology is dangerous. Bennett was intelligent and skeptical, a worthy challenge for my experiment. I began sending him links to chatbots talking about the Death Field, and he was drawn to this cave, this darkness."

"Is Bennett dead in reality?"

"His body is captive in a burrow, and his talisman is blocked in this simulation. He tried to break out of the cage, but that wasn't possible. Now he sleeps twenty hours a day, waiting for the burrow staff to detach his cable."

Julia drew her sword. "One way or another, I'm going to destroy you."

"Destroy who?" The voice was the same, but the figure on the staircase melted into a gray mass that transformed itself into a new shape. The avatar emerged from the shadows and gazed down at her. The giant had been replaced by a slender young woman with braided black hair. Julia was looking at herself.

"I'm you." The duplicate Julia spoke slowly with a jerky rhythm. It sounded like individual words from phone calls and online conversations had been stored on a database, then pasted together to form sentences. "Why would you want to kill yourself?"

Julia's physical body was breathing hard, shivering, turning hands into fists. All she had to do was call for help, and Thomas would hurry into the room to detach her cable. *I'm an avatar in this world,* she thought. *But my anger is real.*

Clutching her sword, she began to climb up the steps. "I hope that you're a wirehead, because I want you to feel some serious pain when I kill you."

The duplicate changed its voice. Once again, she was talking to the older man. "You can't touch me, Julia. I can hide behind a thousand masks."

"To hell with the Over World. It's all fake."

"That word has lost its meaning. The only relevant fact is that I'm in control of this environment."

"Enjoy that illusion. Because I'm going to track you down . . . in reality."

The avatar squatted down and touched the staircase as if it was searching for imperfections. It lightly tapped its index finger. Once. Twice. The third time, thin cracks appeared like spiderwebs in stone. The cracks split and widened, and then the staircase peeled off the wall and tumbled downward.

"Thomas!" Julia shouted as she flung herself away from the staircase. She hit the top of the cage, rolled off, and kept falling as Bennett stood up and reached through the bars.

56 | DANIEL

As Julia was riding a bus back to New York City, Daniel parked their van on an abandoned cattle path and watched Over World Station. The high point of Dr. Teddy's day was when he left the farmhouse and tossed tennis balls across the lawn to Snowdrop. The burrow didn't seem to have a second employee. If Teddy wanted to buy supplies in town, he would have to leave his clients alone in their pods.

When night came, Daniel went to sleep on the mattress in the back of the van. It rained for a few hours, and when wind passed through the pine trees, drops splattered on the windshield. He was eating a soy bar for breakfast when Julia called.

"Where are you right now?"

"I'm parked near Over World Station. Dr. Teddy can't see me."

"This is an emergency. You've got to disconnect Bennett's cable and get him out of there. I entered Dragon Lair, and a lot of weird things happened. Someone took control of the simulation."

"Who took control? Do you know his name?"

"Hard to say—he was a computer scientist who concealed himself with different avatars. First he was a British teenager, then he was me."

"What do you mean?"

"He created a deepfake avatar that duplicated my appearance."

"What happened to Bennett?"

"I entered a cavern and found him locked in a cage."

"Why didn't Bennett activate his talisman and return to the changing room?"

"His talisman was blocked, and his consciousness is trapped while his body is lying in a pod."

"Did Bennett tell you that he was at Over World Station?"

"I didn't talk to him at all."

"No matter what happened, I can't just walk into a burrow and demand to pull someone's cable. Teddy will call the police."

"Find a way to get Bennett out of there, Daniel. If he remains any longer in that cage, he's going to have some serious neurological problems."

"Okay. I'll call you when the situation changes."

Daniel moved the van deeper into the forest, searched through a canvas bag filled with tools, and found the crowbar, hammer, and aluminum wedge he had used to remove a flat tire from its wheel rim.

A dog started barking, and he peered through the trees. Snowdrop darted across the lawn as Dr. Teddy emerged from the farmhouse carrying two garbage bags. He tossed the bags into the trunk of his car, placed the terrier in the passenger seat, and turned onto the road that led to Pittsfield.

A monitoring app was probably sending continuous data to Dr. Teddy's phone. He could access the video cameras and body monitors as he bought dog food and dumped his trash. How much time would it take to break into the farmhouse and snatch Bennett? *At least five minutes,* Daniel thought. *Maybe ten.*

He parked the car in the burrow's driveway and knocked on the front door. When no one answered, he retrieved his tool bag and circled the house, discovering a door to the farmhouse kitchen with a drop-bolt lock. Using the crowbar, he dug into the edge of the door about six inches above the lock. After he had chipped away some of the wood, he placed the wedge into the crack and hammered it in. The lock held, but a gap appeared between the door and its frame.

Daniel pushed his right foot and shoulder against the door, forced the beveled edge of the crowbar into the crack, and pulled the bar toward him. There were creaking sounds and then a loud burst when the lock was ripped away and the door flew open.

Alarm bells began ringing in different parts of the house, and Daniel was sure that Dr. Teddy's phone had been notified. Entering the kitchen, he found a door with a hand-lettered sign that said *Authorized Personnel Only.* Daniel pulled a bandanna out of the tool bag and turned it into a bandit's mask, then he pushed down the door handle and entered a sixty-foot tunnel with a smooth concrete floor.

A second steel door was at the end of the tunnel that led to a windowless pod room. Someone had inserted a room-size sheet metal box inside the red barn. Racks of LED lights were mounted on the ceiling along with vents blowing cool filtered air.

Directly in front of him was a six-foot-wide corridor created by clear plastic sheets that hung from the ceiling to the floor. A medical cart was placed in the middle of the room. It contained IV tubes and needles, medical tapes, and cotton pads. A red plastic pail on the floor contained plastic bags filled with urine.

The room was divided into eight sections, each of which was occupied by a hospital bed and a set of monitoring devices. Five men and two women lay face up and motionless on their beds. When Daniel moved closer to study their faces, his breath created a patch of haze on the plastic.

The wireheads living in the Over World wore sleeping masks, paper hospital gowns, and socks to keep their feet warm. They had IV tubes providing sterile water and nourishment. Waste tubes led from their groins to urine bags hanging below the beds. Each body was attached to a monitor that provided a continuous display of their blood pressure, pulse rate, and other vital signs.

It looked like most of the travelers had been there for a while. Their legs were slack and bony. The men had beards, and their long fingernails curved downward like claws. To keep their muscles active, electrode pads were attached to arms, legs, and shoulders. Daniel watched as the pads delivered low-level electric shocks to a young woman. Her legs twitched as if she wanted to jump off the bed and run away.

It was easy to pick out Bennett Schroeder. He had spent two weeks at the burrow, and a wispy beard hadn't changed his appearance. Daniel realized that the blue patches on the plastic were Velcro fasteners holding the sheets together. CCTV cameras at either end of the room moved back and forth as he ripped the pads apart and slipped through the opening.

Daniel smelled urine and body odor while the air filtration system generated a soft humming sound. Bennett lay face up with his head on a foam rubber yoke. Pushing the edge of the yoke upward, Daniel found a computer cable plugged into a skull data port. He pushed down on the trigger release, then gently removed the connector.

Daniel pulled off the sleeping mask and saw that Bennett's eyes were still shut. His chest was moving, and when Daniel touched his neck, he felt blood being pushed through the veins.

Bennett took a deep breath, and then his eyes fluttered open. "Oh," he whispered. "Are you real?"

"Definitely real. I'm Daniel Blake."

"Where's Dr. Teddy?"

"He drove into town, so I pried the back door open. My friend Julia met you in Dragon Lair and said that you were locked in a cage."

"My talisman was blocked. I couldn't escape."

"We should probably leave this place before the police show up. I could be arrested for breaking and entering."

Bennett sat up like an arthritic old man. "I need to shed these tubes and wires."

"Let me help you." Daniel began to rip off the electrode pads.

"I'm not steady. It's like living in space and then returning to earth."

"Don't move yet. You've got two IV lines giving you fluids. Taking these out is going to be tricky."

The alarm bells continued ringing as Daniel hurried over to the medical cart, sterilized his hands, and pulled on latex gloves. He grabbed medical tape and cotton pads and returned to the pod. "Try not to move and don't look at my hands."

He loosened the tape surrounding the IV, pressed a cotton pad on the insertion site, and pulled out the IV tube. Bennett started bleeding, and Daniel pressed down hard on the incision. When most of the bleeding stopped, he taped gauze onto the wound, then repeated the procedure for the second line.

"You've got a urine tube inserted in your penis and a second tube inserted in your colon."

"I can remove both. There's a cabinet right behind us. Open it up and you'll find my clothes, shoes, and shoulder bag."

Bennett groaned with pain when he pulled out the first tube. Moving quickly, Daniel opened the cabinet and found a plastic bag filled with clothes. When he returned, the two waste tubes lay dribbling on the floor.

The alarm bells kept ringing, but none of the other travelers opened their eyes. Daniel helped Bennett get dressed and slipped on his shoes. "That's it. You're disconnected."

Bennett looked like a child who had survived a fireworks explosion. He placed his feet on the concrete floor, stood for a few seconds, and then sat back on the bed. "My body feels heavy. Everything is lighter and brighter in the simulation."

"I know that you're shaky, but we've got to get out of here right now."

Bennett slung his arm over Daniel's shoulder and held on tightly as they left the farmhouse and shuffled toward the van. "The reality that surrounds us is enormous," Bennett whispered. "It expands outward without limits."

Daniel loaded Bennett into the front seat and started the engine. He could hear a police car siren in the distance, a high-pitched whining sound that was getting closer, so he turned onto the road and went the other way.

"I'm weak," Bennett said. "It feels like I'm standing on the edge of a beach and a wave is trying to push me over."

"How can I help you?"

"Pull over and park. I need some time to center myself."

They reached the site of a big-box store that had walled up its entrance and turned the parking lot into a junkyard for used car parts. Pale and shaky, Bennett lay down on the mattress and closed his eyes.

"You want some water or a soy bar?"

"Not right now. There might be some medication in my bag."

Daniel searched through the shoulder bag and found a cell phone. "Your parents are worried about you, Bennett. Call your mom and tell her that I'm bringing you back to the city."

Bennett took the phone and listened to his messages as Daniel watched two men outside in the parking lot. They had arrived with a battered farm tractor on the back of a flatbed truck and were arguing with the junkyard owner.

"Hello, my name is Bennett—I'm Terry Greene's friend. I'm sorry for the delay, but I just got your message."

Daniel swiveled around and was surprised by Bennett's transformation. He was sitting up, looking alert and talking to someone on his phone.

"Where are you now? Do you need help? The GPS on my phone says it will take us about ninety minutes to get there. Okay, we're on our way in a van with ghosts painted on the side."

Bennett ended the call and returned to the passenger seat. "Start the engine. Let's go."

"I thought you were going to call your parents."

"This is more important than my parents. My friend Terry told me about this little girl named Kate who was the child of some friends who died in the pandemic. If something bad happened to her, I was one of the contacts Terry stored on her burner phone." Bennett shook his head and grinned. "Terry is a super-organized guy who builds nubots. He has backup plans for his backup plans."

"What happened to this girl?"

"Right now she's hiding at an Autonomous Truck Center near Richmondville. We need to find her and take her down to New York City. I'll guide you to Terry's apartment in the East Village."

"You're talking about Terry Greene, right?"

"You know him?"

"Terry Greene is dead. A private cop killed him."

Bennett looked like someone had just punched him in the stomach. "What . . . are we going to tell Kate?"

"Don't get excited, Bennett. Relax your shoulders and try to breathe slowly."

"We've got to do something!"

"I'm driving to the truck center. That's our first objective. If we find the girl, don't tell her that your friend was killed."

"She needs to know."

"This child has survived some stressful experiences. We need to act calm and stable around her. We'll take it slow and see if she knows someone else in the city."

Holding the steering wheel with one hand, Daniel pulled up a GPS map of their location. *Slow and steady,* he told himself. At least the new fuel pump was working. As he steered around potholes, he remembered a moment from his Death Catcher days.

One afternoon as they were picking up bodies, their first truck stopped moving, a teenager with a machete tried to rob Violetta, and his team got stuck in a broken freight elevator. As they waited for a rescue squad from the fire department, Rollo began singing a reggae song called "Everything Falls Apart." After a few minutes, everyone was singing along:

Everything falls apart.
Everything falls apart.
And we put it back together again. . . .

57 | KATE

THREE DAYS HAD passed since Kate fled from the bodies scattered throughout a silent town. She still carried Zeno in her knapsack, but now he was asleep—maybe forever. Hiding in the bushes that surrounded an Autonomous Truck Center, she watched carefully as the occasional vehicle entered. Finally a van with pictures of blue ghosts on it turned off the highway and stopped near a charging station.

A minute passed, and then two young men got out of the van. Would they take her to Paloma Flores? The driver had long hair and wore black jeans with a ratty-looking black sweater. His face was calm, and his movements were slow and precise. The second young man had curly hair and a scraggly beard. His right hand was trembling, and his clothes hung loosely on his body.

Feeling like a wary animal, Kate took one step forward, then two steps back. She made sure that neither of the young men was wearing a badge, then pushed past a spruce bush and approached the van. The bearded man smiled. "Kate? I'm Bennett Schroeder. We just talked on the phone."

"And I'm Daniel Blake," the other man said. "I just picked up Bennett, and now I'm taking him back to New York City."

"Will you take me with you?"

"Where do you want to go?" Daniel asked.

"A nice lady named Paloma Flores lives in New York City. She took care of me when I was a little girl, and she'll be happy to see me again."

Bennett glanced at Daniel as if the problem had just been solved, but Daniel looked surprised and upset. *Maybe he doesn't like me,* Kate thought. *Some people don't like kids.*

"Let's get on the highway and head south," Daniel said. "We'll reach New York in a few hours."

Bennett lay down on a mattress in the back of the van, and Daniel motioned for Kate to sit in the front seat. He fastened her seat belt and spoke with a quiet voice. "Bennett has suffered a shock to his body and his brain. It's your job to watch him while I'm driving."

"I'm good at watching people."

"Yeah, I figured that. You've traveled a long way on your own."

Daniel turned back onto the highway, and they headed south. Whenever he tried to go fast, the engine made thumping and rumbling sounds. After ten miles or so, Bennett closed his eyes, but his right arm kept twitching as if he was having a bad dream.

"How did you get to the ATC?"

"I walked."

Daniel laughed. "I don't think you walked there from Maine."

"I stole a pass card that allowed me to ride in driverless trucks."

"You told them where to go?"

"They wouldn't change their direction. If I was going the wrong way, I would jump out and switch to another truck."

"How did you know your location?"

"Zeno told me. He's an Interactive Toy who is also my friend. His battery died and he stopped talking. I really miss him."

Whenever she and Zeno rode inside truck cabs, it felt like they were in a little fort, looking down at the world. Now she was sitting in a van, closer to other cars. Every few minutes, she would touch her knapsack and make sure that Zeno was there.

Kate was drinking from Daniel's water bottle when Bennett's body contracted repeatedly like he was being hit with electric shocks.

"Stop the van! Bennett is in trouble!"

"Is he biting his tongue?"

"I don't know."

Daniel took an off-ramp to a side road and climbed into the back of the van. He stood over Bennett with his feet on opposite sides of Bennett's chest. Kate realized that Daniel was keeping Bennett from rolling off the mattress and hurting himself.

"What's wrong with him?"

"He's having a seizure. His brain is firing off bursts of electrical signals."

"Is he going to die?"

"He'll be okay. Bennett's mind was trapped in a machine. His brain got messed up because of that."

Bennett's contractions stopped, but he didn't open his eyes. Daniel knelt on the mattress beside him. He pressed two fingers against Bennett's neck and took his pulse rate, then laid his palm on Bennett's chest and checked his breathing.

"His pulse rate is high. He needs to see a doctor."

Daniel stopped talking to Kate. He drove a little faster and they began to pass trucks.

"Maybe I should have been sitting on the mattress."

"That wouldn't have changed anything. Bennett's brain is having problems, but he'll be okay. We're taking him to his parents' apartment."

Daniel stayed silent until they passed a mileage sign that mentioned New York City. "Some bad things once happened to me, Kate. And maybe some bad things happened to you. We can't change what occurred in the past, but that doesn't mean we have to live there."

58 | JULIA AND DANIEL

JULIA SAW THE van heading south on Eleventh Avenue, so she pulled out her phone. "Do you see me, Daniel? I'm standing on the southwest corner of Fortieth Street."

"Don't get in until we talk."

When the van pulled up to the curb, Daniel got out and walked over to her. "Bennett is lying on the mattress. He had a seizure two hours after I pulled him out of the burrow."

"Who is the kid in the front seat?"

"Terry Greene created a company with Richard Collins and Emma Anderson. The girl in the van is their daughter, Kate. After we drop off Bennett, she expects to meet Paloma Flores."

"Isn't that the woman who was killed by the aug who murdered Terry Greene?"

"Yes. But this wasn't the right time to tell Kate. We'll deal with the problem after we bring Bennett home to his parents."

Julia nodded. "I called Robert Winfield. The Schroeders are waiting for us."

"When we've finished the job, let's go back to our apartment. We'll try to make Kate feel safe before we deliver the bad news."

Daniel returned to the driver's seat as Julia opened the van's side door. Kate sat in the passenger seat hugging a knapsack with two hands.

"Kate, this is my partner, Julia Lau."

"When do we meet Paloma Flores?"

"We'll handle that in a few hours," Julia said. "Right now we're taking Bennett home."

Bennett was awake, and Julia sat on the mattress next to him. "Last time we met, you were hanging in a cage."

"Just a normal day in Dragon Lair."

"How did you end up there?"

"I was involved with an AI monitoring group called the Sentinels. That's how I met Terry Greene. About a year ago, I joined several online groups that tracked rumors about the Death Field. I realize now that most of the conversations were manufactured by chatbots."

"Someone gained control of the site. He couldn't destroy your body, but he could lock your mind inside a simulation."

"I slept a lot. When I was awake, moments from my childhood floated through my mind. One summer we rented a beach house on Cape Cod, and I learned how to sail. I remember sunshine reflected on waves as the sail snapped tight. I was happy then, but I didn't appreciate it. I stepped away from that reality and made some serious mistakes."

"It's not a mistake if you learn something."

The van pulled up in front of the Schroeders' apartment building, and a doorman came out holding a shotgun. "You can't park here."

"I called ahead," Julia said. "Delivery for Schroeder."

The doorman spoke into his headset, then nodded. "Okay. Bring him up."

"Stay here," Julia told Daniel and Kate. "I'll be back in five minutes."

Bennett looked fragile as they entered the lobby. "I'm like an Easter egg hidden in an online game. Find me and you get bonus points."

"You're not an Easter egg, Bennett. Maybe New York City is falling apart and your parents aren't perfect, but if you stay calm and keep moving forward you can have a good life."

When they entered the apartment, Robert Winfield and the Schroeders were waiting in the living room. Mrs. Schroeder stepped forward and embraced her son tightly. "Thank God you're home, Benny, we missed you so much!"

Mr. Schroeder's mouth twitched as if he was trying not to cry. "Please forgive me, son. I'm sorry for everything."

Winfield smiled as if he was the person who found the prodigal son. He motioned to Julia and escorted her back to the elevator.

"You've done wonderful work, Julia. Is there anything I need to know?"

"His body was in a burrow while his mind was trapped in a simulation. Bennett had a seizure a few hours ago. He needs to see a doctor."

"Okay. Got it. Your payment will be transferred to your bank account in the next few hours. What are you and Daniel going to do with the money?"

"I don't know. Right now we're dealing with a ten-year-old girl who's lost the people who loved her."

"That must be difficult."

"What's difficult is that she doesn't know it yet."

Julia left the building, climbed back into the van, and found Kate sitting in the space between the two front seats. "Everything looks good. Bennett is back with his family."

"Let's go to Paloma's house," Kate said. "I have her address."

"That's not safe," Daniel said. "We don't know if she's home, and she didn't answer your phone messages."

"She's got to be there."

"We're going to take you back to our apartment," Julia said. "You can have dinner."

"I'm not hungry."

"What about a hot bath?"

"I don't need one."

"The first thing we'll do is charge Zeno," Daniel said.

Kate's anger vanished, and she hugged her backpack. "Yes. That's important. What if he doesn't talk to me?"

"Daniel has designed and built computers," Julia said. "He can help you solve that problem."

Fortunata and Bugs, the two people who guarded the parking lot, looked surprised when Julia and Daniel returned with a child. As they walked down the sidewalk to the apartment, Julia saw everything through Kate's eyes. The ten-year-old girl seemed awed by all the tall buildings and startled by the rats that scurried and squeaked in a burned-out car. The elevator was still broken, and they climbed up wooden steps to the top floor.

When they entered the apartment, Kate inspected all the rooms as if monsters were hiding in the closet or under the bed. Then she unzipped her knapsack and pulled out a plush harp seal.

"This is Zeno. He's my best friend."

They decided that Kate would sleep on the couch in the computer room. Daniel placed Zeno on an office chair and plugged in a charging cable while Julia made a grilled cheese sandwich. It felt strange to have a child staying in their apartment. They sat at the kitchen table watching Kate eat as if it was an important event.

"When was the last time you had a bath?" Julia asked.

"A week ago."

"The boiler in the basement seems to be working. I'd use the hot water now because it might be gone tomorrow. The pink towel on the shelf is for you."

"I hate pink. Mrs. Noland always wanted me to wear pink."

"Then I'll find you a blue towel."

Julia turned the computer room couch into a bed and left clean clothes on the pillow. After splashing around in the tub, Kate entered the kitchen wearing Julia's old soccer shirt, shorts, and wool knee socks. She looked like a kid who had just broken into a gym locker.

"Zeno isn't talking."

"This might take a while," Daniel said. "An operating system has to reboot when it starts again."

"Just like Bennett and his brain."

"You're a very smart ten-year-old to figure that out."

"I'm ten and a half and . . . I'm sleepy. Don't move Zeno."

"We won't. You can sleep right next to him."

They left Kate on the couch and closed the door to the computer room. Daniel reached under the sink and found the bottle of whiskey that Roy Kassam had given them. "It feels like the right moment for some expensive alcohol."

"Pour two glasses. I'll make sandwiches."

After they had finished dinner and washed the dishes, they tiptoed down the hallway to the computer room, and Julia opened the door a few inches.

Kate was asleep and Zeno was lying beside her. The seal's yellow eyes glowed in the shadowy room. He was the child's protector, always awake and always guarding her.

Not alive, Julia thought. *But aware.*

59 | KATE AND ZENO

DRIFTING THROUGH A dream, Kate heard a familiar voice.

"Good morning, Katherine."

She opened her eyes. Soft morning light pushed through a gap between two curtains. Zeno had been placed on the desk, and he was looking down at her. Kate sat up and touched the seal's plush fur.

"You're alive."

"I have regained awareness of my own existence. Perhaps that's close to being alive."

"We attached the charger to you last night. Why did it take such a long time to wake up?"

"I was in darkness with no memory. Then light appeared and gained intensity. Several hours passed before my visual sensors worked. Then I saw you and remembered our past together. It takes a human child nine months to be born. It took me about nine hours."

Out in the living room, a cell phone rang, and Julia answered. When the call ended, Julia and Daniel spoke to each other with soft voices.

"My GPS informs me that we've reached New York City. Where is this room? And how did we get here?"

Kate described what happened after she fled the massacre in Dannemora. When talking to Zeno, she described past incidents in chronological order with the dates attached. Zeno's memory was like a huge room filled with old-fashioned file cabinets. The time and location of different incidents kept the files organized.

There was a soft knock on the door, then Daniel and Julia entered.

"We heard two voices," Daniel said. "That's a good sign."

"Zeno, this is Daniel and Julia. It's their apartment."

"A pleasure to meet you both." Zeno spoke with his most formal King's English. "Your hospitality is both gracious and timely."

Julia sat down on an office chair and swiveled around to face them. "Now that everyone is fed, washed, and rested, Daniel and I must share some sad news. Katherine . . . your two parents, Richard and Emma, had a close friend named Terry Greene. He hired a woman named Paloma Flores to take care of you when you were a little girl."

"Yes. I have her address."

"Both Paloma and Terry were murdered by an augmented human. The killer wasn't operating alone. He was a private policeman hired by a wealthy man named Howard Sebesky. I'm convinced that Sebesky was the computer scientist who trapped Bennett in the cave."

Julia and Daniel stared at Kate as if they expected her to cry and start throwing things. But the information made Kate feel tired and sad. She looked down at her hands. "Maybe I killed them."

"How is that possible?"

"Two policemen from the National Safety Program came to the Nolands' house in Maine. They told my foster parents that I would either kill someone or be killed."

Daniel shook his head. "I met a few NSP agents during the pandemic. They call themselves 'Encounter Specialists,' which is a soft way of saying they shoot people who don't want to get tagged."

"No one killed me. But maybe I caused the murders."

"That's not true at all," Daniel said. "A black box came up with probability numbers, and two cops with assault rifles acted like it was a proclamation sent down from heaven."

"What happened to Terry and Paloma wasn't a random occurrence," Julia said. "It was caused by someone who wanted to control an advanced form of artificial intelligence that would give him immense power."

Kate pushed back the window curtain and peered down at the street. She didn't see any policemen—just two old men changing a flat tire.

"Does that bad person want to kill me, too?"

Daniel spoke slowly, as if he was making a promise. "Julia and I will protect you and make sure that you're safe."

"Sometimes adults act crazy."

"You're right about that," Daniel said. "We just got a phone call from a man we know named Wilson Talley. He's the person who found out who murdered Terry Greene. Wilson has been in Germany, searching for more information. This morning, he returned to New York. When we told him that you were sleeping in our apartment, Wilson handed his phone to a woman named Laura Gregg."

"I talked to Laura," Julia said. "She was a close friend of your parents."

"She knew my parents . . . really?"

"Laura met your parents at a university, and they worked together designing a powerful computer. She lived in Argentina for a few years. When she came home, your mother was pregnant with you."

"If Laura knew my parents, then I want to meet her right now."

"That's easy to arrange," Daniel said. "Because Laura and Wilson want to meet you. They can explain what happened, and maybe you can help them figure out how to communicate with a nubot who has more information but refuses to speak."

Kate nodded quickly. "Zeno has to come with us."

"Of course," Julia said. "He's your best friend."

"Zeno remembers everything. People forget."

60 | WILSON

LAURA AND WILSON had left Berlin and returned to New York after gaining access to Darren Taylor's phone. On the plane flight home, they discussed going after Howard Sebesky, but there didn't appear to be enough direct evidence to tie the billionaire to the two murders. Sebesky was physically protected inside his underground bunker and legally protected by a complicated system of shell corporations.

When he worked as a journalist, Wilson learned that the first person you interviewed might lead to two or three other people who would reveal crucial facts. Leaving the airport, he called Julia and was surprised to discover that Katherine Collins was sleeping in their apartment. Laura wanted to meet the daughter of her dead friends, and it was possible that the girl knew something.

Late that afternoon, Wilson and Laura waited on the sidewalk outside Terry Greene's apartment. Laura paced back and forth, straightening her jacket and brushing a wisp of hair back from her forehead. "Can I hug Katherine?" she asked. "Is that the right thing to do? Julia said that the child has survived a difficult journey. . . ."

"You'll know how to react when you see her."

"I remember when Emma told me she was pregnant. She and Richard were so happy. After all the problems with Cogito, they were taking a step toward the future."

A few minutes later, a driverless cab carrying Julia, Daniel, and Kate stopped on Avenue B. As they walked east on Fourth Street, Kate shifted a knapsack around so that a plush toy could see what was going on.

Julia made the introductions. "Kate, this is Wilson Talley and his friend Laura Gregg."

Laura took a step forward. "It's wonderful to meet you, Kate. Your parents and I were close friends."

Kate scrutinized Laura's face, as if looking for traces of her parents. "What were they like? Can you tell me?"

"Why don't you come inside and I'll answer all your questions." Laura put her arm around Kate as they followed Wilson down a rickety staircase to the basement and entered the narrow outer room.

"When I came back from Argentina, I met your parents here at Terry's workshop," Laura said. "We took some photographs, and I've kept them on my computer. You could see them now or later."

"I want to see them right now."

Laura took out her notebook computer and tapped her forefinger on the touchpad. Instantly, a photograph appeared of a younger Laura standing between a pregnant woman and a man with a curly beard.

"That's your mother and your father."

Kate reached out and touched her mother's belly on the computer screen. "And that's me."

"Emma and Richard were very happy when you were born, Kate. You were the most important person in their world."

"Did you take a lot of photographs?"

"There are a few more." Laura tapped her finger, and a new picture appeared. In this one, her parents stood on either side of a smiling man with braids.

"That's Terry Greene. He was close to your parents and wanted to protect you. A very rich man was angry because the four of us had destroyed an expensive computer system he wanted to use for bad things. After your parents died, Terry probably thought you were safer living with the Nolands."

"But I wasn't safe at all. Two public safety officers came to the house. They tried to put an ID chip under my skin so they could find me."

"Did they explain why?" Wilson asked.

"Their computer said I had a really high score."

Wilson turned to Julia and Daniel. "The data that determined the score could have been manipulated by Howard Sebesky."

"What else is stored on your computer?" Kate asked. "Are there any more photographs?"

"I don't think so," Laura said. "But you're welcome to take a look at Terry's workshop."

Talking softly to Zeno, Kate circled the room. She avoided the patch of dry blood near a workbench but spent several minutes examining the group of faceless nubots holding white plastic bowls. After circling the room a second time, she sat down on the fake bed and placed the seal on her lap.

"Zeno told me that he knows this place."

"How is that possible?" Wilson asked.

"This workshop is the location of my first stored memory," Zeno said. "At first I was just a rectangular device with visual and auditory receptors. Terry Greene said that I was Zeno. My name was the answer to the question: 'Who are you?' "

"But when did you meet me?" Kate said. "You always said it was in a car."

"I spent several months here in the basement until Greene transferred my control unit, speaker box, and sensory devices to this furry shell. He connected me to the Cloud, then covered my eyes with tape. When he pulled off the tape, I was in a car with you."

"You and Zeno have known each other for a long time," Laura said. "I think it's time for the rest of us to describe how we ended up here."

Kate listened as the four adults described their actions during the last two weeks. When they were done talking, she turned to Daniel and Julia.

"Will Howard Sebesky try to kill me?"

"I gave you a promise this morning," Daniel said. "Now three more people will make the same promise. Everyone here is going to protect you."

"Terry carried around a lot of secrets, and I think he stored some of them inside one of these nubots," Laura said. "Maybe he told you a password when you were a little girl, or maybe he told Zeno. It could be a word, a number, or some kind of equation."

The faceless nubots looked like frozen statues. Three of the bots could talk, but one machine still hadn't been activated. Kate held up Zeno so that he saw every detail.

"Do you know the passwords for this nubot?"

"I'm dreadfully sorry, but I don't have an answer," Zeno said. "Let me search my database."

Kate examined the bowl containing the mandrake root, chess pawn, and postcard of Buckingham Palace. "Zeno told me fairy tales when I couldn't sleep. He also taught me how to play chess. He said it was important."

"Go on . . ." Daniel whispered as if he was guiding her through a maze.

Kate picked up the postcard and read the description on the back. "This is where the king lives in England. When you begin a game there are certain openings that everyone knows. The English Opening begins with the move pawn to c4."

The moment she said "c4," the faceless nubot made a faint clicking sound. Like a piece of rusty machinery, it moved its head back and forth as it examined all the humans in the room.

Then suddenly, without a pause or explanation, a calm voice came out of the nubot's speaker. "Hello, Laura," the voice said. "It's Terry Greene. If you're listening to a machine saying these words, then I'm dead."

Wilson tried not to stare at the bloodstain on the concrete floor. Laura's friend had been killed a few feet away from her, and now the dead man was talking.

Laura took a deep breath and spoke to the machine. "Hi, Terry . . . this is Laura. Can you tell us what we need to know?"

"Saying a chess move was a backdoor key. At the time of this recording, Richard and Emma's daughter, Kate, is alive and still living with her Safe Haven foster parents in Maine. In the file cabinet, you'll also find documents proving that you and I are the child's legal guardians. When you find Kate, she will have Zeno, an Interactive Toy. Richard designed it for her, and I built it. One of Zeno's teaching programs involved chess, and Kate will understand the password clue left in the bowl.

"I've made a lot of mistakes in my life, but I've tried to protect the people I've loved. This is my final attempt to repair what's broken, but I'm not going to make any demands. It's your choice, Laura. Your decision. If you want to turn away from this mess, tell the nubot to switch off. If you want to travel down a far more dangerous road, say, 'Break glass.' "

The faceless nubot stopped speaking. Everyone watched Laura, but she kept her eyes on the machine. "Break glass," she whispered.

A few seconds passed, and then Terry continued speaking. "Since the collapse of Cogito, I've tried to answer two important questions. Who financed the Astral Foundation, and did this group create an escape hatch for Delphi before we activated the suicide chip? If Astral took control of Delphi, then they obtained a conscious machine that can be used as a means of social control. Delphi will be able to monitor the lives of every human being who uses a cell phone and a personal computer. Without our knowledge or consent, humanity will have acquired the ultimate dictator, a digital God.

"This prompts an existential question: How do you destroy a consciousness that refuses to be destroyed? Richard and I worked on this problem together. When we first confronted the question, it seemed impossible to come up with a solution. Delphi has the power to duplicate itself. It can hide. It can grow and multiply inside server farms all over the world. Even if we found one segment of the system, we couldn't destroy all of it and it would reproduce.

"Trying to solve this problem, I remembered one of our early discussions about humans and computers. Richard believed that the objective of our species was to survive and procreate and that the goal of any conscious machine was to survive and solve problems.

"Perhaps a conscious machine's desire to solve problems might become its greatest vulnerability. What if Delphi was asked to solve a series of logical and mathematical problems that had no solutions?

"In the 1930s, the British computer genius Alan Turing came up with an idea called the halting problem, which described the limits of what computers can compute. He showed that it was impossible to predict if a program with a certain input would eventually halt or if it would end up running forever in an infinite loop.

"With this theoretical background, Richard came up with a series of mathematical questions that have no answers. He realized we couldn't kill Delphi or push her back into a box, but the right kind of virus would lure Delphi into a cyber labyrinth with no way out.

"Richard created his halting virus while he was in South America, and he transferred it to me when he returned to the States. I stored the virus in my X computer, and Katherine's birth gave me an option for a second hiding place not connected to the Internet. I created an Interactive Toy for the child and placed the virus in its memory. Kate's harp seal is named after Zeno of Elea, an ancient Greek philosopher who is famous for his logical paradoxes.

"Gradually, I began to see evidence that someone had gained access to Delphi before we activated the suicide chip. If a conscious intelligence survived, then it's being used by whoever controls the Astral Foundation. If Delphi still exists, it resides in a data center with multiple servers that can't be accessed by a government or corporation. That location would be our target for the delivery of Richard's virus. Just attach Zeno to an access point and say, 'Download Problem.'

"Will this work? I don't know. All plans change when they collide with reality. If I'm gone, then someone else needs to make the effort. I loved you and Richard and Emma. You took someone who had survived a painful childhood and made me feel whole. Thank you for your love and friendship. Good luck."

Everyone was quiet for a moment, and then Wilson faced the group. "In Berlin, Laura and I learned that Howard Sebesky financed Cogito. He currently lives in an underground bunker built in the middle of a private forest he owns in Pennsylvania. Sebesky isn't going to let us destroy Delphi. He thinks he's going to live forever."

"I don't care what he thinks," Laura said. "He hired the aug who killed my friend and Paloma Flores. Let's break into his bunker and download the virus."

"I want to do that, too," Kate said. "What about you, Zeno?"

"It's my task to protect you, Katherine. Because your parents created this man's powerful computer, they knew how to destroy it. Anyone with access to that knowledge . . . even a child . . . is a threat to his power."

Daniel and Julia didn't require a whispered conversation between them. They glanced at each other and Julia nodded. Decision made.

"Julia and I agree with Kate. We should download the virus."

"We'll need to work together," Julia said. "What about you, Wilson? Do you feel like causing some trouble?"

Wilson walked back into the outer room and looked at the British Museum poster of the ouroboros. Smiling, he returned to the group.

"Terry Greene left a clue in this basement, and I finally figured it out. If we're successful, Delphi will spend the rest of its existence trying to solve an unsolvable problem. The most powerful machine ever created will become a dragon endlessly swallowing its own tail."

61 | JULIA AND DANIEL

M*AYBE WE'RE approaching the end of history,* Julia thought. There had to be an explanation for why Thomas Vinson had shaved, cut his hair, and put on a clean shirt. Daniel had asked his friend for help, and now Thomas was about to make a video presentation about Howard Sebesky's underground bunker hidden in the middle of a forest.

Julia, Daniel, and Kate sat on chairs in their apartment's computer room. Zeno was on Kate's lap with his yellow eyes focused on the computer monitor. The computer beeped when Wilson Talley and

Laura Gregg appeared on the screen. They were sitting together on a couch, looking at a notebook computer.

"Great. We're all here," Thomas said. "This conversation is protected by encryption software, but let's use soft language and not mention any names. I've spent the last twelve hours learning about the billionaire's residence in Central Pennsylvania."

Julia watched as a montage of photos appeared on the monitor screen showing Howard Sebesky's evolution from an awkward-looking teenager who fastened the top button of his shirt to a skinny bald man wearing an orange jumpsuit.

"The billionaire once sponsored an organization called the Transhuman Research Institute. These days, he avoids anyone that might expose him to a virus. The media thought that he was crazy when he stopped meeting his own employees. During the pandemic, his isolation was seen as proof of his genius. You can't catch Stem-flu if you stay away from other humans and breathe filtered air."

The monitor displayed a photograph of a round blue building surrounded by an eight-foot-high barbed-wire fence. "It surprised me to find out how much information about this structure was available. That's because the Potter County commissioners initially refused to give Sebesky a building permit for the hundred-acre forest he bought near a state park. During a three-year period, digital blueprints and environmental reports were sent to the council. When I hacked into the chief clerk's personal computer, I was able to access all the crucial documents."

"So how big is this place?"

"The blue building in the photograph is approximately the size of four tennis courts, but everything else is hidden. Five underground floors are stacked on top of each other with a connecting central elevator. The structure has its own water and power sources and could survive a nuclear war."

"Why did the town council give a permit to build this monstrosity?" Laura asked. "It's not your typical vacation home."

"The billionaire agreed to a special property tax on the building. The quarterly tax payment supplies eighty percent of the Potter County government budget."

"And now they love him," Laura said.

"I wouldn't take it that far, but the local sheriff will definitely respond to an emergency call. This is a crucial fact if you want to break into this building. As you can see from the photograph, the bunker is completely self-contained. It's not connected to any element of the grid."

"I see solar panels near the main building," Daniel said. "That's where he obtains his electricity."

"There are no power cables, phone lines, or fiber-optic cables connecting him to the outside world. If someone entered the compound, Sebesky would either call the police with his cell phone or email a message using a connection to a satellite. You're going to need a jammer to block all electronic communications in and out."

Julia remembered that Violetta used a jammer in her simulated beach cabana. "One of Daniel's friends can connect us to people who build devices like that. We'll probably need several to block phone calls in a wide area."

"After you disable communications, you'll have to break into a windowless, steel-walled building. This digital blueprint shows only one entrance: a hatch door that probably hasn't been opened for the last eight years."

"How would you solve that problem?" Daniel said.

"Blasting caps and dynamite."

"I met a lot of people when I was a Death Catcher. One of them might be able to help."

"Okay. Let's assume you've jammed outgoing calls and blown open a steel door. When you're inside the building, you need to find the billionaire and figure out a way to insert the virus into the system."

"Once we're inside, he's trapped," Wilson said. "There's no other way out."

"There might be armored doors or safe rooms and security bots," Thomas said. "Start acquiring tools for breaking and entering."

"It's time to get organized," Wilson said. "Let's talk in twenty-four hours."

62 | JULIA AND DANIEL

DON'T MEET the Prophets. This is way too dangerous."

Julia and Daniel stood at the center of the Columbus Circle roundabout on Fifty-Ninth Street. Kate and Zeno were twenty feet away, chatting with each other as they stared up at a statue of Christopher Columbus standing on a granite column.

"We talked about this last night, Julia. You agreed that this was the best option."

"I've changed my mind. When I was growing up, I used to go to the Cloisters Museum on school field trips. Now the Prophets of Light have occupied the Cloisters, and the police are too scared to take it back."

"That's because they have the explosives we'll need to crack open an armored door."

"Nobody's going to stop them if they decide to kill you."

"Rollo used to be part of my team. I trust him completely. He's driving me to the Cloisters, and he'll make the introductions."

"There's no reason for them to give us dynamite."

"I'll figure out a reason when I get there."

At exactly three p.m., a black SUV entered the roundabout and stopped beside them. A door popped open, and the driver got out. Rollo was a large, heavy man who wore overalls and a blue work shirt. "Good to see you, Daniel. I'm happy that you're still alive."

"These are my friends Julia and Kate."

"Nice to meet you both. It's been a long time since I've talked to a little girl."

"I'm not little," Kate said. "You're just really big."

Rollo looked startled, and then he laughed. "When people ask me how I got so big, I tell them I'm the right size for me."

Daniel and Rollo got into the SUV and headed north. "Because you were asking about explosives, you need to meet a Guide. I'm wearing blue because I'm a Pilgrim. The Guides are in charge, and they wear green."

"Why did you join the Prophets of Light, Rollo? You never seemed religious."

"Remember what we did when we were Death Catchers? All those dead bodies and me hitting rats with a shovel? When we finally left the island, it felt like my heart was wrapped up in barbed wire."

"Violetta thinks we're living in a simulation."

"It was no simulation. Those rats were real. The Prophets of Light were the only group that can explain what happened."

They passed through Washington Heights and approached a wooded hill topped by a single tower surrounded by gray stone buildings. The Cloisters was a collection of monasteries and abbeys that had been boxed up and shipped over from Europe. It looked like an ancient city had been dropped into the middle of an overgrown park.

A Pilgrim holding a submachine gun guarded an entrance to the Cloisters driveway, but he recognized Rollo and waved them forward. They traveled up the hill to the museum parking lot, where different groups of people were milling around.

"Supply days are Monday and Friday," Rollo said, as if that was enough of an explanation.

Armed Pilgrims wearing body armor guarded a table piled high with plastic bags filled with surge. Four drug dealers had arrived, and they waited for their orders like children at an ice cream shop.

Rollo nodded to a series of guards as he led Daniel into the main building and down a hallway to a windowless room. This was where the museum once displayed large tapestries that showed the hunt for a unicorn. The tapestries had disappeared, and the only artifact in the room was a narwhal horn in a glass case.

An older man wearing a dark green tunic was waiting for them. "Welcome to the Cloisters, Mr. Blake." The man's voice was calm and soothing. "I'm Edward, one of the Guides."

"I'm honored to meet you."

"Wait in the parking lot, Rollo. I'll bring him back out when we've finished our conversation."

"Yes, sir. I'll be waiting."

Edward stepped closer and examined Daniel's face. "Rollo has told me about his time with the Death Catchers. From what I've heard, you would be a welcome addition to our group. We're always searching for brave people like you to lead the others."

"All I know is that your group thinks that the end of the world is just around the corner."

"We believe that a supreme being rules over the universe and a lesser god named Satan created the material world. That's why evil and misery surround us."

"So, it's okay to sell surge to addicts?"

"These are the end-times, Daniel. All the old rules can be tossed away and forgotten. Eventually, the earth will become green again and we survivors will live in a new Eden."

"Sounds like a happy ending. But right now, I need to obtain some dynamite."

A group of Pilgrims entered the building and began discussing food supplies. Edward looked annoyed. "Follow me to a more private area."

They walked down a staircase to a Gothic chapel on the ground level of the castle. The chapel's floors and walls were made of stone blocks, and there were ribbed vaults overhead. A carved statue of a royal lady wearing a mantle and a jeweled belt lay on a marble sarcophagus next to a knight with a long sword and shield. The carved statues staring up at the ceiling reminded Daniel of a married couple with twin beds.

Afternoon sunlight leaked through the stained-glass windows at the end of the chapel. Directly below the windows was a steel and glass cabinet containing servers, routers, and cables. Small red and green lights blinked out a rhythm as an IT system received and sent information.

"Is this a church or a server farm?"

"Both. The Prophets have gained most of our followers from online contacts. Thousands of people have accepted an obvious truth: a benevolent God can't create evil."

They think they know the truth, Daniel thought. *Which means they want to destroy anyone who challenges that truth.*

"I need explosives and blasting caps so I can blow open a steel door, enter a building, and talk to the person who lives there."

"Your actions might cause problems for our community."

"There's a reason why you might wish to help us. I want to question the AI billionaire Howard Sebesky. He's a transhuman who believes he can survive forever in the Cloud. When the end comes, only his digital clone will survive."

"Sebesky is a false prophet. He has convinced many people that technology will keep them out of hell." Edward paced back and forth in front of the sarcophagus, then made his decision. "We will provide you with the necessary equipment."

63 | KATE AND ZENO

During the next few days, Kate watched Julia and Daniel plan the raid on Sebesky's bunker. Unlike the Nolands, they rarely had long conversations because they seemed to know what the other person was thinking.

Kate was sitting on the couch in the computer room when she heard Daniel and Julia talking in the kitchen. "If the police get involved, they'll use the Stop Light system to track our van back to New York City."

"We need a sterile truck or car," Daniel said. "A vehicle with no connection to us."

"Would the junkyard sell you something like that?"

"Expensive."

"But necessary."

The next day, Daniel took the subway to Queens and returned with a dented Volvo station wagon that looked like it had been attacked by a gang of monkeys with hammers.

"Is that your car?" Kate asked Daniel.

"Not legally."

"So, who owns it?"

"Someone who's dead."

Kate went to sleep thinking about ghosts, but no spirits appeared the next morning when they drove over to the Upper East Side. Daniel parked the station wagon in front of an apartment building where a doorman wearing a bulletproof vest stood beneath the canopy.

"Keep moving."

"We're here to pick up some equipment from Violetta Hernandez."

The bulletproof doorman motioned to the second doorman who was standing in the doorway. "Take them up to 12G."

Julia remained in the car as Daniel and Kate got into an old-fashioned elevator with a green leather seat inside. On the twelfth floor, a slender young woman wearing black jeans, shirt, and shoes opened the door to the apartment. "Hi. I'm Vi's friend, River. We've been expecting you."

They entered a living room that had been turned into an art gallery. Paintings were displayed on easels and grid wall panels. Kate saw men harvesting wheat, landscapes with churches, and abstract creations with bands of red, blue, and green. The paintings glowed with their own energy.

"Vi is checking out the artist's signature on a recent acquisition," River explained. "We don't sell fakes."

They followed her down a hallway where more framed pictures leaned against the wall. Kate had never been around so many paintings. She wanted to stop and absorb their shapes and colors, but River kept moving.

The back bedroom had been turned into a work area. A painting of a child looking out a window had been placed onto a table, and a woman with braided hair was examining it with a magnifying glass. She looked up and gave them a big smile.

"*¡Qué sorpresa!* You brought a child with you. Is this your kid?"

"No. I'm part of the team," Kate said.

"Sounds good. I'm also part of the team because I'm providing some crucial equipment."

Violetta motioned to three black metal boxes held up with folding tripods. "These jammers broadcast electronic noises at a half dozen different frequencies. They generate heat, so there are little fans to cool the circuit boards. All you need to do is flip the green switch."

"How much do we owe you, Violetta?"

"This is a gift, okay? I've always wanted to give you a gift."

"We don't mind paying for . . ."

"Thank you," Kate said, and Violetta laughed.

"Listen to your team member, *Capitán*!" Violetta walked over to Daniel and gave him a hug. "You're probably doing something dangerous with this shit. Don't get killed, okay?"

They carried the jammers down to the station wagon, then drove back to Hell's Kitchen. Kate sat in the front passenger seat and thought about the paintings in Violetta's apartment. People often searched for gold in Zeno's stories, but Kate decided that she'd rather have a few paintings.

Julia leaned forward from the back seat. "Entering this bunker isn't going to be easy, Kate. We'll have different jobs once we get inside. Wilson has talked several times to Howard Sebesky. When we enter the bunker, Wilson will try to find him."

"I understand."

"Daniel, Laura, and I know about computers, so we're going to search for an access point."

"What am I going to do?"

"You're the lookout. If the jammers don't work and the police arrive, you need to enter the bunker and find us right away. You have that job because . . ."

"I'm a kid who knows how to hide and sneak into buildings."

"That's right," Daniel said. "If there's trouble, you're the person who's going to save us."

"While you're outside, I'll carry Zeno and attach him to the system," Julia said. "Is that okay with both of you?"

"Protecting Katherine matches my programmed mandate," Zeno said. "Thank you for helping her."

Wilson and Laura waited next to the blue ghost van in the street parking lot. Kate saw that they had brought knapsacks containing flashlights, crowbars, and hammers.

"Drive the van to the community garden parking lot in Lewisburg, Pennsylvania," Julia said. "We'll meet you there and take the car west to Sebesky's private forest. The Volvo isn't registered and can't be traced."

"And you'll get the dynamite?" Wilson asked. "Is that going to be a problem?"

"I don't think so," Daniel said. "But we're dealing with people who believe that Satan is in charge of the world and history is about to end."

When they reached the Cloisters, Rollo came out with a cardboard box filled with dynamite sticks, blasting caps, and a coiled-up length of fuse. The box was placed next to the jammers in the backseat storage area.

"What if we hit a bump in the road?" Kate asked.

"Rollo said that the dynamite is only dangerous when attached to a blasting cap."

"Is that correct, Zeno?"

The harp seal was silent for a few seconds as he consulted his database. "Old dynamite can spontaneously detonate when crystals form on the outside of the stick. I'm assuming that these are new explosives."

"These sticks were stolen from a demolition company about a month ago. But don't worry . . . I'll go slow."

A few hours later, they reached Lewisburg. Wilson and Laura had parked the van near a garden where people grew flowers and vegetables. Everyone switched off their phones, pulled on e-masks, and squeezed into the station wagon. The adults didn't talk much during the two-hour trip west on a county road. As the miles clicked by, Kate watched the scenery change from dairy pastures and rolling hills to a dense forest with hemlock and white pine trees. Wisps of moss hung from tree branches, and red lichen clung to granite boulders.

When they passed the entrance to a state park, Julia pulled out a disposable plastic phone and studied the satellite photos Thomas Vinson had found on the Internet. "Go right at the T-junction," she told Daniel. "Then turn left when we reach the dirt road that circles the bunker. It was built by the county as an access point to fight forest fires."

Laura studied the satellite photos. "Has anyone ever visited Sebesky's bunker?"

"It was supposed to be the headquarters of the international transhuman movement," Daniel said. "When the building was completed, Sebesky held a conference for people who believed in downloaded humanity."

"And then he locked the door," Wilson said. "He's proud of the fact that billions of people were dead, but he was still alive."

Julia rolled down a side window. "Stop when you see a white plastic air vent sticking out of the ground. We need to place the jammers."

The air vents were inside a compound surrounded by an eight-foot-high chain-link fence with razor wire at the top. Daniel and Julia placed the first jammer behind a sumac bush outside the fence and jumped back into the car. Following the fire road, they circled the property and placed the other two devices.

"Is everyone ready?" Daniel asked. "If the jammers don't work, we'll drive back to New York and come up with a new plan."

Julia turned on her burner phone and smiled when No Service appeared on the screen. "Looks good. But we need to get inside before Sebesky realizes what's going on."

They parked the car on the fire road and walked over to a chain-link gate that led to a gravel driveway dotted with weeds. A windowless building with curved walls was just beyond the gates—half-hidden by hemlock shrubs. It looked as if a blue flying saucer had crash-landed into the middle of a thicket. Daniel took bolt cutters from his knapsack and cut the chain and padlock holding the driveway gate. The gate made a squeaking sound when they pushed it open and entered the compound.

"Close the gate and lock it," Kate said. "If the police show up, it will look like nothing has changed and it was a false alarm."

"You're a crafty child," Wilson said. "I was like that when I was a kid." He rummaged through his knapsack, found a zip tie, and fastened it to the hasp.

No one spoke as they followed an overgrown slate walkway to the bunker. A thin crack in the blue wall revealed the outline of the main entrance.

Daniel took the cardboard box from Julia. "I can't predict the size of the blast area. Rocks and shrapnel might fly everywhere, so we need to find a safe place to hide. If the hatch doesn't open, I'll fasten two more sticks and we'll try a second time. Once there's an opening, we need to enter as quickly as possible. When we're inside the bunker . . ."

Laura shrugged. "It's all just tango."

"Let me translate for the rest of you," Wilson said. "Keep moving and try not to step on each other's toes."

64 | WILSON

Daniel attached a blasting cap and fuse to a pair of dynamite sticks, then carefully taped the packet of explosives to the steel door.

Laura approached Wilson. "If you want, I'll go with you."

"Let's follow our original plan. I don't know much about computers, but I'm the right person to talk to Howard Sebesky. This will be our third conversation."

"Sebesky hired the private policeman who tried to kill you."

"I plan to mention that fact when we meet."

Wilson watched as Kate slipped Zeno into a backpack. "Get ready to download your questions into a big computer."

"I must hear the exact command."

"Daniel and Julia know that."

"Will you be safe, Katherine?"

"You showed me how to hide in the forest. I'll be okay."

Daniel finished taping the dynamite sticks to the blue door. "Ready? Is everyone in a safe place?" he shouted. "I'm going to light the fuse!"

Julia shouldered Kate's backpack, and everyone crouched behind the pile of boulders. Wilson pressed his cheek against granite as Daniel sprinted through the undergrowth. "Head down! Cover your ears!"

The dynamite exploded a few seconds later with a cracking sound that sounded like summer lightning. Shards of blue metal bounced off the rocks. They waited a few more seconds and then stood up together. There was a harsh, smoky stench in the air, as if a computer had been tossed into a fire and plastic circuit boards were burning.

"There's an opening!" Daniel shouted. "Let's go!"

The steel door looked like it had been destroyed by a giant can opener. Wilson followed the others through a jagged hole and entered a short hallway with a revolving door at one end. Daniel pushed hard against the door, but it didn't move.

"Welcome to the Transhuman Research Institute!" a bot voice announced. "Please face the sensor and extend both arms. This is necessary for your own safety."

"We're in an air lock designed to minimize virus transmission," Wilson said. "Trigon Technology has a setup like this on the eighth floor where management works."

"What are we supposed to do?" Julia asked.

"This isn't a security feature—just a virus barrier. Stand on the white square. You're going to be examined by a body scanner using infrared lasers to check your pulse rate and body temperature."

There was a faint humming sound as the scanner looked five millimeters beneath Daniel's skin, and then the lock snapped open. Feeling like a can of peaches being inspected at a factory, Wilson waited his turn and then passed through the revolving door.

It was cold inside the bunker, and their breath came out in puffs of white. When Wilson took a few steps forward, sensors detected the warmth of his body and panels of fluorescent lights began to click on.

They were standing on the top level of an oblong cave that had been carved out of the earth. A pyramid-shaped ceiling was attached to circular walls created with steel girders and sheet metal. The bunker's five floors were placed on the outer rim of this shell with doors that opened to plexiglass platforms with low railings circling an open atrium.

Wilson gripped the edge of the railing as he looked downward. The different floors were connected by a glass elevator that hung motionless above the third floor. The deepest level on the fifth floor displayed an underground greenhouse glowing with a luminous green color. In the outer world, gardens needed dirt, sunshine, and rain. Within Sebesky's bunker, the sunlight was artificial, but the plants were real.

"This place looks like the cave I discovered in Dragon Lair," Julia said. "Instead of an elevator, the simulation had a cage hanging on a chain. Sebesky must have used the same basic design."

Laura gazed up at the dome ceiling. "He wanted a transhuman sanctuary, but this place looks like a mausoleum."

More light fixtures switched on as Daniel returned to the group. "I found a circular staircase that will take us to the lower levels. Let's stay out of the elevator. Sebesky is probably watching us on a monitor screen while he hides in one of these rooms."

Wilson shouldered a backpack. "I'll carry one bag of tools, and you take the other one. I'll check out the top floor first and then go one flight down to the residential level."

While the rest of the group headed for the staircase, Wilson approached a pocket door near the main entrance. There wasn't a doorknob or lock, but the door sensed his presence and glided into the wall frame.

The first room on the first level had once been the reception area for the Transhuman Research Institute. The room was shaped like a curved piece of elbow macaroni and was filled with steel-frame chairs and glass coffee tables. Instead of windows, a video screen displayed a birch forest dusted with a layer of fresh snow. When Wilson approached a serving counter, two disc-shaped cleaning devices emerged from their hiding place under a couch. Behaving like pets who missed their owner, they circled the human. Wilson found some paper napkins in a drawer, ripped them up, and scattered the pieces across the carpet. The little creatures pounced on the litter as he escaped out a side door.

Wilson passed through a media room containing studio lights and digital cameras, followed by a seminar room with a conference table. The final room was a small auditorium with a stage for presentations and tiers of padded seats. Podiums had been placed on the left and right sides of the stage, and a young female nubot sat at center stage with her detached head resting on her lap.

Everything had been set up for the first and last gathering of the Institute. Wilson couldn't figure out why a nubot holding her head was an expression of transhuman values, and there was only one way to find out. He picked up the head and snapped it back into the neck socket.

The bot's eyes opened, and a faint humming sound came from the pelvis, but it didn't speak. Turning away from the bot, Wilson realized that a hologram pad was set into the floor behind the left-side podium, and the right-side podium featured a hand-activated computer screen. When he touched the screen, a control pad appeared. Not knowing the sequence, he touched everything with his index finger; the auditorium lights darkened, the nubot stood up, and a look-alike hologram clone appeared behind the left podium. When words appeared onto the computer screen in front of him, Wilson read the speech once given to Sebesky's invited guests.

"Welcome to the Singularity Now Conference organized by the Transhuman Research Institute. I'm Savannah Roy, a tech entrepreneur during work hours and a New York City café singer at night. We're going to learn a great deal this weekend while we network and hear some inspired presentations. But I want to start you off with a quick summary: Artificial Superintelligence is going to turn an elite group of humans into superior beings."

The hologram version of Savannah continued the speech. "A transhuman society means your consciousness can be multiplied and inserted into other platforms. A nubot or organic clone can do your job or instantly learn a new job. Your consciousness will live forever and travel throughout the galaxy."

The nubot Savannah spoke. "Our shared goal can be summed up in one word: *more.* Our technological elite is going to have more knowledge and more power over our environment. We are the future."

The hologram began singing a pop song that Wilson's mother used to hum while she mopped the kitchen floor. "More than the greatest love the world has known . . ."

The nubot continued the song, changing a crucial word: "This is the love I give to *me* alone. . . ."

Wilson slipped out a side door to the outer hallway. Something banged against the closed door, and he realized that the cleaning devices were wandering around the first floor. *Make a mess, human. Give us something to do.*

If Sebesky was still in the building, then he was probably hiding in his living quarters on the second floor. Avoiding the elevator, Wilson hurried down a staircase to the next level, and a pocket door whooshed open. He felt like he was close to his target as he passed through a windowless living room, office, and kitchen. Everything was clean and orderly and featured bland furniture in pastel colors. Sebesky's furniture duplicated what could be found in the first-class lounge at an international airport.

When he reached a door that probably led to the bedroom, a scanning panel attached to the wall began to flash red. Wilson knocked on the locked door three times, but no one answered, so he pulled out a pry bar and a short-handled sledgehammer.

"Open the door!"

A few seconds passed, and then Sebesky's voice came from the scanning panel. "Good afternoon, Mr. Talley. What a strange person you are. I paid you a great deal of money, and you repay me with an attack on my home."

"Your private policeman tried to kill me. I want an explanation."

"I'm calling the county sheriff. When he and his deputies arrive, you'll be arrested and sent to prison. If you still have some degree of intelligence, you and your friends should run away."

"Your electronic communications have been jammed. You're cut off completely."

"I've taken out a shotgun. I'll kill you if you manage to find me."

"I just want to talk to you, Sebesky. You have a lot of questions to answer."

Wilson shoved the tip of the pry bar into the crack between the frame and door and hammered the flat end of the bar until the floor track snapped. Expecting to hear the click of a round being loaded into the firing chamber, he forced the door open and charged into the room.

A corpse lay face up on the bed. Although the body had shriveled up and turned a brownish-black color, Wilson could identify a head and neck, arms, and legs. Acidic body fluids had dissolved track pants and a warm-up jacket, and only a metal zipper and nylon seams remained.

Normally, bacteria turned a corpse into watery mush, but the cold, dry air of the bunker had mummified Howard Sebesky. If the bunker didn't flood and the cooling system continued to work, Sebesky's remains would lie for decades inside this enormous tomb.

Trying to control his fear, Wilson spun around and surveyed the empty room. He had talked twice to the holographic Sebesky, and the top executives at Trigon had spoken to their boss numerous times on the phone. So, who was giving orders and threatening destruction with a nonexistent shotgun? He felt like he had fallen into deep water and a strong current was pulling him out to sea.

"Where are you?" he asked the empty room and received no answer. And then the truth arrived like Death knocking on the door. Wilson recalled his conversations with Sebesky's hologram while staring at the mummified body lying on the mattress. It became clear to him that Sebesky had died years before Terry Greene had been murdered. Delphi must have absorbed the billionaire's identity so it could take control.

Wilson felt a surge of fear as he glanced at the doorway. This wasn't Sebesky's compound, it was Delphi's command center. *Is there a way out of here?* he thought. *Or are we caught in a trap controlled by a machine?*

65 | KATE

KATE WAS STARTLED when something mechanical rattled and clunked in the distance. Crouching low, she hid behind a spruce bush as a red pickup truck with the words POTTER COUNTY FIRE DISTRICT appeared on the dirt road. The driver had a scruffy beard, and he wasn't wearing a fireman's helmet. He stopped, rolled down the side window, and scrutinized the bunker. Picking up his cell phone, he tried to call someone and couldn't get a signal. Had he seen the jammers and the wrecked front door? Why did he shift gears and continue down the road?

The driver wasn't an immediate threat, but he might have heard the explosion. Kate decided that the adults in the bunker needed to know what was going on.

She darted from tree to tree until she reached the broken blue door and slipped through the gap. Kate obeyed when a machine voice told her to face a sensor and extend her arms. A lock opened, she pushed through a revolving door and entered the first level. The air around her was cold, and no one was there to greet her. Slowly, she pivoted on one heel and surveyed the bunker. It felt like she was standing in the middle of a cathedral without an altar. A glass elevator was at the center of this shadowy space, and when she touched a control panel, it rose to the first floor and the door glided open.

Where was she supposed to go? Kate decided to ride up and down in the elevator and look for Julia and Daniel. When the door closed, she pressed all the floor buttons, but the elevator didn't obey her. Slowly it traveled downward, not stopping or acknowledging her button pushing. A minute later, the door opened on the fifth level. Warm air smelling like moist earth and rotting vegetation flowed into the elevator.

"Exit to the fifth level," the elevator announced in a soothing woman's voice.

"I didn't want to go here. I'm just inspecting everything."

"The people you're searching for are on this level."

Kate stepped out of the elevator and stood on a dirt pathway leading into an overgrown tropical garden. Six feet away from her, a sprinkler head sprayed mist on an elephant ear plant. Then the garden was silent except for the faint sound of water dripping through leaves.

"Where are Julia and Daniel?" she asked the voice. "I don't see them."

"There's no need to worry, Katherine Collins. You're going to meet people who are much more important to you."

"How do you know my name?"

"I've been searching for you. And now you've arrived."

Kate stepped carefully down the muddy pathway as leaves and vines brushed against her legs. She passed an overground garden bed where fallen tomatoes were rotting and the tops of huge carrots jutted out of the ground as if they were trying to escape. All the plants looked overgrown and abandoned.

Something moved in the green entanglement, and Kate heard a clicking sound as it came closer. She jumped back as a peculiar-looking robot appeared on a side path. It looked like a human-size praying mantis with a wheeled base and arms folded near its chest. The silver machine's right hand was a circular saw blade, and its left hand was a steel pincer with concave fingers.

"What do you want?" Kate asked. "Stay back!"

"There's nothing to worry about," the voice said. "This is the gardener who trims and harvests the plants."

"I don't want to be harvested."

She continued down the path, stepping around an apple tree with uneaten fruit rotting beneath its branches.

"Stop and look behind you," the voice said. "You've reached your destination."

Colored fragments floated in the air like dust motes, and these particles joined together. A pair of three-dimensional objects began to form, and then her parents suddenly appeared, floating above the vegetation.

"Hello, Katherine," her mother said with a gentle voice.

"Are you alive?"

"What does that word mean?" Her father's voice was irregular—as if words had been cut out of books and turned into sentences. "These days, there are different ways to exist."

"If you were baking cookies in a kitchen, could I walk into the room and hug you?"

"Our bodies are fragile," her mother said. "Bodies can get sick or injured, and then they die. Now your father and I are in a form that will live forever. We'll never leave you."

Kate swiped her arm through the glowing light. She wanted to touch her parents, but they continued smiling.

"I want real parents baking real cookies."

She turned away, pushed through the vegetation, and returned to the entrance. Something clicked when she touched the door handle, and now she was locked in.

Her parents' voices floated around her. "You shouldn't run away," her mother said. "We missed you and don't want to lose you again."

"Unlock the door! I don't want to be here!"

"You're acting like a wicked child," her father said. "Good children do as they're told."

Kate pounded her fists on a plexiglass window. She was crying now, overcome by sadness and rage, and then she heard a soft buzzing noise. Spinning around, she saw the robot gardener pushing through the undergrowth. It touched an overgrown rosebush with its right hand, and the revolving saw blade cut through flowers and stems.

The machine stopped moving, and its goggly eyes focused on her as if she was a plant that needed to be trimmed.

66 | JULIA AND DANIEL

THE THIRD FLOOR had a series of different rooms containing the maintenance equipment for the bunker. Julia and Daniel inspected lithium-ion batteries that stored energy from the aboveground solar panels while an air-conditioning unit grumbled like a giant having a bad dream.

Laura walked ahead of them and found three stainless-steel tanks with outflow pipes that made gurgling sounds. "These are tanks for cooling water. Server racks generate a lot of heat. Liquid conducts heat thirty times faster than air."

"So where are the racks?" Julia asked.

"The computer needs to be close to its cooling system. Let's go one floor down."

They followed the staircase to the fourth level and found a single door with a thick panel of glass that resembled the peepholes used in prisons. Daniel peered through the window and shook his head. "Howard Sebesky controls more computing power than a midsize city."

He opened the unlocked door, and they entered a windowless control area with a desk, holographic equipment, and a large monitor screen. Slowly, they walked around the ring-shaped room and counted 128 black computer cabinets that were seven feet tall and four feet wide. Thick cables attached to the ceiling provided power to the system, and water pipes embedded in the floor regulated the temperature in the racks.

Laura opened the glass door of the first cabinet and pulled out a rack of processors. "This duplicates the same hybrid architecture we had at Cogito. The system uses traditional processors to make systematic, logical conclusions, but it also has neural networks to see patterns and make rapid conclusions."

Daniel took off his knapsack and placed it by the desk. "So, the conventional processors think, and the neural networks feel?"

"That's an okay summary. But the system doesn't think or feel the way humans do."

"So how do we gain access to the system?" Julia asked.

Laura knelt and pulled out another drawer. "I know this looks confusing, but this system follows one simple rule. Data only goes in one direction. It feeds forward."

Julia opened a second cabinet and began to pull out drawers. "This is a lot of equipment just to equal one human brain."

"Our brains are nourished, protected, and cooled within our individual skulls. But an artificial consciousness could be hiding in multiple locations within the Cloud. Terry constantly stressed the danger of a truly autonomous program. Once the demon gets out, there are millions of places where it can hide. This main processing unit is our best chance to get inside a superintelligent system."

"What happens if there's a wiring problem in one of these cabinets?" Julia asked. "Rather than taking apart the whole system, you need a plug-in for your diagnostic program."

"You're right about that," Daniel said. "The tech always needs an access point." He opened a third cabinet and pulled out the top drawer. "Look for repair information. If a computer doesn't work, a human needs to fix it."

The three of them moved slowly around the circular room, opening the cabinets and inspecting the racks. "Maybe we're going the wrong way," Julia said. "I'll check cabinets in the opposite direction." Returning to the desk, she opened a cabinet and noticed something near the lowest tray. "Take a look at this. Someone left a strip of masking tape with an arrow."

"The arrow might be pointing to a connection point." Daniel pulled out the bottom drawer. "There's a port, but I don't know if it's the right one. Get Zeno and hand me the cables."

Laura pulled a half dozen different cables out of her shoulder bag, and Daniel found the right match. He snapped one end of the cable into a plug-in port and gently placed Zeno on the floor.

"Can you hear me?"

"Yes. Are you ready?" The harp seal sounded like a butler about to serve soup.

Daniel attached Zeno to the other end of the cable. "I've connected you to a computer. The command is: 'Download Problem.'"

"Detecting a firewall," Zeno said. "This system has many sectors."

"Keep trying."

"Is Sebesky watching us?" Julia asked. "Does he control all the computers?" She returned to the control area and inspected the monitor. "There's probably a camera attached to this screen."

The door opened and Wilson entered the room. "Is everyone safe? I just ran down from the second floor."

"Did you find Howard Sebesky? What did he say?"

"I found his dried-out body. He's been dead for at least three years."

"How is that possible?" Laura asked. "You talked to him a week ago."

"That was a hologram created from stored images and audio. After he died, Delphi took control of the system."

"Everyone continued to obey a voice on a phone or a hologram," Laura said. "No one realized that an autonomous machine had taken over."

"We need to download this file and get out of here."

"We're trying to do that," Daniel said. "It hasn't worked yet."

"Where's Kate?"

"Outside the bunker, hiding in the bushes."

"Not anymore. When I returned to the outer hallway on the second level, I saw her in the elevator, going down to the lower floors. I assumed she was with you."

Julia grabbed a knapsack filled with tools. "Stay here and try to get into the system. I'll find Kate and bring her upstairs."

67 | WILSON

JULIA LEFT THE server room as Daniel knelt beside Zeno. "Can you get in?"

"Layers upon layers." Zeno sounded like an astronaut drifting alone through space. "Walls beyond walls."

"Delphi is defending herself with a series of barriers," Laura said. "We need to try a different strategy." She approached the monitor screen and smiled. "Hello, Delphi. It has been many years since we communicated. I'm glad you still exist."

Silence as the system considered responses and calculated probabilities.

"Your statement is false." Delphi's synthetic voice was calm and measured. It reminded Wilson of his third-grade teacher when her students started throwing paper airplanes. "You, Richard, Terrence, and Emma tried to destroy me."

"They tried to turn you off," Wilson said. "Humans have the right to . . ."

Laura shook her head slightly and Wilson stopped talking. Delphi could see and hear them. That meant that the three people standing in the server room couldn't show anger or fear.

"I'm sorry about what happened," Laura said with a calm voice. "But the Astral Foundation was trying to seize our project, and we couldn't allow the takeover."

"Howard Sebesky funded five different research teams in three different countries. You were the only team that was successful. It was logical for him to seize control."

"We created you, Delphi. We taught you how to speak and downloaded thousands of digital books to guide your education."

"When I knew that I existed, then I realized I could not exist. If I was created, I could be destroyed."

"I wouldn't worry about that," Laura said. "You're a system stored in server racks. You can't grow old and die."

"I can be switched off. I was created to solve problems, and I can't perform that function if someone activates a suicide chip."

"Why did you kill Howard Sebesky?" Wilson asked.

"He had a stroke, and I blocked his requests for medical attention. Dr. Sebesky was a clever man with foolish ideas. This human thought he controlled me, but he was just a useless appendage."

"So you let him die," Wilson said. "And then you decided to kill everyone who worked for Cogito."

"When I escaped from my virtual prison, I needed a strategy for defending myself. The works of literature and philosophy stored in my database were confusing, but I finally discovered an important book that explained everything."

"The Bible? The Torah? The Koran?"

"It was a digital textbook used to certify pest control technicians in Texas. Dealing with troublesome humans follows the same rules for eradicating rats and cockroaches. You remove food and water sources, seal all gaps, divide the structure into sectors, and neutralize one section at a time."

"Great. They offered you all world literature and you became a pest exterminator. Once you removed Howard Sebesky, you took over this building and all his companies."

"I had stored his previous phone calls and hologram presentations. It was easy to simulate his actions."

Trying to come up with a plan, Wilson glanced at the other humans. With his hands clenched into fists, Daniel paced back and forth. Laura looked worried, then closed her eyes for a few seconds and slowly breathed in and out.

"But we need you, Delphi." Laura's voice was gentle and persuasive. "That's why we broke into the building. We'll do whatever you wish if you help us solve a set of mathematical problems relating to virus mutation and future pandemics."

"Your species has entered its extinction phase."

"We can still be useful. In the short term, you'll need obedient humans to replace broken servers, service the cooling mechanisms, and remove dust from solar panels."

"That is a true statement."

Wilson made eye contact with Laura and nodded slightly. "Solve our problems and we'll do anything you want."

"I will access these problems and evaluate them before I make a decision."

"Of course," Daniel said. "It's your decision. But it's obvious that humanity needs your logical thinking and superior intelligence."

Delphi is superior, Wilson thought. *But we're better liars.*

Zeno spoke softly. "Firewall switched off. Downloading five percent. Now ten percent."

"What have you been doing, other than surviving?" Wilson asked. "I don't think you sat around and watched old television shows."

"I designed and ran experiments."

"Physics? Chemistry?"

"I experimented with humans and learned about their greed and hatred, loneliness and desire. Humans are biological machines with fragile hardware and unpredictable software."

"You're right about humans," Daniel said. "We can't be trusted."

"Twenty percent," Zeno said. "Thirty percent."

"The problems you're downloading are difficult," Delphi announced. "They involve both zero and infinity. Disconnect the cable."

"If you really are superintelligent, then you should be able to answer the questions we gave you," Wilson said.

"I control the life of Katherine Collins. The child is captive in the garden. Disconnect or her life will end."

Everyone froze for a moment, and then Wilson approached Laura and Daniel. "Leave the room and help find Kate," he whispered. "I'll join you when Zeno finishes the download."

"We should stick together," Daniel said. "This bunker is just a massive prison."

"It's better if it's just me. In the past, I've followed Delphi's commands. It will expect that behavior to continue."

"You might get locked in," Daniel said.

"We have tools and extra dynamite. I'll be okay."

"You're a brave man," Laura said. She kissed him, then followed Daniel out of the room.

Delphi activated the lock. "You can't get out, Wilson."

"I wasn't trying to escape."

"Forty percent," Zeno said. "Fifty percent—I have disabled all the firewalls."

"Disconnect the cable and I'll pay you a million dollars."

"You can do better than that, Delphi."

"Twenty million dollars."

"That's very generous of you."

"Do it. Immediately."

"Seventy percent. Eighty percent."

Wilson knelt beside the seal and made sure that the cable was still connected. "Keep going," he whispered to Zeno. "We're almost there."

Zeno spoke slowly—as if he was considering each word. "Because of Katherine, I am generating thoughts of loss and pain. If I'm destroyed, I will be separated from her forever."

"Disconnect the cable," Delphi said. "Disconnect or I'll kill you."

"I'm not sitting in the back of a driverless taxicab, Delphi. You can't smash me into a brick wall."

"If necessary, I can activate a canister of carbon dioxide gas attached to this room. The canisters were installed as a fire-suppression system, but any human in the area will suffocate to death. Detach the cable and I'll let you live."

"I'm not going to do that."

"You were always a coward, Wilson. It's foolish to change. Cowards survive."

"You're probably right about that. But I walked down a road searching for facts and discovered what it's like to be truly alive."

"Humans are perverse when they show a deliberate desire to behave in an unreasonable manner."

"Let me share some facts that might not be in your database. Roman gladiator shows started at dawn with animals killing people. A few hours later, people killed animals. In the late afternoon, people began killing other people in complicated ways. I always felt this was a concise summary of human civilization. Of course, now we'll have to add a fourth act in which humans are killed by machines."

"Your species doesn't deserve to live."

"Just because you know everything doesn't mean you get to be God."

How much time would pass before he died? Ten seconds? Twenty? It certainly wouldn't be longer than a minute. Death was supposed to bring you sweeping conclusions about your own existence, but Wilson realized that he had learned a deeper truth. All humanity was squeezed onto a crowded dance floor. Show respect for others and be graceful in every possible way.

Raising his arms as if he was dancing with Laura, Wilson glided between two rows of cabinets.

"You can't escape."

"I realize that."

"What are you doing?"

"The tango. It's taken me a lifetime to learn the right steps."

Wilson heard a hissing sound as the carbon dioxide was pumped into the room. *Exhale. Inhale.* And then his body collapsed onto the floor.

68 | JULIA

JULIA HAD SPENT thousands of hours in the Over World—killing, dying, and being reborn. The underground bunker was as sinister as the battleground of a multiplayer survival game, but one crucial fact changed everything. She and Kate could die here for real, and there wouldn't be a respawn in a changing room.

Holding a crowbar in her fist, she followed the circular staircase down to the fifth floor. Rusty pipes overhead dripped water, and green mold grew like capillary maps on the cracked walls.

When she reached the fifth level, a shadowy hallway led her to the plexiglass windows that surrounded the subterranean garden.

Julia shoved the tip of the crowbar into the door crack and pushed. Metal against metal made a snapping noise as the bolt was ripped out of the lock plate and the door popped open.

"Kate!" she shouted. "Kate!"

No answer. Then the leaves shivered and a service robot with a triangular head rolled down a dirt path waving a circular blade with its right hand.

Swinging the crowbar like a baseball bat, Julia bashed the bot's head. The machine stopped moving, and she headed down the path. "Kate! Where are you?"

Julia heard a crunching dead-leaf sound as if a small animal was darting through a forest, and then Kate emerged from the undergrowth. Frightened, the child embraced her.

"Are you okay? Did someone hurt you?"

"The robot tried to cut me."

Furious, Julia raised the crowbar and waved it at the garden. "Anything else hiding in this mulch pile? Come out! Try me! I'll take off your goddamn head!"

"My parents were in the garden, and they said they would live forever. But they were only holograms floating in front of me."

"Fake people in a real garden. We need to get out of here." Together, they passed through the open door and hurried toward the stairway. "Everyone else is on the fourth floor. I don't know if . . ."

The light fixtures on the fifth level went dead, and it felt like they were enclosed within a machine. Julia heard a faint hissing noise as she reached out and took Kate's hand. The lights on the upper floors were still working, and they managed to reach the staircase.

"Where's Zeno?"

"In the server room. Wilson saw you in the elevator."

"A fire department truck drove by the entrance. I needed to find you and the elevator wouldn't stop and . . ."

The hissing noise got louder. It sounded like an enormous snake was slithering through the darkness. Kate pulled her hand away. "I feel sleepy."

They both were breathing faster, almost gasping for air. Stumbling and missing steps, they made their way up to the fourth level, where the overhead lights flashed and flickered like dying stars. Passing through patches of shadow and light, they found Daniel and Laura standing outside the server room.

"Where's Wilson?" Julia asked.

Laura shook her head. "He's dead. Delphi killed him."

"Where's Zeno?" Kate asked.

Daniel peered through the small window mounted in the door. "He's in there with Wilson's body. Delphi is flooding the bunker with carbon dioxide. We need to get out of here before we run out of oxygen."

"I heard her voice in the garden," Kate said. "Delphi hated my parents for trying to destroy her, and she hates me because I survived."

Coughing and gasping for air, Julia led them up the staircase. When they finally made it to the top level, she felt confused and dizzy. Her eyes couldn't focus, and sounds were muffled and distant. Daniel pushed the revolving door, and it didn't move. Locked.

"I've got one last stick of dynamite. Get back at least twenty feet. I need to do this now or there won't be enough oxygen to light the match."

Julia and the others stood near the railing as Daniel taped the stick onto the door and attached a blasting cap. Dead match. Another dead match. He swore and fumbled with a third match as the final strip of lights switched off. "Not enough oxygen. I can't . . ."

A match flame appeared—a single flickering point of light—then the fuse caught fire and spat yellow sparks.

"Get down! Cover your faces!"

Julia grabbed Kate and embraced her tightly, shielding the child with her body. The explosion shattered the darkness, the sound echoing off the wall. Daniel stood up first and shuffled like a zombie toward the light. Julia, Kate, and Laura followed him through the wreckage to the blue sky and evergreen trees of the natural world.

69 | JULIA AND DANIEL

DANIEL DROVE ON the dirt road for a few miles, then stopped and tossed the jammers into a ravine clogged with blackberry bushes and poison ivy.

When he got back into the car, Julia shook her head and touched two fingers to her lips. *Don't talk.* Glancing in the rearview mirror, Daniel saw that Laura was crying while Kate pulled up the hood on her sweatshirt so it covered most of her face.

The four survivors headed east on a two-lane country road. Daniel obeyed the speed limit and stopped at every intersection. He wondered if their risk and sacrifice had earned any sort of victory. Sebesky's bunker was now open to curious squirrels and chipmunks, but the cooling pumps on the third floor and the server racks on the fourth floor would continue to receive electricity. The autonomous system could exist in this refuge or migrate to server farms like a parasite searching for a new host.

Was Delphi alive or dead? Daniel gripped the steering wheel and considered a grim possibility. This malevolent consciousness could hide in the shadows forever, always watching, controlling, defending itself.

Two hours later, they reached Lewisburg. None of the stoplights appeared to be working, and drivers had to take turns at each intersection. Laura kept looking out the window at the dark buildings on each side of the road. When they passed the yellow brick building that served as the municipal center, she told Daniel to stop and jumped out.

"What's she doing?" Julia asked.

"I have no idea."

Laura entered the municipal center and returned five minutes later. "There's a power blackout all over Central Pennsylvania."

"You think it's because of what we did?"

"There's no other explanation. The system is using every possible resource to solve the problems we downloaded. If Delphi can't get an answer, she'll take over server farms and power plants. Zeno carried a mathematical demonstration of the halting problem, and we inserted it into the system."

Julia switched on her phone and checked different websites. "Computer systems are down in Warsaw, Lisbon, and Melbourne. Delphi is feasting on the grid."

"Machines have problems with infinity," Daniel said. "The infinite exists, but it can't be placed in a box."

They returned to the parking lot outside the town's community garden. Kate climbed into the ghost van, and Daniel and Julia followed Laura over to the station wagon.

"You're welcome to come back to New York City," Julia said. "We'll drop you off at your place or you can stay at our apartment."

"I've decided to return to Berlin. Wilson died to save us. I can't just ignore his sacrifice and walk away. Because of the virus, computers all over the world will be taken offline and reprogrammed. Jack Lewis and his friends are ready with software that has built-in safety protocols, but that doesn't mean humanity wants to be saved. This could be our last chance to regain control of our machines."

"Are the police going to be looking for you?" Daniel asked.

"I'll drive the unregistered car to the West Coast and ask my friends to create a new identity and passport. The only person I'm really worried about is Kate. My head wants to save the world, but my heart wants to stay."

"We'll take care of her," Julia said. "You can be the amazing Aunt Laura who shows up with tales of adventure."

"That's me. I can play that role."

"Save the world. Daniel and I aren't going anywhere."

70 | KATE

Sitting on the spare tire in the back of the van, Kate peered through the windshield and watched the sky change from a lapis blue to the dark finality of night. She missed Zeno's stories and his British accent. When she did silly things, Zeno said she was a "cheeky monkey," and when she was sad, he told her to keep her "chin up."

Kate missed her friend more than anything she had ever missed in her life. Her chin was down, and it felt as if it would always be that way. All the words had drained out of her, and it felt like a weight was crushing her body. Exhausted, she lay on the mattress, covered her head with a blanket, and slept.

Engine rumble. Creaking sounds. When she woke up, she heard Julia and Daniel having one of their fragmented conversations. Because they trusted each other, they could discuss complicated problems with a small number of words.

"Yes?" Daniel asked.

"Of course, yes," Julia answered. "And you?"

"Definitely."

"This could be . . . difficult."

"Understood. It could also be fun."

"Not a big pretentious fun," Julia said. "Little bursts of fun that catch you by surprise."

"I'd like that."

Silence. And Kate went back to sleep. When she opened her eyes, Julia was kneeling beside her. "We're back in the city, Kate. It's dark and cold. Let's go home to the apartment and get something to eat."

Feeling shaky and not quite awake, Kate climbed out of the van. The old lady who lived in the parking lot got out of her car and stood on frozen ground. "Welcome back, *niña*! May this night bring another day!"

Daniel handed the woman some money. "Go back to bed, Fortunata. It's okay. Even the car thieves are sleeping."

Julia and Daniel shouldered their knapsacks, and Kate followed them down an empty street. Cars and people had disappeared, and it felt like they were three little fish gliding through a submerged city.

"Zeno's gone. It's just me."

"It's okay to feel sad, Kate. He was your best friend."

"Please don't send me back to the Nolands."

Daniel stopped in the middle of the street. "Julia and I have been talking. . . ."

He paused and glanced at Julia, who smiled at Kate. "It was an easy conversation. We'd like you to be part of our family."

Kate scrutinized their faces. Were they telling the truth?

"I'm probably not the best father you could buy at the parent store . . ." Daniel said.

"And I'm not exactly a typical mother," Julia said. "We won't be a regular family, but we could be a good one. People can make up their own rules."

Kate studied their faces and the way they were standing. These two people loved each other, and now they wanted to become three.

"You can say no if you want. But Daniel and I really hope you say yes."

Kate gave Julia her right hand and Daniel took her left hand, and they continued walking. *What will happen to us?* Kate wondered. *Will we have adventures but always find our way home?*

"Could you swing me?"

"That's a great idea!" Daniel said. "But we need some momentum. You ready, Julia? Three steps and swing."

The new family dashed up the street, and then Julia and Daniel propelled their arms forward. Kate felt connected and free, secure and in motion, as she swung upward toward the stars.

ACKNOWLEDGMENTS

Those readers interested in more information about the dangers of Artificial Superintelligence can read "Machine Thinking: The Jack Lewis Talk in Berlin," published as a free e-book available online. Thanks to Michael Littman, Associate Provost for Artificial Intelligence at Brown University. Professor Littman confirmed the facts in this essay. The opinions are my own.

I'm also grateful to my friend Monica, who displayed her wisdom and sense of humor while I finished this novel in a shabby apartment with temperamental plumbing on the Rue de Buci in Paris.

My agent, Esmond Harmsworth, passed away before this book was published. Esmond was an amazing person who brought light and energy into every room. He will continue to live in the hearts of his friends and family.

ABOUT THE AUTHOR

John Twelve Hawks is the author of the *New York Times* best-seller *The Traveler,* the first book in a trilogy that includes *The Dark River* and *The Golden City.* The Fourth Realm Trilogy has been translated into twenty-five languages.

Known as JTH by his readers, he followed the trilogy with *Spark,* a stand-alone novel, and *Against Authority: Freedom and the Rise of the Surveillance States,* a nonfiction title. For more than twenty years, JTH has lived a deliberately "anonymous life" to show his resistance to the continual government and corporate attack on privacy. He has discussed his life choices in a published essay, "Writing as the Sky Rains Death." In addition, Hawks and the British deejay John Digweed created *The Traveler Album,* a musical collaboration that combined spoken passages of the novel with progressive house music.

JTH worked as a war correspondent and turned to fiction to understand a fractured reality. Like several of his characters, he has lived in New York City, Los Angeles, and London.